The Island Club

ALSO BY NICOLA HARRISON

Montauk

The Show Girl

Hotel Laguna

THE ISLAND CLUB

A NOVEL

Nicola Harrison

ST. MARTIN'S PRESS
NEW YORK

This is a work of fiction. All of the names, characters, organizations, places, and events portrayed in this work are either products of the author's imagination or used fictitiously.

First published in the United States by St. Martin's Press, an imprint of St. Martin's Publishing Group

EU Representative: Macmillan Publishers Ireland Ltd, 1st Floor, The Liffey Trust Centre, 117–126 Sheriff Street Upper, Dublin 1, D01 YC43

www.stmartins.com

The Library of Congress Cataloging-in-Publication Data is available upon request.

ISBN 978-1-250-27740-4 (hardcover)

ISBN 978-1-250-27741-1 (ebook)

First Edition: 2026

10 9 8 7 6 5 4 3

For all my tennis girls. I am forever grateful for the fierce friendships I've made through this sport, both on and off the courts.

The Island Club

PROLOGUE

Balboa Island, California, 1956

Balboa Island, tucked neatly inside California's Newport Harbor, might just be the most charming little beach town you've ever seen. With a perimeter of less than three miles and sandy shores lapped by waves with no breakers, the island's front doors are flung open, letting the breeze flow through fairytale-like cottages painted in bright colors on streets named after gemstones. Automobiles approach by crossing a four-hundred-foot bridge from the east or gliding on a ferryboat that plies the bay from the west. To look out from the man-made island at sailboats and canoes putting out from the shore and drifting lazily by is to float in a dream of repose, watching the world pass by—an invitation to join in or to escape.

On an evening stroll down Coral, Ruby, or Amethyst Avenue, you might hear the laughter of freshly bathed children or the clink of knives and forks as families sit down to dinner. The last golden beams of sun make their final glowing performance, showing off sailboats moored in the bay in their most flattering light, and one might assume that life on this magical island is dreamy and perfect. But don't get too comfortable, because behind those white lace demi-curtains, things may not be quite as they seem.

CHAPTER ONE

March 1956
MILLY

At a little past six on a Wednesday evening, after fixing her hair into a smooth S-wave and slipping into her canary-yellow dress with the sweetheart neckline, Milly Kincaid picked up one of her slingback pumps and hurled it down the hallway as hard as she could. Its heel lodged into the wall of her brand-new house on Balboa Island, and it stayed there. She picked up its mate and launched that one too, watching with dissatisfaction as it thumped, sadly, to the floor. She considered grabbing another but stopped and froze, staring at the damage she had caused, and wondered what she'd tell her husband. Only then did she allow herself to acknowledge the feeling that had nagged at her all night as she'd tossed and turned alone in their bed: the feeling that she had made a terrible, terrible mistake. They should never have moved to this godforsaken island.

Her husband Lloyd hadn't been home for three nights, and fifteen minutes earlier they were supposed to have arrived at the house of their new neighbors, the Johnsons, for a welcome dinner. Despite leaving numerous messages with Lauralee, Lloyd's secretary, Milly had no idea if he would actually show his face.

Leticia, the new babysitter, who barely spoke a word of English, was in the yard playing with the children, and Milly didn't know which would be worse—to cancel last minute and make a terrible first impression with her new and rather fabulous neighbors, or to go alone and risk starting rumors about her shaky marriage. Balboa Island was a small community; people would talk, people would gossip, she was sure of it. She had no choice but to face the evening alone.

She powdered her nose, reapplied her Cardinal Red lipstick, and regretfully collected her shoes, dislodging the one wedged in the wall and picking up the other from the floor.

When she reached over the white picket fence and unlatched the gate at the house on South Bay Front, just a short walk from hers on Amethyst Avenue, her hand was shaking slightly. Milly and Lloyd were the new couple in a new town. Having Lloyd by her side gave her stability, comfort, someone to lean on to ensure they came off as a couple worthy of an introduction. As a television executive, Lloyd had far more impressive things to talk about than Milly did. What could she possibly converse about? How Debbie had been crying herself to sleep each night because she missed her old friends, what Jack ate for dinner, or how overwhelmed Milly felt by the sheer magnitude of unpacking an entire house alone? What a bore!

The table on the Johnsons' front patio was already set with a red-and-white-checkered tablecloth, white china plates, and pale-blue rolled napkins. A bowl of fresh strawberries caught the late afternoon sun, and the whole scene had a casual elegance to it, like something out of a magazine. If Milly had been the one inviting the new neighbors over, she would have been a frantic mess, scrambling to get dinner on the table, tidying up the house, and making sure the children were presentable. But Milly could tell even after meeting her hostess only a few times that Sylvia was the kind of self-assured woman who made entertaining look like a breeze.

"Milly!" The front door swung open, and Sylvia sashayed out in a full-skirted royal-blue dress with a pale-pink bowknot collar and a matching pink apron tied around her tiny waist. Her auburn waves caught the sun and looked as if she'd just walked out of the beauty salon. She placed a bowl of melon balls on the table, then leaned in for a kiss on the cheek. "I'm so glad you're here. Where are those adorable ankle-biters of yours?"

"They're at home. I'm trying out a sitter, Leticia. It's so much more relaxing without the children," Milly said, not feeling relaxed at all—worrying if Debbie was missing her, worrying if Jack was acting up, worrying if Lloyd would make an appearance.

"I don't envy you," Sylvia said. "Those early years are exhausting. You need all the help you can get." She smiled, and Milly wished she could be her for a moment, standing there in front of her perfect house, with, no doubt, a perfect, happy family inside. "My Walter will be out in a jiffy. Is Lloyd joining us?"

Milly's stomach clenched. "He'll be here any second," she said an octave too high. "He must be stuck in traffic."

Though it had been a calculated decision to move, the fifty-mile stretch of road between his work in Hollywood and their new home on Balboa Island was beginning to feel precarious, like a piece of bubblegum stretching out between them, growing thinner and thinner, threatening to break at any moment. She never knew when to have dinner on the table or what to tell the children when he didn't come home. In the last two weeks since they'd moved in, he'd barely spent any time with them at all, and his absence made her increasingly anxious.

"Is there anything I can do to help?" Milly asked, trying to change the subject.

"It's all under control." Sylvia pulled out a chair for Milly, then sat across from her. "The food is almost ready. My daughter Judith is upstairs in her room listening to records—'Heartbreak Hotel' over and over again." She rolled her eyes. "He is a peach though, don't you think?" Sylvia fanned herself dramatically with her hand. "That Elvis Presley."

"Oh, sure," Milly said. "Actually, Lloyd was in the same room as him at CBS when he was on *Stage Show* a few months back."

"Do not tell my Judith that; she'll never leave your poor husband alone, pestering him for information." She laughed. "But, more importantly"—Sylvia leaned forward and gave Milly a wink—"it's cocktail time." Sylvia stirred an etched-glass pitcher with a long silver spoon and began to pour the bright red concoction into two tall glasses. "I hope you like a Rangoon Ruby. It's Ocean Spray cranberry juice, vodka, soda, a squeeze of lime, and a sprig of mint. I got the recipe from a bartender in San Francisco, and it's perfect for these gorgeous spring days."

Milly took a long drink. It was exactly what she needed.

A full forty-five minutes later Lloyd entered through the gate, and Milly let out a sigh of relief.

"Sorry to keep you all waiting," he said, looking as dashing as ever, not a hair out of place. "The studio kept me late, but I insisted I had to leave, told them I had a very important dinner." Milly was shocked that he'd come, and angry that he hadn't bothered to let her know, but mostly, she was just grateful not to have to squirm through the evening alone making excuses for his absence.

"Oh, Lloyd, we're so happy you're here." Sylvia opened the door and called inside. "Yoo-hoo, Walter darling, Lloyd has arrived."

She started mixing two Manhattans at a wheeled bar cart. "Milly and I are drinking Rangoon Rubies, but I'm assuming you need something stronger."

"Bourbon's great, thank you," he said.

Walter emerged from the house looking serious, and for a moment Milly thought she might see annoyance or anger on his face. Maybe Sylvia planned dinners like this every night of the week. But, as if stepping into a role on a TV show, he cracked a smile and reached out to shake Lloyd's hand.

"Great to meet you, Lloyd. Sylvia tells me you're a Hollywood man."

"I work in television," he said.

"Good business to be in."

Lloyd nodded. "It's certainly a busy time; everyone wants to watch the box. We're trying to provide longer shows, but we can hardly keep up with the demand."

"Exciting times," Walter said. "And this must be your lovely wife," he said, turning his attention to Milly. "Sylvia's told me so much about you."

Milly couldn't imagine what she could have told him, but she smiled anyway. "You have a beautiful home," she said.

Walter was in his mid-forties, and Sylvia was at least ten years younger. He was tall and well-built with some wrinkles forming on his tanned face, but he was a handsome man, and it was easy to imagine what had drawn Sylvia to him. Sylvia reached for his hand, pulled him in. "There you are, darling," she said, handing him his drink.

"Thanks, Lamb Chop," he said, giving her an unabashed smooch before getting comfortable in his chair. "So, how are you two settling in on the island?"

"We're having a ball," Lloyd said, putting his arm around his wife. "Right, Milly?"

She almost laughed. He'd barely set foot on the island since they'd moved in, let alone been around long enough to have any kind of fun. He hadn't taken even one day off to help unpack. He just went to work as usual and left her to make all the decisions on how the furniture should be arranged and which cupboard should house the plates and dishes and which should house the glasses. She'd rushed to unpack the children's boxes so they had something to wear to their new schools and something to keep them occupied when they got home, but the rest sat untouched. It was a miracle she'd met any of her neighbors at all. In fact, she wouldn't have met Sylvia if she hadn't shown up on Milly's doorstep to introduce herself the first day Milly had arrived, with a casserole and a bottle of wine in hand. The only good thing was that the house they'd bought was reasonably sized and somewhat manageable, unlike Sylvia's, which was easily four times the size, pristine, and beautifully decorated, sitting on a double lot overlooking the bay.

Lloyd squeezed Milly's shoulder, coaxing her to respond. "Oh, yes," she said, nodding. "We came here on our honeymoon several years back. We just loved the calm bay beaches and the quaint cottages. Oh, and the main street is adorable with all the little shops." Milly thought back on that time and tried to remember if they'd been happy then, just days after their wedding, but she couldn't recall; it all felt like a blur.

"It's really something, isn't it?" Walter said, proudly.

Milly smiled. "It's like being on vacation every day."

The truth was, she was miserable.

She had no idea what her husband was up to in Hollywood, and trying to set up a new home and a new life on the island without him was overwhelming. It made it hard for her to even catch her breath, let alone enjoy anything that her new hometown had to offer.

At night she lay in bed, dog-tired from all the cooking and cleaning and organizing and corralling the children into bed one at a time, then she'd stare at the ceiling, unable to fall into the sleep that her body desperately needed, instead making mental lists of all the things she still needed to do. It had occurred to her around four that morning that her fretful focus on what to do next—which box to put where, who to call to fix the hallway light switch—it was all irrelevant if her husband never came home. There was no handyman to call to fix a broken marriage.

"Well, you've made friends with the right gal," Walter said. "Sylvia knows everyone around here; she can introduce you." He swigged the last of his cocktail and gave the ice cubes a shake. Sylvia stood to fill his glass.

"It's true, I do know a lot of people," she said, flashing a grin. "I can tell you anything you could possibly want to know about anyone on this island . . . and plenty that you'd rather forget."

Milly laughed.

"How did you two end up on the island?" Lloyd asked.

"Walter's family was one of the first to buy property here, and I was Miss Balboa in 1938," Sylvia said proudly.

"Miss Balboa?" Milly asked.

"I won the Balboa Bathing Beauty Contest—and guess who was judging." Sylvia nodded to her husband.

Walter shook his head, "I wasn't the only judge. Everyone agreed you were the hottest barbecue in town, and I didn't need any convincing."

Sylvia smiled. "Walter's family has been putting on the Bathing Beauty Contest since it started back in the twenties; it's an island tradition," she said.

"That must have been fun!" Milly said, trying not to let her mind wander to the glamour girls Lloyd mingled with on set day in and day out. But she couldn't help herself. There was one actress, Beverly Douglas, from that daytime show *The Light Within*, which Lloyd had been working on recently, whom he seemed particularly enamored with. She was a gorgeous, slim brunette who, he'd told Milly many times, was a sensation and very demanding of his time. Everyone loved her. Was it Beverly who was luring him away? So clichéd, she thought—a beautiful actress ensnarling a television executive in a tryst to get ahead. Milly forced herself to come back to the conversation.

"I tried modeling after that, but I made a terrible mess of it!" Sylvia laughed. "They said I couldn't stop running my mouth long enough for them to get a decent picture. I found all the posing and primping so dull. I like people, I like chatting. I don't like sitting still, what can I say?"

"She was a stunner," Walter said. "Still is. And I like hearing what you have to say."

Lloyd and Walter got along famously at the dinner table. Afterward, Walter offered Lloyd a cigar. "Do you play tennis, Lloyd?"

"I used to, a little, but not much."

"I just opened up a new tennis club last year, The Island Club. It's just across the bridge." He nodded to Milly. "There's swimming too for the ladies and children."

Sylvia smiled and rolled her eyes, leaning in toward Milly. "He's just trying to get you to join," she said and laughed, putting her hand on Milly's arm. "But I must say it's quite a fun way to meet people. I'm happy to give you the grand tour."

"There are two yacht clubs in the area if boating is your thing," Walter went on, "One's right next door to ours, but I thought we men needed a club where we can knock a ball around, you know, take our frustrations out on the court."

"I happen to take tennis lessons there too," Sylvia chimed in.

"Yes," Walter said. "But you only go in the morning when no one else will see you."

"That's because the coaches don't think I'm trainable; I think they're embarrassed by me," she said, laughing. "Though they might be right. I have two left feet. Milly, you should join me sometime."

"Oh gosh, I don't know if I even remember how to play." Milly hadn't played since high school, and even then it had only been to get out of taking gym class, but she liked Sylvia. She was so different from her—outgoing, carefree, and confident—all the things Milly wanted to be.

"Perfect; then you'll make me look good!" Sylvia said. "And from what I've heard, it's like riding a bike—you never forget."

"All right," Milly said, feeling a tiny ripple of excitement at trying something different with this new acquaintance, or maybe it was the cranberry Rangoon Ruby going to her head.

"How about Friday?"

"Sure," Milly said. "I'd love to."

The next morning it was still dark out as Milly stood at the kitchen counter pouring the boiling water into the coffeepot. She watched the grinds settle, letting the steam warm her face, knowing she'd only have the chance to gulp down a quarter cup of coffee, half if she was lucky; then she had the sudden urge to take her husband's keys, get into the car, and drive far, far away. It was a shocking thought, one she regretted instantly as she heard Jack and Debbie singing along to "Zip-A-Dee-Do-Dah" as they came downstairs. The moments of peace and harmony were blissful and she should be more grateful, she scolded herself, but they were far outweighed by the spells of chaos.

The night before, when they got home from Sylvia's house, Debbie was still awake, hours past her bedtime, struggling with her reading. She stayed up until almost eleven o'clock in tears attempting to finish the first few pages of a book she hadn't taken out of her book bag until it was time to brush her teeth and put on her nightgown. By the time Milly left her daughter's room, shuffled Lloyd from where he was snoring on the sofa to the bedroom, it was almost time to do it all over again.

She'd woken to the sound of Jack calling "Mommy" over and over again, followed by questions from Debbie that she didn't really need help with: "Should I wear this white dress with the yellow sash, or the red one with the white collar?" If Milly gave her opinion, Debbie would undoubtably choose the other. Jack had demanded he have marshmallows for breakfast, because Leticia had let Debbie eat two for dessert the night before and he hadn't had any. For a brief moment he forgot about the marshmallows and put on his new Flash Gordon sunglasses—the red ones with the yellow Flash mask in the center and the two tiny rockets on the side—only to have Debbie come along and snatch them off his face, saying, "Can I try them on?" sending Jack into a screaming frenzy, all before the sun was even up.

Lloyd emerged clean-shaven and gleaming, smelling like Gillette shaving foam and pine-tar shampoo. He grabbed his hat, briefcase, and keys from the kitchen table, kissed his children on their heads, and made a beeline for the door.

"What time will you be home?" Milly asked.

"Not sure." He came back and kissed her on the cheek. An afterthought. "Bye kids. Be good for your mother."

"Yes, Daddy," they said in unison, then they ran to the front window in the living room to watch him drive away.

He'd have the send-off of a king, kisses blown, cheeks pressed up to the window, dramatic waves goodbye from the living room, followed by an hour of peace, cruising along the coast in his Oldsmobile, with no whining, crying, complaining. He'd roll the windows down and listen to the Chordettes or the Penguins, and he'd arrive at his office refreshed and calm and ready to take on the world. Milly resented him for that.

She smeared peanut butter and grape jelly onto white bread and crammed it in Debbie's metal lunch box.

"I don't like that lunch box," Debbie began.

"What's wrong with it?"

"Hopalong Cassidy is a boys' lunch box."

"All right," Milly said, dumping the sandwich and a cookie into a paper sack and adding a small Tupperware container of fruit salad. "Take this instead. I'm sure Jack will happily have it."

"Don't give it to Jack," she whined.

Milly took a deep breath, walked to the bedroom to get herself dressed, and counted down the minutes until the school bus would arrive.

It had been Milly's idea to move. She'd insisted, in fact, that they get out of Hollywood, away from the traffic, the pollution, the hustle and bustle of Los Angeles, where Lloyd was constantly being pulled back to work long after he'd left the office. They'd be at dinner and he'd run into another studio executive or a director, and next thing you knew, Milly would be finishing the last sip of her drink, and Lloyd would be ushering her into a taxi and kissing her goodbye. "I won't be late, I promise," he'd say. "We just need to talk business; you know how it goes—you'd be bored out of your mind." And she'd give him her cheek, and later she'd climb into bed alone only to hear him creep in at four or five in the morning or sometimes not at all.

She was surprised that he'd agreed to the move. Two months earlier they'd spent the weekend on Balboa Island for their anniversary, peeking into windows filled with charm and home-cooked meals and families of four sitting down together for dinner. "It would be good for you," Milly said at the end of the weekend before they drove home. "You could leave all the stress of work behind and come home to this at the end of each day," she said as she looked out to the yachts sailing by, the children building sandcastles by the water's edge, the Balboa Pavilion across the bay silhouetted against the setting sun.

She had thought that if they lived here, an hour south of all that lustiness that Hollywood had to offer, a place where it was picturesque, patriotic, with clean, salt air, then he'd have less time to indulge in all that perfidy. They put down a deposit on a house on Amethyst Avenue, they enrolled Debbie in school, and found a nursery school that would take Jack for two hours in the morning three times a week. They packed up their house in Hollywood and had everything delivered to the new house on Balboa Island. But now, instead of pulling him away from the temptations of Los Angeles, she'd simply taken herself out of the equation, making it easier for her and Lloyd to be apart. She'd had a plan, a grand plan, but she was becoming very concerned that it had backfired.

She had to do something to bring Lloyd into their new life on the island. She had to find a way to entice him to her, to ground them here, to make this new life permanent. And she had to do it fast.

CHAPTER TWO

SYLVIA

Sylvia opened her eyes in the darkness and reached over to Walter's side of the bed. It was empty. Had he fallen asleep on the couch again? He'd been drinking too much lately. That night, she noticed him refill his whiskey glass three times after dinner. He hadn't been in a talking mood; instead, he'd sat, stoically staring out of the window to the bay, rubbing his finger around the top of the glass. Eventually she left him with the bottle and went upstairs to bed. And two nights earlier, with the new couple, she'd watched him swill six Manhattans over the course of a few hours. Lloyd and Milly must have noticed.

She didn't care so much if he wanted to go out with the guys and have his fun now and again, which he'd done the week prior and the week before that—he always regretted the headaches that followed after a night of excess—but she did wonder if he was slipping into his old habits. They were the Johnsons, for goodness' sake; she didn't want people to talk. And she worried about his heart. The doctor said he had to take it easy, consider giving up smoking and booze, something they both knew he'd never do, but he definitely shouldn't be careless about his health. They had too much to look forward to.

She slipped out of bed, wrapped her silk robe around her, and tiptoed downstairs. She'd lure him back to bed, she decided. He'd been working so hard lately they'd barely had any chance to be romantic, and she was hoping to make up for lost time. She felt her way downstairs in the darkness, but her eyes adjusted and she made out his silhouette sitting at the kitchen counter.

"Walter?" she said. "What are you doing down here all alone?"

He grumbled, and she realized she had no idea what time it was. She walked up behind him and wrapped her arms around her husband's chest, pressing her breasts against him with more than a hint of suggestion. But he didn't turn and pull her toward him, as he usually would. This wasn't like him. One touch of skin, even just a glimpse, and he was usually raring to go.

Feeling an unusual sting of rejection, she tried a different approach, squeezing herself between the counter and him. She took his hands and slipped them into her robe, wrapping them around her body.

"Want a little pick-me-up?" she asked as she landed his hands on her rear.

"Ah," he screeched. "Damn it, Sylvia. Leave me alone, would you?"

"Walter, what is wrong with you?" She was getting angry now. Rejection was one thing, but blatant irritation with her was another. She moved out of his way to turn on the light. They both squinted at its harsh glow, and when he raised his hand to shield his eyes, she saw it immediately—the swollen purple pinky finger on his left hand, crooked and bending outward at a horribly unnatural angle.

She gasped. "My God, what happened?" She reached out to touch the mangled finger but he pulled it away. She searched his red, bloodshot eyes, noting his ashen skin and silver-streaked hair sticking up in all directions.

"I haven't slept," he said.

"But what happened to your finger?"

"An accident."

"What kind of accident? Did you fall?" She rushed to the icebox and pulled out a box of frozen peas, and when she turned back to him, she realized he was still in last night's clothes. "Did you go out last night after I went to bed?" She placed the peas on the counter in front of him. "You need to see someone; it looks broken."

"It's fine."

"It's not fine."

He pushed his chair back with a screech, and when he stood abruptly the chair fell back and hit the ground with a loud crash. "I told you," he growled loud enough to wake Judith, "it was an accident, that's all. I don't have to explain my every goddamned move to you."

Sylvia stepped back. He'd never raised his voice to her, ever. It was so jarring, she felt as if she'd been slapped, and she didn't dare move. After a long moment, Walter walked away, stumbling a little as he made his way toward the stairs. When she heard the bedroom door close, she forced herself to right the chair, then she sat in it and didn't move until the sun came up.

She jumped when she heard a knock at the door, and she stared at the entranceway. Who could possibly be calling on them at 7 AM on a Friday morning? Another knock. Nerves already on edge, she marched to the door, irritated at the interruption, and swung it open.

"Yes?" she said, and as soon as she saw Milly standing there awkwardly in a pale-green sweater and what barely passed as a white tennis skirt, she remembered they'd made a date to walk to the club together and play tennis.

"Oh, did I get the day wrong?" Milly asked.

Sylvia had no makeup on and probably looked pale and distraught.

"No, no not at all," Sylvia said. "I just need two minutes. . . ." It felt wrong not to invite her in, but she couldn't risk her seeing Walter this way if he reemerged. The Johnsons were the fun couple, the happy couple, the couple everyone wanted to be around, the couple everyone wanted to be. Angry and arguing was not on the menu, and this whole encounter left her sick and unsteady. "Just wait, right there." She had no choice but to close the door in Milly's face, and she raced upstairs to change.

CHAPTER THREE

ADELE

Adele knelt in her front yard on Onyx Avenue, her orange silk headscarf tied around chin-length brown hair. With gloved hands she snipped the full, fragrant head off the stem of the rosebush with a pair of razor-sharp secateurs. She lay the flower in the wicker basket by her side, then she snipped the next, then the next.

Some might find it ruthless to decapitate a rosebush laden with early blooms, but Adele wasn't sentimental about that type of thing. It could do better. She knew what it took to achieve greatness, and this bush wasn't going to blossom to its fullest potential without someone raising it with a stern hand.

If it hadn't been for Mr. Tucket, who owned the hardware and gardening store on Marine, she never would have guessed that something as fragrant and delicate as a rose would prosper near the ocean. He'd assured her, some twenty years earlier, that because Balboa Island was surrounded by a bay and was protected from the ocean by the peninsula, it meant that her roses wouldn't get too much sea breeze, and as long as they were cared for and pruned properly, they would grow beautifully in her front yard.

She sat back on her heels and stretched her back. She started every morning this way, clipping and pruning or planting or weeding, depending on the season. She liked to enjoy the damp, salty air and the comfort her small but meticulous garden gave her, without busybodies looking her way. She'd been out here for an hour already, when the sun was barely up, trimming the eight-by-six-foot patch of grass with her old lawn mower. As she pressed her shoulder blades back and rolled her head a few times—the way she used to in the seconds before she began a match—she had to admire her handiwork in the garden. It had come a long way since she first bought the place over two decades ago. Back then, she'd used every penny she owned to buy the cheapest cottage she could find on the island. It had cost her $1,500 for a shoebox, really, with nothing but a worn-down pile of dirt out front. But she'd worked hard on that pile of dirt, and it had grown into something quite spectacular.

She'd settled on Balboa Island in 1932, when there were almost no permanent residents on the island. Back then people came for the summer and then vanished the rest of the year, leaving it empty and almost desolate September through April, just the way she liked it. At night, men still used to come in looking to wash away their cares, disappearing into taverns through the back doors. Plenty of steamers gambled their money away as law enforcement turned a blind eye, but by daybreak they were gone. Now, though, the secret was out. People had moved to the island in hoards over the past few years, away from the heat and hustle of the big cities. Beach cottages were being torn down, and in their place permanent homes were going in with heat and indoor showers.

She was about to start on the next rosebush when two women walked along the sidewalk with tennis rackets in hand, hardly even used, by the looks of things. She recognized the redhead, Sylvia Johnson; her husband owned the fancy new tennis club in town. The other one, a blond, slowed as she walked by.

"Oh my, your garden looks lovely," she said.

Adele pressed her lips together and nodded, hoping they'd move on.

"We just moved in on Amethyst. Our garden needs a lot of attention, but it will have to wait until the inside's all organized first. I'm Milly, by the way, Milly Kincaid," she said.

"Adele," she said quietly.

"Gosh you look so familiar," Milly said, staring at her intently.

Adele clenched her jaw and kept her head down, busying herself with her gardening tools. She noticed out of the corner of her eye the way Sylvia took the woman by the elbow and nudged her on.

"Well, nice to meet you," Milly called out as they began to walk away. "Maybe I'll see you around."

Once they were out of view, Adele took out the secateurs and severed the rest of the roses in a wild fury. It had been a while since someone had recognized her—years, in fact—and the encounter left her feeling irritated, jittery. She should lay low, Adele thought, but then scoffed at the idea: How much lower a profile could she possibly keep? She'd changed her name. She'd arranged her life to be bland, routine, predictable, to avoid such an intrusion, and it grated on her nerves that someone like that blond should waltz along and disrupt things.

She looked up and tried to take in the clear blue sky and wisps of clouds, hoping to shake her concerns. She shouldn't worry so much; it was probably nothing, just a passing comment. She'd stay out of her way, that's all, but she knew she couldn't let it go that easily. She'd worked so hard to bury her past, and anytime someone so much as looked her way for a moment too long, she feared that they threatened to dredge things up again. She picked up her gardening tools and went back inside the house, trying to push those old familiar feelings of shame and humiliation down, deep down inside her, where they belonged.

She poured herself a cup of hot coffee and sat down, eyeing her old racket leaning against the wall. She envied the way those women had walked by with ease, likely on their way to the tennis club. They'd be warming up soon, feeling the vibration of the ball hitting the strings, softly at first to loosen up their arms and shoulders. But in fifteen minutes they'd be sending the ball soaring, corner to corner. Just the thought of it made her ache with longing.

She could still remember the feel of the racket the first time she picked up an old wooden Spalding, with peeling red-and-blue paint, from a crate next to the courts at the tennis club in Nice, France. She had been ten at the time and children were not supposed to be in the club, but her father had not been one to follow the rules.

"Can you teach me to play, Papa?" she'd asked her father when he stepped off the court, red-faced and perspiring in what had been pristine tennis whites just thirty minutes earlier.

"*Pas maintenant*," he had said, pushing past her and dabbing his face with a handkerchief before rushing to shake his opponent's hand. Adele followed him with a cup of water.

"Better luck next time, chap," the man had said to her father. He was English, much younger, in better shape, and he hadn't looked nearly as winded.

"Can *you* teach me to play?" Adele asked the man, standing at her father's side. Both men laughed, but her father squeezed her shoulder tightly, suggesting she'd embarrassed him.

"I'll teach you, *mon chou*, just as I promised," he said as he firmly ushered her away.

While her father had lunch with a group of men, also in long white trousers and collared shirts, Adele couldn't help but notice how majestic they looked together in their white uniforms of leisure. After she'd climbed all the trees surrounding the courts to give her shade from the midday sun and had drawn circles in the red clay of an empty court, she asked her father once more.

"Now Papa? Now can you teach me?"

He leaned back in his chair and stretched. "Fine," he said, stubbing out his cigarette and knocking back the last of his brandy. "A few minutes while no one's playing, and then we have to go home so I can take my *sieste*."

Her father stood on the opposite side of the net and threw the white felt balls toward her gently. She swung and missed every ball at first, but then she turned her body to the fence, perpendicular to the net, and stretched her arms out like an airplane. When she swung that time, she made contact.

"Catch the racket," her father said, showing her how to continue the swing up and over her left shoulder in one sweeping motion. When she swung the next time, she hit the ball over the net, and after that she sent almost every other ball over.

"*Trés bon*," her father said. "*Trés, trés bon.*" Adele beamed when she noticed the surprise in his eyes.

Once she had grasped the basic movement, he taught her to step into an open stance as the ball approached, angling the racket face so it hit the ball slightly in front of her body, not behind. She had skinny arms and a pale, almost sickly complexion at that age, having been encouraged not to play outside too much as a child; but soon she was hitting the ball with a power that no one expected, and her cheeks flushed with color, her skin glistening in the afternoon sun. They stayed for two and a half hours that day and only left because the men had returned from their lunch and their naps.

For the next several weeks, Adele's father took her to the club early to watch the matches, and she listened intently as he analyzed the players' strengths and weaknesses, commenting on their ground strokes, styles, and strategies. Eagerly, gradually, she began to make sense of his remarks. Some of the men at the club were experienced players, traveling for tournaments; others were on vacation from England and even America. Adele and her father studied them all.

She relished her father's sudden interest in spending time with her. He insisted that she accompany him each morning to the club—she was the only child allowed in because of some arrangement he must have made—and then as soon as the sun got unbearably hot and everyone deserted the courts for lunch and shade, he'd take her out and work on drills.

They were not a particularly wealthy family, but when her father sold his horse-drawn-carriage business a few years prior, they were able to afford a small and rustic holiday home in Nice. They lived a comfortable, if frugal, lifestyle, her father often bargaining or negotiating for a deal. But the one thing her father was willing to spend money on was the Nice Lawn Tennis Club membership. On earlier visits to the South of France, her father had seen firsthand the popularity of tennis and how its star players enjoyed a privileged place in Riviera society. He had been mesmerized and wanted that life for himself, but he didn't have the athleticism or the youth to excel in such an active pursuit. He was starting to realize, however, that his daughter might.

"Today, work on your forehand," he said. "*Tout de suite.*"

"Again, Papa?" Adele groaned, they'd done nothing but forehand strokes for hours the day prior, and she was eager to learn something new.

He didn't respond and simply began hitting the ball to her. After an hour of practicing the same exact stroke over and over again, he took his handkerchief and set it on the far corner of the court.

"*Alors*," he said. "Aim for the target." For the next hour he focused only on control and placement.

When her time was up, her feet throbbed and her shoulder ached from the repetitive movement. She could taste the dusty red clay in her mouth and feel it in her eyes. Her socks and shoes were orange and her skin felt gritty. But despite all that, she was walking on air because for seventeen of the last twenty shots, she'd hit the handkerchief, and then her father had folded it in half, and then in quarters, and only after she hit the square five times in a row did he finally let her take a break.

She wasn't accustomed to this kind of hard work—sweaty, lung-burning work, running down each ball, but now she leapt and swung as if she were a ballerina performing at the Palais Garnier. Until then, she'd always been taught that her role as a young girl was to be reserved and ladylike, seen and not heard. Her mother had enrolled her in classical Greek dance classes and piano lessons, activities to be pursued with control and restraint. When she was younger she'd been told to sit quietly and read while her parents attended to their business. Now, suddenly, everything she had been taught was being unraveled and retaught.

At night she overheard her mother and father discuss their daughter's new interest.

"It's not graceful to leap the way she does," her mother said, after she'd spent a few hours courtside watching the father-daughter display. "I see her bare ankles. It's not ladylike."

"She needs to be able to run, to leap," her father said, fighting back. "Have you seen the way the men go for every ball?"

"She's not a man. And that noise that she makes when she serves—it's uncivilized," she said.

"All right, I'll tell her to control that," he said. "But Anya, God has given our daughter a talent. I can help her polish it, and if she listens to me and does exactly what I say, I think I can make her a champion. Then, *mon amour*, we could have the life we always dreamed of."

Adele had never heard her father speak about her in such a way, and hearing his words set a fire inside of her, making her desperate to succeed. In the coming weeks, months, years, his belief in her made her work harder, made her strive for more, made her desperate not to make a mistake—leaping, dancing, hitting, following through, shuffling. Prepare, hit, prepare, hit. While her father became obsessed with studying the greats and teaching their techniques to Adele, she became obsessed with being able to follow his instructions and impress him. She wanted to succeed and to be able to give him the life he wanted. If that meant becoming a champion in tennis, then that was exactly what she would do.

CHAPTER FOUR

MILLY

The following week Milly arrived at The Island Club with Debbie and Jack in tow. You just never knew how a seven- and four-year-old might behave, but Sylvia had insisted that Milly bring the kids and that the ladies would have lunch and afternoon drinks poolside while the children splashed in the water.

"Jack, Debbie," Milly said, grabbing their hands as soon as they caught a glimpse of the turquoise pool ahead and tried to make a run for it. "We are guests here, and this club belongs to Mommy's new friend, Sylvia," she said. "Please be on your best behavior." They lunged forward. "Did you hear me?" she said, halting them again.

"Yes, Mommy," Debbie said. "We'll behave."

"Keep an eye on your brother, and stay in the wading pool." Milly looked to Jack as if expecting him to respond to her reasoning.

"Swimming pool," he said, pointing. "I want to go to the swimming pool."

"I know, darling, but just hold on a moment." She opened her large straw bag and pulled out a swim buoy that she'd bought from a store in town. Now that they lived near the beach and close to a swimming pool, she needed to travel with inflatable lifesaving devices. "Let me just try to inflate this thing." She ripped it out of the packaging, turned it around, looking for the air valve as quickly as she could, knowing that she had mere seconds before the children would run off again. Jack was hopping back and forth from one foot to the other.

"Do you need to use the bathroom?" she asked.

"No! I want to go to the pool!"

Milly blew hard into the buoy several times and strapped the thing around Jack's tummy. Standing up too fast, she felt dizzy and lightheaded.

"Mommy," Jack said, pulling at the pocket of her capri pants.

"One second, sweetheart." She placed her hand on the back of a chair to steady herself.

"Mommy," Jack said, tugging at the fabric harder each time. "Mommy, Mommy, Mommy!"

"What, Jack?" she snapped, bending down to his level.

"Mommy, I love you," he said, wrapping his arms around her neck, then kissing her bare shoulder. Then he took Debbie's hand and the two kids started off.

"Let's go," Debbie said as they ran full speed toward the pool.

Milly took a moment to compose herself, regretting her impatience just minutes into what she expected would be a long afternoon. She adjusted the waistband of her capris, pulling it back to her natural waistline, and smoothed down the pocket that Jack had been tugging on. Shoving the packaging of the swim buoy into the depths of her straw bag, she walked toward the group of women sitting at a long table in the shade near the pool. She sighed with relief as she saw several other children playing in the shallow pool and a teenage lifeguard keeping watch over them.

Sylvia sat at the head of the table in a pastel-pink horizontal-striped dress. Everyone else seemed to be equally dressed up, and Milly instantly regretted her choice of cropped trousers and a sleeveless shirt that tied at the waist.

"Sorry, Sylvia," she said in a low voice. "I thought it would be more casual since we were poolside, I didn't realize . . ."

"Nonsense," she said, "You are the picture of poolside elegance.

Here, take a seat." She pulled out the one next to her and began to introduce Milly to the women at the table—Betsy, Faye, Maureen, Joan, and Sadie.

"Milly here has just moved to Balboa from Los Angeles. She lives on Amethyst, and I'm trying to convince her to join the club," Sylvia said.

"I don't think it will take much convincing," Milly said. "It's beautiful here."

"Your Lloyd would love it."

He sure would, Milly thought. This was exactly the kind of wholesome family environment they so desperately needed.

"So," Sylvia asked the ladies, "what's everyone planning for Bal Week? It's right around the corner."

"We're leaving town, going to stay at my in-laws for the week," Maureen said. "I don't mind it, but my husband can't stand being here for all that craziness."

"We're renting out our two guest rooms to some girls from Manual Arts High School," Betsy said. "We always get lovely girls from there."

"How about you, Milly?" Sylvia asked. "Any plans?"

Milly laughed nervously. "I'm sorry I don't know what you're talking about."

"Oh gosh, haven't you seen the preparations already taking place?" Maureen asked. "How can you miss it? They remove the benches from the sidewalks to accommodate the crowds. It's a madhouse."

Milly felt embarrassed, as if she'd been so wrapped up in her own little world that she hadn't noticed any of this going on around her.

"Bal Week," Sylvia said. "Short for Balboa Week. Every year just before Easter, high school and college kids descend on the island and the peninsula for spring break. They rent out rooms, houses, guest cottages. They go to the Rendezvous Ballroom every night for live music and dancing, and they take over the beaches and the Fun Zone. The men, or rather the boys, cruise up and down the streets in their cars eyeing the girls in their swimsuits. It's a little annoying for those of us who live here, but the amount of money it brings in to the area is immense. It's a shot in the arm for the local businesses, so we all try to help out, open up our homes, and suffer through it."

"Sounds fun . . . and hectic," Milly said.

"You might want to let your husband know," Sadie said from the other end of the table. "Most husbands can't stand it and want to stay away."

"And others want to stay and ogle the goods for themselves," Maureen said, and everyone, except for Milly, laughed.

"So true," Sadie said. "Funny how all the husbands come back in time to watch the Bathing Beauty Contest at the end of the week."

"I heard Delores Mason is entering this year, Maggie's daughter," Maureen said, then she turned to Milly. "Maggie and her husband own the pharmacy. Her daughter's been dying to enter for years—such a pretty girl—and she's finally old enough."

"Goodness," Sylvia said. "I just know my Judith will want to enter once she turns sixteen. Already she and her friends want be part of all the fun, so I'm going to have to keep an eye on her."

"Oh, Sylvia, I've been dying to ask," Faye said, leaning in. "What are you doing with your house? I walked in on Teddy and Walter discussing it quite seriously." Faye turned to Milly. "My husband Teddy works in real estate." Then she turned back to Sylvia. "At first I thought they were talking about putting it up for sale." She laughed. "And then I thought, goodness no, not Sylvia's house! Where would we all play bridge? Are you considering renting it out for Bal Week?"

Milly noticed a look of confusion on her new friend's face and a flush of color rise in her cheeks, but then Sylvia swatted the comment away. "No, you're mistaken; I would never allow my Walter to rent out our house for Bal Week. Besides, we have to stick around to put on the Bathing Beauty Contest." She smiled a little too enthusiastically, then she stood and waved down the waiter. "Ready for lunch, ladies?"

As the afternoon rolled on, the children played together in the pool, the older ones helping the little ones, taking a short break for hot dogs from the snack bar, then jumping back in again, while the adults ate seafood salad and sipped iced tea. Milly could already sense how she might really enjoy it here, having a group of female friends. It was something she missed from her college days, which she hadn't really cultivated since she'd married. At Sylvia's suggestion the ladies skipped dessert and opted for a round of Tom Collinses. They were just being delivered on a large silver tray when one of the kids from the pool screamed at the top of her lungs. Milly leapt from her seat and was poolside in seconds, setting her eyes on Debbie and Jack, then counting the other children, eight of them, all hugging the edge of the pool. The red-suited "lifeguard" was up by the snack bar, beside a young man and dangling a french fry above her mouth.

"What's the problem?" Maureen asked as others from the table joined them at the kiddie pool.

"Somebody did a boom-boom," a little girl screeched.

"What?" Milly asked.

"A poop," the girl said, pointing to the center of the pool that was filled with pink-and-blue-striped inflatable toys, and, sure enough, a small brown lump was floating on the surface of the water.

"Eww, a poo-poo," another little boy chimed in.

"For goodness' sake," Sylvia snapped. She was standing at Milly's side now and sounded furious. This was her husband's pool, after all. "Emily!" she called toward the snack bar. "Get over here!" But the girl seemed in no rush to help out. "Who did this?"

When all eyes turned to Jack, and Milly saw him sink his chin to his chest and start to cry, she thought she might begin to cry herself. Of all the things that she imagined might go wrong that afternoon, she hadn't dreamed it would be something as awful as this.

"Jack, Debbie, out right now," Milly said as she searched the area for something she could use to get the offending thing out of the water. She reached down and grabbed the end of a pool toy that she thought she might be able to use to get the thing to float toward her, but it was no good. She might actually have to get into the pool to retrieve the thing herself.

"Oh, just leave it," Sylvia sighed, turning and walking back to the table. "The party's over, anyway." But Milly couldn't leave her son's feces floating in the swimming pool, with the kids traumatized and those "fabulous" women, especially that snippy one, Maureen, sitting there sipping their Tom Collinses, staring at it. She spotted a rectangular skimming net with a long metal pole hanging on the side of the wall just beyond the pool, near Jack and Debbie, who stood wet and shivering, huddled together away from the others.

She marched toward them. "Debbie, I need you to take my bag and walk Jack to the car. I'll be there in a minute."

"He ruined the pool party!" Debbie cried.

"We all make mistakes," Milly mumbled, but she resisted the urge to comfort her little boy beyond a pat on his head, with Sylvia and her friends watching. Then she retrieved the net off the wall, skimmed the poop out of the pool, and carried it away to the bathroom, where she flushed the damned thing down the toilet.

It wasn't until she pulled up and parked on their street, rushed the kids inside the house, and locked the door behind them that she was able to even speak.

"What were you thinking?" she said as Jack cowered into his sister's side. "Why would you do something like that and not just get out and go to the bathroom like every other child?"

Jack started crying again, then Debbie joined in.

"Why?" Milly asked, as if it made any difference now.

"We were having too much fun," Jack whimpered.

"You could have had more fun if you'd used the bathroom or called to me. Now head upstairs and change into dry clothes." She hesitated, but couldn't help herself from going on about it some more. "You can't just poop in a pool. You embarrassed me." She didn't want to look at their sad faces. "Think about that in your rooms for a while." They thumped up the stairs as fast as they could, likely relieved to get away from her.

Milly slumped into the couch, mortified, and thought of all the horrible things those women must be saying about her, about her children, how they'd never invite her back to the club. They'd never accept her now. They would be outcast, ridiculed. She pressed the palm of her hand against her forehead.

When Lloyd's car pulled up outside a little after seven, she rushed to the bathroom to wipe the smudged mascara from her eyes and tidy her hair. She wouldn't mention it. It was too humiliating and he'd blame her. He'd be horrified to know that his own son had done such a thing. He'd be angry with Jack but might be even more angry with Milly for letting it happen. No, she told herself, she'd simply ask him about his day and pretend it didn't happen. But as soon as he walked in the door, she blurted out the tragic events of the day.

"Good God, Milly, why didn't you take him to the bathroom?" Lloyd said once she was done.

"I didn't know he needed to go, Lloyd! The club has a teenager who was supposed to supervise them. Or I thought Debbie would take him, or that he'd at least ask me."

"He's four, for Christ's sake."

"He's almost five, and he always goes by himself."

"Well, not this time." He poured himself a drink and stared out the window. "What's for dinner?"

She shook her head incredulously. "I haven't even thought about dinner. I've been very upset. The other women—"

He sighed and wasn't listening. "I'm starving. Should we go out to eat?"

"We can't!" Milly said. "I can't show my face in this town. Everyone will be talking."

"You don't even know these people. You care too much what other people think."

Then he too marched up the stairs to change, leaving her all alone.

He was right: She cared. She cared deeply, about everything to the point of utter exhaustion, and she was filled with shame, as if she herself had fouled the pool. She felt worse than she had when she was at the club. This was her fault; she'd been caught up in the moment, wanting to make a good impression, too eager to make friends and laugh along with the other ladies, too eager to not feel so alone, that she hadn't paid enough attention to the children. Maybe *she'd* been the one having too much fun.

"I have to do something to make it right," Milly said to the empty kitchen.

She stayed up until midnight baking a pineapple upside-down cake. Then early the next morning, before Lloyd left for work, she transferred it into the prettiest cake tin she could find in her half-unpacked kitchen and snuck out of the house. It was barely 7 AM and slightly foggy as she walked down her street toward South Bay Front. She was in her housecoat and curlers, certain she wouldn't see anyone at that time of the morning, but when she turned onto Onyx Avenue and passed the small white cottage on the corner of Balboa Avenue, Adele, the woman with a French accent, whom she'd met a few days earlier, was kneeling on her lawn, weeding, with that same orange bandana tied around her head. She was older than Milly, in her late forties perhaps, and she looked up, squinted her eyes, then went back to what she was doing. Milly hesitated. It felt rude for her not to stop and say hello, but she didn't have the time or the inclination to chat. She turned onto Bay Front and, as quietly as she could, she unlatched the gate to Sylvia's house and tiptoed down the short pathway to the front door. She was carefully placing the cake tin on the front step, along with a note apologizing profusely for the incident, when the door swung open.

"Milly, what are you doing here?" Sylvia asked, standing there looking confused, in a pleated white skirt and matching top, tennis racket in hand.

"I-I-I made you a cake," Milly sputtered. She felt doubly humiliated, sneaking around like this in her housecoat and curlers.

"Thank you, but why?"

"To apologize for . . ." She couldn't bring herself to say it.

"For what?" Sylvia asked, and then it dawned on her. "Oh, for crying out loud, Milly. They chlorinated the pool. Everyone forgot it even happened."

This made Milly feel moderately better, even if it wasn't true, but she still felt like a fool standing there, a pineapple upside-down cake between them, so she set it down on the step.

"Are you off to play tennis?" she asked stupidly, because wasn't it obvious?

Sylvia gave a little twist and swung her skirt around her thighs. "Yes. You know I'd love for you to join me again."

"Now?" Milly asked.

"Well, you don't quite look court-ready, but maybe another day. It's much more amusing to run around after a tennis ball like a buffoon with someone else in tow."

"Well, I-I'd have to ask Leticia if she could come early again and watch the children," Milly said. "But it sounds like fun." Nothing really sounded like fun at that moment; she just wanted to rush home and get back under the covers, but she was trying, she was really trying.

"Another day then," Sylvia said, stepping over the cake tin. "But you know, if you want to join me on a regular basis, you'd have to join the club." She winked.

"You'd still have us, after yesterday's turn of events?"

"Honey"—Sylvia placed a hand on Milly's shoulder—"at some point in your life someone's going to come along and take a shit in your pool, and you can either sit around and cry about it or you can clean up the mess and get on with your life. In my experience, it's always best to move on with your chin held high."

Milly stared at her, not quite sure how to respond. She wasn't sure how she'd ever move on from her darling son having a bowel movement in the swimming pool, in front of all those women and children.

"Anyway . . ." Sylvia walked toward the gate and left Milly at the steps to her house. "I've got to get to the club. Talk to Lloyd and let me know what he says. Toodles."

CHAPTER FIVE

ADELE

Adele took the promenade on South Bay Front, the route she took every morning to get to work at the Fun Zone, a small amusement park just across the bay. Most days she'd look out at the yachts—the same sleek, majestic types that she used to be invited on years ago. She'd pass the fishermen at the end of the public dock and watch the sailboats glide by. But not today. Today she strode head down, faster than usual, if that was possible. She always moved quickly—it was in her nature to get where she was going at a clip—but today she had her arms bent, elbows tucked in tight to her body as she sped along the pathway toward the ferry.

It seemed odd that this Milly Kincaid lady, who'd only recently moved into the neighborhood, had passed by her house again in the early hours of the morning. For a brief moment it looked like she might stop and talk, but Adele put a stop to that, looking away abruptly, not engaging with the woman. Even so, it made her uneasy, as if she were walking that route on purpose to get another look at her.

Adele approached the ferry and stood in line behind a cyclist as the ferry docked. The water was flat except for the gentle wake rolling in after a man driving a small motorboat went by with a dog at his side in the cabin. The ferry operator lifted the metal bar and allowed the two cars it had carried across the bay to disembark.

"*Bonjour*, Adele," the morning ferry operator said as he did every single weekday morning.

"Good morning, Joseph," Adele replied as she took a seat on one of the wooden benches at the front of the ferry. She tried not to speak French out loud, but it sometimes slipped out, especially if she was feeling anxious or upset.

For the past five years she'd been working as an assistant to Hal Peterson, a big shot in the amusement side of town, who owned the Balboa Fun Zone. The name was ironic to Adele, since she didn't much like the place—a carnival across the bay on the peninsula, complete with a Ferris wheel, a carousel, bumper cars, a penny arcade, and far too many opportunities for children to consume their weight in sugar. In front of the Fun Zone was a beach with all sorts of sailboats and canoes available for rent, which meant the whole place would soon be overrun with those high school and college kids coming to town for Bal Week, followed by an onslaught of tourists and unruly children for a few months that summer.

Fortunately, Adele kept to herself in Hal's office on the second floor of the Balboa Pavilion overlooking the Fun Zone, where she helped keep the books, ordered supplies, and scheduled and managed the local boys Hal hired to operate the rides. But occasionally, when someone wasn't available to work their shift, like today, Adele had to step in and help out. It was her least favorite part of the job. In fact, she despised it.

She unlocked the door to a five-by-three-foot shed next to the Ferris wheel. Inside was a rusty stool, an empty metal cashbox, a crate with an oil dispenser, a can of gasoline for the motor, and some rags. She took out her thermos of coffee—strong and black—and a slice of homemade almond cake, and placed them on the narrow bench, something to look forward to that afternoon.

She arranged the schedules for the boys' shifts for the upcoming weeks and pinned them to the back of the door. She couldn't quite believe that these teenagers were allowed to operate the big wheel. It might look easy, but it actually required a fair amount of skill and some on-the-fly math computation. If two people were to ride on seat 1, she'd have to mentally estimate their combined weight, then she'd have to hold off on operating the Ferris wheel until someone else came along who was approximately the same weight and put them in seat 9, directly opposite seat 1, to balance the ride. Operating the clutch and brake was no easy feat either: It required focus to slow and stop the ride in the correct position and to get the passengers to dismount without dumping them forward or backward, especially if they were overly excitable or overweight.

As the hours dragged on, she hoped it would be a slow and uneventful Tuesday afternoon, but when she saw a small child running full speed toward her screaming, "Famous wheel, famous wheel!" she knew she'd have no such luck.

"*Arrête! Arrête!*" Adele said, holding her hands out in front of her body, fearing the boy would plow right into her.

"We want to ride on the famous wheel," he said, with a clump of cotton candy clenched in his little fist.

"It's not the *famous* wheel, it's the *Ferris* wheel." A girl a few years older caught up with him and grabbed him by the hand. "And you can't run off like that; Mother will make us go home." The boy jumped up and down unable to contain himself.

"I don't want to go home, I want to go on the famous wheel."

Adele involuntarily curled the top of her lip in disgust—the sticky hands, the tantrums. She had no patience for those kinds of things.

"We're closed," she said.

"What?" The girl looked up at her.

"We are," Adele said. "I'm sorry."

"Noooooooo," the boy cried, falling in a heap to the ground. "Noooooooo."

Adele looked around to see if her boss was in the vicinity watching the commotion, then rolled her eyes when she saw a woman running up to join them. It was Milly Kincaid, again. Unbelievable!

"What's going on?" she asked breathlessly.

"It's closed," the boy cried. "The mean old lady said it's closed."

"That can't be," Milly said, looking at Adele and realizing who she was. She gave her head a little shake in apparent confusion. "First of all," Milly said to the boy, "That's very rude. She's not a mean old lady, she's our neighbor. Apologize right this minute."

"No!" He curled his hands into fists and punched the ground, which just made him more miserable.

"Then we're going home," Milly said.

"Sorry," the boy whispered.

"We can't hear you, Jack," she said.

"I'm sorry," he shouted this time.

"Thank you. But secondly," Milly looked back to Adele, "What do you mean it's closed? It says right here that it's open until eight o'clock. We came straight from school. It's our first visit to the Fun Zone."

"It's at our discretion. We can do as we please," Adele said, feeling just like the mean old lady she was accused of being.

"I'm sorry, I think there's been some misunderstanding. I'm Milly Kincaid, and this is Jack and Debbie. I saw you gardening; we live one street over from you, on Amethyst."

"I know who you are," Adele said curtly. "We are doing some repairs." She glanced down at the boy and girl as they stared up at her, the boy's face wet with tears. Then she looked back to Milly, who looked as if she might burst into tears herself.

"Fine," Adele said, sighing. "Come back in five minutes." She walked to the office shed, picked up the rag, and began to wipe down the metal seats.

In her youth she'd trained herself to be cruel, uninterested in other people's feelings. She'd mastered a harshness that allowed her to annihilate her opponents in matches and not even wince when she beat them, game after game. She'd had to. It was what her father had taught her to do, and it had become ingrained in her. She was forty-eight now. She might not be playing tennis anymore, but it was almost impossible to let that part of her go.

When she put the rags away and looked up, her neighbor and the children were waiting patiently at the entrance, and Adele nodded to them to come inside the gate. She opened the latch on seat 1 and the kids climbed in. She fastened the safety belt and released the clutch, sending the children to the very top and bringing seat 9 to the bottom. She nodded for Milly to climb in.

"No, thank you," Milly said. "I'll sit this one out."

"You have to," Adele said, holding the latch open.

"Oh, but"—Milly shook her head fervently—"I can't."

Adele shrugged her shoulders. "Then they can't ride."

"But Debbie is very responsible; she'll take good care of her brother," Milly said. She looked up to the children, "Hold his hand, Debbie," she called out. "And don't let him wriggle around."

"Oh, *mon Dieu*," Adele said visibly annoyed. "It's about balance. They can either sit there and wait for someone to come along and ride, or they have to get off."

"Can't they just—"

"No," Adele said, before letting Milly finish her thought.

"It's just that . . ." Milly looked down at her feet as if she were ashamed. "I'm terribly afraid of heights."

Adele shook her head. People who were afraid of such things were weak, she thought, and then she wondered for a second if she'd said it out loud. Living alone for all these years, she had a tendency to talk to herself, sometimes out loud, sometimes in her head, sometimes she didn't know the difference. She glanced at Milly, who was staring up at her children and waving, and was reassured that she'd made that snide comment only to herself.

"Surely there'll be some others coming along soon, eager to ride," Milly said.

Adele shrugged.

"I really wanted them to have a little fun today." Milly smiled at Adele. "It's just that they've been having a tough time lately. Moving is hard, you know? New school, new friends, and their father." She paused, looked down at her shoes. "Well, it's not always easy; he works in L.A., a lot. We've barely seen him."

Why was she telling her all this? Adele thought. She didn't care. She didn't want to know about them, and she didn't want them to know about her. Minutes passed, but it felt like hours. Milly waved up at her children again, and Adele stared out at the bay hoping they'd all grow bored and want to leave.

"Adele." Milly touched Adele's arm, an alarmingly personal action, she thought. "We have some interested parties."

"What?" Adele pulled her arm away.

"Children! They would like to ride on the Ferris wheel."

Adele looked up and saw that a line had formed behind Milly. More children had arrived, and the after-school rush was finally starting. "Ah," she said. "This way," and she began seating them until finally the ride could start.

As the wheel began to move, Adele stood back and watched the children waving down at their parents, smiling. She always thought it was strange how this piece of machinery could cause people to experience such joy: They weren't even doing anything physical, just being lifted in a big circle. When Milly's kids rose up, the sea breeze blew their hair back from their faces, and they were laughing, mouths open, looking positively gleeful; they even waved to her.

When it was over, the Kincaid children begged to go again, and in a moment of weakness—Adele did feel a pang of guilt for being so mean-spirited to them earlier—she didn't force them to disembark. Instead, she let them, and whoever else wanted to ride, stay on for a second turn. It wasn't a full ride but it would be enough once a few others arrived, she reasoned. She returned to the shed and took a bite of her almond cake, waiting for more to join the line. She was refilling her cup with coffee from her thermos when she heard the commotion from the deck. She rushed out to see the wheel rolling backward, fast. Looking up, she realized she'd made the very error she'd been adamant to avoid earlier. When she'd unloaded some of the passengers, she'd left the wheel unbalanced. The first six seats were occupied and the rest were empty, no spaces in between. She rushed to the clutch, but smoke was billowing out from it.

"*Merde*," she said under her breath, a sick feeling in her stomach.

"Mommy," she heard Debbie call out desperately. "Mommy!"

Milly and another mother rushed toward the wheel, but Adele called out to tell them to stay back.

She took control of the clutch and flung it into neutral. As she ran through the many ways that this could get worse, she felt herself perspire. The cable could slip from the track and jam the wheel in place; the smoke coming from the clutch could escalate to fire; too much accelerated movement could cause an axel to snap; if an axel snapped with seats full of passengers, the whole wheel could topple into the bay. Her stomach twisted at the thought of another inexcusable disaster caused by her own stupidity. *Not again,* she pleaded as her past flashed through her mind. *Please, God, not again.* She glanced out to see that a small crowd had formed, and Milly was now clutching her chest with both hands as she looked up at her children.

It took several minutes, but the wheel began to slow and eventually rocked to a stop. Adele unloaded the seat closest to the platform, then very slowly moved the ride forward to unload the next, then she put it back in neutral and let it roll back in the opposite direction and unloaded that seat, then brought it forward again until she was able to unload in the correct order, restoring balance. When the last passenger stepped off the platform, she was finally able to exhale.

"Ma'am, excuse me, ma'am. Can you tell us your name?" someone called out, and a bright flash blinded her. She quickly held up her hand to her face, though it might have been too late. "I'm with the *Newport Harbor News Press*. What happened to the Ferris wheel? Is it fit to run for Bal Week?"

She turned abruptly, keeping an arm over her face as she retreated to the wooden shed. She hastily collected her belongings, shoved the cashbox under her arm and the key in her pocket, then she pushed past the onlookers and headed to her desk in the Pavilion, where she should have been all along. She never should have been operating that ridiculous ride to begin with. She'd made it very clear to Mr. Peterson that she disliked crowds, and she would remind him once more as soon as she saw him. But when she walked toward his office, he was standing looking out the window onto the Fun Zone.

"Adele," he said, his back still turned to her, "come in and shut the door."

She did as he asked, taking a seat opposite his desk. She waited for him to speak and ran through explanations for the fiasco that had just occurred. Eventually he turned toward her.

"I'm going to have to let you go."

"What? Why?" she asked, stunned. "Is this because of the . . ." She pointed out the window. "The incident?"

"Well," he said. "It's not exactly good for business just before Bal Week. I'm going to have inspectors poking around now." He took a puff of his cigar, then set it down on an ashtray.

She was about to tell him it was a technical issue, assure him it was not her fault, but she didn't even have a chance to lie.

"It's my niece, you see. She's just finished college, and I promised her a job for the summer. I owe my brother a favor." He shrugged. "She needs something to do before she meets a husband and settles down. And I have a feeling she'll be good at keeping the books. You know how it is. Family is family."

"But I . . ." Adele was at a loss for words. "The Ferris wheel is more complicated than it looks, as you just saw."

He waved away her comments. "Ah, she'll get the hang of it."

"But I need this job. Surely there's something else I can do. Odd jobs, errands?" She hated to beg—it was beneath her—but she had expenses and bills to pay. She didn't need much, but she relied on this paycheck for her simple, day-to-day life.

"I'm sorry," he said, though he didn't look all that sorry. "It's just the way it is."

Back home Adele picked up her racket and tennis ball and marched out behind her house to the alley that backed up to Amethyst Avenue. The cottage next to hers was vacant, soon to be torn down and replaced with one of those monstrosities, but for now it served as the perfect place to take out her anger. She dropped the felt ball to the ground, then slammed it into the side of the house. It flew back at her, and she whacked it again. The popping sound the ball made when it hit the perfect spot on her strings sent a hum through her body, and she wound up to swing again.

Now that she had to think about finding another job, dread was pooling in the pit of her stomach, her anxiety rising. Another job meant meeting new people, searching for an opportunity. All the jobs on the island available to a middle-aged woman like her involved serving or pleasing people—shop gal, waitress, checkout clerk. Maybe she'd find another gal-Friday position, like the one she did for Mr. Peterson, but those kinds of jobs came along through word of mouth, and after years of avoidance, of purposefully living in the shadows, her name was on no one's lips.

She looped her racket back behind her and threw her whole body into the stroke, her back foot leaping off the ground. She did it again and again, getting into a rhythm. The force felt good, the power and speed giving her a singular focus. She knew as soon as she stopped hitting the ball that the dread would come rushing back, so she kept on doing it. This was the only thing she was good at, this was the only thing that felt right, and yet this was the very thing that had ruined her.

CHAPTER SIX

SYLVIA

Sylvia didn't know exactly what she was looking for. She opened the desk drawers in Walter's office at the club and rifled through his papers. She pulled open a filing cabinet and flicked through the folders hoping to find some clue as to what was causing him such distress, and some indication why he was talking to the real estate agent about the house. She sat down at his desk and scanned it, finding everything in place—a fountain pen and ink, an ashtray, the Waterford paperweight she'd bought him for his birthday. No hints, no clues.

Glenda, Walter's secretary, opened his office door. "Good morning, dear. Is there something I can help you with?"

"No, Glenda, thank you. I can find it."

"OK," she said, hovering, clearly uncomfortable with Sylvia being there without her husband.

"Can I bring you a coffee or a pastry from the restaurant kitchen? They start baking them around this time to get ready for the lunch crowd. I often sneak one for Walter," she said with a wink.

"I'm fine," Sylvia said, wanting more time alone to poke around.

She was only seventeen when she'd met Walter. Her friend Karen Boston had convinced her to go to Balboa Island for Bal Week, where Karen planned to meet a nice college boy. Sylvia lived in Barstow, two hours inland, and rarely saw the ocean, so she jumped at the chance. There was to be a bathing beauty contest, and Karen was determined to win both the contest and a husband, and she insisted that Sylvia enter too, for moral support. They'd pooled their meager savings together to purchase new swimsuits; they'd borrowed clothes suitable for beach activities, and they'd sewn whatever they didn't have. By the time they packed their suitcases and were ready to set off for their week-long adventure, they had just enough money to share a two-bedroom cottage with twelve other girls they'd never met, with not a penny to spare. They were going to have to work really hard for those dinners and drinks. But as Sylvia walked out the door, her grandmother had pulled her aside.

"You go and have yourself some fun," she'd said, placing a five-dollar bill in her hand and closing her fingers over it. "And you be the kind, honest young lady I raised you to be. There's gonna be some flashy people down that way, rich people, that might make you question what you got back home." Her grandmother stood up straighter, smoothing down the clean yet permanently stained apron she had tied around her waist. "Just you remember now, none of that matters; what matters is your integrity, you understand me?"

"Yes, Ma," she'd said, staring down at the money in her hand. "Thank you."

Her grandparents had raised her. There'd never been any mention of who her father was, though when she was old enough to understand a few things, she'd overheard late-night conversations that implied that the act between her mother and whoever he was had not been consensual. When Sylvia was a toddler, her mother met John—tall and serious with a steady job. He lived in a nice house in a decent part of town, but he wanted nothing to do with an illegitimate child. Sylvia was sent to live with her grandparents. Her own mother went on to have two more children with John, but Sylvia rarely saw them.

Except for the occasional sting when some kid made a comment about how old her "parents" were or how worn down her clothes looked, she didn't feel all that different from everyone else she grew up with. As she got older, though, she realized that her prince was not going to find her working the cash register at Dottie's in the small, dusty town of Barstow. She was going to have to get out of there quickly if she wanted a chance at love. Except, instead of meeting a nineteen-year-old college boy that week on Balboa Island, as her friend Karen had predicted, she met thirty-two-year-old Walter.

She'd left her spot on the crowded sand and was standing in line at the frozen banana stand in the Fun Zone to get a chocolate-dipped frozen banana when Walter had approached, dabbing at his forehead with a white linen handkerchief.

"You look like you're at the wrong party," Sylvia said to him as he got in line behind her, wearing a pale-blue suit and button-down shirt, the only suit among hundreds, maybe even thousands, of swimsuit-clad men and women packed like sardines on the beach by the amusement park.

"I'm working, unfortunately," he said, pulling at his collar.

"Working on a beautiful day like today?" Sylvia asked.

"When you live here, you see that pretty much every day is beautiful."

"Then maybe you have the wrong kind of job," she said. "If you were a lifeguard"—she pointed to the strapping young men perched atop shaded chairs overlooking the beachgoers—"then you'd have a far more suitable uniform."

"This is true," he said, chuckling. "But until I land myself a job like that, I'm just looking for ways to cool down." He turned to the man at the banana stand. "Two frozen bananas, dipped, no nuts; one for me, one for the lady."

"How do you know what I want?"

"An educated guess. This is a banana stand."

She laughed. "That's true, but I can buy my own," Sylvia added instinctively, handing the man at the stand fifteen cents. "And I'll take the nuts, please."

Walter seemed to consider this for a moment. "Well, if I can't buy you a frozen banana, nuts or no nuts, perhaps I could take you to dinner tonight?"

Sylvia smiled. He was devilishly handsome and successful looking, despite the fact that it seemed as if he might burst into flames in that suit in the hot sun, and he had a hopeful smile that lifted on one side. She looked into his hazel eyes and really wanted to say yes, but then she knew she'd have to leave Karen all alone, and they'd planned to eat like birds for the rest of the day to prepare for the Bathing Beauty Contest.

"I'm Walter, by the way, Walter Johnson," he said. "I seem to have forgotten my manners, asking a young lady out for a date without even introducing myself." He put his hand on his heart and bowed his head a little, which made Sylvia laugh.

"Well, nice to meet you, Walter. I'm Sylvia, and while I would like to take you up on your kind offer, I'm afraid I can't tonight because my friend and I have to get our beauty sleep for the beauty contest tomorrow."

"You're entering the Bathing Beauty Contest?" he asked. "Of course you are. And I am quite sure you will win."

"And what makes you so sure?"

"Because you're the most beautiful woman on this island." Then growing bolder, he said, "Heck, you're the most beautiful woman I've ever set my eyes on."

Sylvia laughed, feeling her cheeks prickle with heat and her heart race a little. She was used to having the attention of the men and boys in her small town, often unwanted, but never from a man as handsome, charming, and distinguished looking as this.

"So, tomorrow night then?" he asked. "After your big win, may I take you out to celebrate?"

"You're quite sure about this, aren't you?" Sylvia said.

"Never more sure of anything in my life."

Sylvia took a nibble of her frozen treat so as not to let him see her smiling, then she held his gaze, making him wait a moment more, even though she knew she would say yes.

"And I promise you," he said, "I won't take you to some burger and fries joint where these college boys like to go. I'll take you on a real date, for a real lady."

Comparing himself to the college boys, as if it were some kind of competition, somehow made him even more endearing.

"If I win," she said, "then you can take me to dinner."

"*If* you win?" he asked.

"If I win."

"Oh, you'll win."

"Well," she said, "let's hope you're right."

"I am," Walter said, bowing his head to her and starting to turn away.

"But wait," Sylvia said, despite her best effort not to sound desperate. "You don't even know where I'm staying."

"I don't need to; I'll see you at the contest."

"You'll be there?" she asked, a little shy now, since he was going to see her strutting her stuff down the boardwalk. What if she didn't win? What if she came in last? What if he changed his mind?

"I don't think you leave me any choice," he said. "How could I possibly miss it now?"

"Well, then I'll see you tomorrow," she said. "Nice to meet you, Walter Johnson." As she had returned to the beach, she knew he was watching her, and she had to do everything in her power not to run back to Karen, still sunning herself, and tell her that she'd just met the man she would marry.

There was a rap at Walter's office door. "Just me again," Glenda said, peeking in and jolting Sylvia out of her memories. Sylvia shoved a drawer closed. "I brought you a pastry anyway because they're fresh out of the oven." Glenda placed an apple turnover in front of Sylvia, but the sweet smell of it turned her stomach.

It had been days now since Walter's mood had soured. His behavior had become more and more erratic, with him snapping at her when she tried to help, or avoiding her completely. And he still hadn't offered her any explanation about the injury to his finger. He'd simply come home the evening after his outburst with it all bandaged up, and he hadn't mentioned it again since. It was the first time in their sixteen years of marriage that she began to question their relationship, and she was desperate to know what was at the root of it all.

"You know I think he has a meeting elsewhere," Glenda said, looking through a steno pad. "Though I don't know with whom." A phone began to ring in the reception area out front, and she hesitated "I'd better . . ."

"All right," Sylvia said, standing. "I'll see him later then."

Glenda hurried off.

Sylvia looked around one last time and noticed a slim drawer under his desk with a lock, but when she pulled it, it slid right open. There was a pen, a cigar, and a glass bottle of pills lying on its side. Printed on the label was Walter's name, a doctor's name she'd never heard of, and in bold letters: HEXAMETHONIUM. TAKE ONE PILL A DAY. She opened the bottle and smelled the pills, as if that might give her some insight into what they might cure. She looked around for an accompanying note, but there was none. My God, was he sick? She knew she shouldn't take them with her—he'd know she'd been looking through his things, and he might need them—but she needed to know what was going on with him once and for all. She put them in her bag and left.

Marrying and having a child with a man who was fifteen years her senior meant that she had considered his death before, but in her mind she had only pictured losing him when he was old, and she'd imagined being an old woman herself, sixty perhaps, and having to go on and live another fifteen or so years without him. Never before had she considered the possibility of losing the love of her life now, when he was only in his late forties. He was still relatively young by many measures, and the very thought of him being ill and not feeling that he could confide in her about it gave her a chill. It must be serious; that was the only reason he would be acting like this and keeping it a secret. He wouldn't want Judith and Sylvia to worry. Oh God, maybe the illness had caused him to fall and injure himself and that's why he hadn't wanted to tell her. A sudden dread set in.

Back home, a car was parked outside her house, so she let herself in quietly. The door to Walter's study was closed, but she could hear mumbling voices inside. She tiptoed closer and put her ear to the door.

"Well, I'm sorry, Walt. I really am." It was a man's voice, and it amplified a little as if he'd paced over to the door. "But it's not getting any better; it's only going to get worse with time. One of them has got to go, and fast. I'll check back in a few days." The door opened abruptly and Sylvia stood upright, stepping back so fast she almost lost her balance.

"Oh," was all she could manage. It was Hank Harris, Walter's accountant.

"Good morning, Mrs. Johnson," he said, looking sheepish and brushing past her as he let himself out.

She felt foolish for getting caught listening in on a private conversation, but she tried not to let it show. Her mind raced with the thought of wills and trusts and planning for an uncertain future, and she hated the fact that he was discussing such things without even letting her in on the truth.

"Walter," she said as soon as she heard the front door close. "What does he mean, 'it's not getting any better'?"

Walter glared at her.

"You can't keep these things from me, Walter. Faye said you've been talking to Teddy about the house. What's going on? I'm worried and I want to help." He turned away and looked out the window, and Sylvia tried to steady herself for the news.

After a moment he pulled out his desk chair and sat, dropping his head into his hands. "I'm sorry, Sylvia. I'm so, so sorry." He rubbed at his temples and wiped a tear away.

Sylvia was at a sudden loss for words. She'd only seen him cry once before, and those were tears of joy, the first time he held Judith as a baby. This was something entirely different and he was scaring her. She braced herself.

"I've been worried about our finances. The club has put us in a hole, so many bills, the loan, the mortgage, salaries, taxes. We should be doing better by now." He wiped his eyes with the backs of his hands. "I panicked."

"What are you talking about? What do you mean you panicked?" she said, so confused about where this conversation was going.

"I tried to get ahead, to come out on top." He pressed his hands against the side of his head, then he looked up at her, his eyes desperate. "I'm sorry. I'm so, so sorry."

"For what, Walter?" she was impatient now.

He looked at her again, as if he were willing to do anything not to speak the words. "I lost a lot of money to the wrong guys."

"No, Walter. Not gambling? Again? You promised me."

"I thought I could win big, give us the boost we needed."

Sylvia stood behind the chair opposite, trying to understand.

"How long has this been going on?" she asked.

"Last week was the first time in years, and I got hit hard."

"How hard?"

"Thirty," he said in a whisper.

"Thirty?" she repeated. "You've done much worse."

"Thirty thousand."

Sylvia grabbed the back of the chair for support, feeling as if her knees might buckle under her.

"I went back last Thursday. I was desperate, I didn't know what to do; I didn't want to worry you. I tried to win it back."

"And?" she asked, knowing the answer. Her life, their life, was flashing before her eyes.

"No," he said shaking his head. "No, it's worse. I doubled down. I lost it all. Sixty thousand dollars."

He was sobbing now, and Sylvia couldn't console him. She couldn't even look at him. They didn't have that kind of money in the bank; they'd poured their savings into opening the club. She walked to the other side of the room, her heart pounding in her chest. How could he do this to her, to Judith? They'd be ruined. They'd never come back from this.

"We're going to have to sell the house," he said, as if trying to regain some composure now, to see some path forward. "And the club," he went on.

"Don't be ridiculous," Sylvia said. She needed to think, to absorb what he was telling her, and she couldn't do that if he was talking.

"We'll go to the desert," he went on, as if she weren't there and he was just spewing out ideas to himself. "It's cheaper there."

"We're not going to the desert. We're not selling the house. We're not selling the club."

"You don't understand," he said. "We don't have a choice. I have to pay them, or—"

"Or what?"

"Or they're going to break more than my finger," he said.

Sylvia thought she might be sick, and she realized she was squeezing the glass pill bottle in her hand. "What about these?" she asked accusingly, holding the bottle up to him as if this bit of evidence could somehow change things, as if it could give him some other reasonable explanation.

He looked confused. "Where did you get those? They're my blood-pressure pills." Suddenly she couldn't stay in the same room as him. She threw the pill bottle across the desk to him and walked out of the house, got back in her car, and with shaky hands drove away so she could think.

His father had been a gambler. Walter had told her that when he was a boy, his father used to bring him along to the numerous properties he owned on the island to collect rent from the tenants, and they'd often end up at the Green Dragon on the peninsula. After a drink or two at the bar, his father would head upstairs for one of his not-so-secret poker games, and Walter would be left at the bar for hours. He was eleven at the time, but eventually the bartender gave him the job of ice chipper—breaking the slab down with a pick so that the chips would fit into a glass. He heard a lot while he was chipping away at that slab, and, as he got a few years older, he was allowed to go upstairs and sit in on some of the card games.

Just as he'd taken over his father's businesses and properties, when his dad passed away, Walter had also stepped right into his father's seat at the poker table. It had seemed natural to him: He knew what to do and he knew how to win. But when Sylvia and Walter married and had Judith, she'd asked him to stop. She knew too well what it was to be poor and she wanted those days behind her. There were times over the years when she'd suspected that he had gone back to the table, but as far as she knew, his interest had waned. She now felt like a complete fool.

Without even realizing that she'd driven herself back to the club, she pulled her pink-and-cream Dodge La Femme into the parking lot. Walter had surprised her with this car for Christmas. Pink paint job, pink steering wheel and dashboard, it even came with a pink purse, complete with pink cigarette case, lighter, comb, and lipstick holder, which all fit neatly into the back of the seat. "She's a beauty for my beautiful wife," he'd said on Christmas morning as he handed her the keys. "I wanted you to be one of the first to have a car made especially for a woman." If they'd really wanted to cater this car to women, she grumbled to herself as she wrangled her pink beast into one of the parking spaces, they should have made it smaller and easier to drive. She killed the engine and sat there, hands still fixed to the smooth leather steering wheel.

How could he upend their life like this? Everything had been so perfect. Judith was doing well, the new club was making steady progress, or so she thought, and they were about to gear up for Bal Week, hosting the grand finale, the Bathing Beauty Contest, at the end of the week, just as they always did. How could they go on now as if nothing had happened? And their house, their home—where she'd lived since her wedding night, where she'd nursed Judith as a baby, where she'd raised her, hosted birthday parties, hosted every other imaginable soiree—surely he was wrong about the house. My God, they needed a place to live, didn't they? And what would people say if their beautiful bayfront home, that coveted corner lot, was suddenly up for sale? No one would believe it. This wasn't happening, it couldn't happen. She pressed her head to the steering wheel and closed her eyes, willing it to all just be a bad dream.

CHAPTER SEVEN

MILLY

Milly made a check out to The Island Club and signed Lloyd's signature, leaving the amount blank, as she had no idea, nor did she care, how much the membership fees would be. She'd planned to stride into the office at the club, hand over her check, and head straight home, membership card in her purse. But as she pulled into the parking lot, she saw Sylvia in her flashy pink car.

Milly tapped on the window. "I'm sorry," she said when Sylvia jumped, "I didn't mean to startle you."

"Milly, hello darling," Sylvia said, putting on a pair of large white sunglasses and stepping out of the car. "What brings you to the club?"

"I've decided to join," Milly said. "We. We've decided to join."

"Oh!" Sylvia clasped her hands together.

"Assuming the offer is still on the table."

"Of course. We're going to have such fun!" Milly couldn't help but notice that Sylvia's enthusiasm seemed forced. Maybe she didn't want them after all. But then she linked her arm through Milly's and walked toward the entrance. "I'll take you in and get you all signed up."

The cost was $7.00 a day, for a total of $2,555 annually. Milly had never made any large purchase without first consulting Lloyd. She hesitated for a moment too long as she wrote out the final amount and handed over the check, but if Sylvia noticed, she didn't say so. When she left she was trembling slightly at the realization of what she'd just done, and while it had seemed like a good plan to commit them to this new town, she worried what Lloyd would say when he found out.

Milly decided to make steak for dinner. That afternoon, after Jack insisted upon wearing a shirt that was far too small for him and showed off his belly button, and then refused to put on shoes or socks, she gave in and let him climb into his stroller barefoot, then she walked to Marine Avenue to buy the best round steak they had. He needed his father, Milly thought, and it was becoming increasingly clear that Jack was suffering and acting out without Lloyd's nightly presence. She couldn't do this alone—raise children, manage a household, join clubs, make friends. Lloyd was supposed to be the support she needed with the children and the strict one when they wouldn't listen to her. She needed him to be here to help her.

Milly's parents had hated each other. They'd bickered constantly. She'd feel arguments building and building until they became all-out screaming matches. There were slammed doors, threats of leaving that left Milly shaking. Insults were hurled like daggers, cruelties spoken between two people who were supposed to love each other, all stemming from things that seemed frivolous—the way bread was sliced or the way one looked at the other during a dinner party. She couldn't fathom why her parents had ever married, why they'd had a child and brought her into their mess. She had often wondered what it would be like to be part of another family, to have a sibling who could share some of the burden of all the fighting, someone to talk to.

She vowed that when she was old enough, she would do things differently. She would fix all of this longing and wondering by having children of her own as soon as possible, and she'd be a loving, doting mother and wife. She'd do everything that she was taught in the Marriage Education and Marital Arts course she took in college. She'd keep her home-economics textbooks and refer to them often.

She would succeed at motherhood and housewifery the way she'd succeeded in her domestic-arts courses.

Seventeen magazine was her Bible back then, but she'd also read the magazines that women read when they'd already made it—*Woman's Day*, *Better Homes & Gardens*, *McCall's*, and *Good Housekeeping*. She knew exactly what to expect and what to aspire to.

Milly was only one year into college when she met Lloyd, and he was a senior. With all that marital-arts research and education under her belt, she knew all the right things to do and say. She was taught that one of her jobs when they were going steady was to show him how life with her by his side would be preferable and easier than his bachelorhood. And she succeeded for a short time. But when her mother died unexpectedly halfway through that first year of college, she fell apart and she didn't expect to see Lloyd again. There were plenty of other girls he could charm, girls who were fun and carefree and unburdened by grief.

But he surprised her. Lloyd stuck by her side. He attended the funeral with Milly—a very grown-up thing to do for a college boy, she had thought. He met her father, who later told Milly he approved of her beau. He wiped away her tears and listened to her memories and her regrets, and he gradually brought her back to the world again. He was a distraction and a blessing and she was forever grateful to him for that. *This is what I want*, she remembered thinking back then, *a man who is patient and kind, who loves me enough to stand by my side through good times and bad.*

And yet, when marriage and family came along, she realized it wasn't as easy as all those magazines had promised. It was hard to be that perfect woman they pictured in the articles, happily feeding their children, mopping their floors in full makeup and dressed to the nines. It was hard to decorate and maintain a house and learn how to cook delicious meals and look gorgeous and glamorous while caring for an infant. She was exhausted; she missed her mother, yearned for her advice, and felt betrayed by the images of the life she'd dreamed of for so long.

Becoming a wife and then a mother didn't give Milly the feeling of success and security that she thought it would. Instead, it made her feel trapped and resentful that Lloyd got to go out into the world each day and interact with people, adult people, while she had to stay home and clean and wash and feed and console. She loved her children dearly, and at night when they were sleeping sweetly in their beds, she felt guilty for having those thoughts, but the repetitiveness of it all felt suffocating.

There'd been a brief period of time when things started to feel somewhat manageable, when Debbie was walking and talking and able to play by herself for a few minutes at a time. But almost as fast as that phase came along, Milly was pregnant again, and this time it was twice as tiresome. Lloyd was out late three or four nights a week with work, clawing his way up the ladder at the network, missing bath times and feedings and bedtimes, and Milly did it all, slowly losing herself along the way.

"Good afternoon, ma'am," the produce man at Hershey's Market said as he polished apples and lined them up beautifully. She had half an hour to spare before Debbie's school bus would arrive, and Jack had already fallen asleep in his stroller after tiring himself out with his tantrum. "Anything I can help you find?"

"I'm cooking steak for dinner, for my husband."

"Meat department's all the way in the back," he said, but Milly already knew where to go.

To be a successful wife is a career in itself, she recalled her Family Relations professor telling the girls in class. *It requires, among other things, the qualities of a diplomat, businesswoman, cook, nurse, schoolteacher, politician, and glamour girl.* Milly took a bottle of Worcestershire sauce off the shelf and placed it in her basket. *Think about what you can do differently to prevent your husband from straying, drinking too much, or from being abusive.* If she'd been happier, more content, more competent at being his wife and the mother of his children, perhaps he'd be inclined to be around them, she thought. *When a husband leaves his home, he may be seeking refuge from an unpleasant environment.* More advice from her

Marital Arts class rang in her ears. *Could it be that your husband feels that he is not understood or appreciated in his own home?*

She'd make his favorite, she decided—barbecued steak with potatoes. And then she'd be honest and tell him about the club membership. He'd be surprised, shocked that she'd done such a thing without his permission, but he'd see the benefits of it, surely. Maybe they'd even try to play a little tennis. Or, at the very least, they could swim on the weekends.

Back home, Jack and Debbie sat in front of the television glued to *Buffalo Bill Jr.* while Milly prepared dinner. She opened up her wooden recipe box and flipped through the note cards until she found the one she was looking for. Despite its name, it didn't involve a barbecue at all but was named for its smoky-flavored sauce. She chopped and sautéed the onion and green pepper; added the ketchup, vinegar, Worcestershire sauce, mustard, and brown sugar; and brought it to a simmer. The scalloped potatoes were browning in the oven, the cheese sauce bubbling at the edges of the dish, and she was waiting to drop the round steak into the pan when she heard the car pull up, followed by the usual chorus of her children singing "Daddy" from the living room.

A wave of relief flooded over her, and yet as she untied the apron from her waist, she wondered what excuse he'd give her for not coming home the last few nights. *Never mind all that*, she told herself, *he's home now.* She reapplied her Cardinal Red lipstick in the reflection of the kitchen window, kicked her wool slippers into the hallway closet, and slipped into her pumps. She took two crystal glasses out of the cupboard and poured two gin and tonics, then, once she'd heard the excitement die down from the living room, she went back to the steak.

"Milly bird," Lloyd said, placing his hand on her waist and kissing her cheek. "What happened to the hallway? There's a hole in the wall."

She paused as it sank in that she'd hurled her shoes down the hallway more than a week ago, and he hadn't been home long enough, or cared enough, to notice. "Oh, one of Jack's toys," she said, trying to push her resentment down into the pit of her stomach with a hard swallow. "That darn scooter—the handle went right through the wall," she said, handing him a highball. She tried to force a smile but she just couldn't do it, she couldn't help herself. "Where have you been?" she asked quietly, one hand on her hip.

"Work, dinners—I told you," he said, hanging his hat on a hook behind the door.

"You told me that on Monday, Lloyd. It's Friday."

"Milly, it's been a busy week. You know how demanding Beverly Douglas can be; she wants to be treated like royalty, go to the most fashionable dinner clubs. You know what she's like."

"I have no idea what she's like," Milly said, cringing as she heard her husband casually drop the name of a beautiful actress into his conversation, as if this were normal.

"Well, let me tell you," he went on. "She's brilliant on screen, just brilliant. Everyone is awed by her, but when the camera is off, she's a child; she needs a chaperone, she wants to see everyone, everywhere."

"Your children would like to see you now and again," Milly said, thinking of her husband and Beverly Douglas snuggling in together in a booth, ordering martinis, eating dinner, laughing, drinking, and worse.

Lloyd looked at her crestfallen—so handsome, a face so perfect, eyes a clear, piercing blue. Milly always thought he should have been in front of the camera, not behind the scenes.

"Do you think I want to be away from my children?" he asked in a low whisper.

"I don't know, Lloyd, I don't know what you want. We moved here so we could get away from all that and start acting like a family again."

"'*All that*' is my work, Milly, my work that pays the bills around here and pays for this house. I can't just get away from that." He picked up his glass and took a swig. "If anything, being all the way down here is just making it harder. The commute, the traffic."

"You said you wanted to move," Milly said.

He shook his head. "Let's be honest; you were the one who wanted this. You insisted."

Now, Milly picked up her gin and tonic and took a gulp. "You agreed to it, Lloyd. You even seemed excited about finding the house. If you thought you'd never be home you should have said something; we wouldn't have moved." She slammed the glass on the counter harder than she intended, sending it spilling over the rim.

"You made it clear you couldn't stay in Los Angeles anymore. What was I supposed to do, force you to stay? I don't want to see you unhappy all the time, not again." Lloyd shook his head, and Milly knew he was referring to those months after Jack's birth when she'd been so out of sorts, anxious one minute, unable to get out of bed the next. "Look, I'm here now, aren't I?" he said softening, as he reached over and squeezed her arm. "Let's not argue; the children will hear."

Milly took a deep breath and tried to focus on that; she never wanted to fight in front of the children. She tried to ignore the thoughts of where he'd been and with whom. She tried to erase the image of Beverly Douglas seared in her mind. *He's here now*, she repeated in her head as she turned away from him, stirred the sauce in the pan, and turned the heat down. That's something.

At the table—Jack in his high chair, though way too big for it now, and Debbie seated next to Lloyd—Milly served the barbecued steak with potatoes and Lloyd dug in. "Nothing like a home-cooked meal." He looked up at Milly and smiled.

"I chose a new book at the library today," Debbie said, grinning.

"Is it *Bambi*?" Lloyd asked. Debbie shook her head. "Is it *Lassie*?"

"No," she said.

"Is it *The Red Balloon*?"

"No, Daddy," Debbie said and laughed. "You're not going to know it. It's a grown-up book, a ladies' book for children." She waited to see if he'd guess it anyway.

"*Jiminy Cricket*?"

"No. Daddy," she said, laughing again and pulling it up from her lap and holding it up. *Mary Alden's Cake and Cookie Cook Book for Children*. "I'm going to make the Angel Puffs and the Snowman Cookies and the Polka Dot Roll and the Wonderland Bars. Right, Mommy? Can I make them?"

"Yes, darling, but not all at once," Milly said.

"Do we have marshmallows and chocolate pieces and almond extract?"

"Smarshmallow?" Jack repeated, looking up from the food on his tray. "I want smarshmallow."

"Debbie, let's look at the recipes later," Milly said, hoping to avoid an escalation into a tantrum about "smarshmallows."

"I really want a smarshmallow," Jack whined as if on cue.

"Maybe for dessert, if you eat all your dinner," Milly said calmly.

Lloyd reached over and gave Debbie's hand a squeeze. "It sounds like a wonderful book. It's going to teach you how to become a real little lady."

Debbie beamed at him, while Milly shuddered at the thought of Debbie's early interest in domesticity. She hoped that by the time Debbie was of marrying age there'd be more for her than this.

"Well," Milly said, not looking up from her plate, "today we joined the club."

"What club?"

"The Island Club. You know, Sylvia and Walter's club; they talked about it at dinner, remember?"

"You said you'd like to take a tour."

"Well, I took a tour and I signed us up. We're members now."

"Milly, how much . . ." He glanced at the children and stopped himself, forcing a smile. "We should have spoken about it first."

Milly cut a piece of steak. "How could we"—she smiled right back at him—"if you're never here?" There was a burning silence between them. No one looked up from their plate. Even Jack seemed to know to keep his focus on smooshing his peas on his fork in front of him. "Anyway, I was thinking we could get back into tennis."

"We barely ever played tennis," he said.

"We used to love watching it; maybe we could actually play this time. There's a young girl who watches the children while the parents are indisposed." She waited but he said nothing. "Or we could swim."

"I want to swim," Debbie chimed in.

Lloyd finished his meal, gulped down his gin, then stood, pulling at the tie around his neck. "I'm going to get changed."

Later that night after the kids were in bed and Milly had washed the dishes, wiped down the countertops, and finished the last of their cocktails, Lloyd joined her at the kitchen table.

"I wish you hadn't done that," he said.

"It's too late, I'm all done," she said, wiping her hands on her apron, untying it, and throwing it in the laundry hamper.

"I'm not talking about cleaning up," he said. "I'm talking about joining that tennis club. I wish you'd asked me first."

"Lloyd," she said as calmly as possible, "I shouldn't have to ask your permission for every little thing I do. I have to make decisions about our household, especially in your absence," she said, even though she'd asked his permission throughout their entire marriage. He didn't seem angry—it was disappointment she could hear in his voice, and that was almost worse.

"If you had spoken to me first, I would have told you to wait; I would have told you that we just bought a house and that I just put a deposit down on an apartment near my office."

"You did what?"

"I'm going to need somewhere to stay on those long days followed by business dinners. They won't go away just because we don't live in Hollywood anymore."

"What's wrong with a hotel? You didn't seem to have a problem with staying in a hotel the past several nights."

"It's not a long-term solution."

Milly took the gin from the counter and poured a shot onto the melting ice cubes in her glass.

"Are you saying you want to live apart?"

"No," he said, then hesitated. She could have sworn she saw a glimmer of hope in his eyes. "Do you?"

"Of course I don't. But I don't want to live with someone who's got one foot out the door either." She glared at him, waiting for him to tell her she was wrong about this, that he was committed to her, committed to their family, that of course he didn't have one foot out the door, that he would change, that he would make more of an effort to be home in time for dinner, to be home at all. But instead, he sat down at the table, closed his eyes, and rubbed his temples. He looked exhausted, beaten down. He didn't even have the energy to argue.

"Look," he said weakly. "Maybe it makes sense if I stay up in Hollywood during the week and come here on the weekends, to spend time with the kids."

It stung to hear him say that, no mention of her, just a visit for the sake of the kids. Milly felt her chest tighten. It was happening, exactly as she'd feared. Her master plan to tie them back together on this impossibly happy little island was going to be the thing that would tear them apart.

"Maybe, I don't know, maybe it's best." Lloyd looked up at her as if he might begin to cry. He reached for her hand, but she pulled it away sharply and took two steps back, as if she might catch this thing that had infected him, this thing that was going to ruin them if she allowed it to take hold and spread. "I'm not . . . It's not that . . ." He sighed. "I don't know what I'm saying."

"Oh, I do," Milly said, suddenly very sure of what he was proposing. "I know exactly what you're saying." He'd gone and bought himself a love nest away from her, she thought, away from his children and his wife, so he could carry on up there without her. With that gorgeous young actress from his show. She felt sick. "So you think you can just waltz in here on the weekends like a hero and take them to the beach and build sandcastles and leave me to deal with the upbringing of our children and the cooking and the cleaning and the maintaining of this house and the appeasing of neighbors the rest of the week." Her lips curled in what she knew must be a hideous expression, but she didn't care. "Well, I won't stand for it, Lloyd. I won't live that kind of life. I can't."

The words felt so good hurtling out of her mouth at him with such force, and yet as soon as they left her lips, she regretted it. She'd wanted to lure him back to her, not push him away.

He looked confused, as if he himself hadn't been the one to bring this all about, as if she were the one who was springing this on him, unraveling their lives single-handedly.

"What are you saying?" he asked, almost too quiet for Milly to hear. "Are you saying you want a divorce?"

She stared at him, not quite sure she'd heard the words right. Of course she didn't want a divorce. She wanted their marriage to work; she wanted their family intact. Without him she'd be alone. She'd be shunned before she'd even had a chance to make any friends in this town. Her children would be ridiculed. They'd never become part of the community. They'd have people talking about them behind their backs everywhere they went. Neither one of them had expected it to go this far, and yet here they were, saying that terrible, terrible word. But the fact that he was speaking it meant that he'd been thinking about it. Maybe he'd even had this conversation rolling around in his head on the drive home and she'd just given him an easy way to enter into it.

"Do *you* want a divorce?" she whispered back, a single tear dropping onto her cheek.

Lloyd seemed lost for words. "I would never do that to you."

She knew that another woman would beg him to come back to her, ignoring the fact that the D-word came too easily to him, as if he'd hoped she might want it too. Another woman would put past insecurities out of her head and move forward, not letting him out of her grip. But for Milly this felt somehow inevitable, as if she'd been avoiding it from the day they'd met. He'd always been somewhat elusive—charming and kind, but always a little out of reach. She'd been trying desperately to pull him away from whoever it was who lured him in—Beverly Douglas or some other beauty—but now it was clear he didn't want to be pulled away, and she had a terrible feeling, deep down, that she couldn't make him change his mind.

Terrified that if they spoke one more word they'd say or do something they couldn't take back, she took a swig of the gin, feeling it burn as it went down almost undiluted. "Let's talk about this tomorrow."

But they didn't speak of it the next day, and the weekend was insufferable, both of them pretending they hadn't had that awful conversation, Lloyd busying himself with the children, touring the club just to keep up appearances.

On Monday morning, Milly was already stirring the cream and sugar into Lloyd's coffee when she heard him walk into the kitchen and snap the paper open onto the breakfast table.

"Coffee?" she asked, as if the fresh new week were a clean slate, as if her world had not been cracked open and threatened to swallow her whole.

She glanced over Lloyd's shoulder to the morning paper to see what he was reading: *Rev. Martin Luther King Jr. is welcomed with a kiss by his wife, Coretta, after leaving court in Montgomery, Ala.*

"What a beautiful couple," Milly said, attempting some semblance of normalcy between them. "They seem absolutely in love, don't you think?"

"Sure, but I don't think that's the point of the article here," Lloyd said, and Milly read the rest of the caption: *King was found guilty of conspiracy to boycott city buses in a campaign to desegregate the bus system, but a judge suspended his $500 fine pending appeal.*

"Maybe not, but nice to see he has her support. She looks so proud of him."

"He almost got thrown in the slammer for 386 days; I doubt she'd love that," Lloyd said.

"It's ridiculous, really. Why shouldn't a Black person be able to sit on the bus just like everyone else. Honestly, who cares?"

"People in the South care," Lloyd said. "It's different there." He took a sip of his coffee, then set it back down. "Hot," he said before slipping on his jacket and hat and picking up his briefcase.

"So, I'll see you Friday," he said, trying to make eye contact to confirm their new arrangement. But Milly looked away. She hadn't agreed, and she wouldn't give him her blessing to stay away. "And I was thinking," Lloyd said, lowering his voice to a whisper. "Maybe we should get the guest cottage cleared out."

She looked up at him now. Just beyond their small backyard was a separate garage that the previous owners had converted into a small guest cottage. It was filled with unopened moving boxes that she'd need to unpack at some point. When they'd bought the place, she'd imagined converting it into a separate playroom for the children, or, in an even wilder fantasy, a reading room for her, a place where she could read her books and magazines in peace. Maybe he had a better plan, a joint effort, perhaps. But he seemed pained. "Given the new circumstances, I could sleep there. I know this is hard for you. I don't want to make it . . ."

Milly couldn't let him finish. She was already hurrying toward the sound of the kids racing down the stairs.

"Come along, you two; breakfast's almost ready. Chop-chop."

"What's for breakfast?" Jack asked. "I don't want eggy."

"Chocolate chip pancakes," Milly said as she took plates down from the cupboard, then helped Jack into his chair.

Lloyd walked over and kissed the kids on their heads, then hesitated at the door, but Milly kept on moving, pouring the pancake mixture onto the griddle, flipping them, and dousing them with more maple syrup than she would usually allow. She filled two mason jars with warmed chocolate milk and placed them on the table.

When Jack and Debbie dug into the first batch of pancakes, Milly finally allowed herself to look up. He was gone. She'd blocked his attempt, at least temporarily. If she let him move out of her bed and into the guest cottage, it would be final. There would be no bringing him back to her; he'd be cutting the ties and she'd be releasing him. She could not let that happen. She had to do something and fast, and she had an idea that might just turn things around.

She ripped a piece of paper out of one of Debbie's notebooks and began to write: *One-bedroom, one-bathroom cottage available for rent during Bal Week. May use kitchen in main house as needed. Short walk to shops on Marine Avenue and to ferry. Must be responsible and respectful. Please call for more information.* She scribbled her phone exchange on the bottom right-hand corner.

Before she could change her mind, she walked into town and into Hershey's Market with the listing in her hand.

"I'd like to post a rental opportunity," she said to the gray-haired man she'd spoken to in the store earlier that week. "Are you the owner?"

"Yes, ma'am. Tony Hershey. How did your husband like the steak?"

"Excuse me?" Milly said, taken aback, as if he somehow knew what she was doing with this listing.

"You came in Friday, said you were making your husband his favorite steak. How did he like it?"

"Oh gosh, he loved it," she said.

"Good. We've got a sale on hams today."

But she couldn't think about hams or any dinners that he wouldn't be coming home to, for that matter. "Thank you, but I'm all set for tonight. I just really need to post this." She held up the piece of paper.

He took it and read her listing. "Well, yeah, I see your urgency. Bal Week starts next week, but if you want the college kids to see your notice, you should really post it near the colleges up in L.A. or inland. Once the kids arrive here for Bal Week, they'll already have their accommodations sorted out."

"Oh," Milly said, disappointed. "So I'm too late."

"I'll tell you what: My produce supplier is stopping by this afternoon. If you want to write out a few more of those listings, I can ask him to post them at the markets in Los Angeles. There are always some kids who make a plan to come down last-minute."

"That would be helpful," Milly said, thinking it would be ideal if she could commit to renting out the cottage before Lloyd returned on Friday. She wrote out two more notices and handed them to him. "Thank you very much."

"Sure thing. I hope it works out."

"Yes," Milly said, a tinge of desperation in her voice. "I do too."

CHAPTER EIGHT

SYLVIA

Sylvia had barely seen Walter, between his closed-door meetings with his accountant and his frequent visits to the bank, and she was fine with that—she needed some distance from him—but she refused to sit idly by and wait for him to make some other disastrous choices on her behalf.

She got out of her car in the city of Orange, where no one would know her, and marched into Gems & Wares Pawn Shop, jewelry box tucked under her arm. Her red belted skirt suit would show them that she had expensive taste and that she meant business.

"I'd like to take out a loan," she said to a bearded man behind the counter, barely able to look him in the eye. "Temporarily, of course."

"Yes, ma'am." He was a skinny, greasy man, and when he opened Sylvia's jewelry box and picked up a few rings, slipping one onto the tip of his finger and holding it up to the light, Sylvia got a sickly taste in her mouth. He picked up another, analyzing it under a jeweler's loupe. "How much are you looking to borrow?"

Sixty thousand dollars, she wanted to say, but she knew, of course, that this jewelry wouldn't come close to that. "How much can I get for the whole lot?" she asked, running her thumb over her engagement ring still on her ring finger. She'd be keeping that, for now.

"That's a lot of pieces here. I'd have to take them out back and evaluate them one by one," the man said.

"No." She placed her hands on the box. "Nothing leaves my sight. You can evaluate right here. I'll wait. However long it takes."

"All right." He called another colleague up to the front of the shop to assist him.

She sat in an upright wooden chair, sinking in humiliation yet trying to remain stoic, as two men sorted through her personal collection—each piece of jewelry tied to a very specific moment in her life with Walter—the triple strand of pearls he gave her for their five-year anniversary, the diamond bracelet he had given her this year on her thirty-fifth birthday, the ruby solitaire after Judith's birth, and the heart-shaped pendant for when they learned of her second pregnancy, the baby who didn't make it.

Finally, after what felt like hours, the man closed the jewelry box. "All right, ma'am, we have come to a number."

Sylvia stood and approached the counter.

"One thousand six hundred dollars for the lot."

Sylvia put her hand to her chest.

"I know it's a lot—we don't usually take such a large number of pieces from one customer," he said. "But these are nice, the best we've seen, so we're happy to help you out."

She had walked into the shop with no idea what to expect. She'd never bought a piece of jewelry and didn't know what any of this would be worth, but she thought it would be significantly more than one thousand six hundred. This was barely going to make a dent in the amount of debt Walter owed.

"That seems very low," she said.

"It's a fair-priced loan. I've even had my colleague evaluate the items, and we are in agreement."

Sylvia shuddered involuntarily. "How does it work?"

"We hold on to your jewelry, you take the loan. You've got 120 days to pay back the loan, plus interest, and I'll return your items to you good as new. If you don't pay it back, we are entitled to put the jewelry up for sale."

"Of course I'll pay back the money," Sylvia snapped. "This collection is worth far more than what you're offering me."

The man put his hands up and took a step back. "I'm just telling you how it works, ma'am. You asked."

"Yes," she said, trying to regain her composure. This was her choice to come here, after all, and yet the ground suddenly felt wobbly beneath her. She hadn't told Walter what she was doing, but it was the only thing she could think that might help. "I'll take the money," she said, unable to look as he took the jewelry box from the counter between them and placed it underneath, out of view. He went to the back room for a minute and returned with a detailed receipt and a stack of cash.

"That's it?" she said. It was smaller than she expected, insignificant looking. She expected to walk out of there with three or four bricks of bills and come home the hero.

"I'm going to count it out for you, ma'am," he said with a hint of annoyance, and then he counted out all one thousand and six hundred dollars.

On the drive home she had a terrible stomachache, water gathering in her mouth as if she might vomit. She might never see that jewelry again. But these were just jewels, she reminded herself, replaceable jewels. What was worse, so much worse, was the thought of losing their home and uprooting her daughter. The humiliation of it all was too much to bear. Would she have to change schools and make all new friends? Would they really have to leave the island, as Walter suggested?

And then there was Milly. Sylvia had taken a check from her the day before, knowing full well that the club might not exist a month from now. She'd noticed the trepidation in Milly's voice as she asked the price of membership, and the shake of her hand as she wrote out the check, and yet Sylvia had let her join as if everything were just fine. She gripped the steering wheel, determined to make it up to her and to Judith. She had to make things right.

CHAPTER NINE

MILLY

Milly felt a little ridiculous when she walked onto the court in tennis shoes and a short white collared dress with a green cardigan over her shoulders, as if she were dressing up for a costume party, but she was also excited to take her very first lesson. She and Lloyd had loved to watch the college tennis team together when they were first going steady, and while she suspected half of the appeal for him had been the girls in short skirts, they both grew to love and appreciate the athleticism and finesse that the players had on the courts.

It was silly, but as she dressed that morning, she hoped that lessons might bring out some natural talent she didn't know about. She might be able to impress Lloyd with her newfound aptitude. Lord knew she had followed all the rules for excelling at housewifery, and that hadn't impressed him; maybe tennis would offer the spark that would surprise him next time they made an appearance at the club.

She held a borrowed racket in one hand and ran her fingers along the smooth wooden handle, not quite sure what to do with it. Her first practice session with Sylvia had been embarrassingly bad, but she hoped with some instruction she could improve.

"Ready?" Sylvia called out, bouncing the white ball in front of her, eager to begin.

"I think so," Milly said.

The ball flew past her, but before she had a chance to apologize, Sylvia was bouncing another, ready to serve. This time Milly stuck her racket out and managed to hit it back, but not over the net. Sylvia tried again.

"Do you want to serve?" Sylvia asked.

"Oh no," Milly said. She didn't even know how.

"It's all right." Sylvia bounced the ball in front of her again, and when she tried to serve, it hit the net. She tried again and sent it over.

Milly was terrible, but her friend was no Bobby Riggs either.

"Well, well, what have we here?" A man in an all-white sweater-and-trouser ensemble grinned as he looked Milly up and down and up again. "A doubles partner?"

"Robbie, this is my friend Milly Kincaid. She's new here."

He took Milly's hand and kissed it, letting his lips linger too long.

"Milly, this is Robbie, the best coach we have."

"The pleasure is all mine," Robbie said, finally releasing Milly's hand.

"I'm not very good," she said spinning the racket nervously. "I can barely hit the ball."

"Well, you certainly look the part," he said, eyeing her again.

"She's married, Robbie," Sylvia called out as she jogged to the other end of the court.

"They all are," Robbie said and laughed. He walked to the side of the net, where he had a metal cart full of balls. "I'll feed, you hit," he said. "Let's see what you're made of."

Hitting the ball was easier with a coach feeding her the balls exactly to her forehand and at the correct height and speed. But she still managed to hit them sideways, even backward, with just a few heading in Sylvia's direction. It was frustrating and humbling. He asked them to try a few underhand serves to warm up, but Milly's were so soft and slow they didn't even make it to the net.

"You need to work on your strokes," Robbie said. "And grip that handle, really grip it hard," he said. "No limp noodles."

He turned his attention away from Milly toward Sylvia. "That's it. You've been doing your homework; your wrist is getting stronger."

Everything he said seemed to have some kind of sexual undertone, Milly thought, or maybe she was imagining it. It had been so long since she'd been intimate with Lloyd. Four months, to be exact, and it hadn't gone well. He'd said he was too exhausted from work to finish. And now with his latest disappearing acts, she wondered if they'd ever have relations again. Their whole marriage they'd always been kind to each other, sweet even. He always kissed her good night. Sometimes he'd reach for her hand under the covers and she'd think he might reach for her waist, pull her close, even though she was tired and wanted sleep, but he didn't. Almost never. Instead, he'd fall asleep, and when she heard his breathing slow, she'd gently ease her hand out of his and roll over to her side of the bed.

Robbie fed them more balls, but Milly consistently missed them or sent them where they weren't supposed to go, and Sylvia seemed distracted, as if her mind were elsewhere. It felt hopeless, and Milly wanted to give up, go home. Maybe there was nothing she'd be good at, nothing to make her worthy or lovable. She hated to descend into self-pity but as the thoughts involuntarily ran through her mind, her eyes watered. *Oh, stop it,* she told herself, *just stop it.* When the next ball came her way, she swung at it so hard, she made contact and sent it up and over the fence.

"Well, at least you went for it," Robbie said, shrugging his shoulders. "Maybe try to keep it in next time." Their half hour was soon up. Milly paid Robbie, and he moved to another court to coach some men who seemed far more experienced.

"Are they all like that?" Milly asked.

"Like what?"

Milly tilted her head toward him.

"Who, Robbie? He's harmless," Sylvia said. "And no, they're not all like him. We only have a few coaches, and they all like the attention of a beautiful woman, but he's the best if you want to learn fast."

"I do," Milly said, but her hope of uncovering some hidden talent now seemed unlikely, very unlikely—embarrassing, even, that she'd had the thought to begin with.

That night, after she got the kids to bed, Milly started tinkering with the guest cottage, getting it ready in case she found renters for Bal Week, when she heard a soft thumping coming from outside. Looking out the window across her small yard to her house, nothing appeared to be amiss. The noise seemed to be coming from the alley behind the cottage, and when she unlatched the window that opened onto it, she realized she was right. *Thump*, pause, pause, *thump*, pause, pause. It wasn't an insistent rapping on a door as if someone needed urgent help; it was more rhythmic.

Milly unlocked the door that led to the alley and stepped out into the dark. At the end of her street she could see someone moving in and out of view. As she came closer, Milly recognized the figure. It was her aloof neighbor Adele, whose house on Onyx also backed up to the alley. Racquet in hand, she was whacking a ball against a wall next to her house with such force that it made Milly step back into the shadows of her neighbor's house.

Adele's was the second home from the end of the street. The last house on the block was one of Walter's recent investments—run-down, vacant, and, according to Sylvia, soon to be torn down to make room for a larger house. Adele was clearly taking advantage of the fact that she had no neighbors on one side, because if anyone else were to hear or witness this display of aggression, they would most certainly call the police. What astonished Milly the most as she watched Adele move was not just the power with which she hit the ball, which was something she'd never witnessed before, but also her grace and composure. After she shot the ball at full speed toward the wall, she shuffled gracefully backward, racket looping around behind her, then she'd leap forward like a ballerina, meeting the ball mid-flight, only to slam it toward the wall in exactly the same spot, repeating the motion over and over again.

It was grace and power, strength and beauty and precision all unfolding before her in the most unusual way. How did she know how to hit a ball like this, and why was she doing it here, so late at night in a dark alley?

Milly thought she should get back to the house where her children were, hopefully, sleeping soundly, but she couldn't take her eyes off the dance going on in front of her. Still watching, she began to back away but cursed as she almost turned her ankle on an uneven part of the alley. Adele stopped hitting, caught the ball on the strings of her racket, and turned to Milly.

"Can I help you?" she asked, curtly.

"Oh, hi, hello. I just heard you playing and I came out to see what all the commotion was about."

"Commotion?"

"Not commotion, really, just, wow, you hit the ball with such power and grace."

Adele picked up a pitcher of water and a glass she had placed at the side of the alley and took a long drink. She then wiped her brow with her sleeve. She was wearing a bandanna tied around her short brown bob, but it wasn't enough to catch her perspiration.

"Is there something you want?" Adele asked, sounding irritated. "Because if not, you're interrupting my rhythm."

"Oh," Milly said, slightly terrified by her demeanor. "Sorry, I was just leaving. But how did you learn to play so well?"

"My father," Adele said, tapping the ball impatiently against the ground with her racket.

"It's mesmerizing to watch you."

Adele snorted sarcastically. "Do you make a habit of watching people?"

"No, gosh no, I just heard you, that's all. You could be a professional or something."

Adele glared at her, then started up again, hitting the ball gently against the wall, and Milly knew this was her cue to leave.

"Well, if you ever need someone to practice with, I've just taken up tennis."

"Are you good?"

"No," Milly said, "definitely not."

"Then no," Adele said. "I play alone."

"But it's tennis. How can you play alone?"

Adele gestured to the wall.

"That house is getting torn down, you know," Milly said.

Adele shrugged. "I don't need to practice with anyone. I already play just fine."

"All right." Milly put her hands up in defense and backed away. This woman was not neighborly at all. First the Ferris wheel and now this. "I was just trying to be friendly," Milly said.

But Adele had to have the last word. "Well," she said. "I don't need friends either."

Milly shook her head in stunned disbelief; no one had ever spoken to her so bluntly before. Then she turned and walked back to her house.

CHAPTER TEN

ADELE

Adele shook off her irritation with a cold shower, then she made herself a simple dinner—salmon rillettes on toast and a glass of wine. She did not need to worry about Milly Kincaid. Clearly she had no idea who Adele was, she was sure of that now. If she'd shown any glimmer of recognition, Adele would have noticed. No, she was just admiring, and envious, perhaps. And she was being more than a little ridiculous to think she could practice with Adele. Absurd.

She opened her latest edition of *American Lawn Tennis* magazine. While she no longer played matches, staying up to date with the game of tennis gave her a satisfying yet invisible thread to her former life. On page 8, there was a photograph of Althea Gibson—her light-brown skin almost passing for white in the washed-out black-and-white photograph—holding up her tennis racket and smiling. Adele had been keeping an eye on this rising tennis player for a few years now. There'd been little written about her in the national papers, but in select magazines there had been opinion pieces by tennis stars such as Alice Marble and Sarah Palfrey advocating against the color barrier that excluded Althea from the all-white tennis championships, and it was slowly working. Not only was Gibson an excellent player, but she was now the first Negro person, man or woman, ever to play in American Lawn Tennis championships, and

Adele felt a kinship toward her. She herself had broken down boundaries and biases, but in Adele's case, that had meant attitudes toward women, not race.

The article referenced an international news story noting, "The twenty-eight-year-old Negro has been competing as a special emissary of the State Department in its program for sending representative American athletes abroad." Adele pushed her plate aside, intent on reading more. Althea would stay overseas to train for and compete in the Wimbledon tournament in London that summer, and her pre-Wimbledon itinerary included tournaments in Egypt, France, and Italy.

Adele sipped her wine, feeling a pang of longing for the life she had destroyed for herself, as well as an overwhelming feeling of pride for Althea. She could vividly picture how it must feel to charge ahead like that despite the odds. She closed her eyes and rested her hands on the magazine, wondering if they ever crossed paths, whether Adele might have some sage advice for her. This woman was twenty-eight and seemed to be on the precipice of something big. Adele had been four years younger when everything came to a crashing halt.

When she opened her eyes she was looking directly at the framed photograph on the wall of her father, standing tall, wearing a suit and a straw fedora, with fourteen-year-old Adele standing next to him, tennis racket in hand, both of them squinting into the sun. She remembered the day as if it were yesterday, and her father's absence suddenly took hold in her chest. He'd been gone for two decades now, but still she missed him telling her what to do—whether it was what tournaments to enter, how to play each particular opponent, what to take when she felt her energy flag during a match, or what to think when her fear crept in. When he was coaching her, managing her life, she hadn't had to think, she only had to play. Though painful at times, there had been a comfort in that.

She allowed her mind to return to those early days, when she was still proving herself, when she was surprising her father—and the French tennis world—with her string of wins, beginning at the Nice Lawn Tennis

Club. She'd quickly moved up to the Italian Bordighera Club, then the Carlton Club in Cannes, where she skipped through to the finals and outlasted an English woman who was twice her age, as almost all of her opponents were. But that woman, Carol Lewis, had been a formidable Wimbledon veteran, and the match had not been easy.

Approaching the final set, Adele had become exhausted and begun to feel intimidated by her opponent's seemingly endless energy, precision, and endurance. Adele had expected her to tire after a while, after she ran Carol Lewis from one side of the court to the other, to the net and to the baseline, but she did not. Instead, Adele had felt herself weaken in a frightening way. Losing suddenly seemed inevitable, and losing, her father had taught her, was absolutely unacceptable.

In the break before the next set, Adele hurried to her father and asked if he would allow her to leave the court, knowing a default was better than an outright loss. "*Papa*," she whispered, pleading, telling him she was too tired to go on, "*je suis fatigué. Je ne peux pas continuer à jouer. S'il te plaît, Papa*. Please."

"*Absolument pas!*" he spat, enraged that she would ask such a thing. "How dare you give up, all those hours I have trained you. I did not do that for you to give up. . . . *Tu es faible*."

Standing miserably by the court that day, she felt every spectator's eyes boring through her, her opponent's too, while he berated and threatened her, loud enough for all to hear.

And he had not finished. "Look at me. Do you want to be a failure? If you give up and let us down now, you will be on your own. Do you want to disgrace our family name?"

"No, Papa," she whispered, noticing a young reporter with parted black hair and glasses who'd attended many of her early matches, lingering close to the bleachers, notebook in hand.

Carol Lewis was crossing to her side. She began bouncing lightly on her toes, back and forth, twirling her racket expectantly.

"I cannot hear you!" Papa yelled.

"No, Papa," she said louder now, her voice cracking. With the back of her hand, she brushed a tear from her cheek.

"Get back on the court and win."

Trembling, she gripped her racket, steeling herself to obey. Suddenly, he pulled her back to him, and his face softened. "She is more tired than you, she is older, almost two decades your senior. . . ." He lowered his voice: "Be an animal."

Her startled eyes searched his.

"Rip her head off her shoulders with your fastballs. You can win," her father reminded her. He squeezed her by the arms. "Here, for energy," he said, handing her two brandy-soaked sugar cubes, which she immediately popped into her mouth. "Now finish the match."

In that final set she played with burning intensity, determined not only to win over her father, but to give that young reporter something to write about other than the humiliating scene he had witnessed. After each point she locked eyes with her father as he mouthed words and made exaggerated hand signals, indicating which tactics to use. She demonstrated her signature moves, leaping for the ball, legs almost in a full split as she flew across the court, reaching and sending the ball back to her opponent. In the end she'd persevered; she'd played with newfound resolve, speed, and power, and she won the final set 6–3. Eager to forget that she'd almost resigned herself to failure just forty-five minutes earlier, she strode over to her father's proud embrace. "That's my girl," he said, kissing her forehead.

"We won, Papa," she cried ecstatically, jumping up and down, adrenaline coursing through her veins. "We won! Did you see that last point? I smashed it at the end, I smashed it!"

"The point went on for too long. You should have ended it much sooner."

"Oh, Papa," she said, smiling. "You're right, of course you're right, but in the end I won, we won! Let's celebrate. Where's Mama? Let's go out to eat, let's have cassoulet; I'm starving." Her thoughts were still running a hundred miles an hour, her heart racing; she couldn't slow down, she was too excited, too happy with the way she had turned things around.

"*Calme-toi*," he said sternly, jolting Adele out of her delirium. "You won, but just barely. It was far too close. Eat in your room. Tomorrow, we get up early and train. Six AM on the courts. Tonight, you sleep."

"Papa," she whispered. "One night, please?" She had wanted to hold on to the electrifying thrill that was quickly slipping away. But he had already turned his back on her and was leaving the bleachers.

Adele stood and picked up her old racket and tennis ball from where they were resting against the wall in the kitchen, and she began to bounce the ball gently on its strings. She wondered if it was her talent, her father's strict discipline, or her constant need for that winning thrill that had led to the titles that followed—winning in singles, doubles, and mixed doubles, and the flurry of French newspaper articles that called her a rising star, a "Bébé Peugeot." How good it had felt to see her picture in all the papers that had gushed about her skill, her precision, her perfect and unreturnable serves, her "astounding mid-air flutterings," her strength and superb coordination. How exhilarated she had felt when she saw her father showing the papers to his friends. How young she had been then. It had been almost thirty years since those early tournaments, and yet, no matter how cruel and cold he had been toward her, she still longed for the security of his guidance.

She thought about Milly watching her in the back alley, her look of admiration and awe, and she began to wonder if she could ever find the patience within herself to coach another player, to teach them what she had learned. Or would she be too much like her father—consumed with disappointment and regrets? She'd inherited her father's impatience, his severity and cruelty, hadn't she? Or was it something she'd learned and could unlearn, like the game of tennis itself? The only way to know was if she tried, but she didn't know if she'd have the courage to step back onto the court and risk being known for who she was and the terrible thing she'd done.

Just holding the racket in her hands, with its worn grip and fraying strings, brought her a sense of ease and comfort, and that was enough—at least for now.

CHAPTER ELEVEN

MILLY

Usually, Milly followed a strict schedule of housework, parceling out the chores throughout the week just as her housekeeping guides had taught her—kitchen and floors on Monday, laundry and windows on Tuesday, bathrooms and bedrooms on Wednesday, and so on—but without a regular schedule, not sure when Lloyd would come home, she left everything until today, Friday. She worked hard and fast, and by six o'clock she had a ham baking in the oven, green beans almondine, and boiled potatoes on the stovetop, and she even whipped up some ambrosia salad using up the extra pineapple.

When the phone rang, she was relieved to take a break from dusting.

"Hello, Kincaid residence," she said breathlessly, hoping to God it wouldn't be Lloyd's voice at the end of the line telling her he'd changed his mind about coming home for the weekend. They hadn't spoken since he left on Monday morning, and she hoped he was missing the children desperately and had a chance to think about what a mistake he was making.

"Mrs. Kincaid?" a female voice asked.

"Speaking."

"Hi, my name is Rosie, and I'm calling about the advertisement for a cottage rental for next week, Bal Week, and I was wondering if it was still available."

"Yes," Milly said, thrilled by the last-minute call. She'd assumed, after posting it so late, that she had missed her opportunity. "It's still available. Definitely."

"Wonderful. And how many people can it accommodate?"

"There are two twin beds and a mattress. I suppose a fourth person could sleep on the couch, but I don't know how comfortable that would be."

"Is there a refrigerator?" the girl asked.

"Unfortunately, not in the cottage, but you're more than welcome to keep your perishable food items in the refrigerator in the main house," Milly said, and there was a pause, some whispering in the background. Maybe this was a deal-breaker. "There's an icebox, if that would help; I can have a slab delivered before you arrive," Milly added. "Not ideal, but something."

"Oh, that would be just perfect," Rosie said, perky again. "I know it's last-minute, so too late to send you the deposit by mail. Can it be paid upon arrival?"

"Of course," Milly said. She'd almost forgotten about the money, she'd been so focused on ensuring that the cottage was occupied. "You probably won't have time to see the place first, but I assure you it's very quaint, and I'll have clean sheets and towels, and anything else you need."

The young woman giggled. "Oh, I'm sure it will be just fine."

"It's really quite lovely," Milly went on. "I have to say, sometimes I prefer spending time in the cottage than in my own house. It's just got a nice cozy feeling about it; it's bright and airy too, gets a lot of light through the windows."

"Great," the young lady said again as if she didn't really care and was just happy to have arranged accommodations for Bal Week. Milly gave her the address and told her she looked forward to meeting her and her friends, then she hung up feeling satisfied and slightly accomplished. At least for now Lloyd couldn't sleep in the guest cottage.

Later, Milly stood and watched from the kitchen as the children climbed all over Lloyd the minute he walked in the door. Milly, who cooked all the meals; Milly, who packed all the lunches; Milly who untangled Debbie's hair and braided it again; Milly, who soothed Jack when he fell and scraped his elbow—Milly got none of the thanks. But Lloyd was home as he said he would be, she reminded herself, and she'd be grateful for that.

After dinner while Milly washed the dishes, Lloyd played with the children and even put them to bed. Maybe he was feeling sheepish, guilty for all that he'd said the weekend prior. Maybe he'd changed his mind. Had he realized what a fool he'd be to walk out on this family?

She unbuttoned another button on the front of her collared lavender dress and sat on the love seat waiting for him to return to the living room. She would let him have his say, apologize for speaking so recklessly about the life they'd built together, let him tell her he'd had a long week, the stress of the move and work, then she'd place her hand on his knee and tell him it was all right, no need to say more. It was forgotten, in the past. And then they'd move on, watch some television, have a drink. He'd turn off the set and take her hand, walk her upstairs. It had been a while, yes, but they'd start anew. He'd undress her, he'd kiss her neck, and she'd run her hands through his hair, and then she'd give him the best damn sex of their marriage, to remind him of what he'd been missing, of what was waiting for him here at home, right after dinner.

After a while she got up and refreshed her lipstick. She poured them both a gin and tonic in a highball and added a slice of lemon. She went back to the living room and waited to hear footsteps from the children's room to the landing, or to their bedroom, to the stairs. Nothing.

Ten minutes later she went upstairs. Perhaps he'd fallen asleep in the children's room again. But no, she found him sitting on their bed in his cotton striped pajamas and robe, reading a script.

"Oh," she said. "I thought you were coming back down."

"Sorry, I didn't know you wanted me to."

Milly swallowed. This was awful, as if they were strangers, formalities all around.

"I thought we might watch some television. *I Love Lucy*'s about to start."

"All right then," he said, forcing a smile and nodding. "I'll be right there."

Suddenly the two-seater felt too small, like dollhouse furniture. She'd fought for that sofa, loving its compact modern style with the metal tube legs and the beige wool cushions. Lloyd had told her she was crazy to get such a fabric, it would be ruined with the kids' sticky hands and crayons. He'd suggested a brown tweed in a long L-shaped style, large enough for the whole family, but Milly had insisted. She'd seen these sleek, romantic styles in her magazines that said they were originally designed for courting couples in the Victorian era who wanted to be close while chaperoned. Now it seemed ridiculous. How could two people sit comfortably here and not touch, not nestle into one another. A love seat, by its very name, simply wasn't suited to a husband and wife with one party wanting out.

Lloyd turned on the television and took his place next to her.

"Ah, that's the ticket," he said, sipping the gin and tonic she'd placed on his side table, as he crossed one leg over the other. "Thank you. And dinner was one of your best."

They watched a commercial for the new Oldsmobile convertible with sleek lines and stylish taillights, and Milly imagined, for a moment, driving off down Coast Highway in a car like that, full of possibilities and away from all this gut-wrenching hurt. When the show came on they were in Paris, and after seeing all the chic Parisian styles, Lucy wanted a designer dress by Jacques Marcel. Ricky refused, of course, saying he absolutely would not shell out five hundred clams for one dress, so Lucy went on a hunger strike until he changed his mind. All the while, Ethel was sneaking food into Lucy's hotel room, including a roast chicken that Ricky found in his camera bag.

Usually, Milly loved Lucy and she laughed out loud, but that night she couldn't even manage to smile. She simply stared straight ahead and concentrated on the words and the actions, because she had to focus on something. It began to feel absurd, not funny at all. The sharp, snappy banter between Lucy and Ricky sounded trite and stupid. She couldn't stand it. Lloyd hadn't tried to redeem himself; no apologies had left his lips. He seemed to have no regrets about the words he'd spoken earlier in the week. If this was how her life was going to be now, she didn't even want it.

"I'm going to bed," she said and stood, wrapping her arms around herself, feeling cold. "I'm tired."

"OK." Lloyd didn't take his eyes off the television. He laughed when Ethel walked on wearing a burlap sack that Fred was trying to pass off as a new design by Jacques Marcel. "I've never worn burlap before," Ethel said in her nasally voice. "Honeybunch," Fred said, "you were made for it."

Lloyd laughed again, loudly this time, emphatically, as if he were really enjoying this, completely absorbed in these couples' pranks and their lighthearted bickering. Milly looked at him dumbfounded. How could he laugh at a time like this, when he was ripping her heart to shreds with his need to be away from her?

Lloyd looked up as if he'd forgotten she was there. "Sorry, Milly, they're just so funny, these two; they get me every time."

"I'm heading up," she said. One last chance for him to change his mind.

"All right," Lloyd said, stretching his arms and legs out, his body now taking over the love seat. "Good night."

The rest of the weekend was once again excruciating. On Saturday the whole family dressed up and had lunch at the club, but Milly and Lloyd both knew it was for the sake of showing their faces, showing what a loving, happy, normal family they were. On Sunday Lloyd got up with the children, giving Milly the rare chance to sleep in, but of course she didn't sleep. She lay there with her eyes closed, listening to the glee in her children's voices because their daddy was paying them so much attention. By mid-morning on Sunday Lloyd was walking through the yard and out the back gate toward his car, briefcase in one hand and a packed duffel bag in the other.

"Lloyd, wait," she begged, jogging to keep up. "Please."

When Milly reached the gate and Lloyd already had his hand on the car door, he finally stopped to look at her. "I told you about this last night, Milly. I have to get back."

"But it's only Sunday. Sylvia's having her party this afternoon. It's for all the neighbors before all these college kids arrive for spring break. If you're not there, people will talk. Can't you head back after?"

An elderly couple walked down the back alley behind Milly's house with an equally old dog following along behind them. Milly softened her expression—which she was sure was one of desperation. "Good afternoon," she said.

"Hello, dear," the gentleman said, and kept on going at a snail's pace.

When they finally passed, Milly turned back to Lloyd. "Why did you park back here, anyway?"

"For privacy," he said, through gritted teeth. "You said you don't want the neighbors to talk if they don't see my car out front. If I park back here no one will notice if I'm coming or going."

"Well, you're not going to be able to park here this upcoming week."

"Why?"

"I've rented the cottage out."

"What?" he said. "To who?"

"Some college kids are staying here for Bal Week."

"What the hell is Bal Week?" Lloyd asked.

"I told you already. It starts tomorrow. Students come down here on vacation, and everyone rents out a room or their house or their guest cottage. I was going to tell you about renting it, but I've hardly had a chance."

"You can't just go renting out our house to strangers without even discussing it with me first."

"How am I supposed to discuss anything with you if you're never here?" she said. Then she shook her head. This was not her plan. She had told herself she was going to make Lloyd's visits pleasant and enjoyable, no matter how infrequent, so he would be reminded of what he was missing when he was away. And she certainly didn't mean to air her grievances within earshot of her neighbors. "I'm sorry," she said, placing her hand on his arm, a gesture that now, after nine years of marriage, felt strange and unfamiliar. "I should have spoken to you about it first, but it will cover some of the club fees."

"Yes, the club, that's another thing you should have spoken to me about." He shook his head and closed his eyes as if trying to contain his exasperation with her. It hurt. It burned to see him so annoyed with her mere existence. Was she that intolerable? Was she that hard to be around? How had this happened to them? They used to enjoy each other's company; they used to be companions, friends, but now even that seemed to have faded away.

"I just wish you could stay a few more hours for the party," Milly sighed, then added, "and for the kids."

"The kids are fine; they seem happy."

They were only happy, Milly thought, because they didn't know what was really going on. They didn't know that their father was likely carrying on with some gorgeous young actress up in Hollywood.

"Look, Milly." He softened a little. "I'm sorry about all of this. You're doing a good job. You're a great mother. Beverly's having one of her Sunday socials, and she's insisting I be there. I'm sorry." Then he got in the car. "So, I'll see you the following weekend then, if you've got our house rented out."

"Not our house, just the guest cottage!" Milly cried as he started the engine.

"It's the same thing," he shrugged. "I've left you money on my desk, should you need extra," he said before driving off.

Milly stood for a second, watching the dust rise up behind his car. "But it's Easter," she said in a whisper as she realized her plan had backfired yet again. "Next weekend is Easter."

"Good Lord," Milly said as she turned the corner of her street onto South Bay Front and saw all the people gathered on Sylvia's front yard.

"What, Mommy?" Debbie asked, looking up at her.

"It's so elaborate. I thought Sylvia said she was only inviting a few families."

The barbecue was set up surrounded by picnic tables dressed with Sylvia's favorite red-and-white-checkered tablecloths. There was an entire children's section where kids were playing on the sand, while the adults kept an eye on them from the expansive front yard. The Johnsons' small rowboat was moored at the water's edge. A swimming platform had a slide into the water, and the young lifeguard from the club was standing by. Plastic buckets filled with pretzels, cheese puffs, and chips had mini shovels to be used as scoops, and a tray of watermelon triangles on Popsicle sticks were all arranged beautifully on a snack table, ready to be devoured.

"Suzanna's here!" Debbie screamed with delight as she saw her friend from school and tried to pull away.

"Wait," Milly said. "First we say hello to the hosts and we thank them for inviting us, and then you may play with your friend, but only if you take Jack with you."

Debbie groaned.

"Or you can stay by my side the whole evening."

"Fine," Debbie said.

"I want to stay with you, Mommy," Jack said.

"Mommy has to talk to the grown-ups," Milly said, dreading the very idea of it.

As they walked through the party, all Milly could see was couple after couple after couple. She felt naked without Lloyd by her side, as if she had a spotlight on her as she entered the party single with a child attached to each hand. She stayed on the periphery, hoping not to draw attention to herself, glancing around only to locate Sylvia. She heard her laugh first, then saw her and Walter holding court with four other couples near the outdoor bar. My God, she thought, they really did have it all. Sylvia looked so at ease and fabulous in a full navy skirt with a white-and-blue-striped boatneck top that just grazed her shoulders—dressy enough for the hostess, casual enough for a backyard gathering.

Maybe she should take Debbie and Jack to find the other children first, Milly thought, but then she'd have to reenter the adult side of the party completely alone, and that would be more glaring. She paused for a second thinking that this was a mistake; maybe she shouldn't have come at all.

"Mommy," Debbie said loudly. "I want to see Suzanna!"

Sylvia looked up and waved them over.

"Milly, darling, where's Lloyd?"

Of course, it was the very first thing she asked.

"He had to work," she said.

"Work? On a Sunday?" Sylvia said.

"He must be a pretty important guy if they drag him in on a Sunday," Walter said.

"He is," was all Milly could think to say. Then she quickly added. "He was so disappointed, though; he really wanted to come."

Sylvia looked confused and kept her eyes on Milly as if about to question her further, but Milly turned away and smiled at a few women gathered nearby whom she'd met at the club. Debbie pulled at her mother's sleeve, and Milly nudged her toward Sylvia.

"Thank you for having us, Mrs. Johnson," Debbie said, then she actually curtsied as if she were meeting royalty, not a neighbor throwing a backyard barbecue.

Jack followed suit. "Thank you," he said, then he also curtsied, further convincing Milly that he needed his father around.

"They're adorable," Sylvia said. "Just the cutest little things. My Judith is around here somewhere." Sylvia looked down toward the beach where some of the children were. "Or she might still be in her room getting ready, but I'm sure she'll watch your two and give you a break. You deserve it. You're doing all the hard work bringing these two without Lloyd to help."

"Oh, that's sweet. I'm sure they'd love that," Milly said. When the kids ran off hand in hand, Milly stood there feeling idle. No children to fuss over, no husband to hang on to, just her, exposed, likely the only guest alone at the party. She saw people walking past her with tropical-looking cocktails and pink umbrellas poked into floating pineapple. One of those would give her something to do with her hands, and the alcohol might help her relax.

"I'll take one, thank you." She lifted a pink fruity drink off a passing tray and walked by a buffet table filled with platters of deviled eggs, shrimp cocktail, finger sandwiches, toothpicks with cubes of cheese and cucumber sticking out of a half melon. There was a fondue table and a couple of different Jell-O salads that looked too perfect to cut into. White paper lanterns were strung from the trees, and the whole thing was quite lovely—if only she didn't feel so out of place. There must have been at least fifty guests, some she recognized and some she didn't. As she cut her way through the crowds, a woman tapped her on the shoulder.

"Oh, hi, Milly," she said. "I'm Maureen. We met at the club."

"Of course. Nice to see you, Maureen."

"And this is my husband Jack."

"Great name," Milly said. "I have a Jack."

"I thought you had a Lloyd."

"I do. Jack is my son." She pointed to Jack's little blond head of hair poking out from behind a deck chair, where he was digging a hole in the sand. "My husband is Lloyd."

Maureen and her husband seemed to wait for her to say more, to point him out. "He's not here, unfortunately."

"Oh, too bad. Is he sick?"

"Yes," Milly said, thinking that would just be easier—he was just sick, poor guy—but then she remembered she'd just told Sylvia and Walter that he was working. "I mean no," she quickly corrected. "No, not sick, perfectly healthy, just had to work."

"On a Sunday?" Maureen's husband said, and Milly almost rolled her eyes. *Yes*, she thought, *on a goddamned Sunday. Why does anyone care?*

Don't they have enough going on in their own lives to worry about where Lloyd is?

"It's called a weekend for a reason," Jack went on. Maureen nodded in agreement, and Milly wanted to punch him in the face.

"He works in television," Milly said. "He has clients in town, big names."

Maureen's eyes widened. "Television!" she exclaimed, clasping her hands together. "How exciting! What does he do? Hey girls," she called out to several ladies grouped next to them, "Milly's husband works in television."

All heads turned toward her, and Milly had the feeling that she'd gone too far, explained too much, too soon. Drawing attention to herself was exactly what she was trying to avoid. She'd have to work on her delivery, drop snippets of information more slowly.

"Does he work on any shows we might know?" a short, full-figured woman gushed.

Milly racked her brain. All she could think of was that soap opera that consumed him and that horrible, beautiful, Beverly Douglas, but she didn't want to mention her or the show. She tried to think of another single show that the station produced, but she was coming up blank under pressure. What kind of wife knew nothing about her husband's career? She began to panic, she was going to blow her cover of being a perfectly normal married wife within minutes of seeing these women. "CBS," Milly blurted out the minute it came to her. "He works for CBS Television Networks." It was something at least.

"Oh my gosh, I love *The Light Within* on CBS!" Maureen said clasping her hands together. "And Kay Grant's my favorite. What's she like in real life? The actress Beverly Douglas, I mean. Surely you've met her? She's so gorgeous."

The mention of the woman her husband might very well be gallivanting around with made Milly want to vomit. She shook her head. "No, unfortunately not."

"It all sounds so glamorous," another woman, Joan, chimed in.

"Yes, it's quite a production. They film the shows live every day, but there are rumors they might be able to prerecord them soon." Milly smiled, hoping that this new piece of revolutionary information would be what they'd remember about her, not the fact that her husband was strangely absent.

"Do you ever get to be on set?" Joan continued, still fascinated.

Milly tried to recall. It had been so long since she'd been anywhere near Lloyd's work, certainly before children.

"I had a walk-on role once," she said. "As a secretary. I walked across the set and handed someone a stack of papers. It was my big break." She laughed. "My only break."

She thought back on the day, how Lloyd proudly displayed her around the studio and introduced her to his colleagues, how he'd accompanied her to the makeup and costume departments and even helped pick out her outfit, how someone had said she could be a model or a movie star, and how she'd known they were only being nice to an executive's wife but she'd hoped Lloyd had heard them anyway.

"You must tell us what happens with Kay and Doug on the show, Milly, please. Surely your husband spills the beans," Maureen insisted.

"Sorry, I can't say." Milly shrugged; she had no idea. "It's top secret. But I have to check on my little one; so good to see you all." She felt a bead of sweat trickle down her temple as she walked away.

A couple pushed a baby carriage along the pathway that encircled the entire island and was the only divider between Sylvia's property and the beach. She let them go by before crossing. Being surrounded by all these people at Sylvia's party made her feel overcome with loneliness, worse than sitting alone in her kitchen. Here she was reminded of everything she was losing—a companion, a comfort, a crutch—as well as everything she had at stake if people were to find out.

She wouldn't even be invited to this kind of gathering if they thought her husband only came home to save face on the weekends, and she certainly wouldn't be invited if they suspected a divorce. Divorce was contagious; divorce was a threat. No one would want their children spending time with children of a single mother. Tears welled in her eyes as she looked over at Jack and thought of him and Debbie getting caught up in her heartache. Jack was so deeply immersed in carving out a hole in the sand and was now taking a bucket to the water to fill it, only to have most of the water spill out before he got it back to his trench. She saw Debbie notice his attempts and she expected her to ignore it; she was, after all, deep in conversation with her friend Suzanna, sitting on the edge of the pier, legs swinging in synchrony. But after a moment, Debbie got up and ran to Jack, taking the bucket from his little hands, filling it, and bringing it back for him. She did it three more times before returning to her spot on the pier. Already full of swirling emotions, Milly felt a single tear fall onto her cheek and she quickly wiped it away. She had to get hold of herself.

CHAPTER TWELVE

SYLVIA

They should have canceled the party, Sylvia thought as she looked around at the opulence of it all, but it was too late for that now. Every year she said it would be a small beach get-together, and every year it blossomed into a bustling neighborhood affair. The only problem was that she and Walter were friends with everyone, and it cost them a small and ruinous fortune. But there was nothing Sylvia could do. Invitations had been sent out weeks ago, food and entertainment had already been ordered and paid for. Canceling would have only sent tongues wagging, and that was the last thing she wanted.

She stepped away from Walter. He was deep in conversation with the Hersheys about the new Village Inn restaurant that had opened in a property the couple owned and leased out on Marine Avenue. She might have been interested before—she always wanted to know about new ventures happening in her town—but now every conversation seemed fake and pointless. What was Walter going to do? Invest in it? Hardly. She almost muttered her sarcasm out loud, as she surveyed the scene and recognized every single face—friends she'd known for years, business owners from town and from the peninsula, new members from the club, as well as part-timers who lived on the island only in the spring and summer months. She felt a pang of sympathy when she saw Milly standing alone over by the children's area. She imagined it would be tough breaking into this crowd if you were new in town; everyone here had known each other for years, and to navigate it alone would be even harder. Milly's husband Lloyd was strangely never around, but at least he was working, making money, not gambling their lives away.

"Mom." Judith came up behind her wearing a white-and-pink-print summer dress with a pink sash and white gloves.

"Oh, you look absolutely darling," Sylvia said. "Is that my dress?"

"Yes," Judith said. "Everything of mine is getting too tight across the bust," she said in a hushed tone, while giving a small swooshing gesture across her chest. "I need new dresses."

"Well, I'm glad you found something you like in my closet. What's mine is yours," Sylvia said.

"Good," she said. "So can I also borrow your gold bracelet, the one with the rose diamonds that you usually wear with this?"

Sylvia froze. It was gone. It was sitting with the rest of her jewelry collection in the pawn shop, likely in the back room, just waiting to be put out for sale when she didn't return with the money she'd borrowed. But of course she couldn't tell Judith that.

"Mom," she persisted. "Can I? My friends are already here; I just need to put on my finishing touches."

"Not this time, sweetheart."

"Why?" she asked. "You always let me."

"I said no, Judith. This is just a barbecue. You don't need fancy jewelry today."

"But you're wearing . . ." Then Sylvia watched as Judith's eyes went to her mother's bare neck and wrist. "Well, everyone else is dressing up. Why can't I borrow it?"

"Don't argue with me in public, Judith Anne, or you won't be seeing your friends at all today."

"That's so not fair." Judith scowled at her mother, then stormed off. Sylvia instinctively looked around to see if anyone else had noticed the tension between her and her daughter, or that her jaw was likely clenched shut, her hands in fists at her side. She took a deep breath and slapped on a smile when it appeared that everyone was either too preoccupied or too tipsy to notice.

Sylvia took one more glance around, her pleasure bittersweet at seeing so many friends gathered and having a good time at their beloved home. She felt tears well up and she quickly blinked them away, thinking she should probably get back to Walter, keep up appearances, when she suddenly felt someone's eyes upon her. She turned and noticed a man standing on the public fishing pier next to her beachfront, smoking a cigarette, staring at her intently. He might be one of Walter's friends, she thought, but he wasn't anyone she recognized. He didn't look away, and for a brief second she allowed herself to think he might just be passing by, impressed with the grand party; after all, everything looked pristine. But his intensity unnerved her. Someone touched her shoulder and she almost screamed.

"Oh, Sylvia." It was just Milly. "I didn't mean to startle you. Gosh, you're shaking."

Milly looked over to where Sylvia had been focusing all her attention. "Who is that?" she asked.

"I don't know," Sylvia said, looking again, then linking her arm in Milly's and steering them away, picking up a pink cocktail from a passing waiter. "But I don't like the look of him."

Milly's brow furrowed. "Should we tell Walter? Maybe he should send someone over there. He looks a little menacing."

"No." Sylvia grabbed Milly's arm a little tighter than she'd intended. "Not in front of all these people. I'll handle it later."

Milly moved in front of Sylvia and stopped her from walking back into the party crowd. "Is everything OK? You seem rattled," she said.

Sylvia shook her head, afraid she'd start sobbing here at her own party. She was so filled with rage and fear and uncertainty that it might all just pour out of her. "Oh, Milly," she said, her voice shaky. "It's Walter. I can't talk about it, not really, but he's got himself into some trouble, financially," she whispered. "I'm terrified about what it's going to mean for us and I'm furious with him, just so furious I can barely even be around him."

"I'm so sorry," Milly said, genuine concern taking over her delicate features. "What can I do to help? Anything—just say the word."

Sylvia took a deep quivering breath and tried to regain some of her composure, and when she looked out to the pier again, the man was gone. "Don't speak a word of this, please. I shouldn't have told you. I was just . . ." She held up her drink. "I'm a little tipsy, and it's been hard to keep it all to myself. It's just so much to keep inside, you know?"

Milly nodded. "Oh, I know," she said. "I can guarantee you're not the only one harboring secrets around here."

Sylvia cocked her head, but Milly took Sylvia's hand in hers. "I won't say a word, I promise. Your secret is safe with me."

CHAPTER THIRTEEN

MILLY

On Monday morning a car pulled up to Milly's house earlier than expected, but the garage, or rather, the guest cottage, as she was now calling it, was all ready for them. She'd just taken a date-and-nut loaf out of the oven and had fresh-squeezed lemonade in a pitcher waiting, as she expected the girls to be hungry and thirsty after their drive down from Los Angeles. She slipped off her apron, stepped into her pumps, and freshened her lipstick before she opened the door to greet them. It was silly, she thought, but she wanted to look good for them—chic and stylish. But it wasn't them. This car was full of boys, young men, actually, and they pulled into the open parking spot outside her house, squinting in the sunlight at the numbers painted on Milly's house.

"This parking spot is taken," Milly called out from her doorstep. "I have guests arriving who'll be pulling up here shortly. Try a little farther down, where there's plenty of space." She tried to wave them on, but they killed the engine and the young men started piling out of the red convertible, seven of them from a car that was clearly meant to seat five, and they began unloading bags onto the sidewalk.

"Mrs. Kincaid?" One of them said as he walked up the garden path to Milly's front door and held out his hand.

"Yes?"

"Hello, ma'am, I'm Johnny Walsh." He took off his sunglasses. "Lovely house you have here."

"Johnny?" Milly said, confused. "I'm expecting a Rosie and her two friends."

"Oh, sure thing. Rosie is Mikey's girl." He pointed back to a young man with jet-black hair pulling a duffel bag from the trunk. "She was nice enough to find us a place to stay. The girls are staying on the peninsula near the Rendezvous Ballroom, lucky dogs. We were a little late to get our act together and book a place, so we got stuck on the island, but we're just happy to be here. It's going to be a great week."

"But you're men!"

"Yes, that we are," he said with a wink. "But we're very well-behaved men, and we won't cause you a lick of trouble. In fact, you'll barely even know we're here. Oh, and before I forget . . ." He reached into his pocket and handed her a wad of cash. "Here's what we owe you."

Milly took the cash and stared at it, then quickly tucked it into the pocket of her blue-and-white-gingham dress, because standing there with money in her hands while seven men descended on her felt somehow indecent.

"Now, hold on a minute," she said as they all started walking through her gate and toward her front door. "There seems to have been a misunderstanding. This is not the guest cottage; it's out back." She pointed to a gate that led down the side of her house and out to the cottage in the back. The boys, or men rather, filed past her one by one, each nodding to her as they went. "Hello, Mrs. Kincaid . . . I'm Mikey. Great to meet you, ma'am, I'm Wesley. Thank you so much for having us, I'm Luke. . . ." And on they went, reciting names that she couldn't possibly remember.

She stood for a moment, after they'd all headed to the back, to see if any of her neighbors had seen the stream of men flood her front yard, but no one was out on the sidewalk, and she didn't notice anyone peeking out from behind their curtains, but that would just be a matter of time, she thought, and what on earth would she tell Lloyd about all of this?

"I think there's been a mistake," she said, chasing after them, heading in through the door of the cottage. "This place is only big enough for three, maybe four, tops."

"Don't worry about us, Mrs. Kincaid. We're going to be at the beach all day and out dancing all night," Johnny said. "I promise, you won't even know we're here."

How could she not notice that seven young, handsome men were squeezed into her little garage/guest cottage and beaming at her expectantly? They'd come all this way with their duffel bags, and she hardly wanted to be the killjoy that ruined their vacation. It felt like just yesterday that she'd been that age—carefree, looking for fun.

"Mrs. Kincaid?" Johnny said.

"All right," she said and shrugged. "If you can manage in here, all seven of you, then be my guests. But it will be tight. I'll bring some more towels from the main house, and I have a date-and-nut loaf fresh out of the oven and some lemonade." The boys groaned with anticipation.

"Thank you, Mrs. Kincaid, we're starving," one of them said.

She shook her head and smiled. "I'll be right back."

As she walked into her house, she did wonder if she should let the neighbors know about the misunderstanding, but she thought it was probably best to leave things alone. Besides, it seemed quite common for local residents to rent out their guesthouses or extra bedrooms, so maybe this wouldn't be such a catastrophe after all.

She carried a tray of sliced nut loaf and lemonade to the guest cottage, and the boys just about lunged for it.

"This is delicious," Mikey said.

"Best nut loaf of my life," Luke said. "Don't tell my mother I said that."

"That lemonade—" Wesley said, gulping it down. "I didn't know how thirsty I was."

"Made from fresh lemons," Milly said, pointing to the small lemon tree growing outside the guest cottage window. She warmed at the sight of them all gushing over her baking skills, watching them eat and drink as if they hadn't been fed in weeks, seeing someone grateful for the effort she'd made. It had been so long since anyone had thanked her for anything, really.

"Well, I'll leave you to it," she said. "Let me know if you need something. I'm in the house just there." She pointed. "But this is a quiet neighborhood, and I'm new to the area, so I don't want to be bothering my neighbors. You're going to have to be on your best behavior."

They all nodded politely. "Yes, ma'am," a few said.

Maybe she'd make them meatballs tonight, she thought, as she crossed the yard to her kitchen door, even though dinner was not supposed to be included in the rent. She'd be cooking for Jack and Debbie, anyway, so what harm would it do to cook a few dozen more? She delivered the towels and a few extra pillows, then set off to the market to buy several more pounds of ground beef.

When she returned, the boys were gone but the car was still parked out front. She peeked in the cottage window and saw socks and pants strewed about the place. She quickly carried her groceries into her house. There, slipped under the door, she saw a scribbled note:

Dear Mrs. Kincaid,
Thank you for letting us stay. We've gone to the beach.
Be back later,
The Boys

Milly smiled. It felt quite nice to have someone care enough to leave a note. She rolled up her sleeves and quickly got to work. She only had a few hours before the children would be home from school.

The next day, during her lesson with Robbie and Sylvia, Milly felt as inept as she did the first time around. She couldn't keep the ball in play, and a mounting sense of disappointment consumed her. When Robbie stood behind her and adjusted her grip on the racket, moving her arm to replicate the swing, she was not fooled by his intentions and she quickly assured him that she understood and stepped aside. When the lesson was over, she was relieved.

"Should we stay and try to play a little?" Sylvia asked. "I've got a few minutes."

"I don't think so," Milly said. "I might be a lost cause, and I think someone wants to use the court."

"Oh," Sylvia said to a woman standing at the gate. "I didn't realize you were waiting." But the woman didn't respond, just opened the gate and walked on. As she approached, Milly realized it was Adele.

"I'm not waiting for the court," Adele said. "I'm waiting to speak with you, Mrs. Johnson."

"Me?" Sylvia asked.

"I looked for Mr. Johnson but he was not available. His secretary said I could find you here."

"We just finished a lesson. How can I help you?"

"I'm Adele Lambert."

"I know who you are, Miss Lambert," Sylvia said.

"I would like you to hire me," she said. "To work here."

Sylvia looked confused. "Don't you work at the Fun Zone?"

"Not anymore," she said, glaring at Milly.

"Oh no, did something happen?" Milly asked, feeling somehow to blame. "Did the ride malfunction cost you your job? That doesn't seem fair."

"It doesn't matter now." Adele returned her attention to Sylvia. "I'd like to work as a tennis coach," Adele said.

"Goodness." Sylvia almost started to laugh. "I'm sorry we don't have any lady coaches." She picked up her pocketbook and put it on her shoulder.

"Maybe you should," Adele said.

"The coaches here are all male. Same as at any other club." Sylvia said. "Do you even play?"

"Yes," Adele said. "She has seen me." She looked pointedly at Milly.

"It's true, I did," Milly said. "In the alley behind my house. She's very good. Excellent, actually."

"I could beat any of the coaches here," Adele said.

"Ha!" Sylvia laughed. "Good for you."

"And every single man."

"You're very confident," Sylvia said, beginning to step away.

"You do not play well, either of you. You're terrible actually. You don't even hold the racket correctly, and your serve is weak," Adele said.

"Excuse me?" Sylvia turned back.

"You play like girls, like delicate little flowers. You hit the ball with no power, with arms like soft spaghetti," Adele flopped her arms around. "How can you expect to have power and control if you play like that?"

"All right," Sylvia said, irritated now. "I'm not going to stand here and be insulted in my own club." She linked her arm through Milly's and pulled her toward her. "We have to go. And you're not allowed on this property unless you are a member."

"May I give you a few tips?" Adele asked, picking up a ball off the ground and not waiting for a response. She took a step back to the baseline, angled her body perpendicular to the net, tossed the ball in front of her, then jumped up to meet it, sending it crosscourt low and fast like a rocket.

"Wow!" Milly perked up and slipped her arm out of Sylvia's grip. "See, I would really like to be able to do that."

"I could teach you, for a fee of course," Adele said, picking up another ball and doing the same serve again. "I could also teach you to keep the ball in play." She picked up another, tossed it gently in front of her, and sent it down the line, picked up another, jogged to the net, and volleyed it at a tight angle. "No one can get a short ball like that; you would win every time with that angle. Go to the other side of the net."

Milly immediately ran to the other side and held out her racket. Adele hit a ball in her direction and Milly returned it.

"Turn your shoulders," Adele said, and Milly hit it back and forth to her several more times.

"Loop your racket back before you swing, and finish over your shoulder," Adele said and demonstrated, then sent her another ball. This time

Milly returned it straight to Adele, and they rallied for a few miraculous minutes before Adele caught the ball in her left hand and Milly jogged back over.

"That was amazing. I actually hit the ball, a lot of times," Milly said.

"Well, as I said," Sylvia chimed in. "Our coaches are . . ."

"I'll hire you," Milly said.

"What?" Sylvia looked from Adele to Milly.

"I'll hire her. I'll pay the same rate that Robbie charges." Milly turned her attention back to Adele. "Look, if you really can teach me how to hit the ball the way you did, then I'd like you to coach me."

"Hold your horses," Sylvia said. "You can't just hire her; she doesn't even work here."

"Sylvia." Milly lowered her voice. She liked Sylvia a lot; she liked her confidence, her charisma; she liked how sociable and inclusive she was, how she was taking Milly under her wing and helping her navigate life on the island. She didn't want to dismiss her at her husband's club, but she felt strongly about this. "Those lessons with Robbie were awful. I didn't learn one thing, except that he would like to sleep with me, even though I made it very clear that I'm married. Look around, the male coaches are too busy coaching the male patrons and don't seem to want to waste their precious time with us, and when they can, they squeeze us in early in the morning and spend half the time looking at our legs. I want to learn, to really learn, and get good like her."

"Well, honestly, you'll never get as good as me," Adele said. "And you'll only improve if you put in the work."

"But you'll at least teach me what you know?"

"Of course. I will make you a lot better. I can make you both so much better in a few short weeks that soon you will be able to beat your husbands."

"Yes!" Milly said, exuberantly. "I want to get good really quickly."

"Then you need to play every day," Adele said.

"That's fine," Milly said, justifying in her head that she could use the money from renting out the guest cottage to pay for her lessons.

Sylvia looked from Milly to Adele and seemed to consider it. "You'd have to pay me twenty percent of your earnings, just like the other coaches," Sylvia said.

"Fine," Adele said.

"And we can try it for two weeks and see how it goes," Sylvia added. "I reserve the right to cancel this arrangement at any time."

Adele nodded.

Milly felt giddy with excitement. If she could improve, then she hadn't joined this club for nothing. She'd lost so much of herself since having children; she'd been so swept up in them and their well-being and Lloyd and the house and the move that she'd forgotten about herself, forgotten to care for herself, forgotten who she was, even. She'd grown soft around the middle and soft in the brain. She had nothing exciting to add to the conversation; it was no wonder that Lloyd was looking for excitement elsewhere. Suddenly everything came into focus. She might not have that innate talent she'd hoped for, but she was going to take lessons with this brash French lady, and she was going to get so good at tennis that Lloyd wouldn't be able to take his eyes off her. She was going to win her husband back—she was sure of it.

CHAPTER FOURTEEN

ADELE

Adele rummaged through the very back of her closet and dug out her white drop-waist tennis dress, as well as her signature Jean Patou cardigan. Though the length of the dress had been shockingly short in her day, it was too long for today's tastes, a fact that she laughed at as she tried it on. She had stunned the world by showing off her knees. She had paved the way for women like Milly and Sylvia to wear their comfortable and stylish tennis dresses and skirts, and yet they had no idea who she was or what she'd done for them, and she liked it that way. She stayed up late taking up the hem, then she washed it, hung it to dry, and the next morning she ironed it crisply so she'd be ready for her first lesson with Milly.

But walking to her first coaching lesson now she felt strangely exposed. Out in the open, wearing tennis attire for the first time in years brought on a fresh wave of panic. After all this time hiding from the public eye, she would be working at a tennis club, of all places, where she risked being recognized. Was it reckless to do this after leaving the tennis scene in disgrace more than twenty years earlier, or was it necessary to survive? She wanted to hear her father's voice in her head telling her that it was all right, that all had been forgotten, that it was time to move forward, but all she could hear was the blood pulsing through her veins and throbbing in her ears.

She fastened two buttons on her pale-pink cardigan against the morning chill, then she touched the monogram of her initials, AML, embroidered above her heart. After the scandal, she'd shortened her name from Adeline to Adele and changed her last name from Léglise to Lambert, but her initials remained the same.

She had kept every single one of Jean Patou's designs, unable to part with them after he died, every piece reminding her of a specific match, a victory, a gala, or a night out. She remembered the exact time the designer had come into her life.

It was 1924, the year she won her first singles title at Wimbledon against Dorothy Mills, when she was just seventeen years old. She'd dressed the same as the other women on the courts in that game, wearing a mid-calf-length white cotton skirt, a short-sleeved middy blouse, and a ridiculous brimmed bonnet. But after she had won the long and difficult match against her opponent, who was at least a decade older with several Wimbledon titles under her belt, her father decided it was time for a transformation from little girl to tennis queen.

"Adeline, meet your very own personal couturier, Jean Patou," he'd said, grinning from ear to ear as he ushered his daughter into the designer's studio in Paris.

"*Enchanté*," Jean Patou said, kissing the back of her hand.

"*Mon Dieu*," Adele said breathlessly. "It's such an honor to meet you." She was not quite able to believe she was standing face-to-face with one of the most famous couturiers in the world. There was Coco Chanel and there was Jean Patou, and he was arguably the most elegant man in Europe.

"I have extreme admiration for you," he said, impeccably dressed in a charcoal three-piece suit, knit tie, and a bowler. "Your athleticism, your grace, your speed. You are a very talented child, and you must not be restricted by your attire."

"Yes, well," her father said. "That is the exact transformation we are looking to make, from child to woman. Elf to sphinx. Princess to queen. *La reine du tennis*."

Patou nodded his head as if with deep understanding. "*La Divine*," he said, quietly eyeing Adele from all angles. "I am an athlete myself. Not of your skill, of course, but I have studied the sport and I have studied you. I see the way you leap and dance across the court." He stretched out his arms dramatically. "How you move and run and spiral your body when you wind up to strike the ball. I understand the needs of an activewear garment, but I want to understand your needs too. What do you want, what do you need to win?"

Adele thought for a moment. "When I play tennis, I come alive. It's the only time I am completely myself, but I want to be free. When I wear these long and restricting tennis clothes, I feel like I am in someone else's costume," she said.

"You need a more liberated silhouette," he said.

"Yes, but . . ." Adele paused and looked at her father, then stopped.

"Continue," Patou urged her. "*Dites-moi.*"

"Well, I play better when I feel good about myself, attractive. I would like function and fashion, if possible." She looked down at the ground, worried her father would tell her she was being ridiculous. She knew she wasn't a beautiful girl—she never had been—but with Jean Patou dressing her, she could at least feel beautiful.

Jean Patou turned Adele to the mirror and stood behind her. "*La femme moderne*," he said. "I love to dress a woman to enhance her feminine appeal. Tennis is not just a game, it is a lifestyle, and when you wear my creations and move across the court the way you do, no man or woman will be able to take their eyes off you. I know exactly what you need."

With his help Adele got rid of the corseted undergarments and stockings that were customary and wore a short, pleated silk skirt, like that of a ballerina, hitting a few inches above her knees and astonishingly short for the time. Patou made her a sleeveless silk blouse that allowed her to move her arms freely, and a striped V-neck sweater for postgame interviews. He replaced the bonnet with a brightly colored silk bandeau, for a better line of visibility, fastened at the front with a diamond pin.

"Relaxed and comfortable with unexpected flare," Monsieur Patou said when he admired his creation for Adeline during their next visit. "You will never be held back by your clothing again."

He added a light cardigan, color-coordinated to match the bandeau, a sweater that she only ever needed until she was warmed up enough to stun the crowds with her bare, tanned, and toned arms.

In her new attire she felt much freer and less restricted in her movement, as he had promised, but more than that, she also felt fabulous and, dare she admit it, attractive. The following year, she started wearing full makeup on the court, a gold bracelet above her elbow, and she would arrive at her matches in an oversized white mink coat. The extravagance made her feel special, superior, and untouchable. She was stylish and functional, and the press went crazy for it, and for her. When interviewed, Patou called her by his nickname, *La Divine*, and the French papers ran with it. She recalled one male opponent speaking about her attire in the press, and he'd said her outfit was a cross between that of a prima donna and a streetwalker. But that just added to her allure and the frenzy that surrounded her. Afterward, she was in all the magazines. Women started following her every move and copying her looks. They wanted to embrace her freedom and have a taste of it for themselves. Her father may have made her a champion, but Jean Patou made her an icon.

Now, her hands were sweaty as she walked into the club, her heart beating too fast, and she looked around nervously to see if anyone noticed her. They didn't. She checked in with Glenda, as Sylvia had instructed her, and was given her court assignment for the morning.

"Good morning!" Milly almost pounced on Adele as she entered court 4. She was bouncing on her toes, attempting some kind of frenetic warm-up, as Adele put her bag on the bench. "I'm so excited for this," Milly said.

"I can see," Adele said. "Do you need to go to the bathroom?"

"No," Milly said.

"Then stop jumping; you'll give yourself an injury."

"Oh, all right."

Adele saw some of the enthusiasm drain from Milly's face and felt a pang of guilt. This wasn't going to be easy, trying to train this woman, or anyone, for that matter. It didn't come easily to Adele to be pleasant or patient, but she was going to have to try harder if she wanted to get paid. She looked around again, checking to see if anyone had spotted her yet, if anyone had made a connection between her as a middle-aged, irritable recluse and her former outgoing, outspoken self. But no one was paying them any attention.

"*Alors*, let's get to work," Adele said. "First we start with the basics—forehand and backhand. I will feed you one ball to your right and one ball to your left, and we'll see how things go."

"Great," Milly said, standing tall, her racket hanging by her side.

"Ready?"

"Yes," Milly said.

"No, you're not ready," Adele said. "You stand as if you wait to catch the bus. When I say 'ready,' you get into the ready position." Adele crouched in a squat, gripping her racket in front of her as if it were a hammer, her heels off the ground, ready to pounce. "Like that."

Milly copied her. "Like this?"

"*Bien.*"

Adele stood a few feet in front of Milly and gently tossed the ball to her left and to her right, correcting her as she went. "Turn your shoulders. . . . Loop your racket back. . . . . Transfer your weight from your back leg to your front leg as you make contact with the ball. . . . Do it again."

The backhand was worse than her forehand, if that were possible. Adele set her racket down, crossed to Milly, and stood behind her, taking her wrist and moving it for her, showing her how it should feel to sweep the racket back toward the fence, then hit the ball out in front of her. She adjusted the face of the racket to face down a little, and eventually Milly began to get the hang of it. "At your level, you hold the racket with two hands for this. The force has to come from your left hand, the hand at the back. That's why it's called a backhand," Adele said. Milly listened and made corrections easily. She was coachable, Adele thought. She could be trained. "Finish your swing over the opposite shoulder, all the way. Make sure the racket scratches your back as you finish."

After a while Adele realized her focus was intense, the way it used to be during a match, only now it was intensely scrutinizing Milly's movements. She realized she hadn't looked out to the other courts once; she had forgotten to pay attention in case anyone was watching them. Earlier that morning she had wondered if she could tolerate coaching someone else in the one thing that she loved most in the world, or if she'd find it infuriating, but Adele was enjoying this. She was relieved to know that she was able to put into words the actions that came to her intuitively. There was a satisfaction in being able to tell Milly exactly where to hit the ball or how to brush her racket around it to develop some topspin, and to see the desired result unfold. It was magic. She wondered if this was how her father had felt when he'd coached her. Over the years she'd thought so much about the way he pushed her too hard, how he drove her to the edge of her limits, but was it possible that he was simply mesmerized by the ability to pass on what he knew and see it come to life in his daughter?

When Adele looked at the clock mounted on the fence, she realized they'd gone ten minutes over their time, but she didn't mind. She felt better than she had in months, years maybe.

"That was incredible, truly," Milly gushed as she handed Adele eight dollars for the hour. "I feel as if I learned weeks' worth of valuable skills in just one lesson."

"I'm glad," Adele said. "You weren't as terrible as I expected." Her attempt at a compliment.

"Oh, well that's good, I suppose," Milly replied.

The gate creaked open and Sylvia walked onto the court. "You looked quite good out there, Milly," she said. "Well done."

"It was all Adele. She's the most brilliant coach, Sylvia. You have to try for yourself."

Sylvia smiled tightly and Adele handed her $1.60, as they'd agreed upon—20 percent of anything she earned for the use of the court.

"Well, it turns out tennis is not the only thing you have a talent for," Sylvia said, taking a folded newspaper from under her arm and snapping it open. Right there on the front page of the local paper was Adele's face, up close, her arm just out of the frame as she attempted to shield herself.

"*Mon Dieu*," Adele said, moving in to take a closer look. The headline read, LOCAL WOMAN RESCUES CHILDREN FROM OUT-OF-CONTROL FERRIS WHEEL.

"What a hero," Sylvia said, a hint of sarcasm in her voice. Adele shook her head. "I used to work there," she said quietly, gathering her things. She had to get out of there, away from these women before they asked more questions. She had to get back to the safety of her house. This was terrible—the worst possible thing that could happen. She'd been so careful for all these years to live a reclusive life, and now she was exposed, on display for all to see. She panicked, her breath getting shorter as if she couldn't take enough air into her lungs. It had been a long time since she'd had an episode, but she didn't want to have one here in front of these women. She threw her bag over her shoulder and headed for the gate.

"Wait." Milly ran after her. "Are you all right?"

Adele kept walking and raised her hand. "Yes," she managed.

"So, I'll see you again tomorrow, same time?" she called out after her. But Adele had already rounded the corner and was out of sight.

CHAPTER FIFTEEN

MILLY

When the children got home from school, Milly realized she'd been so busy unpacking the last of the moving boxes, she still hadn't bathed or changed out of her tennis clothes. Debbie and Jack started happily playing with blocks in the living room, so she took the opportunity to freshen up and change.

"Debbie, please keep an eye on your brother until I get back down," Milly said from halfway up the stairs.

By the time she got out of the shower and heard the Mouseketeers counting off their names in roll call, she was grateful that Debbie had turned on the television for Jack, and she allowed herself a few extra moments to fix her hair. But when she heard a squeal of laughter coming from outside, she rushed to the window. She had made it very clear, on multiple occasions, that the children were not to leave the house without her permission. They were still new to the area and could easily wander off and get lost—especially Jack. She pushed back the curtains to see them both in the yard playing croquet with one of the young men from her guest cottage.

Ducking from view and pulling on a yellow plaid sundress, she rushed downstairs to the yard.

"Jack, Debbie," she called from the back door, "please don't bother our guests."

"Hi, Mrs. Kincaid," the young man greeted her. His name was Wesley, if she remembered correctly. "They're no bother at all. In fact Jack's really getting the hang of croquet."

"Look, Mommy," Jack said as he swung the wooden mallet toward the ball and let go of the handle, sending it flying in the air toward the young man.

Wesley quickly stepped aside, out of the way, then bent down to pick up the mallet and hand it back.

"You've got to hold on real tight, buddy," he said, taking Jack's hands and placing them on the handle again, this time directing his aim. "That's it, champ," he said as Jack tapped the ball more gently this time and sent it rolling through the wicket.

"It worked," Jack called out, jumping. "I scored."

"Nice work," Milly said. "But you must leave poor Mr. Wesley here alone. I'm sure he has much more pressing things to attend to."

"It's no problem at all, Mrs. Kincaid, really. They are great kids, and we're having a blast."

"See, Mommy," Debbie chimed in, "he said we can stay. I'm really good at this game too." Milly looked to her guest and he nodded.

"I promise, it's fine."

"Well at least let me bring you something to drink." She remembered seeing a few of Lloyd's beers in the back of the fridge.

"That would be swell," he said. "I just rented a board and paddled around the island, so I'm parched. The rest of the boys are sleeping off last night's fun."

Milly nodded. "I'll be right back."

She grabbed two beers, two glasses of milk, and chocolate chip cookies that she'd baked the night before and placed them on a tray. Before returning to the children, she watched from the window. Debbie and Jack were squealing with laughter as Wesley chased them around the yard, and she smiled at their youthful innocence, how easy it was to laugh and smile, and how free they were with their limbs as they leapt to escape his reach. She too felt more youthful since her tennis lesson that morning, giddy almost with the promise of what was to come. She had never played a sport before, nor had she had any interest, but she'd loved being so active and was already thinking about what she might learn in her next lesson.

She stayed a moment longer, enjoying the laughter and squeals of delight coming from a home that was in such a state of silent upheaval. Milly had expected her guests to be female and hoped it would be a treat for Debbie, but maybe having these young men around wouldn't be so bad after all, especially for Jack, since Lloyd wasn't planning to show his face anytime soon. While she was at the window, she opened the kitchen drawer and put on a touch of lipstick, just to make herself presentable, then she carried the tray out to the yard.

"Those look amazing," Wesley said, sitting down across from Milly at the patio table and picking up a cookie.

"I think I've perfected the recipe," Milly said, waiting for him to take a bite.

"Oh, you have," he said, catching a crumb as it fell on his lip. "You definitely have. What's the secret?"

"I can't reveal that," Milly said. "Or I'll have nothing to bribe you with when I need someone to play with the children."

Jack and Debbie launched themselves toward the plate of cookies, then took off again running.

"Don't eat and run," Milly said. "You might choke." She shook her head and laughed when they took absolutely no notice of her.

"It's good advice," Wesley said. "I'll heed your warning." He picked up his beer and held it up. "Cheers."

Milly clinked his. "Cheers." She couldn't help but notice, now that she got a good look, that he was quite a catch, with those dark-brown eyes and disheveled, wavy brown hair. If he wasn't already going steady with a college girl, he was sure to win one over this week. "So where do you all go to school?" Milly asked.

"UCLA," he said. "I'm in my final year."

"UCLA? That's where I went too!" She was excited at the coincidence at first, then a little embarrassed. "Well for a year, before I got engaged and left."

"That's too bad," Wesley said, "that you didn't finish up, I mean, not that you got married."

"Oh." She laughed. "I know, I should have stayed, but you know what it's like . . . or maybe you don't. Everything felt so urgent, like I had to hurry up and do all the things—get married, have children—as if the world wouldn't wait for me."

Wesley nodded, but Milly was sure he had no idea what that was like; the world waited for men like him.

"Well, you've got some great kids here, Mrs. Kincaid."

"Please, call me Milly. Mrs. Kincaid makes me sound so old."

"All right, Miss Milly," he said grinning.

"Now I sound like a schoolteacher," she laughed.

"Well, if I should call you Milly, then please call me Wes—that's what all my friends call me. Every time I hear Wesley I think of my grandfather. Probably because I'm named after him, but still . . ."

"You're the one who introduced yourself as Wesley," Milly said, smiling.

"I wanted you to think I was respectable."

"You seem respectable to me, Wes," Milly said.

He smiled and held her gaze until she looked away, blushing a little.

"Thank you so much for the cookies," he said after a moment. "And for the meatballs last night. We didn't pay you enough for that kind of generosity."

"I like to cook when I know someone will appreciate it. It's actually very satisfying."

"Well, good, we do appreciate it." He took a swig of his beer.

Jack ran up to the table and swiped another cookie. "That's your last one," Milly said as he ran off again. She watched them play for a while. Wes got up to help Jack with his swing and almost got hit in the face a second time.

"I should probably take them inside before you lose an eye," she said to Wes, though she didn't really want to. She was enjoying sitting out in her yard with the warm afternoon sun on her shoulders, and she was enjoying his easy company. "I have to start thinking about dinner."

"Yeah," Wes said. "And I'd better wake up these guys, otherwise they'll sleep all day."

"Yes, yes," Milly said. "You do that." She turned to Jack and Debbie. "Come along, you two, let's go."

"Can we have pancakes tonight?" Debbie asked, running to Milly's side and taking her hand.

Milly thought about it for a minute. Lloyd wasn't coming home for a week; she and the kids could eat whatever they wanted. And she loved the idea of not making another trip to the market. "Why not?" Milly said. "I love pancakes for dinner."

Later that evening Sylvia knocked hard on Milly's door.

"Can I come in?" she asked, as Milly swung the door open, sensing an emergency.

"Of course. Is everything all right?"

"Yes, absolutely fine," Sylvia said, flashing one of her beaming smiles, but Milly saw a strain in her face.

"Can I get you something to drink? A glass of wine? A gin and tonic?"

"No, thank you." Sylvia said. "Do you have a smoke?"

"I doubt it," Milly said, digging through her kitchen drawers. "I thought you didn't like them?"

"I don't, usually. But desperate times . . ."

"Well, hold on, I might be able to find one." She'd seen a few of the boys from the cottage stand out in the back alley and smoke from time to time, so she walked across the yard and knocked on the door.

"Oh gosh, sorry to bother you," Milly said, looking away when one of the young men opened the door in his underwear.

"For Christ's sake, Mickey." Wes rushed to the door to take Mickey's place and pulled the door closed behind him. "I apologize for him, he's . . . we're getting dressed to go to dinner." Wes was in athletic clothes and had a deep V of sweat down his T-shirt. When he caught her looking at it, he placed his hand on his chest. "Sorry. I suppose none of us are all that presentable."

"Oh. No, sorry." She did a quick calculation: First he paddled around the island, now he'd done what? Gone running? "I was just wondering if you maybe had a cigarette to spare."

"You know"—he raised an eyebrow—"I read a study recently that smoking might not be all its chalked up to be."

"Well, it's good for nerves, and that's all I care about, but anyway, it's not for me, it's for my friend."

"Oh, well in that case, I think Johnny has a pack, and Mickey too." He stepped away from the door and came back with a cigarette and book of matches.

"Thanks, Wes, I appreciate that," she said, and she walked back into her house. She set a crystal ashtray on the table and handed Sylvia the goods. She lit it right away and inhaled deeply.

"What's so desperate?" Milly asked, joining Sylvia at the table.

"Oh, it's nothing urgent," Sylvia said, but Milly didn't quite believe her. She had an edge to her; she wasn't her usual calm self.

"You said it was desperate times," Milly said.

Sylvia waved away the comment and the smoke unfurling from her cigarette. "I have a favor to ask of you." She hesitated. "I was just wondering if you could ask your sitter, Leticia, to watch your children Friday night."

"I could . . ." Milly said, "but for what reason?"

"I'm assuming Lloyd won't be home to watch them, right?"

Milly sat up abruptly and suddenly wished that she'd asked Wes for two of those smokes. "Why do you say that?" she asked. How could Sylvia know about Lloyd? Had she started noticing his absence? Had she somehow found out about their arrangement, that their marriage was in shambles, a farce? Maybe people had started talking after she'd shown up at Sylvia's party alone.

"You said he was working lots of late nights?" She put her hand on Milly's arm. "Milly, it's fine, it's normal; men have to work."

"Oh yes, a lot of late nights and early mornings," she said as calmly as possible, but her mind had already begun to race. If Sylvia, of all people, caught on to the fact that she and Lloyd were living as occasional roommates rather than as man and wife, surely the whole town would find out. Sylvia knew everyone.

"It's just that Judith, as you know, loves music, and she thinks that the Rendezvous Ballroom is just 'coolsville'—they've got all the hot acts coming to town for Bal week—and she's absolutely desperate to go."

"Will you let her?"

"How can I not? She'll despise me if she's the only one of her friends who doesn't get to go, but I don't want her getting in with some greaser, you know?"

Milly looked at her and squinted. "Are you sure that's what you're worried about?"

Sylvia's eyes widened. "Of course it is."

"Does this have anything to do with that man hanging around your party?" Milly asked.

Sylvia took a deep breath and cradled her head in one hand, her cigarette shaking in the other.

When she looked up she looked fragile and breakable in a way that Milly had never seen in Sylvia before. "I'm worried, yes."

"Who was he?" Milly asked.

"I don't know, but I think it's got something to do with Walter and the money problem." Sylvia straightened up as if she knew she'd said too much. "So, will you go with me? To the Rendezvous?"

"I don't know, Sylvia. I want to help but I'm a mother of two. Won't the place be crawling with eighteen-year-olds?"

Sylvia forced a laugh. "It'll be a bash, I promise. It's not just the young kids who go; everyone loves to go dancing there. I just need to keep an eye on things, and I can't go alone."

"What about Walter?"

Sylvia stared at her cigarette. "He's been a little under the weather," she said, bringing the cigarette to her lips and taking a long drag. "Come on, Milly, that's what friends are for, right? I scratch your back, you scratch mine."

Milly nodded. Sylvia was right: She had been such a good friend to her in her short time on the island, and besides, a night out on the town might be fun.

"All right, I'll go with you."

"Thanks, Milly." Sylvia stood up and hugged her tightly. "You're a doll, you really are. I'll pick you up at eight."

CHAPTER SIXTEEN

SYLVIA

Walter was home, working in his study, but Sylvia marched in and placed two stacks of cash firmly on his desk, then sat in the brown leather chair opposite him and waited.

"I have to go," Walter said into his phone. "We'll talk more about this later." He hung up.

"I've pawned my jewelry and I've sold my car," Sylvia said, not waiting for him to speak.

"What? Why would you do that?"

She looked at him incredulously. "What else am I supposed to do, Walter? Sit around and wait for you to destroy our lives even more?" She hated this. She hated the anger and resentment she felt toward the man she had loved for seventeen years. How immediate her reaction had been when he revealed what he'd done; how sudden her feelings toward him had changed from love, desire, and respect to utter disdain. She wondered if she'd ever be able to reverse her outrage and if she and Walter could ever return to their old selves, even if they dug themselves out of this mess.

"That"—he pointed to the stacks of cash wearily—"that's not even going to make a difference, Sylvia. I don't think you realize how much debt we're in."

"I realize. We are sixty thousand dollars in debt; you made that very clear. But this is better than nothing, surely. Give them this and tell them we need more time to come up with the rest."

Walter shook his head. "It doesn't work that way." He tried to reach across the desk for Sylvia's hand, but she pulled it away. He sat up in his chair, looking dejected and hurt. "They're charging interest. Weekly interest. They want their money and they want it now." Walter paused, then lowered his voice. "We have to sell the house, fast. We're going to have to take what we can get for it; we can't wait for the right buyer to come along, or this debt is going to double in no time and cripple us. We really will lose everything. I've already spoken to Teddy, and he knows a family that's looking to buy right away, cash."

Sylvia put her hand to her mouth as she felt her stomach churn. She wanted to get up and storm out of this room, leaving behind all these awful, terrible things Walter was saying about their home, about their life. But this was real. Walking out wasn't going to make this go away, so she closed her eyes and rubbed her temples, trying to make sense of it all.

So, he had been talking to Teddy about selling the house, and now she wondered if Teddy's wife Faye knew about Walter's gambling problems before she did. He'd worked with Walter on several of his property acquisitions, but she never imagined having to ask for his help to sell their home. She took tremendous pride in what they had built. Their house was decorated with love for her family, exactly to her taste, filled with trinkets, mementos from their happy life. At this moment, a funny little buffalo statue smiled up at her from Walter's desk, a souvenir she had insisted she buy for him on their last trip to Catalina. She felt safe at home, here, surrounded by her favorite people and things. She'd always imagined they'd live in this house for the rest of their lives, and when they were gone, they'd pass it down to their daughter. A tear dropped involuntarily to her cheek and she quickly wiped it away. "But Judith. She was born here, she's grown up here; everything she knows and loves is on this island."

Walter walked around to Sylvia, moved the statue aside, and sat on the desk in front of her. "You've grown up here too," he said in a whisper. "And I am so sorry. I made a stupid, stupid mistake."

For a moment, Sylvia saw a flash of forgiveness far, far in the corner of her mind, and though she wasn't ready, not even close to being able to forgive him, she felt a glimmer of hope that she'd find it in herself someday. But then her mind snapped back to the present; anger and fear swallowed her whole.

"Where will we live?" she demanded, panicking about what he had in mind. "I refuse to go to the desert. Barstow was bad enough, and I left there long ago with no plans to return."

"We can stay on the island for now," Walter said. "We can move into the property on Onyx Avenue."

"That place? It's a dump, Walter, we're about to tear it down and rebuild."

"Well, that's obviously not happening now."

"Why can't we sell that instead?" Sylvia asked, though she knew the answer.

"We'll get barely anything for it in the state it's in. But we can stay there temporarily; we can make it decent. We can bring some of our furniture, a few of the smaller pieces, until we figure out what's next."

"And live next door to Adele Lambert?"

"I heard you hired her at the club."

Sylvia shrugged. She didn't want to talk about that. The humiliation of moving out of their house and into that tiny cottage next to Adele would be all-consuming. What would everyone say? They'd all be talking behind Sylvia's back, making assumptions about what happened. It wouldn't take long for them to all find out what Walter had done. Usually her husband was her confidant, the one she talked through all her worries with, big and small. How strange that she could barely be in the same room with him now. She had no one she could confide in, and it was unbearable carrying all these secrets alone.

"Someone was watching me at our party on Sunday," Sylvia said.

"There was a man out on the dock. At first I thought he was one of your friends, but he never came into the party."

"I know," Walter nodded. "I saw him too. They're keeping an eye on us."

"So they're following us now?" She shook her head, horrified. "You know, Judith's planning on going to the Rendezvous this week. There are going to be hundreds of people there for Bal Week. Anyone could approach her."

"They won't do anything, so long as they get their money."

"And if they don't?"

"That's not an option," he said grimly.

"Well, I'm not going to let her go alone. I've had a bad feeling ever since the party, so I've asked Milly Kincaid to tag along with me."

"Don't drag her into this mess," he said, looking down to his hands as if ashamed, and Sylvia hoped he was. "If you do see anyone," he said, "be careful. Don't try to approach them or reason with them. They want you to know they're there, they want you to feel their presence, that's all." The front door opened and closed, and Sylvia checked the clock on the wall. School was out already. "But you shouldn't have sold your car, Sylvia. How much did you get for it?"

"Eighteen hundred dollars," she said.

Walter shook his head. "How are you going to get anywhere now? How are you going to get to the Rendezvous?"

"We'll take the—"

"I'll drive you," he interrupted hastily, "of course."

"No! We'll take the ferry and walk like everyone else." She was angry all over again. The fact that her selling her car was going to be of no consequence was infuriating. "You've done quite enough already."

"Mom?" Judith called out, then she appeared at Walter's study door. "You sold your car?"

Sylvia turned to Walter and glared.

"Why would you sell your car?"

"Because, sweetheart, I didn't need it. I barely drove that clunky thing anywhere," Sylvia said, determined to shield her daughter from this, to protect her. If Judith knew the truth, she too would feel differently toward Walter.

"But Mom—" Judith looked from Sylvia to her father—"how am I supposed to go anywhere now?"

"You can walk, and I will too." Sylvia tried not to look at Judith straight on for fear that she'd burst into tears. She looked so beautiful in her burgundy plaid skirt and bobby socks, her hair a little frizzy from her day at school. She'd likely be heading to the Jolly Roger soon; she and her friends often met there after school for malts and Frosties, and this week was especially busy with all those high school and college kids hanging around. She was a smart girl, excelled in her studies, and took pride in her schoolwork, but she was getting so distracted these days with all the attention she was getting from the boys. Sylvia hoped to God she'd go to college and stay long enough to finish. She didn't ever want her to be in a situation like this, where her husband held all the cards.

"Jude, we want you to be careful this week," Walter said. "There are a lot of people here from out of town, and we don't want you going anywhere by yourself. Make sure you have a friend with you at all times, or one of us will accompany you."

Judith rolled her eyes.

"Your father's right," Sylvia said. "No walking home alone."

"Well, if you hadn't sold your car, you could have driven me," she said.

"Sweetheart, please," Sylvia said, exhausted. "I'll accompany you to the Rendezvous tomorrow night, then you won't have to worry."

"Mom," Judith said, screwing up her face, "that's so embarrassing."

"I'll keep my distance," Sylvia said. "You won't even know I'm there."

Repulsed, Judith turned on her heel, her full skirt swishing around her, and marched off toward the stairs "You ruin everything," she called out in her wake, then she went upstairs and slammed her bedroom door.

Sylvia took a deep breath. Her relationship with Walter was in tatters, and now Judith hated her. She stared at the money sitting on the desk, realizing now how insignificant it was, given the calamity they faced. If they sold the house in a flash sale, by the time they paid off their debt, paid Teddy, paid the movers, they'd have very little left to live on. How could they possibly afford to keep the club running with no money to spare? Even if they could keep it afloat, would they even want to? Or would they be perpetuating a lie by running a fancy club while living in squalor? She couldn't fathom leaving the island and leaving their life behind, but in some ways she couldn't imagine staying either, if their circumstances were so drastically different. She would be forever ashamed, forced to endure a downgraded version of her former life. The better option was likely to sell the club and leave the island, start fresh somewhere new, but as soon as she considered this, her insides seemed to fold in on themselves. She couldn't do it. She wouldn't allow it. They might be losing their house and their prized possessions, but they had to save the club—that was the one thing that would keep them here. She had to fix this; she was determined. She didn't know how yet, but she would.

CHAPTER SEVENTEEN

ADELE

With the exception of one hour in the morning to coach Milly, Adele didn't leave her house. She had picked up a copy of the paper on her way home from the club on Wednesday, and her face had stared back at her from the kitchen table ever since. She was furious, and terrified. After more than twenty years in hiding, away from the public humiliation and disgust, she'd thrown away all of her anonymity with one idiotic moment. *I should never have let those kids stay on the Ferris wheel for a second ride*, she said to herself as she paced the living room. *It was their choice to get on the ride, their risk for the chance of a thrill.* But those were just words. That was anger spewing out of her. She wouldn't have been able to live with herself if something had happened to them.

When she did force herself to dress and meet Milly for her second lesson of the week, she was skittish and jittery. She kept her sunglasses on for the whole lesson and barely spoke, feeding Milly the ball from the far side of the court.

"Is everything OK, Adele?" Milly called out about half way through. "You left in such a rush yesterday, and you're awfully quiet today."

"Fine," was all Adele could manage.

"You know I never thanked you for averting danger that day on the Ferris wheel," Milly said. "It's good they acknowledged you in the paper."

"Hardly!" Adele stiffened at the thought of other people reading it, everyone seeing her picture. It was a matter of time before someone made the connection between who she was then and who she was now. Just the idea of that brought up all those old feelings of fear and regret. How sickening it had felt to be hated the world over.

"You deserve the praise, Adele. You got everyone to safety," Milly said. "Why does it bother you so much? Are you camera-shy?"

"You wouldn't understand," Adele said.

"Try me."

Adele shook her head. "Let's just take a break, OK?"

Milly filled her cup with water and took a long drink. "Do you think at some point you can teach me how to play a real match?" she asked.

Adele sighed but didn't respond. She could barely focus on today's lesson, but she needed to try because Milly had helped her get this job, and, however small, it was something, and it helped.

"I know I'm not ready, not yet," Milly went on. "But eventually. You see I'm new here and I don't know many people. Sylvia introduced me to some of the women, but"—she lowered her voice to a whisper—"I don't know if we have that much in common. Their lives, well, their home lives mostly, are a bit different from mine, so I thought maybe if I arranged some matches with a few of the women, it would give us something to talk about. And doubles, that would be my dream; having a partner to play with would be such a good way to make friends around here."

In the midst of her panic and frustration, Adele felt an unusual pang of sympathy for Milly. She didn't know any of the other women either, except Sylvia a little, but this Milly woman did seem to be a bit of an outsider, as if she didn't quite fit in, a little like her. But while Adele had good reason for her situation, she hadn't figured out what was different about Milly yet.

"None of them know how to play," Adele said. "At least, not well."

Milly bounced the ball on her racket and seemed to think about this.

"And," Adele said, "you cannot serve, and neither can any of these women. Have you seen them serve? It's not tennis. They serve underhand. You cannot play a match until you can serve."

"Well, then I'd better learn," Milly said, smiling. "No time like the present."

When the hour was up, Adele took her earnings from Milly and bolted off the court. She'd bring Sylvia her share of the earnings tomorrow. She'd made it through the lesson, she'd taught the basics of a serve. Milly had a long way to go, but she would get there. Right now, Adele had more urgent concerns. Hurrying home, she felt as if she were drowning. The photo in the paper had swallowed her up in an overwhelming flood, leaving her awash in memories from her distant, earlier life and forcing her to relive a time when she was losing control, giving in to dissolution, a time that would forever end with that fateful match in 1932.

She had been in London to defend her championship at Wimbledon. By then, she had taken home the silver salver from Wimbledon six times, but this time was different. Everything had intensified. She was twenty-four years old, beloved by her home country and both admired and critiqued by other European and American news outlets, yet she was having a difficult time living up to all the expectations for her. Especially her father's.

They traveled like royalty—her mother, father, and Adele—everything paid for, staying at the most luxurious hotels or private homes, eating at the finest restaurants, traveling by chauffeured limousine. She was not rich—there was no money in the game—but as long as she was winning, there were significant benefits. In Paris for the French Championships at Stade Roland-Garros the previous month, Adele and her family had been hosted at a millionaire's lavish mansion. When he and his wife dressed for dinner and noticed that Adele was wearing a simple gold necklace with her gown, the couple took her to Cartier on the way to dinner at La Coupole and insisted she accept their gift—an emerald double-strand choker that complemented the green layered-tulle design that Jean Patou had delivered that day.

She was treated to luxury everywhere she turned, but that only heightened the pressure on her to win. Drinking and dancing helped her forget—the booze relaxing her, loosening her from constraint. The press followed her wherever she went, and, when asked about her training, she both shocked and delighted them by confessing that she drank Sancerre before most matches, "as a tonic." And when they questioned her further, she added, "Nothing is so fine for the nerves, for the strength and morale. A little wine tones the system up just right. One cannot always be serious; there must be some sparkle too." After a few drinks she was confident and sassy, and her outrageous and often flirtatious remarks always landed on the front page the next morning.

Men fawned over her and complimented her skill, speed, and precision, then often promptly took her to bed. She loved the attention. It was a way to blow off steam, to push the pressures of the court to the very back of her mind. But in the morning, she'd feel shaky, often sick. As she woke in a haze, often in a stranger's bed, she'd tell herself that if she weren't skilled on the tennis courts, she would never have the attention of these men, or of her father, and she needed both in very different ways.

She showed up to her appointed matches thick with makeup, heavy with perfume—Joy by Patou—and layered with her white mink coat and gold bracelets. The crowd cheered and roared when she appeared, and then she put on a show and won, again and again. After a while though, the numbing drinks, the attention, and the enthusiastic sex weren't distracting enough. She began to feel so anxious in the hours leading up to her matches that on occasion she had to postpone or delay them, blaming some sickness. "A serious indisposition caused by heat," or "an attack of grippe following a swim in the cold ocean."

Her father, who was also enjoying the riches of opulent dinners and prestigious company, would deliver his brandy-soaked sugar cubes to whatever luxurious hotel they might be staying at that night and begin drilling into her head tactics and strategies to beat her opponent. He would tell her all the weaknesses of whoever she would be playing that day and instill into her what she must do to win. When she lay in bed, the covers shielding her eyes from the sun, he would rip them from the hotel bed, pull open the curtains.

"*Tu dois la battre*, do you hear me? *La battre*," he'd say, "you have to beat her."

"*Oui, Papa*," she'd say, reaching for the sheets only to have them pulled away again.

"Get up," he'd yell. "If you lose this, we lose everything. We have no more travel, hotels, nice dinners. If you lose we go back to our *trou de merde*."

She hated hearing him say this. She'd always loved their little house in Nice, but it was no longer her father's taste. He had moved beyond that, and it was Adele's job to maintain his new standard of living.

Her pre-match anxiety grew more and more intense as the matches went on. Even so, at Wimbledon that year, she excelled in the early rounds and was set to play the final round of the tournament. She should have been confident, feeling victorious on the heels of her wins, but on the morning of her final match against Margery Horn, she froze. She'd lost to Margery in New York the previous year and was haunted by the crowds who had cheered for her opponent, chanting the name of the British champion. Her father woke her early with such intensity and cruelty, spelling out exactly how she would disappoint him if she failed.

Rain postponed the match until 7 PM. Adele waited in her dressing room during the long delay, the pressure of being the defending champion building and building until it overwhelmed her. Her usual anxiety turned to palpitating panic. She paced, she argued bitterly with her mother and father, and then she cried and apologized. She changed her outfit several times and reapplied makeup.

The king of England had requested to visit with Adele and her opponent courtside just prior to the match, but Adele could hardly breathe. Wearing her signature pleated short skirt and sleeveless blouse, her heart beat so fast and so loud that she thought everyone else could hear it. She couldn't banish the fear of defeat from her head. She'd had several nips of brandy and felt dizzy and lightheaded, insisting she needed more time, that they should delay the match further, but her father said she was being ridiculous. He sent her to the press suite, where she was told to sit next to Margery on a scratchy gray sofa and wait to be escorted to the court.

"I can't believe we're going to meet the king," Margery said excitedly. "Did you know that his son, the Duke of York, played in Wimbledon with his wing commander and they lost in straight sets?"

Adele stared straight ahead, ignoring her. *Never speak to your opponents, never smile, never nod.* She heard her father's orders in her head. *Intimidate your opponent and impress your audience. For them you are a star, for them she is nothing.*

"Something to drink?" a waiter asked.

"Water, please," Margery said, and Adele nodded in agreement.

"Perrier, *s'il vous plaît*," she said, hoping her French would cease any further attempted conversation from her opponent.

"One sparkling and one flat water coming up," the young man said.

Adele closed her eyes and pictured the upcoming match in her mind. She would toss the ball up into the air, high enough to take a full breath, then bring the racket down on it fast and sharp, propelling the ball across the court, but it slammed into the net. Her eyes shot open. *No!* This was a bad sign. She took another deep breath and envisioned beginning the match again. The same thing happened. This time when she took a breath it was shaky, and she was sure Margery noticed.

"What's wrong, Adele? Are you worried about the match?" Margery asked with a laugh. Adele ignored her.

When the waiter returned with two glasses and set them down on the table in front of them, Margery got up and walked to the window. "I can't believe we're actually going to meet King George," she muttered to herself.

Adele didn't care about meeting the king of England. She cared only about the match. She cared about the expression on her father's face when she won, or, she dared herself to imagine, the look of disgust and his denouncement if she lost.

That could not happen.

She eyed her opponent's glass, then reached into the side packet of her tennis bag and felt for the medicine her father gave her to sleep. She rolled the glass bottle around in her hand, consumed by visions of humiliation and defeat in front of the huge crowd. She unscrewed the medicine bottle and slipped a pill into her hand. She pressed it between her thumb and forefinger, digging into it hard with her nails until she felt it come apart and break into gritty white powder between her fingers.

"I always knew I'd get to play tennis at Wimbledon and meet royalty someday," Margery said, looking back at Adele, then out the window again. "I suppose I also knew that I'd get to beat you too," she said, still staring out the window. "Twice."

Adele didn't think through what she did next. She took her hand out of her bag, leaned forward to pick up her sparkling water, but first sprinkled the powder that she had pinched between her fingers into Margery's glass of still water. Not the whole pill—maybe half had broken off into her bag—but enough to make her a little less excitable, Adele thought, a little less confident.

"Time to go." A gentleman in a navy suit stood at the doorway of the press suite.

"Oh my gosh," Margery said under her breath. "I can't believe it. I can't believe I'm going to meet the king." She walked from the window to grab her tennis bag from the sofa and joined Adele to accompany the gentleman out. "Oh," she said, stopping short, "I almost forgot." She rushed back to the table, picked up the water glass, and knocked the whole thing back, then pushed past Adele, eager to be first in line to meet royalty. Adele watched, agape, then followed her out of the press room, down a hall, and out to center court, where a red carpet had been rolled from the royal box.

Only then, when Adele stood at the end of the red carpet and saw

King George and his wife Queen Mary approaching them, looking majestic and not at all affected by the humidity that the rain had brought, was she struck by two things: the astonishing magnitude of what was happening—she was meeting the king and queen of England—and by the irreversible evil of what she had just done to Margery.

Both women curtsied as they had been instructed and bowed their heads slightly as the king addressed them. Adele's mind was suddenly functioning only in French. "*Votre Majesté*," she said when he addressed her, inexplicably unable to find the words in English.

"I wish you both the very best of luck," the king said. "I must say you are both a delight to observe. Very entertaining indeed." He smiled. "And I know the tremendous amount of skill and desire needed to play this sport at this level. I commend you both." Queen Mary stepped in and smiled. "May the best girl win."

But nobody won that day. And Adele had never returned to the court, until now.

CHAPTER EIGHTEEN

MILLY

Milly laid her clothes out for the next day's tennis lesson. She only had two tennis-appropriate outfits—one skirt and top, and one dress, and she had to wash them daily to ensure she had something ready for her next lesson. Was it excessive to take daily lessons, she wondered as she smoothed the pleats of the skirt hanging over the back of the chair in her bedroom. Yes, probably, she admitted, but she loved it. She looked forward to her time with Adele, and in just a few days she was seeing improvements in controlling the ball. She'd felt quite excited when she'd seen a few women gather at the court, watching her take lessons with the only female coach at the club, as if she'd had some small part in ushering in that change.

She rushed downstairs when she heard the telephone ring, wondering if it might be Lloyd. She hadn't heard from him since he left on Sunday morning and it was now Thursday.

"Kincaid residence," she said.

"Good afternoon." It was a man's voice, and Milly thought she heard a hint of an English accent. "I saw a posting for a guest cottage for rent, and I wondered if it was still available."

"I'm afraid not; it's already rented for Bal Week."

"Bal Week?" he asked.

"Oh, I assumed you were inquiring about this week. It's a busy time here; the colleges and high schools have a spring break."

"I see. How about next week?" he asked. "I'm a journalist and documentarian, and I need to do some research in the area."

"Oh," Milly said, her interest piqued.

She hadn't planned to rent the guest cottage out again. Lloyd hadn't been thrilled that she'd rented the cottage to college kids in the first place, but the extra money would allow her to keep taking lessons with Adele without having to ask for Lloyd's permission. And the more she played, the better she would become, and the more chance she'd have to impress her husband when he finally came back around.

"Well, I suppose it wouldn't hurt to rent it out for one more week," she said. "It's nothing fancy, just a small space behind our house. My current guests will be leaving Sunday."

"It sounds perfect," he said. "I could be there by Monday."

"All right," Milly said, jotting down his name and giving the him the address and the weekly rate. "I'll need a letter of reference," she said, wanting to ensure that this man was reputable.

"Not a problem," he said.

"See you next week."

As she hung up the phone a small thrill ran through her. It was the first time in her life that she was making her own money, not being given pocket money from her parents or a marital allowance from her husband. It might not amount to much, and she already knew exactly how she was going to spend it, but something about the fact that she'd posted the listing, she'd made the place cozy and welcoming, and she was now taking on a second tenant—something about that gave her hope.

Later that night, Jack and Debbie fell into an easy sleep the minute their heads hit the pillow, tired from an impromptu afternoon of digging for sand crabs on the bay. They were bathed, fed, in clean pajamas, and now, hopefully, happily dreaming—something else Milly took some satisfaction in. Lloyd had been away for four nights already and wasn't expected to return for another week. She hadn't called him at work and she vowed not to. She wouldn't beg him to come home; instead she would wait for him to miss her, or at least miss the kids, and she was surprisingly calm about it. She'd had a glass of wine with dinner, which helped. She was alone, yes, but she didn't feel particularly lonely. The children were taken care of and occupied, and the house was coming together, slowly. Things were far from perfect, but the day had gone smoothly, and for at least a brief moment she felt stable.

Later in the kitchen, she poured herself a second glass of wine. When she noticed she still had her apron on from cooking dinner, she stood to hang it on the back of the door. Out of the corner of her eye, she thought she saw a man in her yard. She gasped, instinctively picking up the serrated knife that she'd just washed and left to dry by the sink, but when she pulled back the corner of her lace demi-curtains, she saw it was one of the college guys, sitting by candlelight at her outdoor table.

"Good Lord," she whispered. She set the knife down and opened the kitchen door. "You'll get yourself killed sneaking around in someone's yard like that, you know," she called out.

He looked up sheepishly, and she recognized Wes. "I hope it's all right that I'm here. The guys went out, but I've got some studying to do and the night air helps me stay awake."

Milly picked up her wineglass and walked out to the yard. "Now that I know it's just you and not a stalker, it's fine, but studying during Bal Week? Shouldn't you be out dancing the night away?"

"I have a big exam coming up. I don't want to wait until the last minute."

"How responsible." Milly would not have had the same kind of fortitude when she was a student.

"How's your evening?" Wes asked, glancing at her glass.

"Oh, I'm celebrating a relatively easy bedtime. Would you like some?"

"No, thank you, I need to stay sharp," he said, "but I could use a little breather."

Milly took a seat at the table. "What are you studying?" She tried to peek but he closed the notebook and placed his hands on top.

"I don't want to bore you with this," he said. "Did you have a nice dinner with Mr. Kincaid? I haven't seen him around yet."

Milly laughed dryly. "No one has." She took a sip of her wine. "He works a lot." Wes raised his eyebrows, waiting for more. Oh, what the heck, Milly thought, this kid doesn't live here, he doesn't know anyone in this town. It wouldn't hurt to lighten the load, get some of this secrecy off my chest. "He doesn't come home much. He loves his kids, but the two of us . . ." She shrugged her shoulders. "I don't know, it's a mess. He doesn't want to be here."

"Damn," he said. "What a fool."

Milly blushed at his comment, even though she could sense he was just being kind.

"The funny thing is he's a good man, actually, but it seems there's obviously something going on that I'm not privy to."

"I'm sorry to hear that."

"He works with a lot of beautiful women," Milly said, shrugging. "It's hard to compete with that."

"Jeez," Wes said, lowering his voice. "Then he's missing what's right in front of his eyes."

Milly waved away his comment; she wasn't fishing for compliments. She couldn't believe she was blurting all this out. Maybe it was the wine helping her release more misery than she realized she was holding inside; either way, it felt good to get it off her chest. "I can't tell anyone about it, obviously. I'm new in town. I've got a reputation to maintain and children to raise. It won't do them any good if people get to talking, so I have to keep up the charade of being a happily married, perfect family of four. It's tiring."

"I'm really sorry," he said, a seriousness overtaking what should be a carefree, youthful face.

Milly had to stop talking, stop burdening this poor fellow with her problems, but it was such a relief to speak freely. "I'm getting used to it, and the children are fine; they don't know there's anything going on, just that he's working a lot. And quite honestly, the more I settle in, the more I realize it's not so bad to be alone."

His brow was furrowed now, and she noticed how much better he'd looked moments ago, burden-free. Dear God, she was bringing him down too. She quickly changed the subject.

"Can you see to study with just the candlelight?"

"It's fine."

"How about you?" she asked. "Is there someone special you're going steady with?"

"Not right now," he said. "I have to focus on school, and then I'm sure the right girl will come along."

"Things must have changed since I was in school, because all anyone wanted to do was find the one and settle down. No one was all that concerned about their studies, not even the guys, as far as I could tell."

"Yeah, I see that too sometimes, but I love what I'm learning."

"I used to love learning too," Milly said, thinking back wistfully on her school days before things got complicated. "It's funny, I sort of forgot that. I'm taking tennis lessons now. I know it's not the same as actual studies, but in addition to being physically challenging, it's also got my mind going. There are so many things to think about—where to hit the ball, how to hit it, how to move your legs, how to anticipate what your opponent will do, all the coordination."

Wes leaned in. "I bet you're really good."

"No," she laughed. "I just started, but it's good to have something else to focus on other than my crumbling marriage."

"I hope things get better for you," Wes said. "I really do."

"Oh, it's fine, well, it's not fine, but you know . . ." she said, suddenly embarrassed for saying too much and worried she'd already stayed too long. "I won't keep you from your studies." But she didn't want to leave; she liked sitting out here with him, talking freely. "Are you sure I can't pour you a splash?"

"Thank you, I'm very tempted," he said. "But I'll decline. I'll study now so I can let loose the rest of the week."

"Yes. Get back to work," she said smiling. "And good luck with your test."

"Thank you, Milly. Good luck to you too."

CHAPTER NINETEEN

SYLVIA

There was no turning back. The house had been sold, fast, at a dramatically reduced price for an all-cash exchange. They were to move out on Saturday, which felt unimaginable: This was her home, her refuge, the place where she'd transformed from a seventeen-year-old wide-eyed girl into a wife and mother, a pillar in her community. Life had happened here on South Bay Front. It felt sacred, and leaving it, allowing another family to take over its rooms, its hallways, its quiet corners on the patio, it felt as if she'd be leaving part of herself behind.

On the same day they were to move out, Walter had explained that he would deliver the entire sum they received for the house, which would pay off the debt and ensure their safety but leave them almost penniless.

She had allowed herself a full hour, head under the covers, used tissues piled at her side, to sob and wallow in self-pity. She knew there were people far worse off than she was. She knew she should be grateful that they at least still had a place to stay, even if it was a fraction of the size and barely livable, but she wanted to mourn her old life for just a few moments longer. And then, when the hour was up, she got out of bed, threw the pile of soggy tissues in the trash can, bathed, dressed, and made a plan for what was next.

She was going to have to try to steer this ship now. They still had the club, and that ensured a connection to the island, but the monthly costs associated with keeping it up and running it were vast, and the memberships were still far too low to even come close to covering the overhead. On Saturday afternoon, the same day as the move, they'd be hosting the Bathing Beauty Contest, which Walter and Sylvia had orchestrated at the Fun Zone every single year that she'd lived there, and despite everything, the show had to go on. There were sponsors; everyone was looking forward to it—the visitors, the locals, the contestants, the onlookers. It was the final shiny bow that signaled the conclusion of Bal Week, and it brought the island a lot of press and business—much-needed money for the local stores, which kept them going until the busy summer months and enticed people to return year after year. But Sylvia's reasons were personal: She needed to let everyone know that they were fine, that they were not going anywhere. They might be moving into a shack that they had planned to tear down, but she needed to make it clear that they were still the Johnsons, and they weren't leaving town. This was just a hiccup.

Her housekeeper, Maria, had already started packing up their belongings and when Sylvia walked downstairs, she found her quietly crying as she wrapped their good china in newspaper.

"Come on, Maria," Sylvia said. "I promise I'll do my best to make things right." She hated that her husband's bad behavior was not only causing her family upheaval, it was also costing Maria and the rest of their staff their jobs too.

When Judith came home from school, she took one look at her mother and Maria amid the packing crates, and the tears began all over again.

"I can't believe we have to move," Judith said, rubbing her eyes. "I hate this."

"I hate this too," Sylvia said, putting an arm around her shoulders.

"I've been looking forward to Bal Week all year, and now I can't even enjoy it because I can't stop crying."

"I know, darling," Sylvia said, kissing her daughter's head, but Judith didn't want to be consoled and squirmed away. "You can still have fun, Judith. Let us deal with everything here."

"I just don't get it, I don't understand why we have to do this," Judith said.

"It's hard to understand," Sylvia said. "It's business-related. Your father has to sell the property so that we can focus on the club."

"Why didn't he just sell the club?"

"There's not enough money in the club," Sylvia said. "Not yet; it's too new and very costly."

"It doesn't make any sense," Judith said, more tears streaming down her face, her cheeks getting red.

Of course it didn't make sense. She was being lied to, but if she was told the truth—that her father had gambled away their life savings—she'd resent her father the way that Sylvia resented Walter. She had to shield her from that.

"Well, I'm going to the Rendezvous tonight. Everyone's going, so please don't ruin that for me as well."

"Of course I won't ruin it for you. You won't even know I'm there."

Judith slumped into a pale-blue linen armchair tucked into the corner of the room.

"Margaret heard girls talking about me today in the locker room," she said quietly, as if she weren't sure she should share this information.

Sylvia frowned, immediately feeling protective of her daughter. "What were they saying?"

"That we're going broke."

"Who said such a thing?" Sylvia asked, angry now that fourteen-year-old girls would be the ones spreading rumors.

"Apparently Mary-Louise's mom was talking about it and Mary-Louise overheard, and now everyone at school is talking about us moving out of the house. They're trying to decide who's going to host the end-of-school party since we'll no longer be able to."

"Who says we won't be able to host?" Sylvia said, feeling defiant, and burned by Helen, Mary-Louise's mother, whom she'd always thought of as a friend, or at least an acquaintance through Judith's school. It was awful to think of people talking behind their backs, and for Judith to get roped into it too—the whole thing made her sick.

"Where would we host it?" Judith asked sharply, then rolled her eyes.

Sylvia wanted to say the club, but she didn't want to make any more false promises, then she was about to suggest a beach party, but who knew if they'd even still be on the island by the time June came around.

"I'll have a word with Mary-Louise's mother," Sylvia said, knowing it was too late for that; the whispers had already begun.

"No, Mom," she said, the irritation bubbling in her voice. "You'll just make it worse."

Before she got ready for the Rendezvous that evening, Sylvia took a ride to the club with Walter. He needed to pick up some paperwork, and Sylvia needed a break from the sight of packing crates and the heartache of deciding what she could fit in the new house and what they'd have to leave behind. She walked through the grounds and shook her head at the empty courts. The pool had a few kids splashing around and a couple of mothers keeping watch nearby, but it was not the picture of a thriving enterprise. On the weekends and early mornings, the courts were relatively full with men playing matches before work and a few taking lessons, but it wasn't busy enough. It was a beautiful club, Walter had got that right—pristine courts, lush landscaping, clear blue pool, and comfortable spaces to lounge and socialize—but it wasn't gaining the traction it needed to get off the ground. The Balboa Yacht Club and the Balboa Bay Club, both catering to the watermen in the area, had been around much longer and were more established, so it was hard to compete. Maybe no one needed a tennis club; maybe Walter had miscalculated the numbers needed to succeed.

When she walked toward the last court, thinking she should get back out there to play tennis while she still could—it could help take her mind off things at home—she heard voices and realized that Milly was taking her daily lesson with Adele. Milly looked good, fast and sporty. She and Adele were rallying back and forth. If Sylvia didn't know her, she never would have guessed that Milly was so new to the sport. As she rounded the corner, she saw that five or six women were sitting in chairs lined up around the court, with a few more women standing around. They had an audience.

"Hi there, ladies," Sylvia said. "What's going on?"

All heads turned toward Sylvia, and she felt the women's eyes collectively settle on her, uncomfortably, as she approached. Did they all know about the move? Was it possible they could know about Walter's gambling? For the first time in as long as she could remember, Sylvia wanted to slink away, out of sight. She hated the thought of her beloved friends thinking any less of her or Walter.

"We're watching the new coach," Susie said. She and her husband Mitch had been good friends with Sylvia and Walter and early supporters of the club. If these women knew what was going on behind closed doors, then they'd likely be wondering about the future of the club too.

"Where did you find her?" Susie asked. "She's fantastic."

"Who, Adele?" Sylvia thought about it for a moment. "She found me, actually. But you're right, she's really something. We're very lucky to have her." She stood and watched as Milly raced from one side of the court to the next, drops of sweat actually flying from her brow as she leapt for the ball and hit it back to Adele, then sped to the net to catch a short ball that dropped in just before her reach.

The ladies watching broke into applause, despite the fact that Milly didn't make that last ball.

"What a point," Susie called out.

"Fantastic," said another.

Milly and Adele looked over to the small crowd that had formed.

"Oh, you guys," Milly said, swatting the air. "Don't exaggerate." She laughed and poured a tall glass of water from the pitcher.

"That was magnificent, Milly," Joan called out, clapping.

When the applause settled down, Sylvia could have sworn she saw a couple of the women glance back to her, then murmur something to one another before looking back to the court. But maybe she was just on edge. She stood back and tried to shake free of her insecurities. She had always prided herself on her confidence. She observed how the women were enraptured by Milly—still mediocre by all accounts, but she had improved greatly in just a few lessons—and more so by Adele, who seemed wonderfully skilled at explaining to Milly how to move, how to swing, how to angle the racket. More than anything, though, Adele had taught Milly how to fall in love with this sport. It was clear as day that despite the troubles that Milly was having at home, and there was obviously something going on there, she was thoroughly enjoying herself on the court, and Sylvia admired her for that.

She looked from Milly to Adele and could feel the beginning of something forming in her mind, the wheels spinning, the idea solidifying. Maybe this was her ticket. The ladies hadn't been given a chance to succeed at tennis with the likes of Robbie and his counterparts, with their off-color remarks and their gross underestimation of their potential. But Adele could help them, and help Sylvia at the same time.

She waited for the lesson to end, then rushed onto the court, energized by her ideas.

"Ladies," she said excitedly, "you both looked great out here. Did you see you had an audience?"

Milly was dabbing her face with a towel, and Adele was packing her racket and balls into her bag.

"I have great news," Sylvia went on. "I'm going to run an ad in the local paper and maybe even the *Register* too—I know the publisher—and I'm going to advertise tennis for women, by women." She ran her hand across the space in front of her as if she could envision the headline. "And we'll run a picture of you, Adele, or maybe even the two of you training together."

"No," Adele said abruptly. "Absolutely not!"

"Yes!" Sylvia insisted. "It will be great. No other club is doing this." She turned to Milly. "You said yourself the male coaches cater to the male patrons. This will be new and different. It could attract a lot of new members, and Adele, you'll be the star attraction."

"I said no," Adele growled. "I don't want my picture in the paper, not now, not ever, and I do not want to be the attraction."

Sylvia looked at her stunned, baffled. How could she just shut down this idea, this brilliant idea that could potentially help with some of their financial troubles if it took off? "Look, Adele," Sylvia said. "I took a chance on you; I hired you when you needed a job, and we have a chance to turn it into something big."

"Big is the last thing I want," Adele said, turning to leave. "As you pointed out, I already had my picture in the paper, and I don't want it to happen again."

Sylvia grabbed her arm. "I don't expect you to understand this, but I'm in a tough situation here, very tough. If I don't figure something out fast, I don't even know if this club will be open two weeks from today."

Adele hesitated, then shook her arm free.

"Is it that bad?" Milly asked. "What about the dues I just paid?"

"That's why I'm trying to keep it afloat," Sylvia said, desperation rising in her voice. "So I'm begging you to help me, Adele, otherwise you won't even have a place to coach."

Adele glared at her. "I'll coach more women. Tell your members, tell those women who were watching us, that I'll coach them all day long if that will help, but I do not want my picture in the paper. I do not want the attention on me."

"But why?" Sylvia asked. "You're so good at what you do."

Adele shook her head. "There are things in my past that I am not proud of. I live a private life for a reason, and if you knew about it, believe me, you wouldn't want to advertise it either."

Sylvia watched her, wondering if she could press her for more. What kinds of things was she talking about? Should she be worried about who she'd brought into the club? Was she some kind of criminal? Alarm bells started ringing in her head, but Sylvia had to ignore them for now. She needed this, she needed her, she didn't know what else to do.

Adele zipped up her bag. "I will try to help you, Sylvia, but if you put my picture in the paper, it's over. I won't set foot on this court again."

CHAPTER TWENTY

MILLY

It was a tiki-themed night at the Rendezvous Ballroom on Friday. Milly wore a Hawaiian halter dress, peacock blue with a bold red floral print on the full skirt. Sylvia plucked a red hibiscus from her garden on their way out and put it behind Milly's ear.

"To match your skirt," Sylvia said as they linked arms walking toward the ferry. "Now you look the part."

Sylvia teetered along in a fitted, sarong-style dress that hugged her waist and hips, looking feminine and gorgeous, as always. "So, what's the plan of action?" Milly asked, as they walked. "Do we just keep an eye on Judith, make sure no one suspicious is lurking around?"

"I think so," Sylvia said.

"And is there a particular beau she has eyes for? Anyone you want to steer her away from?"

"No one in particular," she said. "Just boys in general. Walter says it's the music that's putting them all in the mood for love. That Elvis, he's so lively and suggestive."

"And he's got a movie coming out later this year," Milly said, "*Love Me Tender*."

"I know! I'm going to see it," Sylvia said. "He's so velvety-smooth."

"But I don't think Elvis Presley is going to be at the Rendezvous tonight." Milly gave a playful nudge.

"You never know," Sylvia said with a laugh. "Anyway, I just want to keep an eye on things, that's all."

"How are you feeling about the move?" Milly asked. She couldn't quite believe it when Sylvia had told her, in a very matter-of-fact way, that they were moving from their beautiful, sprawling, waterfront house to the run-down property they owned next door to Adele—a house she had said was not even fit for college kids to rent during Bal Week.

"Oh, fine, I suppose. Maria's helped me get all packed up, so there's not much more to do." She shrugged.

Milly looked at Sylvia, unconvinced. How could she be so calm about all this happening so quickly, leaving the home that she adored, that was also a cornerstone of the community, a place where she brought people together so beautifully?

"Must be a big change," Milly said.

Sylvia stared straight ahead as they walked. "It's temporary. We've had the same view for years. I've got my eye on a few other properties. Once Walter sorts things out, we'll buy again."

Sylvia was putting on a brave face, but Milly didn't push it, not yet.

"How's Lloyd?" Sylvia asked, abruptly changing the subject.

"Good, great," Milly said. Now they both had topics they didn't want to linger on.

"And your lodgers? How's that going? Hopefully they're not too rowdy."

"It's been quite nice, actually," Milly said, relieved to have settled on a more comfortable topic of conversation for both of them. "The guys have been very sweet to the children, playing sports with them in the yard. Jack is really enamored of them."

"You have boys in the guesthouse?" Sylvia asked, shocked.

"I know, I wasn't expecting them either; I thought it was a nice group of college girls coming. But it's been fine, really, no trouble, and I have another renter coming next week, a gentleman who needs to stay in the area for research."

"Careful, Milly." Sylvia squeezed her arm. "You don't want people to start talking."

"Oh no, it's fine. It's a separate little house; you've seen it. It feels very removed from us. Besides, it pays for my tennis lessons."

"Oh, well, in that case, yes," Sylvia said, smiling. "Go for it."

They reached the ferry landing right as the boat was pulling in.

"Good evening, Mrs. Johnson," the captain said, rushing to give her his arm and leading her and Milly to a seat at the front of the ferry.

"Hello, Joe," she said, handing him the paper-wrapped box she'd carried with her. "Butter cookies," she said. "Maria made them."

"Bless her," he said.

"Joe, have you met Milly Kincaid? She's new to the island. Milly, this is Joe, our fearless ferry captain. He's been running this ferry back and forth from the island to the peninsula for some thirty years."

"Well, not this exact ferry. Started off as a rowboat, then I added a motor to it, then I got the *Arc*—that one carried twenty passengers—then this one, the *Joker*, which can transport cars and passengers."

"He's an island treasure," Sylvia said. "You *are*, Joe, and so is your ferry, that's why I bring you sweets every time I ride—to be sure you keep things moving."

"No place I'd rather be than on this here ferry," he said.

"It's lovely to meet you," Milly said, noting his scruffy gray beard and the kindness in his eyes. "I've taken a ride with my children, but I think it was a younger fellow commandeering the boat."

"Ah yes, my son Seymour."

One of the cars honked its horn, and Joe scurried off to place the box of cookies in the cabin, then he went around to collect the passengers' fares as they made the short crossing from the island to the peninsula, just in time to open the gate at the other end and let everyone off.

"See you on your return, Mrs. Johnson and Mrs. Kincaid," Joe called out.

"Will do," Sylvia called back, giving him a small wave as they walked off the ferry, passing the Fun Zone and heading toward the Rendezvous Ballroom.

They arrived a little after 8 PM, just as the band was starting to play. The parking lot was packed with cars, and Sylvia looked around, skittish, presumably looking for the man who'd been watching her at the party, but nothing seemed out of sorts. When they paid their dollar to get inside, Stan Kenton and his orchestra were taking the stage. Milly had heard him on the radio plenty of times but had never seen him perform in real life. He was a tall stork of a man, with long arms, awkwardly yet masterfully driving the orchestra.

The place was alive, crammed with people of all ages, though heavy on the young college and high school kids. Sylvia took Milly's hand and pulled her toward the bar, where they ordered Mai Tais in coconut shells with a flower perched on the side. It had been a while since Milly had been around this kind of heaving energy. A trombonist played a solo, then Stan took to the piano. A crowd formed around a couple dancing the Lindy, and Milly couldn't take her eyes off them, the way they anticipated each other's moves and knew exactly how to respond to one another. They were so in tune, so perfectly synchronized, and she marveled at how they had learned to work together, knowing exactly what their partner might do in each situation. She began to wonder, how did she and Lloyd get so disconnected? In the beginning they had a connection, didn't they? A partnership, a family they both wanted? Now everything seemed so foreign and forced, it was hard to imagine what they had once had.

When the song ended the crowd swarmed in again and caused her to spill a little of her drink. Everyone was dancing now, a staccato-style dance with much smaller steps.

"Ah, the Balboa," Sylvia said.

"Balboa?"

"We have our own dance, compact and fast, so lots of people can squeeze on the dance floor at once. It started right here at the Rendezvous. Come on." Sylvia linked arms with Milly. "Let's take a look around and see if we can get eyes on Judith."

Milly followed Sylvia in and out of the swaths of Hawaiian-clad dancers in the cavernous space. Tabletops were decorated with pineapples and other tropical fruits. Some people wore flower leis around their necks. A few girls even wore their swimsuit tops with full, Hawaiian skirts. After a while Sylvia spotted Judith and her friends near the stage and stopped Milly in her tracks so they could observe. They seemed to be having a whale of a time laughing and swaying to the music. Judith was talking to a boy about her age, but it all seemed respectful and suitable, and Milly felt intrusive spying on them like this. Judith seemed like a lovely girl, she thought, polite and responsible and the double of her mother.

"Let's sit at the bar for a bit," Sylvia said and ordered another round of Mai Tais. Two couples that she knew from the club approached and joined their group.

"Where's Walt?" one of the men asked. "Cutting a rug on the dance floor?"

"Not without me by his side," Sylvia said. "He's home, a little under the weather."

After the second drink Milly was feeling flush and happy, maybe a little tipsy too, and she excused herself to go to the powder room. On her way back through the crowds someone touched her on the shoulder.

"Hey, Milly!" It was Wes and all of his friends.

"Hello, boys," she said. "Having fun?"

"The best time. Can't beat the music." His face was glowing, a slight sheen from the warmth in the room. Some of the others, Mickey and Luke, were talking to a group of beautiful young girls, and there was such a youthful innocence about it all that made Milly smile. It seemed like just yesterday that she had been that young and wide-eyed, hopeful and excited for all that was to come.

"Can I buy you a drink?" Wes asked.

"Oh Wes, you don't have to do that," Milly said. "I've already had two."

"I insist." He took her hand, a strangely personal thing to do, Milly thought, and yet it sent a surprising thrill through her. He guided her toward a bar near the back of the ballroom. It was less crowded back there and, she justified, it was difficult to weave through the crowds. At the bar he dropped her hand. "What are you drinking?"

"Mai Tais," Milly said. "Probably too many."

"No such thing," he said.

They took a seat at the bar while the bartender mixed their drinks.

"So, how's your week been going so far?" Milly asked. "Are you enjoying Bal Week?"

"Oh, it's swell," Wes said. "I just love it down here and being so close to the water; it's good for the soul. Don't you think?"

"Yes, absolutely," she said, though she hadn't had a chance to take full advantage of her newfound beach life yet.

"And how are you . . . without Mr. Kincaid around?" he added quietly.

"Fine," she said. "I'm actually having a little fun, as you can see."

He smiled at her, holding her gaze. "I'm glad; you deserve to."

She smiled back and appreciated for a moment that he knew a little about her situation, and then she wondered if the Mai Tais had gone to her head. "You know what? I should get back, actually," she said. "I told my friend I was just going to the powder room."

Mickey, Luke, and the others approached the bar and slapped Wes on the back. "We're hitting the dance floor," Luke said.

"How about one dance before you go?" Wes asked Milly.

She shook her head, then looked up to the mirror behind the bar and caught a glimpse of herself. She too had a flush in her cheeks. Maybe it was the tinted mirror, or maybe it was the Mai Tais, but for a moment she liked the way she looked in this light, glowing in the dimly lit room, a sheen on her bare shoulders, a flower in her hair. There was something about the live music and everyone dancing that sent a hum through her and made her feel alive.

"Come on," Wes said, standing and holding his hand out to her. "One dance."

She hesitated, shaking her head. "One dance," she said, trying to hide her smile as he led her to the dance floor.

"It's the Bal," Wes said.

"The Balboa? Oh no, I don't know that one," she said, slowing her pace.

"You know how to swing, right?"

"Of course."

"Then you can Bal. It's an eight count." He put his left hand on her back and took her right hand in his. "Don't worry, I've got you."

It was a subtle dance with the smallest shuffle movements, but with his lead, her feet somehow knew what to do. As the music continued, he twirled her a couple of times, still somehow compact and contained, then brought her back to the closed position. The music slowed and they moved in time to the beat, but they weren't really dancing anymore, rather swaying gently. She fit against him, his arms encircling her, then after a brief drum solo, it changed to Carl Perkins's fast-paced "Blue Suede Shoes."

"May I have this dance, Mrs. Kincaid?" Johnny, the blond, stepped in.

"Oh gosh." Milly laughed; they were being so funny, indulging her like this. "I have to get back to my friend," she said, but as the music picked up, he took her hand, and she was surprised that she remembered the moves and was able to keep up. It was fast and invigorating, her body falling right into the rhythm and her feet moving under her as if they were not her own. After a while, Johnny stepped back, spun Milly out, and she ended up back in Wes's arms. She hadn't been dancing in years, and she suddenly realized what fun she was having and how much she'd missed it.

"I should do this more often," she said.

"Do what more often?" he asked, his cheeks flushed, his dark eyes searching hers.

"Get out of the house, go dancing, all of it!"

She found Sylvia sitting at a high-top table with some friends, and everyone seemed to be too caught up in conversation to have noticed her absence. Sylvia insisted they stay until ten, her daughter's curfew, and then follow behind Judith and friends at a safe distance, letting them take the first ferry, Milly and Sylvia taking the next.

Once Milly was back at her house, had checked on the children, and helped Leticia settle into the guest bedroom, where she'd arranged for her to stay since it was late, Milly looked around in the kitchen for something to eat. She hadn't had a proper dinner before she left for the Rendezvous, which explained why the drinks had gone to her head, and now she was starving. She munched on a few handfuls of the baked Chex mix she'd made earlier that day and thought about what an unexpectedly fun night she'd had. The Chex mix was the perfect antidote to her Mai Tais—salty, crunchy, and satisfying, and she had a feeling the boys would appreciate it when they got home too. She took a tin down from the cupboard, filled it with the mix—there was still plenty left for Jack and Debbie the next day—then she filled a pitcher with lemonade. She walked out to the guest cottage, leaving the tin and pitcher outside the front door. As she turned to walk away, she wondered how long it would be sitting there, the lemonade exposed to the night air. Would it be swarming with ants by the time the boys came home? They might still be a while. She picked it up again, debating if she should return it to her house and just leave the Chex, but that mix always left her so thirsty. She'd leave them both inside the guest cottage, she decided, trying the door handle and finding it open.

"Hello," she called out, though she could tell no one was home yet; the lights were out and it was still.

She stepped inside, set the pitcher and the tin on the counter, and took a quick look around the space. It was a mess, their clothes and belongings everywhere, and she took a moment to appreciate, almost envy, the carefree feeling of it all. Out of habit, she picked up a jacket off the floor, folded it in half, and laid it on the back on the sofa. As she put her hand on the doorknob to leave, the door swung open toward her, and someone tried to step inside.

She gasped and instinctively kicked the door closed with her foot, then stepped back, horrified that she was about to be caught intruding on their space and snooping.

"Milly?" the door inched open again slowly. "Is that you?"

"Oh my God," she said, recognizing Wes's voice. "You scared the daylights out of me!"

"You gave me a start too," he said.

"Sorry, I was just . . ." Milly pointed to the tin and the lemonade. "I wasn't snooping, I promise. I thought you all might like . . ." she stopped when she realized Wes was holding his right hand. "Are you OK?"

"I trapped it in the door," he said.

"I'm so sorry," Milly said, feeling terrible. "I thought you were an intruder."

"It'll be fine," he said, running it under cold water.

"I'll get you some ice."

"No, really, it's all right," he said, drying it off with a dish towel. "What did you bring us?"

"Oh"—she felt so foolish now—"just some baked Chex mix that I made earlier."

"Chex mix?" he said, opening the tin and popping some into his mouth. "It's good," he said, offering the tin toward her. She took a few pieces, though it was the last thing she wanted now.

Wes poured them both a lemonade, handed a glass to her, and took a drink of his.

"I really am sorry about your hand," she said. "I feel so silly. I planned to leave it on the stoop, but then I thought there might be bugs. . . ."

"Milly," he said, stopping her. He placed his glass down and unwrapped his hand, turned it over, and wiggled his fingers. "See? You shouldn't apologize for being kind and thoughtful."

"Wes," she said, shaking her head.

"No, really," he went on. "I've never met him, so I don't know what's going on, obviously, but I get the sense you aren't appreciated, that you've been taken for granted. And I hate to think of that. You're generous and considerate."

It had been so long since anyone had said anything so nice to her. She knew she should go, but she let it soak in for just a moment.

"Thank you," she whispered. "That's kind of you to say."

"And you're beautiful," he said, his eyes landing on hers, almost daring her to look away.

A moment passed between them, as if he had something else to say, and she didn't want to leave without hearing it. In the silence, she could hear him breathe. He took the glass from her, placed it on the counter, then took her hand and pulled her ever so slightly toward him. Tiny waves rippled all over her skin. She should step back, she knew that, but she was so surprised, shocked by him—what was he doing?—and by her body's reaction to his touch. He placed his hand on her cheek, and she lowered her eyes, her stomach flipping, every inch of her body on high alert. He lifted her chin with his fingers until her eyes reached his—they looked darker in the dim light of the cottage—and they searched hers as if asking permission. No man had ever looked at her like this, ever, and it mesmerized her. Slowly, incredibly slowly, he inched toward her, and when she closed her eyes she felt his lips on hers, warm and soft. She felt herself melt, every part of her suddenly awakened and filled with desire. His lips stayed on hers for a second, maybe two. His fingers moved to the base of her neck and into her hair. She felt the warm rush of desire flood her and she wanted to give in to it. And then, reluctantly, so very reluctantly, she placed her hands on his chest, feeling the rise and fall of his breath, the outline of his muscles under his shirt, and pushed him away, hard.

Then she slapped him across the face.

With his face turned to the ground, he put his hand to his cheek and looked up at her for a second, then away, hurt or ashamed, she couldn't tell.

"I'm sorry," he said in a low whisper.

"How dare you?" she said.

"I'm really sorry. I don't know what came over me."

"I am a married woman," she said, her voice sounding unfamiliar and sharp. "And you are a student, in college. My God."

"I'm in medical school, actually," he said quietly, still looking down.

"What?" she said, trying to calculate how old that would make him, but she was so flustered that her brain wasn't cooperating, and her hand was stinging from the slap. "It doesn't matter," she said, horrified at what she had let unfold between them.

He shook his head. "You're right. I'm very sorry. It won't happen again."

"You're damn right it won't," she snapped, studying him, unsure if there was something else she should add to ensure that he understood her outrage, but her mind was spinning and she couldn't think straight. She walked toward the door, opened it, and turned back to him.

"You will not mention this to any of your friends, or anyone at all, do you understand?"

"Yes, ma'am," he said.

"Good." She left the cottage, marched across the lawn to her house, stepped inside, and locked the door behind her.

Upstairs, she was shaking. She stared at the hand that had slapped his face, his handsome, smooth face. She brushed her teeth and tried to focus on herself in the mirror. Her blond hair fell around her face in soft waves, messy now from his fingers running through them, and she stared back at herself in wonder. What had she done? When he took her hand, she had let him. When he pulled her toward him, she had let him. When he kissed her, she'd let him. She closed her eyes and took a deep breath, reliving the moment, so sensual and forbidden, feeling his hand on her cheek, his soft lips on hers, the taste of rum on his warm breath, the look of shock on his face when she slapped him. Dear God. She squeezed her hands into fists. She had slapped him.

Suddenly a hundred questions were running through her head. Why had he come back from the Rendezvous alone without the others? Had he planned to seduce her? Was he really in medical school? Why was he even here for Bal Week? What was he thinking, kissing her? She rushed back downstairs, and before she could change her mind she walked back across the lawn to the cottage and knocked.

When he opened the door in his undershirt and trousers he didn't say a word.

"Can I come in?"

He looked at her warily, his wavy brown hair disheveled, but he pulled the door open and let her in. She walked into the main sitting area that had clearly been converted to a bedroom for the week and awkwardly paced the small space, not sure whether to sit or stand. Wes cleared the sheets off the sofa that sat in the middle of the room, but she remained standing.

"Where are the others?" she asked.

"They're still out. They stay out pretty late, squeezing every ounce of fun out of this week."

"I have some questions," she said, her arms crossed.

"Shoot," he said, perching on the arm of the sofa.

"What do you mean you go to medical school?" she asked.

"I'm in medical school. I've finished my classes and I'm about to start my residency. Listen, Milly . . ."

"I'm not done."

"OK."

"Why did you come here? Isn't Bal Week supposed to be for college kids and high school kids?"

"Luke is my brother. He and his friends had been planning it for a while. They're seniors, so it's their last year. Luke and I are close, but he can get a bit wild sometimes. He asked me to come; he thought it would be good for me to have a break before my residency starts, and I thought it might not be a bad idea to keep an eye on him, keep him out of trouble, you know." He shrugged. "It was a last-minute decision to come."

"Shouldn't you be keeping an eye on him now?" she asked.

"I'm not his babysitter," he said. "I'm just here if he needs me." He sighed. "Sometimes he drinks too much. I just want to make sure he's got things under control."

Milly nodded, trying to remain calm and absorb all he was telling her in her flustered state.

"He gets that from my father," he said, looking away. "It's as if he doesn't have an off button: Sometimes he doesn't know when enough is enough."

"I understand that," Milly said, then cleared her throat. "I need to know something else."

"OK."

"Why did you do that?"

He raised his eyebrow. "Do what?"

"You know what," she said.

"Milly, I'm sorry, I didn't mean to . . . I thought you . . ." He looked at the ground. "I guess I hoped you were feeling what I was feeling."

She was. She wanted to tell him that every part of her body was filled with longing then and now at this very moment, but she couldn't. How could she? She had a husband and children, a marriage to salvage, or she'd be ruined, shunned, destitute. He shook his head, and she watched him, arms crossed on his chest, his muscles taut and tense and even more pronounced under his tanned skin.

"I made a mistake," he said in a whisper. But she couldn't let him believe that. She took a tiny, trembling step toward him.

"Wes," she said, "you didn't." He looked up, his dark eyebrows lifting, pieces of his tousled hair falling over his eyes, making her catch her breath. "You didn't make a mistake." She moved closer and was standing right in front of him now, inches apart, a lingering question between them as he sat on the edge of the sofa. He uncrossed his arms and put his hands on his knees, likely not wanting to make assumptions after the last time. She looked at his hands and she wanted them on her, she needed to feel his touch again, for him to pull her toward him. The thought of his hands moving from his knees to her hips, up her torso, and onto her skin made her heart pound and her breath quicken, but she could tell he wasn't going to make the same mistake twice.

Milly brought her hands to his thick brown hair and ran her fingers through it, brushing it back from his face. The sensation of his hair in her hands was so heightened, it was as if she'd never touched another person before.

"Milly, we can't," he said, turning away slightly. "I shouldn't have . . ."

"Yes," she whispered, "you should." He studied her for a few seconds, then she leaned toward him and kissed him. He quickly wrapped his arms around her, all hesitation gone, one hand reaching back for her rear and pulling her into him, the other traveling up her spine. The kiss wasn't gentle now, it was hungry. His lips parted and she felt his tongue, the taste of him unblocking something primal in her. She ran her hands across his strong shoulders and down his back, pulling him to her, wanting him closer. She could feel the heat emanating from him, warming her. They were pressed together but it wasn't close enough.

He slowly unzipped her dress all the way down her back, kissing her neck, her collarbone, her chest, the soft touch of his fingers following the zipper down. He began to unfasten her bra.

"I was not expecting this," she murmured as she looked up to the ceiling, then her eyes closed as she felt his soft fingers on her skin, each touch a new wave of ecstasy.

"Neither was I," he said, his lips hovering over hers now. "But I've never wanted anyone as much as I want you right now." He kissed her again, slowly this time, letting her savor every second. "You're so damn beautiful."

She pulled his T-shirt over his head and felt her stomach flip again at the sight of his tanned, smooth skin on his sculpted body.

"They could come back," Milly said, almost too overtaken with lust to care.

"They could," he said, "but they won't, not for a while."

Wes got up from where he sat and locked the door.

When he returned, he slipped the straps of her dress off her shoulders and stepped out of his trousers, then he walked the two of them backward to the sofa where he lay Milly down. He lowered his body on hers, the weight of him, the heat of him, the sensation of so much of him against her making her crazy with desire.

Milly couldn't think straight as his mouth traveled down her neck, his hands moving down her stomach and slipping beneath her lace underwear. She had never been touched like this before, ever, and it was a whole world of pleasure opening up to her. His chest on hers, her thighs wrapping around him, pulling him closer. She wanted to feel every inch of his skin pressed against hers and she couldn't wait any longer. She felt for him fast and desperate. He groaned, bowing his head to her shoulder.

"Milly," he murmured, "are you sure?"

"Yes," she said, pulling him into her. "Yes," she repeated, breathless now, when they finally moved together as if they had been made for this.

She pulled him toward her, pressing herself to him, desperate to feel more of him, and he did everything her touch asked, moving deeper into her as she arched her back, gripping the back of the sofa until she couldn't take it anymore. His name rushed out of her in a desperate cry. Wes groaned into her neck and pulled her hips to him again and again and one final time before collapsing next to her, pulling her close and not letting her go.

Milly let out a sigh of deep and dreamy relief, pleasure, and utter, melting relaxation.

They lay in a sweaty heap, content. "I think I'm in a state of shock," Milly said softly.

"I'm in a state of bliss," Wes said, tracing the outline of her collarbone with his finger.

"So, medical school?" Milly said.

"That's right," Wes said. "I always wanted to be a doctor."

"Well, you certainly understand the human body," Milly said, and he laughed.

"I just can't believe I'm here with you."

"Me neither," he said, "but somehow I think it was inevitable."

"What do you mean?" she asked, smiling.

"I don't know, there's just something about you, something magnetic. You undid me. But I think I may have been a bad influence on you."

"You certainly have," she said.

She didn't want to move, to leave his side. She wanted to stay tucked into his warm embrace, her body pressed against his until the sun came up, but she couldn't.

After a while she turned to him. "I have to go; I don't want to, but I have to," she whispered. "The others could be back any minute."

"I know," he said as she stood and picked up her dress, then he leaned down to kiss her again before zipping her up.

He threw on his shirt and trousers and pulled her toward him. "You . . ." He breathed into her hair. "You're incredible."

And she carried that with her across the lawn, into her house, and upstairs to her room, where she turned out the light and lay on the bed, staring up at the ceiling feeling as if she were forever changed. She couldn't sleep right away, her mind racing, her body still wound up and buzzing. It wasn't until she lay there and tried to still her mind that she realized how perfunctory things had been with Lloyd, how detached they had seemed from one another. She'd been so young when they married, and never having known any other way, she'd thought that was normal. But after being with Wes and experiencing how much he wanted her and how he even seemed to need her, she realized what she'd been missing. A strange and unfamiliar surge of femininity ran through her—an energy, powerful and womanly pulsing from her head to her toes. It was a feeling that she had lost, or maybe she'd never had it to begin with. But now she knew what was possible.

CHAPTER TWENTY-ONE

SYLVIA

Sylvia linked her arm through Judith's and walked out of their house on Saturday for the very last time. She closed the door behind them and forced herself not to look back. She was distraught and all she wanted was to race back inside, curl up in a corner of the living room, and sob amid the chaos of her crumbling life. But she had to be strong for her daughter, and besides, there was no point standing around watching everything she owned get packed into the back of a moving truck when there wasn't a darn thing she could do about it.

They'd agreed to sell most of the large furniture to the new owners for an extra few thousand dollars. The movers were in the process of carrying the rest of their belongings to a truck parked outside and would deliver them to the cottage on Onyx Avenue later that afternoon.

"I don't see how we can just sleep at the new place tonight; it's all happening so fast," Judith said through tears.

"I know it's hard, but we have to remember it's just a house," Sylvia said, giving her a squeeze and trying to believe it herself. "We'll make the next place cozy, I promise."

The Bathing Beauty Contest was starting at 2 PM, and she needed to get to the Fun Zone fast. Sylvia put her arm around Judith, who was feverishly dabbing her eyes with tissues, desperate not to mess up her makeup before the contest she'd be attending with her friends in just a few hours.

"Let's do a quick check," Sylvia said once they were out of the front gate. "Do you have the corsages with the numbers?" Sylvia asked.

Judith nodded, lifting an elbow to indicate they were in her heavy tote bag.

"The sashes?"

"They're with the numbers. In the box."

Judith was watching her expectantly, no longer sniffling. Maybe focusing on the details could help her—and Sylvia too, for that matter—pull herself together. What other choice did they have? "Good. I've got the trophies and the crown," Sylvia said, patting a large bag looped over her shoulder. "Milly said she'd bring fans in case the girls get warm. I've got a first aid kit: Someone always needs a Band-Aid for a blister or smelling salts if they're feeling faint after starving themselves to fit into their swimsuit!" She gave her daughter a nudge and shook her head. "You wouldn't believe the theatrics!" And Judith managed to smile back. "I was certainly guilty of that the day before my contest," Sylvia went on. "Anyway, I think we're all set. Let's at least try to have some fun."

They started down the promenade, but any sense of camaraderie faded too soon.

"This would be so much easier if you still had your car," Judith grumbled under her breath as they made their way toward the ferry.

"Yes, it would," Sylvia said. "I wish I'd thought to ask your father to leave us his car this morning, but there was so much going on."

Walter had left for the bank earlier that morning to fill out paperwork and hand the deed over to the new owners. If all went well, after he'd awarded the Bathing Beauty Contest winner her prize, he could at last deliver the money he owed later that afternoon, upstairs in some dingy bar on the peninsula. The mere thought of it made her heart ache and her eyes sting.

"Can't someone else announce the winners, Lamb Chop?" he'd asked Sylvia wearily the night before. "Hal Peterson would be happy to do it." Clearly the contest was the last thing on Walter's mind, but he had awarded the prize for the past two decades, and before that his father had done the presenting, so Sylvia insisted that he not break with tradition now. They had to maintain their reputation; they had the club, just barely. Everything was riding on it, and she was going to do everything in her power to hold on to it and make it a success. People in town seemed to know about the sale of the house by now, and she was sure rumors were flying. She had to keep her chin up, keep moving forward and project the image of a welcoming community family as they always had, so that no one would question Walter's shaky finances, wonder about the club's potential longevity, or the status of the memberships they'd eagerly sought when it opened last year.

"The Bathing Beauty Contest will be a vital demonstration of community action and generosity, Walter," she'd reminded him. "And after the trouble we're in now, it couldn't come at a better time."

The beach next to the Fun Zone was already packed when Sylvia and Judith arrived. As usual, the high school and college kids came early to claim their spots, blanketing the sandy beach with their brightly colored towels, lined up one next to another as far as the eye could see. Some reserved space on the wooden pier, while others packed themselves into the viewing area in front of the boardwalk, rocking to the live music, waiting for the festivities to begin. Some picnicked in rowboats, others were perched on surfboards and kayaks, happy with a view from the water.

Milly was already there with Jack and Debbie by her side.

"Thank you for offering to help," Sylvia said. "We need it."

"Of course; it's your big day," Milly said. "Leticia couldn't work today so we've got two extra helpers." Milly nodded to her children and shrugged just before lunging for Jack as he tried to sprint off into the crowd.

"The more the merrier," Sylvia said. "Can you check in the contestants and give them each a number? Judith and I made the numbers into corsages so they can wear them on their wrists. And then, Judith"—

she turned to her daughter, who was scanning the crowd—"I know you want to find your friends, but can you please help Milly for now? I'll go and check on the gentlemen."

The judges' booth was front and center with seats for six local businessmen who'd volunteered to be part of the highly coveted Bathing Beauty Judging Committee. Walter's seat sat empty. Sylvia was starting to perspire when she realized it was five minutes past two and Walter wasn't anywhere in sight. If they were ever to vanquish the threat of exposure, today had to go like clockwork. She prayed nothing had gone awry.

It was unseasonably hot. The men, though shaded in the booth, were squirming in their suits and ties. The contestants, all fifty of them, were hopefully now lined up and out of sight inside the Pavilion in their glamorous swimsuits and white pumps.

"Mom," Judith called out to her mother when she saw her pacing outside the Pavilion. "Should we just start? I don't know how much longer I can hold these girls back. They're hot and raring to go."

Sylvia hurried over and peeked inside to an earful of complaints about the hot, stuffy hallway where they waited, the warm air trapped in the building threatening to deflate everyone's perfectly coiffed hair and give a shine to their freshly powdered faces.

"Two more minutes, sweetheart," Sylvia said as she checked again to see if her husband had arrived. The whole point of the contest, of Walter's announcing the winners, was so that he would maintain his good standing in the community and, hopefully, mention the club to a captive audience. She didn't want some other big shot from the judges' booth to take the stage and claim all the credit for the well-attended contest they'd worked so hard to put on year after year.

She took the steps to the stage and grabbed the microphone.

"Welcome everyone, welcome," she said as the crowd began to hush. "Welcome to the annual Balboa Bathing Beauty Contest, where the first-place winner will win a vacation to Catalina Island with boat passage, and all runners-up will win a weekend pass to The Island Club, lunch and dinner included!" People gave a few cheers, others clapped appreciatively.

The Catalina trip had previously been planned and donated, but she'd decided on the club prizes last-minute, hoping it would get mentioned in the papers. "We'll be getting started soon." She looked over at the judges again and tried not to guess what could be keeping him. If there was any problem with the sale or with getting the cash, he'd be panicked. She thought of the man on the pier who'd been watching her at her party. What if he'd been waiting for Walter outside the bank? What if there'd been an altercation? She tried to remain calm.

Before she could think of what to do or how to prolong the start of the contest, the band started to play and the door to the Pavilion burst open. Judith was shoved out of the way, and the girls started to walk, single file and a little too hurriedly, down the boardwalk in front of the crowd. The girls, ranging in ages from sixteen to twenty, paraded down the long wooden boardwalk, all smiles in their swimsuits and heels, waving to the crowds and the judges as well as to the beachgoers. Number 1 wore a daring cream two-piece, pursed red lips, and her short blond hair parted and curled to perfection. Number 2, a brunette, followed in a black one-piece with two white stripes forming a V down the front. She looked out to the crowd anxiously, then down to the ground, speeding up and almost crashing into the girl in front. Number 3 was a stunner with a tiny waist and full bosom, high arched brows, and a coy side glance. The judges gaped at her and all jotted something on their papers. Sylvia rushed to help her daughter at the Pavilion door and managed to get the girls to slow down a little, spacing them out so that each contestant would have a moment to shine. When she saw Delores, Maggie's daughter from the pharmacy in town, Sylvia approached her in line.

"You go out there and give them your brightest smile," Sylvia said.

"They're all so pretty," Delores said.

"So are you," Sylvia said. "But you've got the smarts and the charm to go with it."

Milly had hightailed it to the other end of the boardwalk now, kids in tow, directing the girls to loop around behind the Fun Zone and back to the Pavilion to find out if they made it through to the next round.

Once they were walking in an orderly manner, Sylvia allowed herself to step back and enjoy the spectacle for a moment, remembering her own walk down that very boardwalk. Remembering how she'd dared to glance over to Walter in the judges' booth and seen that look in his eye, a look that made her feel like she was the only girl on the stage. Oh, how her life had changed that day, eighteen years ago, more than she could have ever imagined. Everything was filled with promise and possibility, youth and beauty. Back then she had nothing and everything. She could have ended up with another husband in another life. A thousand roads lay ahead of her then, leading to unknown futures. Now her life's path was determined. She didn't long for the youth or the beauty or the possibility; she longed for her life and her marriage to return to the way it was, she longed for stability and assurances. She belonged here with her family, and she only hoped they could stay.

When the last girl, number 50, made her way down the boardwalk, the crowd cheered, and Sylvia went to the judges' booth to collect their votes for the next round. The band played another set, and people took breaks to grab ice cream Balboa Bars and frozen bananas. But Walter's seat was still empty, and Sylvia couldn't shake the queasy feeling in her stomach that something was wrong.

"Who's going to announce the winners in Walter's absence?" Hal Peterson asked from his seat in the booth.

"He'll be here," Sylvia said as cheerfully as she could. "He just had some business to attend to."

Hal raised his eyebrows. "I'm sure he does," he said, which garnered a chuckle from Herb, who ran a tiki hut on the peninsula.

It took everything in Sylvia's power not to snap back at them, ask Hal exactly what he meant by that and find out what he'd heard, but that would do her no good. It was possible these men knew about the high-stakes poker games that had been going on in these parts for years.

Heck, they probably participated in them, but with better luck by the looks of things. There was no point engaging with them now.

"I'll be needing your votes," she said, holding out her hand to collect the judges' scoring cards.

When the contestants walked again, it was just twenty of them. She was glad Delores had made it into the second round; she hoped a local girl would be part of the winner's circle. All the young ladies strode down the pathway glowing and radiant in their youth and the warm spring sunshine. Each one in this round had the figure, legs, and charisma to win. They sure made them pretty these days. This time they took a seat on chairs lined up on the stage, right ankle crossed over left. The judges had to select their choice for first, second, and third place as well as a winner for Miss Poised, Miss Personality, and Miss Suntanned, but not before each one was given a chance to wow her audience with a glimpse into her character. Walter always asked the questions, but Sylvia would have to take charge this time.

Before anyone could protest, she walked onto the stage and took the microphone again.

"Congratulations to every single young lady who was brave enough to come out and take a chance today." She waited for the audience to applaud. "And now it's time to get to know our contestants. Number Seventeen, please join me."

Seventeen sauntered to the center of the stage in a stunning white one-piece halter-style swimsuit with a large bow at the bust and stood slightly angled to the judges with a hand on her hip.

"You clearly follow fashion," Sylvia said. "But what else makes you interesting?"

"Well, I love to cook, sew, and spend time with my friends. I like music and dancing, and I think that makes me interesting. And I hope it'll make me a good wife to my husband."

"Thank you," Sylvia said and called up number 23.

"If your life is like a novel, what do you think will happen in the next chapter?"

Number 23 didn't miss a beat. "In the next chapter of my life I hope to find a wonderful husband to love and support, and I'd like us to have three babies."

As she called the rest of the contestants onto the stage and tried to coax differing responses out of them, she got similar answers over and over. Marriage. A husband. Children. She didn't blame them, she'd wanted that too, and she hoped Judith would find love and happiness someday, of course. But she also hoped for more. Marriage wasn't the only measure of success. Couldn't they also strive for a little self-sufficiency and independence? If she had, would things be different now? Could she have helped Walter avoid this mess he'd got them into?

"Number Forty-Five," she called out, and Delores joined her center stage. "Hello, dear," Sylvia said. "How do you envision making a difference for future generations?"

Sylvia expected Delores to give the same trite response about raising children and feeding them and her future husband nourishing meals.

"My parents own Mason's Pharmacy in town, and it's my hope to take over the family business someday. I've grown up on Balboa Island, and it's important to me that it keeps its character and charm as a small, family place to call home with plenty of fun stores and family businesses. I work there part-time now but I hope to save up enough money to buy it from them when they are ready to retire."

The audience cheered, especially the islanders.

When Sylvia collected the judges' votes once again and began to tally them up, Hal Peterson stood, presumably to take his place on the stage and announce the winners, but Sylvia wasn't going to let that happen. "Time to announce Miss Balboa," she said, heading quickly back to the stage, sorting through the slips of paper as she walked. Delores hadn't made the cut for Miss Poised, Miss Personality, or Miss Suntanned; but for the big prize, Miss Balboa, she was tied in first place. Sylvia made an executive decision. Miss Balboa should go to a Balboa girl.

"Thank you so much for coming out today to celebrate our very own Bathing Beauty Contest, sponsored by The Island Club, where we have tennis, swimming, and fine dining." She looked around at the crowd, pleased with herself for squeezing that into the announcement early on. As she surveyed the hundreds, maybe even thousands, in front of her, she saw mostly young men and women eagerly awaiting the results, tourists who'd traveled in for the day and pockets of neighborhood folks too. Mina and Tony from Hershey's Market, Teddy and his wife Faye were there, and Sylvia wondered if he'd been at the closing with Walter earlier. Teddy looked carefree; that might be a good sign, but where was Walter? Delores's mother Maggie was cheering her on. Even Joe had taken a break from his ferry service to witness the contest. Seymour would be working the ferry; it never sat idle, especially with crowds like these.

Sylvia was doing her best. They were in the homestretch and were going to get through this. She smiled and waved to a group of women from the club, but their expressions were not joyful or enthusiastic like those of the others watching. They looked sour, maybe even angry. Perhaps, if they knew of her family's financial troubles, her mention of the club was making them worry about their memberships and the dues they'd already paid for the year. Could they be talking among themselves about getting taken for a ride? Calling her and Walter frauds, thieves, spendthrifts? She couldn't stand the idea that they might think differently of her now, that she could have lost their respect and might never be perceived the same way again. She looked away, back to the smiling, carefree students eagerly awaiting the announcement of Miss Balboa, and tried to stay focused on the task at hand.

"We are so thrilled that you are enjoying everything that our community has to offer, and we're just so excited to announce our 1956 Miss Balboa." The crowd roared with applause, and Sylvia smiled but couldn't help glancing back out to the women once more.

When the sashes had been placed, trophies awarded, and Delores crowned Miss Balboa 1956 and celebrated, Sylvia escorted the six winners to the front of the banana stand for a group photo. Nothing said Bal Week like six gorgeous swimsuit-clad gals with a backdrop of saltwater taffy, Don's fresh homemade candies, and hand-dipped frozen bananas. When the pictures were taken and the reporters took down the winners' names, Sylvia made sure to speak to the reporters herself and mention the club once again.

As the girls shuffled excitedly back to the Pavilion, Sylvia found herself standing alone at the banana stand.

"Can I get you anything, Mrs. Johnson?" the man behind the counter asked.

"Oh, thank you, Don. Sure, I'll take a banana, dipped—"

"With nuts, I know," he said and smiled.

She handed him her change, but he shook his head adamantly. "You must be kidding me. You keep us in business with this here celebration you put on. I couldn't be more grateful to you and your husband."

"Thank you," she said, turning to scan the crowd for Walter again, praying he was all right. She was about to take a bite of the banana when Milly came up behind her.

"What are you doing here all alone? You were wonderful," she said, excitedly, pulling her in for a hug. "Really, you looked like a star up there on that stage."

"Thanks, Milly," she said, grateful that she now had some company. "I didn't really have a choice; Walter couldn't make it in the end."

"That's a shame." Milly looked concerned. "I wish he could have seen how fantastic you were. You should always announce the winners. And next time, tell them you're our very own Miss Balboa 1938!" Milly linked her arm through Sylvia's. "Your Judith is such a doll; she offered to watch the kids while I came to find you."

"I'm glad you did," Sylvia said. She hadn't known Milly all that long, and she certainly seemed to have her own set of challenges, but as they walked side by side through the crowds, she thought maybe Milly was exactly the kind of friend she needed right now.

Sylvia couldn't bring herself to walk past her house on South Bay Front and risk seeing the new owners through the windows, so when she exited the ferry, she walked up to Balboa Avenue, strolled past Ruby, Diamond, and Sapphire Avenues and kept going until she reached Onyx. She stood outside for a moment staring at the run-down cottage, then she reluctantly let herself in through the front door. There were boxes stacked from floor to ceiling with only a narrow pathway leading through the living room.

"Hello?" she called out.

"I'm over here," Walter called back. She followed the sound of his voice to the staircase, where he sat with a coffee mug and a bottle of whiskey next to him.

"Where the hell have you been?" she asked, furious. She'd been panicked all day that something horrible had happened to him, and now, instead of relief at the sight of him, she felt mildly repulsed.

"I couldn't do it," he said, looking miserable. "I handed the money over, all of it, and I just couldn't get up in front of all those people at the contest and put on a happy face."

Sylvia knew how he felt. She hadn't wanted to get up in front of all those people either—it had felt wretched—but she did it anyway.

"So you just left it all to me," she said, grabbing his bottle and taking a swig.

"I'm sorry," he said, closing his eyes and shaking his head.

"Yeah, that's what you keep saying." She set the bottle back on the staircase and walked into the living room, took a deep breath, and ripped open the first box.

CHAPTER TWENTY-TWO

MILLY

Before the children woke on Easter morning, Milly got up to put the finishing touches on the Easter Glory Cake she'd made using Swans Down cake mix. She frosted it, sprinkled the cake with shredded coconut, and arranged the jelly beans on top. She'd already assembled the Easter baskets with Pez dispensers, a Milky Way each, some Dubble Bubble gum, and an assortment of Brach's Easter candies. She was going overboard, and all that candy was going to turn the children into sugar monsters, but she had to make up for Lloyd's absence, as well as her mounting guilt over Wes, any way she could.

She laid out the clothes that her stepmother had sent for the children—a turquoise ruffle dress and matching bonnet for Debbie; shorts, a button-down shirt, and blazer for Jack. She'd never really bonded with her stepmother: Milly had been too old to appreciate anyone new stepping into her mother's shoes, and she'd stepped into them way too soon after her mother's death for Milly's liking. But she'd dress her children in the clothes sent to them because that was the right thing to do. Besides, they'd be adorable—Jack with his knee-high socks and Debbie with her grown-up Mary Janes—but Milly still hadn't decided if they'd actually go to church that morning. She was sick of making up lies for Lloyd and she couldn't think of a single plausible reason for his absence. When the children woke up, however, racing down the stairs chanting "Easter Bunny have some honey" and told Milly how they couldn't wait to meet him at the Easter egg hunt, scheduled to take place outside the church immediately following the service, the decision had been made for her.

They arrived, intentionally, as the service had just begun. It would be better to be a few minutes late to avoid all the small talk prior, but when they walked through the double doors and an elderly usher talked in a loud whisper advising them on where to sit, almost the entire congregation turned to see who was making the commotion. She caught eyes with Sylvia sitting in the front row, who waved Milly over, but she wasn't going to parade her kids to the front of the church like that. They squeezed into a pew in the very back.

Milly barely heard a word of the sermon; instead she questioned how Lloyd could stay away from his children for this long. What kind of man doesn't show up for his children on Easter? It was unfathomable. Was this her life now? Would he ever come back to them? And then she found herself wondering if she even wanted him to.

When it was over, the children lined up on the grass outside, and the Easter Bunny, in his purple overalls and pink ears, made his way down the line, greeting them one by one. And then they were off; the hunt had begun.

"Hello, darling," Sylvia said. "I saw you sneak in the back like you were in trouble for your sins or something."

"In trouble? For what?" she said, thinking of just how much trouble she was in. She began ruminating about exactly *how* she had sinned—and how she'd like to sin again in a multitude of ways—but then she looked out at the children running frantically around the field searching for eggs and felt a painful stab of guilt. Yes, Lloyd might be running around with Beverly Douglas, and he didn't seem to feel any shame, but Milly was different. She'd never so much as looked at another man. How was she going to live with herself after what she'd done? How was she ever going to pull her family back together after this?

"I'm only joking. Don't take things so seriously," Sylvia said, watching Milly and linking her arm through hers as she walked her to a coffee-and-cake table situated by the front entrance. "Just the three of you today?" Sylvia asked quietly, keeping her eyes straight ahead.

Milly cleared her throat, running through all the possible, ridiculous excuses she'd conjured up while they sat through the service. But this was Sylvia she was talking to; she wasn't going to believe any of that nonsense. "Yes, just the three of us," she said, resigned. And then, whether it was the guilt of what she'd done, or the desperate need to unleash some of her inner turmoil, she added, "Lloyd hasn't been home all week, and, quite honestly, I don't know when he'll show his face."

Sylvia patted her arm, which surprised and comforted Milly. Sylvia wasn't shocked by the confession. She clearly already knew something was awry, but she wasn't going to judge her.

"Well," Sylvia said, "I would invite you to lunch with us, but we haven't even unpacked the kitchen yet, and I don't know if we can fit more than the three of us around the dining room table in our new place." She laughed. "That's if Judith graces us with her presence. She's so furious at us for moving."

Milly knew this must be hurting her. "I know a little about unpacking," Milly said. "I can swing by this week to help you, if you'd like."

"You're a doll," Sylvia said.

At the Bathing Beauty Contest, Milly had noticed that some of Sylvia's friends were a little standoffish, and she wondered if it was due to Sylvia's move from her extravagant house on the bay to the little cottage next to Adele. It seemed a paltry reason for them to keep their distance. My God, she thought, if they couldn't stand by their longtime friend when she was moving out of her home with her husband and daughter, what would they think of Milly if they found out that she was likely getting a divorce, that Lloyd would probably be leaving her for a famous television star, and that she'd just slept with a younger man? She almost laughed at the mess she'd made of her life.

"Why don't you jump in on a lesson with me and Adele this week to take your mind off things?" Milly suggested. "Moving can be so stressful, and Adele says I need to find women who can actually play if I ever want to learn how to play a match."

"Sure thing," Sylvia said. "That would be nice. I could use the distraction."

That afternoon, instead of baking a ham with pineapple sauce, her cheesy potato casserole, and a peach custard pie, Milly decided to make a picnic and take the children out for an adventure instead. They took the ferry back to the Fun Zone, where it felt desolate compared with the previous day's chaos. The Ferris wheel was still closed, but they rode the bumper cars and played in the arcade. As the children ran from one arcade game to another, using the pennies she'd given them, Milly sat on a bench and relived her last encounter with Wes.

During the madness of the Bathing Beauty Contest, she'd looked for Wes, expecting to find him ogling the beautiful young women in swimsuits. Instead, she'd found him hitting the high-striker strongman game with his brother, and he'd rushed over as soon as their eyes met, smiling when he saw the children.

"Well, I didn't realize I'd get to see two croquet superstars at the Fun Zone today."

Jack and Debbie had beamed at him. "We can beat you now, Mr. Wes," Jack said. "We've been practicing. Right, Debbie?"

"That's right," Debbie said. "We would like a rematch."

"Oh, I am afraid, very, very afraid, because I haven't practiced at all since we last played," Wes said, then he reached into his pocket and pulled out some change. "Have you two been on the carousel yet?"

"Yes. But not today," Debbie said.

"I heard that the horses are feeling very lonely. Everyone's been giving all their attention to the girls gallivanting in swimsuits instead of those beauties." He handed them each a nickel, then looked up to Milly. "Is it all right if they ride the ponies?"

"Of course," she said, smiling at the easy way he had with them.

"The pink horse is the fastest," he whispered to Debbie before she ran off holding Jack's hand.

"Thank you," Milly said, "That was sweet of you."

"I was hoping I'd see you here," he said. "We're leaving early tomorrow morning." A look of disappointment came over him.

"I know," she said.

"Milly, I want to tell you . . ."

But she shook her head. It was too crowded—someone could overhear them—but also, she didn't want him to pity her. She wanted to remember everything exactly as it was between them. Magical. "You don't have to say anything, please."

The week had been a collision of days, of moments she'd never expected.

And that morning, Easter, when she'd heard them packing up the car, she'd forced herself to stay in bed and not look out the window. They'd already said their goodbyes, but she relived their moments together in her head all the same.

What she'd done was wrong. She'd allowed herself to be swept up in a fantasy. She was married and she loved Lloyd, she did, but she'd never had with him the kind of physical attraction or sensation that she had with Wes. She hadn't even known that kind of passion and wanting was possible. The way her body responded to his touch, the way she was able to convey to him what she needed without saying a word, the way he could make her forget everything around her for those few blissful, ecstatic moments. It was a powerful magic she hadn't known existed. It almost felt like a sin to have the capacity for that kind of pleasure and not use it, not submerge yourself into it, not to experience it at least once in your lifetime.

Lloyd had made it quite clear by now that he was not in love with her and that he'd fallen for someone else. Why else would he leave his family like this and not come home on Easter? It was only a matter of time before someone found out, or his new lover insisted he desert them completely. She couldn't live in fear of what people would think, but she didn't know what to do about it.

There was no future for her and Wes; she wasn't naive enough to think otherwise. For one thing, he was young—though, in fact, more like twenty-five than the twenty or so she'd first assumed, not so very far from her twenty-nine years, it occurred to her. But that was beside the point. He was back at UCLA now, around his peers where he belonged, eager to embark on his residency. She'd been a holiday fling for him, and that had to be fine. It wouldn't be anything else; it couldn't be.

But the fact was, she was not the same woman she was before she met him. He had brought something in her to life, and she knew now what her body could do and feel, what it craved, what it needed, and she didn't want to deny that or pretend otherwise. It made her feel different about everything; it made her see the world around her in a different light. She was feminine, she was desired, and she deserved to have that kind of magic in her life.

"Mommy," Debbie sang as she ran toward Milly, holding Jack's hand. "Mommy, can we play Skee-Ball?"

"Of course you can, my darlings," Milly said, standing up and giving her children a kiss on the tops of their heads. They were far too dressed up to be running around this arcade, but she didn't care. "You can do whatever you want today. Do you know why?"

"Because we're having an adventure," Jack said clapping his hands.

"That's right, we're having an adventure."

"And because it's Easter," Debbie said.

"An Easter adventure," Milly said taking her hand and walking them to the Skee-Ball lanes.

"Mommy," Debbie said. "Why isn't Daddy here? He's always with us on Easter. Is he going to miss Thanksgiving and Christmas too?"

Milly swallowed hard, caught off guard in the middle of her own exuberance. "Well"—she hadn't prepared for this—"well, honey, I think he had to work this time."

Debbie nodded. "Mommy?"

Milly braced herself. "Yes, sweetheart?" she said crouching down and looking her in the eye.

"Is God calling on Daddy to do a new life?"

"What?" Milly said, shocked.

"That's what the priest said today."

"He did?" Milly realized she hadn't paid any attention to what was being said in the service that morning.

"He said God is calling on us to a new life through Jesus, but I don't want a new life, because we just got a new life here on Balboa Island, and I didn't like it at first, but I love it now because Suzanna is my best friend."

Milly hugged her daughter. "We don't need a new life, honeypie, we have the best life right here."

"Come on, you slow pokes," Jack called out, already at the Skee-Ball game holding the wooden ball in his chubby little hands. "You can't beat me."

"Oh yes I can," Debbie said, breaking away from Milly's embrace and rushing to her brother's side to play.

CHAPTER TWENTY-THREE

SYLVIA

Tennis was exactly what Sylvia needed—something to get her mind off the move to their tiny, damp-smelling house. It also gave her a much-needed break from Walter. She could barely look at him, still furious with him for putting them in this awful and humiliating situation and for standing her up at the beauty contest. She also needed a respite from her daughter's daggerlike glares.

"It smells like moldy old cheese," Judith had said to Sylvia that morning as she dressed for school, as if this were all Sylvia's fault. "And I can't find any of my things."

"I know the feeling, Jude, believe me. I'm having a hard time too, but we have to do the best we can with this new situation," she'd said, having to try very hard now not to throw all the blame on Walter, which she desperately wanted to do.

The situation they were in was still dire. Walter had paid off his debts, but there was barely anything left in their accounts, and the club still had significant bills to be paid, monthly, with money that they simply no longer had. Money was so tight and accounted for that Sylvia had to cherry-pick her groceries, opting for what was cheap and on sale, something that reminded her of going to the market with her grandmother in Barstow and seeing her count out her coins at the register, sometimes asking Sylvia to return something to the shelf when they couldn't afford it. Walter was constantly anxious, often at the bank or with their accountant, and it was painfully clear now that their days of keeping the doors to the club open were extremely limited.

On the court, though, she was able to put it out of her mind for a little while.

"I'm glad you asked me to join," Sylvia said to Milly as they stretched their arms over their heads and rotated their torsos from left to right, as Adele had taught them to do. "I haven't played for a while."

"Well, you've been busy with the move," Milly said. "Speaking of moves, I've got a new tenant moving into my guest cottage." She stepped into a lunge, then straightened her leg, reaching forward to touch her toes. There was a smile on Milly's lips.

"You're enjoying this," Sylvia said, teasing.

"Enjoying what?" Milly said, her smile growing now.

"Taking in these new tenants, making money," Sylvia said. "It probably feels good to have money handed over to you and not your husband for once," she said, lowering her voice. "Making your own money."

"It does," Milly said. "I've never had a real job. There's something thrilling about earning some of your own cash, even if it's just a little."

"Oh, I believe it," Sylvia said. "These new women that Adele is coaching now—that was all my doing, not Walter's."

Milly raised here eyebrows.

"OK, fine," Sylvia said. "You were the one who convinced me to let her coach here. I have you to thank, but Adele is coaching seven or eight women now. It's not a lot of money, in the grand scheme of things, but it gives me a little hope that I could do more to help improve things around here."

"I hear my name," Adele said, approaching in her usual white tennis outfit and her headband holding back her short wavy hair.

"I was saying how you're becoming quite popular around here."

Adele shrugged. "I'm glad."

"The ladies seem happy with their lessons," Sylvia said.

"Good. Now come on, let's get moving."

Adele taught them the basics of match play that day, two chances to serve from the deuce side, then two chances from the ad side. She'd taught them how to score—love, 15, 30, 40, deuce—how many games to play in a set, how many sets to play in a match. Sylvia knew all this, but it had been so long since she'd attempted an actual match that she was grateful for the refresher. Milly seemed excited too, despite the fact that she kept counting to 45 instead of 40, claiming that it didn't make any sense. She was eager to start playing matches with some of the other women and had a pep to her, Sylvia noticed, an energetic spirit that had come about since she'd started taking private lessons with Adele. It made Milly seem even younger somehow, more vibrant, and her enthusiasm was contagious.

When the lesson was over, Adele and Milly packed up their bags and headed off the court.

"No more bookings today?" Sylvia asked, trying not to look disappointed.

"You were my last two," Adele said. "But you are both coming along quite nicely. You've got a long way to go, *bien sûr*, but you played well. Soon you can play a practice match with each other. Maybe I will watch, to see how you do."

"You'd do that?" Milly asked, excited.

"*Oui*," Adele said. "You're not as bad to spend time with as I once thought." Sylvia laughed, both at the backhanded compliment and at how Adele was turning out to be quite fun, not at all the sourpuss she'd pinned her for all these years.

When Milly and Adele left the club, Sylvia marveled to think that the two might even be walking home together. "Incredible," she said to herself. "What a turning of the tide."

She was on her way to Walter's office—in a better mood now after an hour on the court, and she decided to make the effort to be pleasant around him, try to be supportive, even, if their marriage was going to survive this—when she heard an unfamiliar voice at the front desk.

"Oh, Mrs. Johnson," the receptionist said, "there's someone here to see Miss Lambert."

It was a man in his fifties or sixties with a mustache, glasses, and bushy gray hair.

"Oh, she just left," Sylvia said. "Is there something I can help you with?"

"So, she does work here?" he said, giving away a hint of an English accent and clasping his hands together.

Sylvia frowned. Why would he come here if he didn't know she worked here, she wondered. Something wasn't quite right.

"By any chance do you know which way she went?" he asked.

"No, I do not," she said firmly, not about to give the location of her—dare she say—friend to a complete stranger who was clearly not from around here.

"I apologize," he said. "I didn't mean to pry. Would it be possible to get a message to her, or for me to come back at a later date, when she might be available?"

"What is this regarding?"

He looked from the receptionist to Sylvia. "Is there somewhere we could talk in private?"

Sylvia eyed the gentleman. "Come this way."

She led him to the restaurant, which wasn't open for lunch for another half hour, and gestured for him to take a seat at the corner table. She sat down opposite.

"What did you say your name was?" Sylvia asked.

"Right," he said. "I haven't had the chance yet to properly introduce myself. I'm Jonathan Rutherford. I'm a senior reporter and host for a television show called *Lives & Stories*, and I'm interested in interviewing Adeline for a segment I'm working on. I saw her photo in the paper, something to do with a Ferris wheel malfunction, and I couldn't quite believe my eyes. She hasn't been seen in nearly two decades."

Sylvia didn't follow—Adele on a television show? And why was he calling her Adeline? She wanted to hear more. "Go on," she said.

"Well, when I realized she was in the United States, in this area, and then I heard about this relatively new tennis club, I put two and two together, and I thought she must be here. In fact, I felt it in my bones. I knew she would be here. You must be thrilled."

Not wanting to give away her ignorance on the subject, Sylvia tried to keep her expression neutral and prompted him to keep talking, hoping she might be able to piece it together if she knew more.

"And what exactly do you want to interview her about?"

"Well," he said, his eyebrows raising, causing his forehead to crease, "her past, of course."

"I see," Sylvia said, her stomach clenching.

"I've been on the lookout for Adeline Léglise for years, years," he said.

"Adeline Léglise? That's not her name. . . ."

"My mistake. I hear she goes by Adele Lambert now, understandably so," he added, looking a bit ruffled. "But to interview her, after all this time, would be an absolute coup for me. I suggested the story to my network, and they want it as much as I do. They've given me carte blanche to tell her story."

Adeline Léglise. Sylvia repeated the name in her head. She knew that name. She was the tennis champion who nearly took out her opponent's eye at Wimbledon. My God, Sylvia thought, she was once a star. When Sylvia was a teen she had idolized her, had followed her in the papers. She was a glamour girl and a fashion icon. This was crazy! How had she overlooked the similarities between her then and now? And yet of course she hadn't pieced it together. Adeline Léglise had been glamorous then, so outspoken and sassy. The Adele she knew had been closed off, cantankerous, and rude—until recently. She couldn't believe they'd both lived on the island for so long as neighbors and as strangers. How could this be? One thing was certain, Adele Lambert wasn't who she said she was at all. Adele Lambert was *the* tennis champion of the twenties and thirties. Unbelievable. Adele Lambert was Adeline Léglise.

Suddenly the wheels in Sylvia's head were spinning. Once this got out, she would have women lined up around the island, intrigued, wanting to take lessons, and men too. Adeline Léglise had won Wimbledon and just about every other world championship in her day. This was astounding. If it came to light that she was working at her club, this could change everything. This could help save them. Adele had protested when Sylvia had suggested running an advertisement in the local paper, but this was different. This was a reporter who had come to her—she hadn't sought him out—and he clearly wanted to shine a light on her achievements.

"Mrs. Johnson?" The gentleman interrupted her thoughts. "Do you think you might be able to make the introduction?"

"Yes," she said, thinking it through. "Yes, absolutely I can."

CHAPTER TWENTY-FOUR

ADELE

Adele pulled her old bike out of the garage and wiped it down, oiled the chain, and pumped up the tires. She was busier now, coaching Sadie, Marlene, Joan, Milly, and more, and she needed to be able to get to and from the club fast, sometimes stopping at home for lunch before heading back for an afternoon session. She propped her racket in the basket she'd already filled with balls and thought about the drills she'd run today for each of her ladies.

Joan and Sadie were first-timers and had never even held a tennis racket before. The others were slightly better, having played as kids or in school, but Milly was her best student by far. It wasn't that she had some surprising skill; it was her passion and her desire to learn that was uplifting. In some ways it reminded Adele of herself as a child, desperate to prove something.

As she cruised along Balboa Avenue, up Marine, and over the bridge, she felt herself smiling as she watched the sailboats moored and bobbing on the north side of the bay, and the American flags flying proudly in the warm spring breeze. It was a strange and unfamiliar feeling she was experiencing. Contentment. She had left everything that she knew and loved behind twenty-some years ago to start a new life here on the island, and it dawned on her that this was the first time in all those years that she was doing something worthwhile, something that people appreciated and made her feel valued. It was the first time in more than two decades that she was actually living her life instead of hiding from it.

It was different, of course, to be coaching instead of playing competitively. It didn't produce the same kind of thrill, but it gave her real satisfaction and pleasure in being able to pass on her knowledge and her experience to these women. Sure, at some point they could have started taking lessons with the male coaches, as Sylvia had tried with Robbie, if they'd wanted to learn badly enough, but men often underestimated the power that women had. Adele knew that with the right angle and timing, any one of these women could serve an ace. It was about throwing the toss high enough and coming down on it just a touch earlier than you might expect, to rip it across the court and sail it past your opponent. No one at the club was going to teach them that; they didn't think the women had it in them. But that was a mistake. No man should underestimate the power a woman held when surrounded by other women who believe in her. And Adele did believe in these women. They were all capable of far more than they gave themselves credit for. She was excited about her rise from the shadows and she was excited to bring them with her—her own little team.

She parked her bike at the club entrance and made her way to the courts. As she passed court 3, she saw Robbie look up at her. She kept walking.

"Hey, Miss Tennis Lady," he said, "I hear you've been stealing our students."

Adele wanted to ignore him, get to her court, and set up for her first session, but that was simply untrue: Most of these women hadn't been taking lessons with Robbie before she came along; she was the reason they'd wanted to start. She stopped and turned to him.

"I'm sorry, but you are incorrect."

"Oh, really? Those are our students you're taking—me and Jim and Christoph. We've all been here a lot longer than you."

"First, this club opened only one year ago," she said calmly. "And second, the ladies needed someone who respects them and actually wants to teach them how to play and how to win."

"If they want to win, then they should be learning from me, from a man, and that's just how it is."

"Why don't you let us show you how it is?" Adele said, forcing herself to disengage and turn toward her court.

"Do you even know how to play, lady?" he asked, laughing. "Yeah, I'd like to see you try to play a match and win."

She stopped and stared. "Oh, you will," she said. "You will."

For the rest of the day, she was on fire: He'd ignited something in her that made her even more determined to see these women succeed. It wasn't about her anymore, it was about passing the torch. These women were hardly training for Wimbledon, true, but if she could get them to play well enough to prove that *idiot* wrong, or maybe, maybe even good enough to beat their husbands at their own game, they would be victorious.

By noon she had completed three private lessons, and she was ravenous. She was just leaving the court, feeling accomplished, and was already thinking of the sandwich she'd packed for lunch with the spring radishes that had cropped up in her vegetable garden and the homemade bread she'd baked the day before. She'd sit at one of the tables by the pool and have just enough time to eat it before her next lesson with Milly at twelve thirty. Maybe she'd also buy a packet of potato chips from the snack bar to go with it. She was getting settled, unwrapping the wax paper on the table in front of her, when she heard Sylvia's voice.

"Here she is," Sylvia said, walking with a smartly dressed man. "Adele, I'm so glad I caught you. There's someone I'd like to introduce you to."

Adele looked to the man, and she hoped he wasn't going to ask her to train him. Taking that on would certainly cause an even bigger rift between her and the other coaches.

"Adele Lambert, or should I say Adeline Léglise?"—Sylvia winked and Adele's stomach dropped—"I'd like you to meet Mr. Jonathan

Rutherford. He's a reporter and he's interested in interviewing you on television," she said, sounding excited, as if this were some sort of joke.

Adele felt the blood drain out of her face.

"Actually, we met many years ago," Jonathan said. "I used to be a sports reporter for *The Times*."

Adele couldn't believe what was happening. Just moments ago she'd foolishly allowed herself to feel something that resembled happiness, and now her world was tumbling in on itself.

"I have to go," she said, pushing the metal chair back from the little table and standing abruptly.

"Miss Léglise—I mean, Lambert, please . . ." the man pleaded, but she pushed past them, head down. She had to get out of there, away from them, as fast as possible. She rushed away, through the lobby of the club and out the front door. She shoved her racket into her basket, then stumbled as she tried to turn the bike around and mount it at the same time. As she peddled shakily out of the club parking lot, she saw Milly walking toward her.

"Adele," she called out, but Adele rode straight past her. "Adele, are we still on for twelve thirty?"

CHAPTER TWENTY-FIVE

MILLY

Milly walked into the club, confused, and saw her new tenant standing near the entrance with Sylvia.

"Hello, Mr. Rutherford," Milly said. "I see you've found the club. Do you play tennis?"

"No," he said. "Unfortunately not."

"Well, I'll be home later this afternoon if there's anything you need to make yourself more comfortable."

Sylvia gave Milly a strange look.

"Quite comfortable, thank you, Mrs. Kincaid," he said, tipping his hat to them both and walking out the way she came in.

"You know him?" Sylvia asked.

"He's my new tenant in the guest cottage. Do you?"

"I just met him yesterday. He wants to interview Adele."

"Adele?" Milly asked. "Why?"

Sylvia glanced around looking uncomfortable. "It's a long story. Do you have time for lunch?"

"I think so," she said. "I'm supposed to have a lesson, but Adele just sped off on her bike, all out of sorts."

They sat in the far corner of the restaurant out of earshot of other members, and Sylvia explained what she knew.

"I just can't believe it's her, and that she's been coaching me, of all people," Milly said. "I remember my mother and her friends used to talk about her. They didn't care much about tennis, but they loved her style and panache."

"I remember her too; she was such a star. It's incredible that she's been living here right under our noses like a hermit for all these years. I mean, when I first met her, I never for a second considered she might be Adeline Léglise. She was so strange and ignored everyone."

"She seemed quite distraught when she was leaving," Milly said. "I thought she was going to crash her bike right into me."

"Now I feel terrible about the whole thing," Sylvia said. "I really didn't mean to upset her."

Milly looked at her and raised her eyebrows.

"What?" Sylvia asked.

"You know she's a very private person. And she was so distraught when her picture was in the paper."

"All right, I got ahead of myself. I didn't think about what it would mean to her. The look of shock on her face when I introduced Mr. Rutherford to her—she looked terrified."

"What a slug, Rutherford. He lied to me, or at least he wasn't forthright about his research." Milly took a sip of her iced tea and swirled the ice cubes in the bottom of her glass. "Gosh, I hope she still keeps on with my lessons."

"Me too. I can't afford to lose her." Sylvia shook her head. "She's going to be so angry with me; I really betrayed her trust."

"I'm the one who's housing the guy who's after her. When she finds out he's staying one street over from her . . . phew, she'll be mad."

"We have to do something to make this right," Sylvia said. "Or her name could be splashed all over the national papers by morning. And if that happens, I won't be surprised if she leaves the island by the afternoon."

Milly went home in a state, and before setting foot in her house, she went straight up to the guest cottage and knocked hard.

"You have some nerve, Mr. Rutherford," she said, before he had a chance to greet her. He was wearing glasses now with a pen in his hand, and that somehow infuriated her more. He must be crafting his piece about Adele in Milly's very own cottage.

"Excuse me?" He seemed shocked by her outburst.

"You have a lot of nerve to come here and think you can use my cottage and my goodwill to expose my friend to who knows what."

"You know Adeline?" he asked.

"Of course I do," she snapped. "And I have a feeling you knew that too. You must have known she was coaching me."

"Look, I have tremendous respect for her, but a story's a story, and we're going to run it with or without her."

"She's not a story, she's a human being who deserves her privacy just like anyone else."

He put his hands up in defense. "I thought she'd want the chance to tell her side of the story."

"What's that even supposed to mean?"

He took a deep breath and let it out slowly. "You say she's your friend, but you clearly know nothing about her. That's doesn't sound like much of a friendship to me."

Milly was so angry she wanted to shove him. How dare he tell her what kind of friendships she had or didn't have? And yet, when she considered it, she was lying about so much of her life too. Were these even real friendships if they were all keeping so much from each other?

"If she doesn't agree to it," he went on, "maybe I could interview you about your experience with her, what she's like now."

"How dare you even ask that," she said. "I would never betray my friend's trust like that."

"Fine." He shook his head. "Fine. But you should talk to her," he said. "Let her know it would help her case if we heard the truth from her."

She studied him. What a weasel, she thought, feeling deeply regretful that she'd taken his rent money. "Fine," she said. "I'll speak to her. But don't expect much."

"I'd be so grateful," he said.

"I'm not doing it for you," she snipped. "I'm doing it for her."

"Right," he said, nodding. "Well, you know where to find me if she wants to talk."

CHAPTER TWENTY-SIX

ADELE

Adele couldn't eat, she felt so nauseated. She'd opened a bottle of Beaujolais and poured a glass, but she couldn't drink that either; she just held it in her hand like a prop as she paced. A knock on the front door almost sent the glass flying. What if it was Rutherford, with a photographer? What if they ran a picture of her, startled, wineglass in hand? They'll call her a drunk, a recluse, a lunatic.

She raced to the living room and peeled back the curtain just an inch to peek outside.

"Adele, it's Sylvia and Milly. We know you're in there. Please open up."

"We want to speak with you." It was Milly's voice now. "We want to help."

Help? How could they help anything? They'd likely brought this reporter in. It could all be a setup; maybe they'd known who she was all along and had planned the takedown. They'd buttered her up, connived to get her to teach at the club only to rip her to pieces.

"Adele, open the door," Sylvia said. "We don't want to cause a scene out here."

Adele stood behind the front door thinking. She didn't want to cause a scene either. That was the last thing she wanted. She opened the door a few inches and looked around.

"Adele," Sylvia said, "may we please come in?"

Adele moved out of their way, and they stepped into the living room.

"Well, congratulations," Adele said. "You figured it out. You figured out who I am, that I'm the person who ruined Margery Horn's life." She clapped her hands sarcastically.

"Rutherford came to us; we had no idea, honestly," Sylvia said. "But I should not have brought him to you the way I did. I should have asked you first if you wanted to meet him, but I didn't realize—"

"Well," Adele interrupted, "it's too late now. Because you brought that man to my place of work, I now will not be able to leave my house, I will not be able to work, and my life will become a repetitive, lonely hell all over again. The last twenty-plus years living under a shell was now all for nothing."

"He says he has a lot of respect for you," Milly said, though she could hear how pathetic that sounded when she said it out loud. "He claims he wants you to tell your side of the story."

"Of course he's saying that," Adele said. "He wants to get me in the chair and expose me for the monster that I am."

"Don't say that, Adele," Sylvia said. "You're no monster, we know that. You've clearly been punishing yourself for way too long."

"You don't know the whole story." Adele shook her head. "You have no idea what was really going on; you only know what the papers told you."

"It's true," Sylvia said. "I don't know, but I will listen anytime you want to talk. Look at what you're doing now; look at all these women who are currently taking lessons with you. You're giving them so much. You're changing their lives."

"You really are," Milly said. "But you don't have to do this interview. Just because he showed up and requested it doesn't mean you have to say yes."

"I don't need you to tell me what I should or should not say," Adele said coldly.

"OK," Milly said. "I know you're angry, Adele, but I need to tell you something else. And you're not going to be happy about this either."

"Great," Adele said.

"The journalist, Mr. Rutherford, he's staying in my guest cottage."

"What?" Adele raised her voice now. "Why would you let that *homme terrible* stay in your house?"

"Not in my house, in my guest cottage," Milly said. "It was so that I could pay for my lessons with you, if you want the truth. But I will send him on his way. I'll tell him he can't stay, if that's what you want me to do. Please believe me when I tell you, I didn't know who he was or why he was here."

"Well, now you do. And now that you know my big dirty secret, that I've been living a lie, then I suppose you can splash it all over town," Adele said, sneering.

"We would never do that," Milly said.

"We are your friends, Adele. Friends take care of each other." Sylvia stepped toward her. "And, besides, you're not the only one who has a big dirty secret."

Adele raised her eyebrows and waited for more.

"Can we sit?" Sylvia asked, and Adele begrudgingly gestured for them to sit on the sofa while she sat in the armchair across from them.

"As you both know by now, Walter and I have been having some money trouble."

Milly nodded. "You don't have to talk about this if you don't want to, Sylvia. You don't have to tell us anything, but if you do, I won't tell a soul, I promise you that." She looked to Adele for her agreement.

"Who am *I* going to tell?" she said.

"To be quite honest, I *want* to tell you. It affects you both and it's been eating me up inside, keeping such an enormous secret." Sylvia paused briefly. "Walter gambled away all of our money. All of it. He's been involved in these high-stakes poker games for years, but I thought it had stopped."

"No!" Milly said.

"I'm not exaggerating. Every last penny. That's why we sold the house, that's why we've moved in next door. We can barely afford to put dinner on the table. He's ruined us. It's absurd, really, that we're even trying to hang on to the club. We've got huge loans out on it, and if we can't make the payments, the bank will take it from us, foreclose, seizure—whatever it's called—along with all the money we've put into it so far. And if we lose this, we lose everything. That little shack we're staying in, they'll take that too."

"It's horrible," Adele said.

"My God, Sylvia, I'm so sorry. I had no idea it was so grave. Can't you sell the club?" Milly asked. "I know it's not what you want, and it's obviously not what we want, but at least you'd have something."

"I suggested that to Walter. We're friendly with John Wayne—"

"John Wayne?!" Milly said.

"Yes, you know Walter, he's friends with everyone. Apparently, he's been poking around showing interest in opening some kind of a club around here himself, but Walter says it wouldn't help. The club's too new, we don't have enough members yet to make it profitable, and it's not worth what the bank loaned us for it."

Adele snorted a laugh.

Sylvia stared. "You find this amusing?"

"*Je suis désolé*," Adele said. "I am sorry, I just always thought you were the richest family on this island."

"I did too," Sylvia said. "It's amazing how fast your luck can change."

Adele nodded. That part she could agree on.

"When I realized who you were, I selfishly thought of my dismal situation and the club and how an article or a documentary or whatever it is Rutherford wants to do might bring attention, and members, to our doors. I thought about how it might save us, get us back on our feet, how I might be able to shield my daughter Judith from this embarrassment and upheaval. But I should have thought of what it would mean to you, and I didn't. I'm sorry."

The three sat in silence for a moment. Adele briefly considered offering them a glass of the wine she'd opened before they showed up at her door, but decided against it. She felt bad for Sylvia and could imagine her shame, but she wasn't sure she wanted them to stay.

"I've been lying about the house," Sylvia continued, "telling you that we were looking at other properties, that staying in our little shack was temporary, that we wanted a change of scenery. I even lied to my own daughter. What a load of baloney. I'm shocked you believed it."

"I didn't." Milly gave Sylvia a kind smile.

"I didn't either," Adele said.

"To be honest, we all have our secrets," Milly said. Adele and Sylvia both turned to her.

"What's yours?" Adele asked. She'd always sensed that Milly was keeping something to herself. She might as well hear about it; after all, these women knew all her business now.

"Lloyd is leaving me," Milly said.

"What?" Sylvia gasped.

"I don't know exactly when or even why, though I suspect he's having an affair with that gorgeous actress Beverly Douglas. He's obsessed with her. He hasn't been home in almost two weeks, and when he has shown up, he's made it very clear that it's just for show, to keep up appearances and to protect the children. He wants nothing to do with me. He even wanted to sleep in the guest cottage, but I put a stop to that."

"Oh, Milly," Sylvia said. "You've been alone so much, but I thought whatever it was would blow over."

"It's serious." Milly felt a weight lifted off her shoulders. "But the tennis—maybe it's stupid—but it really made me come alive. I thought that if I could excel at tennis, really excel, and then show Lloyd what I could do, I thought I might impress him." She looked to Adele sheepishly. "I realize that probably sounds ridiculous to you, a tennis champion."

"It does not," Adele said.

"He sees me as the mother of his children and the person who delivers a hot meal to the table at night and a clean shirt to his closet. It's as if he's lost sight of who I really am, who he fell in love with. I wanted to do something to show him this new side of me, this fun, athletic, fit, maybe even sexy woman he's married to."

"You are sexy, darling," Sylvia said. "Any man who fails to see that is a fool, an absolute fool!"

Milly brushed away her comment. "Part of the reason I rented out my guest cottage for Bal Week was so that Lloyd couldn't move into it! That would be the final nail in the coffin, and then once I started earning a little money, I used that to pay for my lessons. It gave me some power back. That's why I agreed to let Mr. Rutherford stay, so I could keep on with tennis."

At this Adele took two wineglasses out of her buffet and poured them each a generous serving. They deserved it.

"To secrets," Adele said, holding up her glass.

"To secrets," Milly and Sylvia repeated, clinking their glasses with hers.

Adele spent the next few days alone, gardening in her yard in the morning hours, or staying inside the house, doors locked the rest of the time. She was grateful for a light drizzle of rain because she had a good excuse to cancel her lessons. She'd be losing out on her earnings, but that would be over as soon as the news came out about her, anyway.

She'd been making good money during those past few weeks of coaching, double what she'd made at the Fun Zone, and for fewer hours. More importantly, she'd been enjoying it. With all this time back on the court she'd even felt the itch to play again, just for fun. She'd have to find someone who could keep up, of course, and if that coach Robbie hadn't been such a jerk, she might have asked him, but that was a pipe dream now. There would be no coaching and no playing. Not unless she wanted to be watched, photographed, and shamed.

She didn't know how she was going to return to a life of seclusion, nothingness. Shockingly, she had begun to enjoy Milly's and Sylvia's company; she'd even enjoyed the other women, Joan and Sadie specifically. She'd looked forward to their lessons together. She hated to admit it to herself, but she even enjoyed hearing little tidbits about their lives, the funny things their children would say and do, the ridiculous amount of effort they put into making dinner, cleaning house, and looking good for their husbands. She'd found it humorous and sometimes even charming.

She stretched her body, feeling stiff without the brisk walks or bike rides to and from the club and without her constant movement on the courts. Adele realized now that she had pegged Sylvia all wrong, assuming she didn't have a care in the world with all that money. She'd heard the other women talk on the courts, of course—how could she not?—and she knew that something must be very wrong if they had to move into that dingy property next door. That place was only decent enough to hit a tennis ball against, but she just hadn't believed that something so devastating could happen to Sylvia, who'd always seemed invincible. She could imagine Sylvia's pain in trying to protect her daughter from her husband's mistakes. Adele's relationship with her own father had been so fraught, so complicated. If only he'd protected her instead of throwing her out to the wolves and putting so much pressure on her at such a young age.

And then her mind went to Milly, with two young children and an absent husband, and how she would be treated when he left her for good. People around here would distance themselves from her. No one liked a divorcée, especially if children were involved. It was like an illness that everyone was afraid of contracting. The fact that Milly was willing to send that reporter on his way and give back the money he'd paid for rent said something about her character. Maybe she'd underestimated both of these women.

Restless, she sat down on the armchair in her living room and flipped through the pages of *American Lawn Tennis*, but she'd already read it cover to cover. It always opened to the image of Althea Gibson. She stared at her picture. What would Althea do about Jonathan Rutherford if he continued to hang around? She saw Althea's smile and that look of determination in her eye, despite all the times she'd had the door slammed in her face, all the times she'd been turned away from a tournament and shunned or ridiculed because of the color of her skin. The thought of all Althea had fought for, and all that Adele had hidden from, made her cringe. She picked up her racket, laced up her shoes, and went out into the back alley to do the only thing that helped in situations like this, before remembering that the cottage next door was no longer vacant. She was forced, instead, to think.

CHAPTER TWENTY-SEVEN

MILLY

There was a gentle tap on the kitchen door, and Milly tensed, expecting it might be Rutherford asking if she had any news about Adele—which she didn't, and she wouldn't reveal it even if she did. It was warm and sunny this afternoon but had been raining on and off for two days, so Milly hadn't seen Adele for her lessons. The children were engrossed in a game of Chutes and Ladders with Leticia in the living room. She took a deep breath and opened the door.

"Wes," she whispered, barely able to speak.

He had no reason to be there anymore, no excuse of renting the guest cottage or looking out for his brother. She glanced out to the back alley to see if anyone was walking by.

"What are you doing here?"

"That's not the greeting I was hoping for," he said, joking.

"Sorry, I'm just surprised," she said quietly. "I didn't expect to see you again."

His eyes widened. "Ever?"

"Well, no," she said, stepping out and pulling the door closed behind her. She felt a shocking rush at the sight of him, but this wasn't the right place for that: There were neighbors, that reporter in her cottage, and her children all within earshot.

"Are you all right?" he asked.

"I just don't know where we can talk; I have a new tenant."

"I have something I want to show you. Can you get away for a little while?"

She popped her head back inside the kitchen and heard the children laughing. "*Tu turno, Leti*," she heard Debbie saying in Spanish. "*Tu turno.*"

"OK," Milly said, turning back to Wes, "but I can't be gone too long."

She went into the living room. "Kids, I have to run to the market and drop something off at the post office."

"Can I come, Mommy?" Jack said.

"No, sweetheart, stay with Leticia; it's almost your dinnertime."

"Not fair," Jack said, but he was immediately back in the game when Debbie told him it was his turn. Before she returned to the kitchen Milly stopped in the bathroom, smoothed her hair, and pinched her cheeks. She shook her head. *This is ridiculous*, she thought, slipping on her shoes in the hallway.

"Where are we going?" she asked.

"It's a short walk, maybe fifteen minutes," he said as they made their way up the alley toward North Bay Front. "Is that all right?"

"It's fine," Milly said.

They walked in silence for a brief moment, and their night together flashed through Milly's mind.

"So," she said, forcing herself to think about something different, "how's it been back in L.A.?"

"Good. I had my first exam on Monday. It was eight hours straight. I was exhausted."

"Eight hours? Good Lord! How did you do?"

He smiled. "I aced it."

"That's great, Wes, I'm so happy for you."

"One down, many, many more to go."

As they walked, the back of his hand lightly brushed hers and she looked up at him, catching her breath, as if he'd done something far more explicit.

"Sorry," he said, giving her a half smile that suggested he wasn't sorry at all. "I've missed you," he whispered.

"Wes," she said, looking around. "Not here." Then a moment later she said, "I've missed you too."

When they crossed the bridge off the island and turned left, she wondered if he was taking her to the club, and for a brief second she envisioned him swimming at the pool, her sitting on the edge, letting her feet hang in the water as he swam up to her, his shoulders glistening from the sunlight.

"Where are you taking me?" she asked.

"Almost there, I promise."

They passed the club and kept going, then turned down a pathway through a gravel parking lot, toward a marina. She followed him along a wooden boardwalk, passing yachts of all sizes, until they reached a turquoise wooden boat about thirty feet long with a white cabin.

"We're here," he said.

"What do you mean?"

"Come on," he said, climbing the ladder aboard and reaching back for her. "Take my hand."

"Are we allowed to do this?" she asked, confused.

"Yes," he said. "Trust me."

Once on board she walked around the deck and ran her hand around the rail.

"Do you like it?" he asked.

"Yes, it's beautiful," she said, opening the door to the cabin and peeking down the stairs to the lower deck.

"Good. Because I just bought it," he said. "I'm going to live on it while I do my residency."

"Live on it?"

"Live on it," he repeated.

"But your residency is in Los Angeles," she said, bewildered.

"Actually, it's here," he said. "It's at the new Hoag Hospital in Newport Beach."

None of it made any sense, and yet the idea of having him so close sent a thrill through her.

"But you're at UCLA. I assumed your residency would be there too."

He shrugged his shoulders.

"Why didn't you tell me?"

"You kind of left in a rush, remember?" he said and smiled. It made her blush to think of their last moments together, putting her clothes back on, him still shirtless on the sofa, then standing to zip up the back of her dress, almost as sensual as his taking it off. "The residency at Hoag was another reason to spend the week down here with my brother. I had some appointments lined up to see boats."

"Do you know anything about boats?" she asked, though she had a hundred other more important questions running through her head, along with a flood of emotions. She had really believed that she wouldn't see him again. She'd thought about it a lot and was convinced that he'd come into her life to unlock some part of her, to show her what she was missing, what she needed, but that was all. It had been crushingly disappointing to think that their time together was so brief, but over the past few days she had been forcing herself to accept it. He was a young doctor-to-be, a heartthrob for any gal, and she hardly expected him to look her up again. She couldn't understand what she could possibly have done for him. And jumbled up in her thoughts there was a rush of panic. He was here, he had come to her, and with him living here, so close to her, how would she ever have any restraint? If he found a new girlfriend and she had to ever see them together, it would be the end of her.

"I know a thing or two," he said smiling. "This, where you're standing, is the cockpit. It looks like it was set up to have a tiller here." He pointed to a small handlelike contraption on the floor. "But it has a helm"—he grabbed the wheel—"which I prefer." He took a few steps to the front of the boat and Milly followed. "This is my favorite spot." He lay down and put his hand behind his head. "You can do a little bow riding here, feel the breeze, feel the waves. And then the salon is downstairs."

He reached toward her, took her hands, and pulled her closer to him. "I can see the thoughts spinning through your beautiful mind," he said. "We have a little time, right?"

She nodded.

"Talk to me." Sitting on the bow, he leaned his back against the window, gesturing for her to sit beside him. The late-afternoon sun was a deep orange, reflecting off the still, glassy water and putting the most beautiful glow on his face. A seagull cawed in the sky above.

She sat down next to him but didn't know where to start. "I am happy to see you, so happy. Relieved, actually."

He took her hand in his, linking his fingers through hers, enclosing it in his other hand. "You have no idea," he said, his dark-brown eyes steady on hers. "I have not been able to stop thinking about you."

Milly felt her heartbeat race. She'd never felt this kind of longing, and it had been years since she'd felt seen, wanted. But even then, it was never like this. As he studied her, she couldn't help wondering what he saw in her. Jack and Debbie's mother? A lonely housewife? Or could he somehow see the woman trapped inside? She'd been thinking of him far too much since their night together, her yearning stretching out in all directions, but to know he thought of her too was shocking. She wanted to know more: *What* had he been thinking, specifically? But she also needed to calm her thoughts and racing heart, to be levelheaded, sensible, so she brought the conversation back to the present. "So you know your way around this thing, but tell me more," she said. "Why a boat?"

He laughed. "My dad used to take me out on his boat when I was little, and Luke too sometimes; it was kind of our thing. I used to love it. So peaceful, so calm. Just us, away from the distractions in his life, away from school, away from home. I looked after Luke a lot. Mom hated it when Dad drank; she'd lock herself in her room, away from him." He looked out to the other yachts moored in the marina. "Anyway, once he stated drinking more, he couldn't keep up with the maintenance. Boats are a lot of work, and it became too much for him, so he sold it. I was devastated when I found out. I always told myself I would buy one someday, reclaim the peace that it brought me as a kid. I've been saving for it ever since. I figure now's as good a time as any: I've got to find a place to live anyway, and I didn't think you'd let me stay in your guesthouse."

She laughed and shook her head. "Listen, Wes," she said turning toward him, "that night that we spent together, it was the most incredible night of my life. I will never be able to forget how you made me feel. I didn't even know that was possible, that kind of"—she blushed but forced herself to go on—"that kind of pleasure." Just saying the words seemed to raise her body temperature, and he ran his hand up her arm, but she stopped him. "But I'm still a married woman, I have children, it's complicated; you don't need complicated. You're young, you've got your whole life ahead of you."

"Milly," he said, his dark eyes searing into hers. "I don't expect anything from you. I know you have a life here, and I will not bother you. I just had to see you again."

"I'm glad," she said. "We didn't have enough time."

Milly forced herself to stand. As much as she needed him to understand that this could not go on, she couldn't bear the thought of this being the last time, and she didn't want to dwell on that in these moments they had together now. "You want to show me around?" she asked, opening the cabin door. He nodded and led her down the short ladder to a tiny kitchenette with two burners, a small built-in sofa and drop-down table, a washroom, and a full-size bed. His head was half an inch from touching the ceiling. "It's a small space for a tall, strapping man like you," she said. "Are you going to manage OK in here?"

"I'll be fine," he said. "I'll get a grill for the deck, but I'm going to be at work a lot. I'll be down here mostly to sleep."

"I don't know much about boats, but this one seems like a winner,"

Milly said, looking around at the navy-and-white-striped sofa cover and matching bedspread and pillows. "It's adorable."

Wes stepped toward her in the cramped space and took her face in his hands. "You're adorable," he said, pulling her to him.

"Wes," she whispered.

Just one small touch from him and it made her woozy. He moved his hand down her neck to her collarbone, tracing the line to her shoulder, examining her.

"God damn," he said. "You are so beautiful."

Just hearing his words, feeling his breath so close to her, she thought she might unravel all over again.

When he finally kissed her, running his hand down the side of her body, caressing the curve of her breast, she melted into him, craving his touch, wanting more, desperately needing him. "I can't," she whispered, kissing him again as if it might be the last time their lips touched. "I have to get back." But even as she said it, her heart pounding under his urgent touch, she knew she wasn't leaving, not yet.

Later, he stood on the slip and watched her leave. She'd stayed much longer than she'd planned, two hours longer, but she just couldn't pry herself away. After they made love once, he found new ways to make her stay. She could feel his eyes on her as she walked away, and she wished she didn't have to leave. She yearned to fall asleep in his arms, just one time, the gentle rocking of the water below them, but that was impossible; she needed to get back to the children, and she'd insisted she could walk home alone. On the way, she tried to imagine having him living so close to her. At first it worried her—how would she have any willpower?—but by the time she reached her house and walked past the guest cottage where that heated night had unfolded, she had begun to give herself permission.

I don't belong to Lloyd, she told herself. I don't have to be obedient and faithful to a man who wants nothing to do with me. Lloyd put me in this position: He's withheld attention from me for months, years even. He clearly has a lover. Why couldn't she see Wes? She rationalized the crazy, reckless thoughts racing through her mind. Why shouldn't she be happy? She deserved to be happy, to be desired. She deserved to feel something real.

She opened the back door to the kitchen realizing she had no grocery bags to show for herself, and Leticia rushed into the kitchen.

"*Ah, gracias a Dios*," she said.

"Is everything OK?" Milly asked.

"*Es Jack. Está triste*," she touched her face as if to show tears. "*Es el padre*."

"His father?" Milly began to panic. "Where?" She touched her face and smoothed her hair back, wondering if her lips, swollen and raw from so much urgency, would give her away.

"*Ya se fue*." She pointed out the front door.

"*Se fue?*" Milly repeated, not understanding.

Leticia placed her hands on an imaginary steering wheel and acted out Lloyd driving away.

"He left?" she asked. "He came here and then he left?"

"Yes, *sí*," Leticia said.

"Did he see me?" she asked frantically. "Did he see me leave with the . . . my friend?"

Leticia looked at her blankly.

"Did he see me? Did he ask about me?" But it was no use. "Oh God. Is Jack awake?" Milly asked.

"*Jack está triste*," Leticia repeated.

When Milly opened Jack's door he was whimpering and Debbie was curled up in his bed next to him. "What happened, my loves?" she asked, sitting on the side of his bed, brushing his hair off his damp, red face. "Did Daddy come to visit?" Jack took a deep breath, but it came out shaky, as if he were trying not to cry. "Oh, Jack, love."

"I want Daddy," he said, tears streaming down his cheeks no matter how hard he tried to keep them in.

Milly picked him up from his bed and wrapped his arms and legs around her, holding him tight. "I know, sweetheart, I know you do." Then she pulled Debbie in too.

"What did he . . . ?" She didn't want to interrogate the children but she needed to know what he knew, if he'd seen her leave the house with Wes, if, God forbid, he'd followed her to the marina. "Did he have to get back to work?"

"He said he was waiting for you, but then it got late and he said he had to return to the studio," Debbie said, surprisingly calm. "I asked when he'll be coming home again, and he said he doesn't know." Jack, still squeezing Milly tightly, took several more staggered breaths. "Why can't he stay?" he asked.

How could she respond? "Well, I'm not sure exactly, but he must have a very important assignment, because I know he would much rather be with you right now than doing whatever silly work he has to do."

Jack rested his head on his mother's shoulder, and she rocked him the way she had as a baby. She felt him trying to catch his breath, and then she felt it get easier, peaceful, and she slowed to a sway.

Once the crying stopped and his breathing calmed, Milly lay Jack down and smoothed his cheek until he fell asleep. She tucked Debbie into her own bed and read a few chapters of one of her Polly and the Wolf books until she too began to give in to sleep. She kissed her forehead and went downstairs to see Leticia off.

Finally, alone in the living room, she felt wretched. Everything she'd told herself as she walked home from the boat, everything she relived now—giving in to Wes, all of it—suddenly made her spin. How could she be so selfish, putting her needs and desires before her children's? She had one job, and that was to protect them. They needed their father, and they needed their mother to love their father, to fight for him, to do whatever it took to bring him home, not to be off in the guest cottage or on a secret boat making love with another man. She felt dizzy with the realization, disgusted with herself for indulging in a salacious affair while her son was left at home, crying to the nanny. Milly put her hand to her mouth, horrified at her actions. *I have to get him back*, she told herself. *I have to bring Lloyd home for good.*

CHAPTER TWENTY-EIGHT

MILLY

As soon as the children were in school the next morning, Milly got in the car and drove to Hollywood. It had felt strange as she'd dressed for Lloyd that morning. She'd styled her hair for him, applied her makeup for him. She wore the pastel-pink cap-sleeved dress he'd bought for her birthday several years ago, back when he'd had enough room in his heart and in his mind to go to the dressmaker and select the fabric and style. She hoped it would remind him that he used to care.

On the drive, she tried to come up with what she would say when she saw him and how she would respond if he'd seen her leave with Wes, but she couldn't find the words. She was sure something would come to her when they were face-to-face. There would be no upset, no arguing. He had had his break from them; maybe that was what he'd needed. He had made his mistakes, and she had certainly made hers, but now it was time to reunite and for him to come back to them. She would force everything else out of her head: She would not allow herself to dwell on whom Lloyd may or may not have been with, and she would not allow herself to relive any of her own stolen moments with Wes.

When she finally pulled into the studio parking lot, her palms were clammy. She felt nauseated. Whether it was fear that he'd be angry that she'd shown up at his place of work without warning, fear that he'd reject her again, or guilt for what she'd done, she had to get beyond all that.

She announced herself to the receptionist at the front desk and waited while the girl ran her manicured nail down row after row of names in a blue binder.

"What did you say his name was again?"

Milly smiled. "Lloyd Kincaid."

"Hmmm," she said, picking up her telephone and putting it to her ear. "I don't see his name. But I'm new here. Hold on a second." She dialed a number, then spoke into the receiver. "Hi, Lauralee, it's Missy at the front desk. I've got a Mrs. Kincaid here looking for a Mr. Lloyd Kincaid." There was a pause, and a concerned look came over her face. The girl glanced uncertainly at Milly. "Oh, I see. All right. I'll let her know." She hung up the phone. "You can take a seat; someone will be right down to see you."

"Thanks," Milly said, feeling uneasy.

She sat in one of the hard, upright gray seats and looked out the window, trying to calm her nerves. Why must she be nervous, embarrassed even, about seeing her husband? This was silly. But there was something about the way that girl looked at her. After what felt like fifteen minutes, Lloyd's secretary walked over to Milly.

"Hi, Lauralee," Milly said, standing. She'd only met her a couple of times, but she'd spoken to her on the phone frequently, and she suddenly felt a little foolish showing up like this unannounced; he could be in a meeting or on set. She should have at least called ahead and spoken to Lauralee, even if she'd told her it was to be a surprise.

As Milly watched her walk toward her in her fitted two-piece suit, her full curves just tempting those pearl buttons to spring open and reveal what was underneath, she had a terrible thought that maybe she'd been wrong about the actress all along; maybe it was Lauralee who was stealing her husband's affection.

"Hi, Mrs. Kincaid," she said, her perfectly plump lips drawing it out longer than necessary. "Lovely to see you. What brings you by the studio?"

Milly stood a little taller and cleared her throat. "I'm here to see my husband."

"Um . . ." Lauralee took a few steps toward the window, away from the receptionist, and Milly followed. "Mr. Kincaid hasn't worked here for almost two weeks," she said in a low voice, making eye contact with Milly as if to be sure she heard her.

"I'm sorry, what did you say?"

"He doesn't work here anymore," she said. "I'm sorry, Mrs. Kincaid." She looked very concerned. "I have an address," she said, "for mail, but I don't have any other information. I'm so sorry." She held out a folded piece of paper. Milly stared at it, speechless, then at Lauralee, and then at the receptionist, who quickly looked away as if she hadn't been listening to every word they'd said. Milly took the paper, folded it again, opened her pocketbook, and slipped it inside.

"Well, thank you for letting me know," she said, with as much composure as she could manage, and walked briskly to her car.

She pulled up outside a white apartment complex with an orange sign that read THE LOCO and sat in her car, unable to peel her hands from the steering wheel. She looked out her window to the building and saw through its facade—a recent fresh coat of paint to tart up a tired and worn-down structure. She couldn't believe he was living here. And yet everything started to make sense now. He'd been too ashamed to admit that he'd lost his job; that was why he hadn't come home, that was why he'd been pushing her away. And she, dear God—her stomach clenched—she had responded by falling into the arms of another man, a young medical student. What kind of woman did this? The father of her children was struggling, and she had taken a lover. If only he'd told her sooner, she would have understood.

Eventually she got out of the car and took the concrete stairs to the second level. She stood at the door to 2B, the number scribbled on the piece of paper, and heard the sound of a television on inside. She waited, feeling as if she were not actually there, as if she were watching someone else, as her hand lifted to knock at the orange door.

The TV turned off. She heard footsteps, an unbolting of the door, and then Lloyd stood before her, unshaven in his flannel pajamas and a wrinkled T-shirt.

"Milly," he said. It was almost noon, and the look of shock on his face made her want to cry. "What . . ." He ran his hands through his hair and wiped the stubble on his chin and cheeks. "What are you doing here?"

All those words that Milly thought would come to her when she saw him, all those persuasive and loving things she thought would innately flow from her, convincing him what a terrible, terrible mistake he'd made—they didn't come. She just stared at him.

"I went to your work," she said finally, her mouth dry.

He shoved his hands deep into the pockets of his pajamas and rounded his shoulders, making himself smaller. "I see," he said. Then he asked, "Where are the kids?" as if he suddenly remembered that he had them.

"They're at school. Leticia is picking them up and staying with them until I get home. They were so upset that you came to the house yesterday but couldn't stay," she said, waiting for him to question her about her whereabouts, but he didn't.

She looked past him to a relatively bare apartment—just a sofa and a coffee table, on it a milk carton, a cereal box, and a half-filled bowl.

"Do you want to come in?" he asked, following her gaze. "It's a bit of a mess."

"No," she said. She hadn't known what to expect. She had half expected to walk in on him and another woman, but seeing him like this, scruffy and ragged, she knew there was no woman there.

"Please, Milly," he said, "we should talk." He walked back into the apartment, picked up the milk and cereal from the table, and took them to the kitchenette. He picked up a shirt strewn over the back of a chair and threw it in a closet, then pulled sheets off the sofa, where he must have been sleeping. "I wanted to talk yesterday but you weren't there."

She didn't respond. Instead she took a step into the single space and looked around, bewildered. He'd rather live like this than be with her?

"Lloyd," she swallowed hard. "What's going on?"

He looked at her, then unfolded a metal seat from the corner, turned it around, and sat down, motioning for her to take the sofa. Reluctantly, she sat on the very edge.

"Milly, I um . . ."

She waited patiently for him to go on.

"I lost my job. I was fired, actually." He looked at the ground, as if he were unable to meet her eyes.

"Why?" she asked quietly. And when he didn't answer: "Why didn't you tell me?"

He shook his head, still looking down at the ground.

"Lloyd, we're your family," she said, persisting.

"I couldn't," he said, barely loud enough for her to hear. "I was . . ." He paused. He was having trouble getting the words out. "I was ashamed."

Milly didn't know what to do or how to feel. She wanted to go to him, put her arms around him, tell him everything was going to be all right, but how could everything be all right after what she'd done? And she had the distinct feeling that whatever he would tell her next was going to split her heart in two. She needed to brace herself.

"I had an affair," he said, his eyes still glued to the ground. "And the studio found out."

There it was. The words she had been expecting to hear, and yet somehow they didn't break her the way she thought they would. It was almost a relief to know that she hadn't made it all up in her head, and that she wasn't the only one who'd faltered. The confession hadn't changed anything. They were just words, words familiar to her because they'd been floating around in her head for weeks. She just hadn't known if it was something he'd ever actually admit to. It hadn't shocked her to her core, because she'd already known it to be true, and she'd cemented his cracks in loyalty with her own. She'd had an affair too. She realized as she sat in front of him now how fundamentally broken things were between them.

When he finally looked up at her, Milly's eyes met his blankly.

"I had an affair Milly," he said, louder this time, as if disappointed at her lack of reaction.

"I heard you," she said.

And then he leaned forward, resting his elbows on his knees and meeting Milly's eyes with pleading intensity. "I had an affair with a man."

CHAPTER TWENTY-NINE

SYLVIA

Sylvia lit the candles on the dining table, stood back, and surveyed the spread. It was a far cry from the sturdy walnut table that sat fourteen in her last dining room. At the old house this table sat in the corner of her patio—but at the new house it was the only thing that would fit. With the sage-green tablecloth, her floral china, matching napkins folded and perched atop the plates, and a few small vases with wildflowers from her overgrown yard placed in the center, it looked quaint and cozy. She opened the wine, placed three glasses next to their table settings, and brought the salmon spread and crackers to the table. She'd leave the chicken salad casserole and green beans in the kitchen until they were ready to eat, she thought, realizing she was actually a little nervous.

She hadn't cooked a full meal, unassisted, for years, maybe not ever. She was so used to having Maria by her side doing most of the work and all of the cleanup, she just hoped she hadn't messed this up. It was important to her that Milly and especially Adele, if she came, felt that she'd put forth her best efforts to try to make amends.

Milly arrived first, looking pale and windswept, as if she hadn't had a chance to fix her hair and had quickly pulled it into a loose bun instead.

"It beautiful, and it already has your touch," Milly said as she walked through the tiny living room, looking around. "Warm and inviting."

"I'm getting used to it," Sylvia said. "But it feels cramped. None of us want to be in the same room with each other, and there's nowhere to escape to."

"You've still got the club, those big open tennis courts," Milly said.

"For now." Sylvia walked to the back of the house. "Can I pour you a drink?"

"Yes! I could use a stiff one," Milly said.

"I have gin."

"Perfect."

Sylvia poured a tall gin and tonic and sliced a lemon. This she had plenty of practice in; it was the dinner she was worried about.

When Adele knocked, Milly answered and brought her back to the dining room.

"I'm so glad you came," Sylvia said, walking over to give her a hug. Adele tensed in her arms.

"I'm not a hugger," Adele said, standing stiffly.

"I know, but I am," Sylvia said, "so get used to it."

Adele handed Sylvia a small bouquet of roses, their stems beautifully wrapped in paper and dusty-pink ribbon. "From my garden," she said.

"They're gorgeous." Sylvia took them from her, surprised by the gesture. She inhaled their sweet scent and placed them in a vase on the table.

"Your front yard needs some work," Adele said. "It's a wilderness."

Sylvia suppressed a smile. Classic Adele. "Maybe you can give me some gardening tips," she said.

Adele shrugged. "Start by pulling up all the weeds and plant some roses."

"I'll do that," Sylvia said, laughing. "Cocktail or wine?"

"Wine, thank you."

"So, Sylvia," Milly said as she took a seat at the table, "how are things with you and Walter? Any improvement?"

Sylvia shook her head. "Honestly, I can barely look at him. I'm still so sick—about the money, the house, but also that he's made it impossible to save the club. And he had no excuse for missing his part in the Bathing Beauty Contest. I don't know if I'll ever be able to let all of this go."

"You have to," Milly said emphatically.

Sylvia looked up, surprised.

"He messed up, but he's a good man, Sylvia, and he loves you so much—anyone can see that. And you love him."

"I know," Sylvia said, though she barely believed herself when she said it. How could he love her and be so reckless with her life? How could he be so stupid?

"He made a huge mistake, there's no getting around that; he shouldn't have done it, but marriage isn't about being perfect. If you really love each other, which you two do, it's obvious to anyone who's been around you both, then it's about growing together and lifting each other up when you fall and when you fail, and becoming more than you could ever be alone."

"How can we be more together? There is no more. He's taken everything from us."

"That's just money," Milly said.

"Money and a house and our self-respect, our livelihood."

Milly reached over and put her hand on Sylvia's. "What you two have is worth so much more than that."

Sylvia nodded and took a sip of her wine. "I suppose," she said.

They were quiet for a moment, possibly the longest Sylvia had stayed quiet ever, but she was trying to absorb all that Milly was saying. Milly was a good friend, but she was usually a listener more than anything, not one to push so hard for something she believed in.

"What do you think, Adele?" Milly asked.

Adele shrugged. "I am not one to give advice on relationships. I have never been married. But I would think if you can find it in yourself to forgive him, then you should forgive him, for your sake as much as his."

"I know you're both right, but I'm having a hard time getting to that point." Sylvia said, sighing. "Anyway, enough about me. Has Lloyd shown his face yet?"

Milly sighed. "I've seen him, but not here. I went to Los Angeles to find him."

"You did?" Sylvia said, shocked. "What did he have to say for himself? Good God, don't tell me you caught him red-handed. Was he with that actress?"

"No." Milly shook her head and looked down at her hands in her lap. "No, but it was awful. He lost his job. He was fired, and he couldn't bring himself to tell me. He was so ashamed."

"So there was no affair after all?" Adele asked.

Milly shook her head again. "If only it were that simple." Milly kept her eyes down, as if thinking how much to share, but weren't they beyond that by now?

"What do you mean?" Sylvia persisted. "Milly, either he is or he isn't," she pressed, but Milly shook her head.

"He is having an affair, or he was, I don't know, it's just not with the person I thought it was."

"Oh, Milly. I'm sorry," Sylvia said. "What a mess. All three of us. We're a disaster."

Milly took a long drink of her gin and tonic.

"What are you going to do?"

"I don't know. I have two young children. I don't have a job. I can't support us. And what would people think? We'd be the disgrace of the island. I suppose I have to accept the fact that I'll spend my days with a man who doesn't love me, who can't love me," she said, "ever." She knocked back the rest of her drink.

"Well," Adele said after a while, "I've been thinking about the reporter."

"And?" Milly asked.

"And I realize now, it's not your fault, either of you; you didn't know who I really was or why I was keeping my past a secret. I was wrong to blame you when he came snooping around."

"We really didn't know," Milly said.

"I should have recognized you," Sylvia said, "but I just didn't put two and two together."

"That was my plan, to not be recognized," Adele said. "And it worked. It was just a matter of time until someone figured it out."

"Have you spoken to him?" Milly asked. "Mr. Rutherford. Has he bothered you? I made it very clear to him that he should not disturb you."

"If he knocked, I didn't answer," Adele said. "I have barely been outside, and I have not opened my door."

"I can attest to that," Sylvia said. "I began to wonder if you were alive in there."

Adele shrugged. "Yes, well, it's why I came today. I cannot play dead forever. I've done that for too long."

"So what happens next?" Milly said when Sylvia brought out the next course. "I know I already said it, but I'll make him leave the guest cottage; just say the word and he'll be gone."

Adele shook her head. "No, let him stay, let him pay you rent a little longer. If he doesn't stay with you, he'll just find someone else to put him up. Hopefully he'll get bored and go home eventually."

"Just let us know what we can do to help," Milly said. "We're in this together now." She took a bite of the chicken casserole. "This is delicious, Sylvia."

"Is it really?" Sylvia beamed. "I had to call Maria three times today to make sure I was doing it right," she said, laughing. "Good Lord, I miss having her around."

There was a noise at the back of the house, and they all looked up.

"Is that Judith?" Milly asked.

"No, she's staying at her friend's house tonight. I wasn't expecting Walter home for dinner, either." She got up and pushed in her chair, mildly annoyed. "Walter? Is that you?" He'd said he'd eat at the club with Hank, their accountant, and she thought she'd have more time with Milly and Adele. They couldn't talk freely with him around, and there was no space for privacy in this house. "Walter?" she called again.

No answer. Maybe he hadn't heard her. *Please don't let him be drunk*, she thought, hurrying toward the back door. "Why are you—"

She stopped and gasped.

Walter was stooped over, leaning on the counter holding his ribs, his white shirt covered with blood. "My God," she cried, rushing to him.

When he looked up, his face was almost unrecognizable. One eye was swollen shut and blood was covering his mouth, chin, and clothes. Walter moaned and allowed Sylvia to put his arm around her shoulder and steer him to a chair. "What happened to you?" she asked after he slumped into a chair at the kitchen table, Milly and Adele now joining them.

"Oh my God," Milly said, hands over her mouth.

Sylvia imagined possible scenarios—a car accident, a bar fight—but in the pit of her stomach she knew it was something to do with the men he'd paid off. "Walter, please, tell me what happened."

Adele had already grabbed a kitchen towel and drenched it with water, rung it out, and handed it to Sylvia, who dabbed at the blood on his face. He winced and pulled away. "This is bad, Walter," she said, breathless. "I need to call Doc."

"No." He shook his head. "It's too late," he managed. "Don't." Doc lived in the next town over and was nearing his seventies. He'd retired years ago but was still who they called in a medical emergency. He lifted his head and took one look at Milly and Adele. "I don't want people to know," he managed to say, but he looked so terrible that Sylvia didn't know how to help him. Just seeing his face made her lightheaded. She reached for the counter to steady herself.

Milly brought a chair to Sylvia and poured them both a glass of water.

"You need stitches," Adele said, taking over. "Bones could be broken. you need a doctor, or your face will stay like this, *hideuse*."

"I don't care about my face," Walter mumbled sorrowfully. He turned to Sylvia. "I care about you and Judith." He looked from his wife to Milly and Adele, then back to Sylvia.

"Don't worry about them," Sylvia assured him. "They know everything; they won't say a word."

"I still owe them interest," Walter said. "I paid them what I *owed*, but they're still insisting on getting their lousy ten percent for each day I was late." He took a few short breaths, holding his ribs.

"They're still charging interest?"

"I told them it was bullshit. I told them to get lost!"

"Oh, Walter," Sylvia said, shaking her head. "I'm so sorry." He'd done this to them, ruined them financially, but she'd made sure he knew she hadn't forgiven him. She'd been so intolerant, she'd put so much pressure on him to fix it. She'd let her immense disappointment in him be known, as well as her rage over selling the house and moving to this one. If she hadn't been so obstinate, if she'd given him even a glimmer of hope that she might someday be willing to forgive him, that they might be able to move on with their lives, he might have simply paid the interest he owed and been done with it. Instead, he'd tried to hold on to what little money they had left. And they'd come after him. "I'm sorry, Walter, I'm so, so sorry."

She dabbed at his mouth and chin to wipe away the blood so she could see what injuries lay beneath, then she carefully unbuttoned his shirt. His chest and stomach were bruised and bloody, and he winced when she tried to move the hand that clutched his ribs.

Adele poured him a shot of whiskey from the bar, and he sipped it, sucking in air when it touched his split lip, but he gulped the rest down anyway.

"I know someone who might be able to help," Milly said, stepping forward. "A doctor—well, a doctor-in-training, but I'm sure he can help. He lives nearby, and he'll be discreet."

Sylvia gave her a puzzled look but there was no time to explain. Walter had set his glass down and was now slouched over the table as if he might pass out. He gave an almost imperceptible nod.

“I’ll go now,” Milly said.

Sylvia nodded. “Thank you.”

When Milly returned to the kitchen with a handsome and vaguely familiar young man by her side, Sylvia was surprised: Wasn’t he one of the college kids who’d stayed in Milly’s guest cottage during Bal Week?

“This is Wes,” Milly said, avoiding Sylvia’s eyes. “He’s completed medical school at UCLA and is going to be working at Hoag Hospital just up the road.”

“I’m happy to help,” Wes said. “I haven’t completed my residency yet but I have basic supplies.”

“Thank you, Wes,” Sylvia said. “We appreciate whatever help you can give him.”

“OK,” he said, “let me take a look.”

Within thirty minutes Wes had examined him, sutured him with three stitches above the right eye, and cleaned and dressed the wounds.

“Do you have anything in the house for pain?” he asked.

“We have a few leftover Percodan pills in the medicine chest.”

“That would help,” he said. “You’ve got at least two broken ribs,” he said, “but it seems they’re nondisplaced fractures.”

“What does that mean?” Sylvia asked.

“They don’t appear to have moved out of place or splintered, which could have caused a laceration of the lungs or kidneys, so you’re lucky in that regard. They should heal at home. There’s not much else you can do for them except take the pain medication to ease the discomfort, but switch to aspirin after tomorrow. Percodan is pretty strong stuff.” He started to pack up his things. “It’s going to be painful to take deep breaths for a while. Try not to cough—that will hurt.” He checked the stitches on his face. “I’ll stop by in a couple of days to change the dressings and check on these stitches. In the meantime, try to get some rest and drink plenty of fluids.”

"Thank you," Walter said.

"You're welcome." Wes stood and picked up his bag.

"We won't forget your kindness," Sylvia said. "Really, we are so grateful that Milly asked you to come."

"Anytime," he said, and Sylvia watched him look back to Milly, nod, and head out the door. She didn't know why Milly had stayed in touch with that young man, or how she even knew how to find him, but there was something between them; innocent or not, there was definitely something.

After Milly and Adele left, Sylvia slowly, very slowly, managed to get Walter from the kitchen to the bedroom, where he winced and groaned until he was lying flat on his back in their bed. When he was finally there, he lay with his eyes closed, as if it had taken every part of him to get that far. Seeing him like this, disfigured and swollen, made her want to cry. She knew every millimeter of that face; she'd known it and loved it for eighteen years. Every expression, every subtle movement of the eyebrow or tightening of the jaw, she could read. Lately, in their crisis, she'd read telltale signs of stress on his face too, but mostly, at least before their money troubles, he was happy, always smiling, always laughing. And their friends, neighbors—everybody—respected him, loved him, valued him for all he did for the island.

You made a mistake, Sylvia thought as she sat watching him on the edge of the bed, *a huge, stupid mistake—and it changed everything for all of us.*

But Milly was right. When you marry someone, you vow to spend the rest of your life with them, and there are going to be mistakes and missteps. There are going to be some wrong turns, some bad decisions, and she needed to decide, right now, what she could forgive and if there was a chance for them to find their way again. She had to let her anger go. She had to believe he wouldn't make the same mistake again. She had to revive the trust that she'd put in him for so long. She had to love him.

"Walter?" she said in a whisper, placing her hand gently on his arm.

"Mmm," he murmured, though she wasn't sure if he was awake or just stirring.

"Walter, pay them the money, please; just give them what they want."

Walter took great pains to reach over and take Sylvia's hand in his.

"They could have killed you, Walt. And I"—she brushed a tear away—"I cannot live this life without you. I love you. Just pay them the money."

She had never once imagined leaving here. Their life was on Balboa Island, they had built it together, planned for their future here, developed so many friendships, but, she realized now, as she looked at him, bruised and beaten, that he was her life, Walter and Judith. She lay down next to him.

"I know I have to hand it over," Walter said, his voice faint and hoarse. "I'm worried what they'll do if I don't, but it's going to empty us out. We'll definitely lose the club. I'm already behind on loan payments. If we don't make the next one, the bank will repossess it and we'll lose it all."

"We don't need it, Walter," she whispered. "None of it matters. As long as we are together, you, me, and Judith, that's everything, and that's all I care about."

Walter looked over to her and a tear fell down his cheek. "I've failed you," he said.

"You made a mistake," she said. "None of us can be expected to walk through this life unscathed. But honestly, Walter, I failed you too."

"How could you even think that?"

"Because I let you do all this alone—provide for our family, worry about money—it led you to do this, to take a chance with our money. I wish I'd let you know you could come to me, talk to me. Maybe I could have helped, but you should never have carried this burden alone, and for that I'm sorry."

"I didn't let you in."

"Let me in, Walter, please. In the future let me try to help, let me be part of building our new life together."

"I don't know what that's going to look like once I pay them," he said. "The bank will take this house from us too. They'll want to recover whatever losses they can."

"I'll call on family in Barstow. I'll call my mother and see if we can stay there until we sort things out," Sylvia said.

"You haven't seen your mother since your grandmother died."

"Now's as good a time as ever," Sylvia said, forcing a smile.

"I love you, Lamb Chop," he said, squeezing her hand.

"I love you too," she said, and she meant it.

CHAPTER THIRTY

MILLY

Lloyd called early on Sunday and announced that he'd be returning home that afternoon. He insisted that Milly not go to any trouble making dinner, but she was immediately filled with panic. She busied herself by cleaning and tidying the house, bathing the children, and baking a cake, but it didn't stop the constant loop of questions and confusion running through her head. How could they return to normal after he'd dropped this bomb on her? How could they ever live as husband and wife again?

When he'd confessed his affair, with a man, in Los Angeles, Milly had stood up and stormed out of his apartment, running down the stairs, catching her dress on the rough concrete step, and ripping it free until she got into the safety of her car.

A man, she'd screamed into her steering wheel. He'd been having an affair with a man? Handsome, charming Lloyd, who'd proposed to her, who'd asked for her father's blessing, who'd impregnated her twice—he was having sexual relations with a man? She felt not only betrayed but utterly dejected and horrified. Had she driven him to this, or was this always his disposition? And if he was always this way, why had he taken a wife? Why had he wanted children? She pictured him kissing a suit-clad, blank-faced man and began to sob. In her mind the man looked in stature and style exactly like Lloyd, two Lloyds in love with each other, and she pounded her fists on the steering wheel.

After fifteen minutes, twenty, maybe even more, her breath had begun to slow and she was able to think again. She had wiped her eyes dry and put on her sunglasses. She couldn't leave, not yet. She feared that if she did, she might never see her husband again.

She returned to Lloyd's apartment, door still ajar as she'd left it, Lloyd still sitting on the chair. His eyes were red and puffy like hers.

"Tell me everything," she said quietly as she sat back down on the couch. "I might not understand it, but I will try."

And he did, to the best of his ability.

"He was an actor that we had on contract; you wouldn't know him," he said.

"Are you in love with him?"

"Does it matter?" he asked.

"To me it does," Milly said.

"Yes, I think so, but I don't know. It's all so confusing. I love you, Milly, I do. You have to believe me."

Milly shook her head and looked away.

"I do love you, Milly, but not in the way you hoped I would. I am horribly ashamed of what I've done and of how I feel, but the truth is, I've felt this way my whole life."

"Then why did you marry me?" Milly said loudly now, standing.

Lloyd got up to close the apartment door.

"I thought I was doing the right thing. I didn't know how else to survive. I'm so sorry."

"The right thing? For who? You used me. You stole my youth. I didn't finish college because of you. You used me up and spit me out."

"You deserve better and I'm sorry. I will make it up to you, I promise."

"How?" Milly asked, incredulous. How could he possibly make this up to her?

"I've got to get out of here. The studio, they found out and fired me instantly. It's a crime, Milly. They're terrified of being put on a list, and so am I. McCarthy's put the fear of God into all of them, the politicians too."

"McCarthy's over," Milly argued. "He lost his influence two years ago with those army hearings. Him and his Red Scare—it's finished; everyone knows that."

"OK, the hunt for Communists may be over, yes. But the fear he put into the public about homosexuals—easy to blackmail into turning against their government—that's stuck."

"He's just a drunk now, Lloyd, a laughing stock."

"I'm telling you, Milly, it's not about him anymore; it's about what he sprinkled, convincingly, in the public consciousness. Men at work don't go out for a drink in pairs anymore. They'll be suspected. They only go out in groups. Haven't you heard Dirksen calling homosexuals 'lavender lads'? He and his pals want to purge politics, government, Hollywood. . . . They say the 'lads' have secrets and can't be trusted. It's real, Milly."

Milly had heard about it, but she'd never paid it much attention. Now it was all she could think of. What would happen if Lloyd were reported? What if the studio had already turned him in? What would that mean for Milly and the children? She shuddered to think of how her children would be ostracized if the truth came out now.

As she relived the conversation, waiting for his return to their family home, she vacuumed faster, dusted more frantically. Every time he'd touched her must have been an act, a forced gesture. Everything inside her felt as if she were being squeezed, crushed, with the realization that anytime he'd held her hand, kissed her, or worse—when he'd made love to her—he was simply doing his duty. It was never what his heart had desired. She was never what his heart had desired.

At noon his car pulled up, and Milly was so anxious about seeing him she thought she might vomit.

"Where are my little monsters?" he called out as he walked through the door, and the children went crazy, running wild as Lloyd pretended he was going to eat them for lunch. After the initial excitement had calmed down, Jack didn't leave his side, playing next to his feet as he sat on the sofa, or curling up next to him.

That afternoon he suggested they go to the club, and she was sure it was either to make his presence known and seen or that he didn't want to be alone with her in the house. Since she felt the same way, she agreed. They walked in together, Lloyd all smiles. It was as if she hadn't visited him in Los Angeles just a few days earlier, as if he hadn't admitted that their whole marriage was a farce. For a moment she wondered, had she somehow made that up, dreamt it, hallucinated? But no, it was seared into her mind. Lloyd opening the door unshaven and unkempt, his head in his hands as he told her his truth. She couldn't have made that up. Her imagination didn't even have the capacity for that.

The children splashed in the pool while Milly and Lloyd sat poolside and ordered lunch, she a Cobb salad, he a Reuben sandwich.

"So," Lloyd said to Milly after the waitress brought them drinks and a bread basket with soft dinner rolls and salted butter. "Have you been liking it here? Have the kids been swimming much?"

"Yes, they like it" she said, unable to believe they could have polite conversation about daily goings-on. It felt so hollow. Maybe he'd always resorted to that. And yet, what else could they do? "And I've been taking tennis lessons," she added, glad to have something real to tell him.

"Really?" Lloyd said. "You—tennis?"

"Don't sound so surprised."

"I never thought of you as a sporty kind of gal," he said.

She wanted to come back with some snide remark, that he clearly never thought of her at all, or that all he ever thought of her was as a prop to conceal his dishonest ways, but she stopped herself.

"Well, as I said, I've been taking lessons, from our neighbor Adele, on the next street actually; she works here."

"A lady coach?" Lloyd asked.

"Yes, it's quite astonishing what a woman is capable of these days." She couldn't help herself.

"Hey, Milly," he leaned in and took her hands. She resisted the impulse to pull them away. "I know you're angry with me. But can we talk?"

She nodded, though it was the last thing she wanted to do. What could he possibly say that would change this? Everything she'd ever known was a lie, and she had merely been a ploy, a facade for him so he could live his deceitful life while appearing to be the perfect family man. It made her sick to think she'd been so naive, so stupid, playing house for a man who never would be, never could be, attracted to her. She picked up her iced tea and took a gulp, feeling nauseated but desperate for something to do with her hands other than be held by his.

"I've been offered a job," he said.

"A job?" Milly said flatly. She was glad he would be employed again—they had a mortgage to pay and children to feed and clothe—but it was hard to gather up much excitement or enthusiasm for him.

"It's in New York."

She stared at him.

"I know, it's a long way from home but it's a good job, a promotion, increase in salary. They're offering a nice signing-on bonus." He lowered his voice. "And they don't appear to know anything about the scandal."

The scandal? That's what he was going to call it? New York? She could hardly follow what he was saying.

"It would be a fresh start, away from all of this. It would be a clean slate, as a family."

She was dumbfounded. Speechless. How could they possibly have a fresh start? He was in love with a man, not her, not his wife. And no, she didn't want to go to New York. She didn't want to start all over just for him to start this up all over again with someone new, some man on the East Coast! She was furious that he would suggest such a thing, and yet, in her anger, she felt the acute sense of powerlessness, as if she were falling backward into the deep end of the turquoise pool with nothing to hold on to, nothing to reach out and grab. This was happening to her whether she wanted it or not. What choice did she have? He was the father of her children; he was her husband. He was the breadwinner. She didn't have money of her own to pay for this house, this life. And even if she did, she had her children to think of.

"Mommy, Daddy," Jack called out, his floatation belt wrapped around him. "Watch me!" He jumped off the side of the pool, curling himself into a ball as he leapt and splashing water everywhere.

"Cannonball!" Lloyd called out.

"Daddy, watch me again," Jack said, swimming back to the side of the pool and climbing out. Lloyd clapped his hands as Jack repeated the maneuver.

"Look, it's a lot to think about, I know," he said, leaning back into his chair as if he belonged here, as if he hadn't left them for several weeks to fend for themselves, as if he could just slip right back into their lives, as if nothing had changed.

"Why can't you just get a job at a new studio in L.A.?" she asked, though she knew the answer. He looked at her as if she should know better.

"I'm in a tough spot, Milly; I think you know that." He leaned in again and lowered his voice. "Once word spreads, I'm not going to be able to set foot in Hollywood again."

She looked out to her children playing happily in the pool. Their innocence overwhelmed her. She wished they could stay that way, blissfully naive. She closed her eyes and allowed her mind to drift to Wes, the ease of it all, his warm embrace, the way he wanted her. She wished she could get lost in all of him.

"I have to go," she said, standing suddenly.

"What are you talking about, Milly?"

"I need to get some air," she said, grabbing her purse.

"We're sitting outside."

"I need space to think," she said. "When the kids are ready, you can bring them home. I'll walk." She pushed in her chair and walked away.

It took everything in her power not to walk straight to the marina.

Wes felt like an escape, a powerful magnet pulling her toward him. Feeling claustrophobic and trapped by her marriage, she had trouble catching her breath. Wes would ease her mind, soothe her, temporarily take away her pain, but he couldn't fix anything, not really. She had to deal with her real life in front of her, to think of her children. So she put one foot in front of the other, and she slowly walked back home to start on dinner.

CHAPTER THIRTY-ONE

SYLVIA

Sylvia walked hand in hand with Walter into the club. They had an end date now: May 9, 1956. One month to either make their late mortgage payment on the club or the bank would repossess it. Now that Walter had handed over the last of the money he owed for interest on the gambling debt, there was no way they would make it. They had thirty days to shut things down with as much dignity as they could muster. Sylvia insisted on working alongside Walter; no more solo missions, she'd told him. From here on out they would together tackle the challenges that came their way. She volunteered for the hideous job of letting all the staff know, one by one, that their jobs would be ending.

As she walked through the hallway, past the restaurant and ballroom, she wished they could have had more time. She had so many ideas that she'd planned to share with Walter. Weddings, for one, could have been a big draw. She could have handled that part of the business—working with the brides and their mothers to arrange the décor and menu, bringing in local florists and bakeries. It could have been a profitable venture for both the club and the local business owners. They could have done Easter brunches and Christmas dinners. Her mind flooded with possibilities now that the possibilities were gone. She squeezed Walter's hand and kept her chin up as they made their way toward his office.

"I can have a desk set up for you over here," Walter said, pointing to an open corner in his office. "Or we can find you your own space, if you'd prefer."

"With you is perfect," she said, thinking it would be easier if they could talk through all the arrangements that needed to be made in private.

He provided her a list of all their employees, their schedules, and salaries, and since it wasn't a huge staff, she planned to explain that the club would be closing to each person individually. Next, he gave her a stack of invoices for suppliers to call. She'd let them know they would no longer be needing their products and services.

"Walt," she said, "what happens to all the money we collected for memberships?" She thought of all her friends and acquaintances she'd encouraged to join, and Milly, whose hand was shaking when she'd handed over the check for the entire year.

Walter sighed. "We don't have the money to pay it back, so it depends what the bank does with the club. If they keep it as a club, then the members, I would think, would keep their memberships. But if they shut it down, sell it, knock it down and build some houses here instead, then there's nothing we can do."

Sylvia put her head in her hands and groaned.

"I'm sorry," Walter said quietly.

Sylvia forced herself to stand, walk over to Walter, and kiss him on his head. "We'll get through this," she said.

By noon she was weighed down with sadness and went outside to stretch her legs and take a breather.

As she walked past the pool and admired the turquoise water sparkling in the midday sun, she thought about the letter she'd sent her mother earlier in the week, letting her know that they were considering a move inland to the desert, possibly to Barstow, and asking if she had any recommendations on where to stay until they got settled. She knew it would come as a surprise to receive a letter in early April; after all, they usually only sent each other Christmas cards once a year with a brief "Merry Christmas, Hope you are all well" kind of greeting, but she couldn't bring herself to tell her mother about their misfortune or to ask, flat out, for a place to stay. She didn't have addresses for her half-siblings; in fact, she had no idea where they lived or how they lived their lives. She had never wanted to be part of a family that hadn't wanted her, and now, she thought, she didn't want to look desperate, but she did need to provide some kind of stability for Judith until they found their way out of this mess, and that desire rose above her pride.

She wandered over to the courts, past Robbie rallying back and forth with one of his regulars, and on to the back court where Adele was teaching a group of four women. Sylvia pulled up a chair and watched her in her element, feeding the ball, then calling out instructions on how her students should respond. She noted the satisfaction in Adele's face when her guidance resulted in a point or a win, and Sylvia hated that she was going to be taking this away from her, both the place to coach and the community of women she was building around her.

"Looking good out there, ladies," Sylvia said as the class ended, and the women filed off the court.

After they left, she approached Adele.

"Hey there," she said.

"*Bonjour*," Adele said, taking a drink of water.

"I wanted you to be the first to know," Sylvia said, "we have a date now. The bank's going to take the keys from us in one month. I just wanted you to have time to find something, somewhere else, maybe, to coach."

"There's nowhere else that will take me, but it's all right," Adele said. "I know how much you love it here and I'm sorry it's come down to this. But I have an end date too."

Sylvia studied her friend. "What do you mean?"

"I've decided to do the stupid interview with Rutherford and get him out of everyone's hair. Now that he's found me, he's going to do the piece with or without me; I know how these journalists work. I might as well have a say in it. But you know as well as I do that once I do and everyone knows who I really am, I'll be shunned. No one will want to train with me."

"Not necessarily," Sylvia said. "The women love their lessons with you. Look what you've given them."

"Maybe so, but it doesn't matter," Adele said. "I've seen scandals play out before. It's bad for people's reputations to be any part of it. And it was a scandal. You don't know the whole story, but I ruined a young woman's life. Margery Horn was a skilled athlete who would have gone far if it weren't for my jealousy, my fear of losing. I did a terrible, terrible thing, and I went from being a beloved tennis star to the most hated woman in Europe and even the United States."

"Well, you're loved around here; I hope you know that," Sylvia said.

Adele gave a slight nod and put her racket in her bag. "Thank you," she said. "Not just for saying that. For the chance to coach here. Rutherford was going to find me one way or another, but it was nice to have all this back, even if just for a few weeks. Even if it's all going away and if everything else is falling apart—it has been nice to feel the way I felt, to immerse myself in the thing I love most, for a little while. And I have you to thank for that, for giving me a chance."

Sylvia put her arm around Adele's shoulder and pulled her toward her. "That's not a hug," Sylvia said. "That's just a squeeze."

Adele rolled her eyes and smiled. "Would you come with me to the interview?" she asked. "I'm sure it will be a whole production with all the television equipment and people fussing around. It would mean a lot if you and Milly could be there when he rips me to shreds for all the world to see."

"Of course," Sylvia said. "And we would never let him humiliate you on live television."

"Well, you might not have a say, but at least you could be waiting with a whiskey on hand."

"That I can do," Sylvia said as she linked her arm in Adele's and they walked off the court.

CHAPTER THIRTY-TWO

ADELE

One week later, Adele sat down in one of the armchairs in her living room across from Jonathan Rutherford. A huge light box shone down on her from its spindly metal legs, and a large camera faced her and Jonathan from the back of the room. Wires and clunky equipment were everywhere, and it was hot as hell.

"Can we open a window?" she asked.

"Sorry, ma'am," a young man in a charcoal suit replied as he adjusted the two large microphones. "We can't risk picking up any outside noise."

"*Mon Dieu*," Adele mumbled under her breath, dabbing at her forehead, which caused the young makeup woman to rush forward with a powder puff. "Can we just get this over with?" Adele added impatiently.

"We're about to get started," Jonathan said, setting an unlit cigarette and a box of matches on the table next to him.

"You can't smoke in here," Adele told him. "It's too hot, and I can't stand the smell."

"A French woman who doesn't smoke?" he said. "You used to be known for always having a cigarette in your hand after your matches."

"I quit years ago."

"All right," he replied, handing them to one of the camera crew. "I usually light one as a prop, but I don't have to."

"Good." She eyed him. She'd tried to prepare for the interview, for every imaginable invasive and personal question he might ask, but she had no idea how much he knew about that awful day.

There were far too many people crammed into her tiny living room. Sylvia and Milly had been relegated to the kitchen out of view, but they could still hear what was going on, and just having them there was a comfort. Adele rubbed her hands together and realized her palms were sweating. The director announced something to get everyone's attention, then called out, "And we're on in five, four, three, two . . ." and he mouthed "one."

"Good evening, and welcome to *Lives & Stories*," Jonathan said, sounding like a different version of himself. "I'm Jonathan Rutherford, and tonight it is my absolute pleasure to bring you one of the most famous, and infamous, female tennis players of our time, a woman who revolutionized women's tennis and wowed us with her speed, her power strokes, her elegance, and balletic moves on the court from Paris to New York, to London, to California, and beyond. She became possibly as well-known for her fashion choices as she was for her prodigious talent in tennis. She has been out of the public eye for more than twenty years, following an altercation with her fellow tennis champion Margery Horn, which turned her biggest fans against her. On air tonight to tell her story in her own words, for the first time since 1932, please welcome the one and only Adeline Léglise."

The camera turned to Adele and she stared, momentarily stunned, at the bright light. Realizing she should respond, she looked back to Jonathan. "It's Adele," she said. "I go by Adele now."

"Of course," he said. "We are filming live today from Adele's home in sunny Southern California, some six thousand miles from where she grew up in the South of France. Now, Miss Léglise, you were a champion, a star. You won eight Grand Slam titles in singles and twenty-one titles altogether. You were a four-time World Hard Court Champion, and you won Wimbledon in singles six times. You were arguably the best female tennis player in the world. Would you agree?"

"*Oui*," she said. "If I'd been given the chance to compete against the men, you'd likely say I was the best tennis player in the world, *la fin*."

Jonathan laughed. "It's possible," he said. "It's very, very possible. You were on top of the tennis world and then on one Saturday in July 1932, things went terribly wrong. Can you take us back through the events of that fateful day?"

Adele took a deep breath. She'd hoped perhaps he would ease into this—first ask questions about her career or how she began to play tennis in the first place—before diving headfirst into her worst nightmare. But she knew what made news. They wanted viewers, and they wanted them right away. She braced herself as the events of that day flashed through her mind.

She had walked to the baseline and was already sweating. She hated herself for what she'd done. She knew she could win without cheating, without drugging her opponent's drink. Now, Margery could trip and fall, she could be pounded by a ball if she didn't move fast enough. When the powder kicked in, Margery would likely have to default the match. Adele could get caught and her career would be over, but there was no turning back. The damage had been done.

A Wimbledon official tossed the coin. Margery was to serve first, but Adele couldn't stop thinking, wondering, if it had taken effect. Frozen with fear, she faltered, stepping too late to return Margery's serve as it aced her, shaking her resolve. Margery took her own service and broke Adele's to take a 2–love lead.

"*Idiote*," Adele cursed herself. "*Tu es une idiote stupide.*"

The pounding in her chest was thunderous. When Adele looked up to her father, his face was beet red and he stood, motioning with his hands so firmly and dramatically that she thought he might hit the people next to him. She squinted to make out what he was saying but, as if in a nightmare, she couldn't. He was yelling but the pulsating in her ears was louder. Her opponent was bouncing on her toes eagerly awaiting Adele's serve in the third game. Why wasn't she getting tired? Why wasn't the crushed pill working? She had regretted it at first, but now with her own inner agony and her father screaming from the sidelines, she wanted it to do its job, make Margery drowsy, make her slow. Make her lose.

When Adele lost the first set, unable to control herself, she approached the net and screamed at Margery, then she turned her attention to her father, who was now courtside.

"*Que fais-tu?*" he screeched. "You have no energy, you have no focus; you play as if you've never picked up a racket," he snarled in a rage. "What is wrong with you? Where is your power, your drive? Watching you is an embarrassment. And to think the king of England is here, watching this pathetic spectacle." Spit fired from his mouth as he hurled insults at her. *"Qu'est-ce qui ne va pas chez toi?"*

Adele looked down at the ground, holding back tears. She was ashamed, humiliated; reporters were everywhere, watching. She knew she could play better than this, but the panic, the thumping in her chest, the fear of losing and facing her father afterward was paralyzing.

Her confidence shattered, Adele lost the first game in the second set. She never suffered losses like this. She had to do something to turn it around. She didn't dare look up to the stands to see the disappointment in her father's face again, so she began to yell at the umpire in his tall wooden chair.

"That was a bad call," she shouted, pointing to her last ball, which had landed just outside the white line. "It was in." It had been close, possibly in, but more likely out, but Adele didn't know what else to do. The umpire gave her a warning, and when Adele looked up to her father for guidance, he was gone. She looked around the stands to see if he was there, pacing—she knew this was as stressful for him as it was for her—but he was nowhere to be found, and her mother, who looked so small and insignificant sitting there alone, had turned her face away from the court, as if she couldn't bear to watch.

Margery took a step toward the umpire's chair to defend the call that Adele's ball was out, but the sight of this woman, about to beat her, exhilarated and on her feet despite the crushed pill, only terrified and enraged Adele further.

"It was in; it was clearly in," Adele screamed, throwing her racket with all the power she could muster toward the spot where her ball had hit the court. But by now Margery was inexplicably charging toward the umpire, equally passionate in her defense, and at that very moment the racket spun upward and hit her in the face, hard. There was a yelp as Margery cupped her hands over her left eye and collapsed to the ground.

"*Mon Dieu*," Adele gasped, hurrying toward her. There was blood trickling though Margery's fingers.

"Get away from me," Margery cried out. "You're a monster!"

"Adele?" Rutherford's voice jolted her out of her thoughts. "Adele, can you tell us about that day?" She looked up at him and caught his concerned expression. She wondered how long she'd been sitting there, eyes closed, reliving it all. Had it been seconds, minutes, longer?

She nodded. "Yes." Her throat was suddenly dry. As she reached for her water and gulped down a few sips, she realized what a heavy weight she'd been carrying on her shoulders for so long, a secret that only she could know. She realized now how she desperately wanted to be free from it. She looked up at Rutherford.

"I regret that day deeply," she began. "If you are interested in the truth, then I will give you the whole truth," Adele said.

Rutherford nodded eagerly. He wanted viewers, he wanted ratings. Fine, she thought, she'd give him what he so desperately wanted.

"The truth is, I drugged her."

There was a gasp. Adele didn't know if it had come from Rutherford or one of the camera crew or from her friends in the kitchen, but she couldn't stop now and she didn't want to. The words poured out of her. She explained everything that had happened before the match, including the crumbled pieces of a sleeping pill that she had sprinkled into Margery's drink.

"It was a stupid, childish thing to do, and I've wanted to tell that truth and to apologize to Margery, for many, many years now, but I've been too cowardly to do it, hiding away from the world instead."

"My goodness." Rutherford looked shocked, but Adele forced herself to continue on relentlessly. "The thing that the press got wrong," Adele said, "was that I did not intentionally throw my racket at that woman. That was an accident. I was angry, yes, I was furious, I was confused; I wanted the pill to affect her. That's a hideous thing to say, but in that moment, I was so obsessed with winning, I threw that racket, yes, I admit that. But I did not throw it *at* her. It ricocheted off the court and hit her eye. I did a terrible thing that day, but I never, never intended to do that."

When she finally took a breath, she saw the disturbed look on his face. There, he had it, the full truth. The papers would go wild after this.

"Well, I have to say, you've rather astonished me and likely our audience, Miss Léglise. I had no idea."

Adele looked away, not sure what to make of the feelings swirling around inside of her. Was that relief she felt, to finally get the truth out, or was that dread and fear of how everyone would now react?

She took a deep breath and hardened her face, preparing herself for Rutherford to demolish her on television.

"I was there that day," he said, and Adele tilted her head in confusion. "I didn't know about the sleeping pill—I don't think anyone did—but I witnessed the incident just as you describe it. I tried to speak with you at the end of the match, but you were too distraught. I saw up close everything that happened, and I saw your frustration and rage. But I can attest that you did not throw your racket toward Margery; I saw you direct it toward the line where you asserted the ball was in—"

"It wasn't in." She cut him off. "That was another act of desperation."

"But you didn't intentionally hurt her with your racket. I know that, and I think every other journalist on the court that day saw that too; they just chose not to report it. You have your regrets, but my regret,"

Jonathan said, and he looked at her sincerely now, "is that I didn't fight hard enough to tell the truth about that. I wrote the story the way I saw it, but my editor didn't want that story; he wanted the villain and the good-girl story, the sensationalized version, the story that sparked a fire, that caused the greatest public outrage. I was just a junior reporter, and I wrote what he wanted in the end, but I should have fought harder to print the truth, and for that I'm truly sorry."

Adele tried to absorb this information. She couldn't quite believe it. Had he really been there? Was he too using this moment to assuage his guilt?

"How can you defend what I did, after what I just told you?" Adele said.

"If I had succeeded in getting an interview with you that day," he went on, "and not just writing what was expected of me, maybe you would have told me what was really going on. I had been following your career for several months, and I noticed you had a fraught relationship with your father."

She tried to arrange an expression of neutrality on her face, but she felt the camera zooming into her and realized she was too late.

"He was strict. Yes." she said, sitting upright.

"If I may, he was more than strict; he was abusive," Jonathan said. "I noticed the way he spoke to you. He berated you in public, at tournaments, and humiliated you. You were a child when you started to compete. Most would say that he was cruel in his treatment of you. Would you agree with that statement?"

She shook her head; she couldn't have her father's name tarnished on television like this. "You need to understand," Adele said, "he was very gifted, but his life had not provided the opportunities he gave me. My father needed me to win. He could be cruel because he himself was crushed anytime that I let him down. As a child, I could see that winning made him happier, but it never lasted." Adele paused and looked down at the floor, flooded by memories that threatened to consume her. "Both as a child and then a young woman who knew nothing about the real world outside of tennis, except what he taught me, I knew I had to do better, always, that I always had to win, above all else, or I would lose my father."

Adele stared past Jonathan to the framed photograph of her father and her that hung on the wall behind him, and a tear rolled down her cheek.

"Adele," Jonathan said, "did he demand too much? Was he responsible for your downfall?"

She wiped away the tear, then forced her eyes back to his and shrugged. "I don't know," she said quietly. "You would have had to ask him, but he died soon after that day."

When the match was over, officials and Margery's family and coach had rushed to the court along with the press. As reporters were shooed away from Margery, they turned to Adele, harassing her with questions.

"What happened today? Why were you so angry? What happened to your game? Why did you strike her?"

They closed in on her, and Adele had to push them away, feeling the breathlessness and panic rise up in her. She looked around for her father, or even her mother, to help her out of the situation, but they didn't come.

"I didn't mean to," Adele had whispered. *"C'était un accident."*

She watched as they carried Margery off the court, limp and fatigued. With the energy and excitement of the match behind her, replaced instead with pain and disappointment, her body must have finally given in to the powder. Adele wanted to shrink into herself, to disappear into the darkness that was enveloping her, to never be seen again.

A young reporter came to her side. "Adeline," he said, "are you all right?"

She looked at him, but everything was going blurry. She needed her father, she needed *him* to ask her that very question. She pushed past the reporter.

"Adeline." He jogged to keep up with her. He pressed a piece of paper into her hand. "I'm with *The Times*. Please contact me when things calm down." But she threw the paper back at him and ran off the court, alone.

Adele looked up at Rutherford. "You were there that day. I remember you now."

He nodded.

Adele was stripped of her previous years' Wimbledon titles and shunned by the public for her horrific display of poor sportsmanship. Margery suffered an eye injury that took months to heal, and though she did eventually return to tennis, she never won another championship. It was a media frenzy; the papers went after Adele, calling her La Bête, La Reine Vicieuse, Le Monstre. She couldn't go out in public without being harassed and hounded. Her parents retreated to their home in Nice, and Adele got as far away from it all as she could. She left London, couldn't bear to return to her beloved France for fear of adding to her parents' humiliation, so she went to America to hide until she could figure out what to do next. She wrote letter after letter to her father, begging forgiveness for her outburst and for wasting all those years he'd spent training her when she'd just thrown it all away. She wrote to her mother, asking her to try to explain her feelings of regret to her father, but none of her letters could fully express her guilt and shame; nothing seemed sufficient, so she didn't send a single one. Instead, she let them pile up on her bedside table. Three months later she read in the national paper that her father, "Beloved coach and father of disgraced former tennis champion Adeline Léglise," had died of a heart attack.

Adele was sure she had caused his death. And when her mother didn't call or write to share the news or ask her to come to the funeral, she was convinced that she blamed her too. She stayed in the quiet, almost desolate town she found on Balboa Island, and she used the last of her money to buy a small, cheap house where she wouldn't bother anyone else, and they, hopefully wouldn't bother her.

"I tried to reach your mother before this interview, yesterday, actually," Rutherford said. "I was able to get in touch with her caretaker in Nice, but as you likely know, your mother is quite ill and was not available for a comment."

"You spoke to my mother?" she asked, but it came out in a whisper.

"Only her caretaker," he said.

At this Adele stood abruptly. "Cut," she said, glaring at the cameraman. There was some commotion among the staff behind the lights; someone rolled their hands in circles, someone else encouraged her to sit down.

"We're still live," Jonathan said calmly, "but we will pause for a word from our sponsor in just a few moments."

Adele obliged and sat back down. She was angry and wanted to know more. What had the caretaker said? How long had her mother been sick? She could have inquired about her mother's health and whereabouts at any point over the past twenty-four years, and her mother could have inquired about hers, but neither had. Now hearing this unexpected news made her desperate.

"What would you say to your father today, Adele, if you had the chance?"

The question rolled around in her mind for what felt like several long minutes, but no one urged her to respond faster, and she hoped it might be her imagination. She could say that her father broke her, that he had ruined her, that he had crushed her spirit. She stared at Jonathan for a moment longer and then said, "I'd tell him I forgive him."

At the ad break for Lucky Strike, she marched over to Jonathan.

"Why didn't you tell me you'd been in touch with my mother?" she asked.

"I apologize," Jonathan said. "I'm not allowed to discuss the questions or topics of conversation prior to the on-screen interview," he said. "But I can give you her address and phone once we're done."

"I don't need that. If I wanted to contact her, I would have done it myself," she said, "at any point over the past twenty years or so."

"Why didn't you?" he asked softly, but she only glared at him, then rushed outside, away from all the cameras, away from all the lights, the heat, and the questions. She was pacing when Milly and Sylvia found her.

"My God," Milly said. "You've been through so much; I had no idea."

"I couldn't keep it in any longer," Adele said. "The guilt, the disgrace, I just had to get it out."

"You did the right thing," Sylvia said, handing her a glass of whiskey, as promised. Adele knocked it back.

"You could have told us," Milly said. "I hope you know that we would never judge you."

"She's right, Adele," Sylvia said. "You've been living with that secret for way too long. You don't have to do this alone anymore; you've got us now." She looked to Milly, who nodded emphatically. "Whatever happens, we're here for you. You'll never have to hide out again."

Adele nodded and tears began to form in her eyes. She looked up to the sky, willing them to disappear. She didn't cry. She never cried, but this was the kindest thing anyone had ever said to her.

"*Merci*," she whispered.

When Adele went back inside, the makeup gal started powdering Adele's face, applying more rouge, a touch more lipstick. Adele waved her away.

"Are you ready to resume?" Jonathan asked. "I'm sorry I caught you off guard. This is an exceptional interview."

"Fine," she said. "I just want it to be over."

"And we're rolling in five, four, three, two . . ." The director mouthed "one" again, and the small green light on the camera appeared.

"We're back with Adele Lambert, formerly known as Adeline Léglise." He turned to her. "Adele, I'm sure our viewers would like to know: Do you still play tennis?"

"No," she said abruptly, but Rutherford tilted his head. She forgot, briefly, that he'd first approached her at the club. "I coach at a local tennis club, all women." She looked to the back of the room where Sylvia and Milly now stood pressed against the kitchen door, and she wondered for a moment if she should say which club. Sylvia might be grateful for the publicity, though maybe not the kind of publicity that Adele would bring after this interview. Then she thought of the letters she'd received from former fans after the incident, letters filled with hatred. She recalled how despised she became and how difficult it was to bear the collective loathing—not just from her beloved France, but the world. All that would resume after this, she was sure of it.

"Have you ever considered a rematch?" he asked.

Adele looked up and almost laughed. "A rematch?"

"Yes, with Margery."

"Don't be absurd," she said. "I haven't played an actual match in more than two decades."

"Margery has said several times in interviews over the years that she would play you again. You didn't know that?"

"I don't read the gossip papers," she sneered.

"Now that you do know, would you consider a rematch? In London or France or New York?"

"Absolutely not," she said.

"All right, then," Jonathan said. "Let's move on to a less-heated topic." He laughed tightly. The production crew began to air film clips of Adele in her golden years, showing some of her shots, some of her wins, her signature leaps across the court. As she watched, she thought not about the good old days, when she was winning, because in truth, even when she was on top, she had been miserable most of the time, desperate to impress, desperate not to disappoint. Instead, she thought about her new friends. When she was at the top of her game, she hadn't had friends—there wasn't time—and she'd had only acquaintances since. For this brief moment, when the camera wasn't focused on her, she considered how Sylvia and Milly had changed everything for her. Meeting them had ended more than twenty years of hibernation, brought her out of her loneliness, and welcomed her into life again. She had pushed them away when Jonathan Rutherford showed up; she had blamed them for his intrusion, when it wasn't their fault. In many ways, getting this burden off her chest, finally coming out from the shadows, no matter how harsh the reception might be, was a relief. It was finally going to be over, and she was glad she no longer had to hide or lie about who she really was. She had Milly and Sylvia to thank for that, for everything, really.

"I'll do it," she blurted out while the footage was still running.

"What's that?" Johnathon asked, motioning with his hand for the cameraman to cut to Adele.

"I said I'll do it. You say Margery Horn would be willing to play a rematch. If she's still interested after hearing what I confessed to today, then I'll play her."

"My goodness," he said.

"But it has to be here."

Jonathan glanced to his cameraman, then back to Adele, looking somewhat shocked and slightly confused, though it seemed he was trying hard not to show it.

"It has to be here in Newport Beach, at The Island Club," Adele said. "That's the only place I'll play, and it would have to be soon, in two weeks." She reached out of the camera's view for her daybook.

Jonathan's jaw dropped.

"How about Saturday, May fifth, two and a half weeks from now, to give time for organizing." Adele looked back to Sylvia, who looked startled, eyes wide, but she didn't shake her head no or motion for her to change course. Adele then looked directly at the camera. "Margery, if you are watching, and if you would still like to play, it would be my honor."

"Well . . ." Jonathan seemed genuinely shocked and thrilled and maybe even a little giddy. "Well, in that case, I'm going to take the liberty of saying that we, the network, would provide Margery a plane ticket to California for that date, if she can travel by then. And we would be glad to televise the event."

"*Bien*," Adele said, feeling a little giddy herself, and also quite nauseated at the thought of what she'd just done. "*Très bien.* It is a date."

CHAPTER THIRTY-THREE

SYLVIA

As soon as the lights turned off, Sylvia rushed to Adele. "What have you done?" she asked, panicked. "You do realize we are shutting the club down! It's being repossessed by the bank mere days after you just proposed, on national television, that we will be hosting a televised tennis tournament."

"I know it is a crazy idea, and I would have asked you first, but I couldn't," Adele said. "But if this works, maybe, just maybe, I could help you save the club."

A rush of trepidation and excitement surged through Sylvia's veins, but she tried not to get ahead of herself; she wasn't even sure if this was possible. "We are not going to be set up for this kind of thing. We won't have a staff or food or beverages. I've just canceled all of our vendors."

"We have more than two weeks to arrange everything," Adele said calmly.

"And seating. And who's going to pay for all this? We don't have extra money floating around."

"I'm going to set up a meeting for tomorrow morning with everyone—Rutherford and his staff, you, Walter. . . ."

"Me." Milly rushed over to join them. "I want to help however I can."

"Walter's not going to like this," Sylvia said. "It's been stressful enough."

"What if we can raise enough money to keep the club running?" Adele said.

"And if we can't?" Sylvia asked.

"Well, then this can be your last hurrah," Adele said. *"La grande finale."*

Sylvia closed her eyes and took a deep breath. "Let's say we can raise enough money to put on the tournament. How do we then make enough money to save the club?"

"Ticket sales, of course, but more importantly, there will be prize money, a purse, mostly coming from sponsorships, and they can be significant; winner takes eighty percent and loser takes twenty percent."

"So you're saying if you win, you'd put that money into the club?" Sylvia asked.

"Yes. We'd have to discuss the terms, but, yes, I could invest," Adele said. "It's not unheard of."

Milly clasped her hands and squealed. "I think it's a brilliant idea."

"Yes," Sylvia agreed. "That would be incredible."

"You have done a lot for me," Adele said. "Both of you. You have given me my life back. Having the opportunity to coach you and the women at the club has made me realize what I've been missing. It's made me face my biggest fears. If I can help you now, I will. It's a long shot, but let's at least try."

Sylvia was right: Walter was not thrilled about Adele's impulsive announcement.

"This would have been a grand opportunity three months ago, six months ago," he said as they sat down for dinner at their small dining table. "I would have jumped for joy at this opportunity, Lamb Chop, you know I would. But we are not in a position to put on this kind of grand spectacle now. We're about to hand over the keys." He reached over and took her hands in his. "I'm sorry. We just need to let this go."

She nodded, taking in all that he said. Sylvia's mother had called her after receiving her letter and said they could stay with her and her husband for a week in Barstow. While the thought of it made Sylvia want to curl into a little ball and hide, she was glad that they had a plan and a place to go once all this was over and they handed the keys to the bank. Walter had told her it would only be a matter of time before the bank came after the little cottage too, and Sylvia didn't want Judith to go through a second round of humiliation. At least now they were not going to be left scrambling, and she needed that security; she needed it for Judith. But this little glimmer of hope that Adele had set into motion, it felt like a lifeline. She had a feeling, a tingling in the pit of her stomach, that they could do this. She wasn't ready to give up this fight, not yet.

"Walt, you promised me that we were going to do things together from now on. We are the only club I know of that has a female champion coaching tennis. After that interview, Adele is going to be all over the newspapers."

"She admitted to drugging a woman!" he said.

"But she didn't have to. She was forthright and vulnerable. I think women will admire her honesty and strength, I really do."

Walter seemed to consider that.

"This is the kind of publicity we could never have even dreamed of," Sylvia continued. "People are already talking; imagine how many women might become interested in joining the club after this."

"Not if there's no club to join," he said.

"Adele thinks there's potential to raise a lot of money with this one event. She's done these kinds of tournaments before; she knows what to do."

Walter shook his head and sighed. "I've never seen you like this before," he said. "I see the glint in your eye. You have a feeling about this."

"I do, Walt, I really do." She ran her fingers along the top of his hand and down the side of his pinky finger, the one that had been broken and had healed at a slightly imperfect angle. "It's our last chance to keep the club and stay on the island."

"I just want you to be realistic. Even if we can pull this off, it's highly unlikely that we'll raise enough money to save the club. Adele said herself that she doesn't even play matches anymore. Playing is very different from coaching. The chances of her winning are slim."

"I know," she said. It was an almost impossible feat, but she wanted to at least try, to give it everything she had. "Let's do this, you and me together," she said. "What do we have to lose? And at least if we go down, we go down fighting."

Walter exhaled. "All right," he said. "Let's do it together."

The front door swung open. "Mom?"

Sylvia tensed, ready to face the fury that seemed to have overtaken Judith ever since they moved. Everything was Sylvia's fault; she was taking the brunt of all of it, and she was trying to do it with grace. It wasn't fair for Judith to unload all of her misery onto Sylvia, but it was hard to be a teenager too, even without all the change and upheaval they were going through.

"Jude?" Walter called out. "Judith, can you come in here for a moment? Your mother and I would like to have a word."

Sylvia looked to Walter, perplexed. "It's time we start treating her like the young lady she is," he said.

Judith walked into the kitchen and slung her satchel over the back of the chair, looking annoyed.

"Sit down, sweetheart," Walter said.

"I'm meeting Margaret at Jolly Roger in five minutes; I have to get ready."

"Sit down, Judith," he said.

Judith looked from Walter to Sylvia and frowned, slowly sliding into a chair. "Oh my God, are you getting a divorce?"

"What?" Sylvia said.

"No, Judith," Walter said. "God no. What on earth gave you such an idea?"

"It hasn't exactly been peaches and cream around here lately," she said, looking down at her hands and picking at her cuticles.

"That's true, it hasn't," he said. "And that's what we wanted to talk to you about. Listen, Jude." He sighed deeply. "I made a big mistake recently. Really big." He looked up at her and she was staring at him expectantly. "I got caught up in some gambling. That's why we lost the house and it's why we'll likely lose the club too. It's all my fault and I'm so sorry."

Sylvia looked from him to Judith, shocked. She'd expected to take this to her grave, to shield Judith from her father's wrongdoings. She couldn't believe he was relieving her of that burden. She felt the weight of it lift immediately and was able to take what felt like the first real deep breath she'd taken for days.

"Your mother has been working really hard to keep this family together, to put on the beauty contest and maintain our family's legacy, to move us from our house to here, and to be a support for all of us during this really difficult time. So it's time to stop sassing her."

Judith looked up at Walter as if she'd been caught red-handed.

"I mean it, Judith. She is the reason this family is still functioning."

Judith nodded slowly, then turned to Sylvia. "I'm sorry, Mom. I didn't know."

"Of course you didn't, and this is a lot to take in." Sylvia put her hand on Judith's and squeezed.

"My mistake," Walter continued, "is that I didn't come to your mother and confide in her right away. But we're working together now to make things right. If there's one thing that I've learned from this nightmare, it's that you don't have to go through the hard times alone."

"Your father's right. If ever you have problems," Sylvia said, "and you will at some point in your life, please know you can come to us; we can support you, we can help you."

"OK," Judith said, looking slightly lighter herself, her shoulders less slumped. Maybe it was the not knowing that had caused her to act out. "I'm glad you told me," she said. "I was really worried when I walked in here that you were going to tell me you were getting a divorce. Then my life would really be over."

"Dear God, no," Walter said. "We've realized now more than ever that money isn't what matters; what matters is that we are together as a family."

The following morning Jonathan and his TV crew, as well as Adele and Milly, joined Sylvia and Walter at the club for their first meeting.

"We have good news," Jonathan announced once everyone was seated in the empty club restaurant. "We were able to reach Margery, and she's agreed to the rematch."

There was a collective sigh of relief, and, at the news, Walter snapped into business mode.

"We need to make sure it's advertised well and that people know to buy tickets," Walter said. "I have friends at the local and national papers, so I can call in some favors there, but your station should start running ads right away."

"We're already on it," someone from the network said. "We need this to be a success as much as you do; we're going to run TV and radio ads nonstop to get the word out."

"What about sponsors?" Adele asked. "At matches I used to play, there were often posters and banners from businesses local to the area of the tournament. Can someone contact businesses in the area and see if they'd be interested?"

"I can do that," Walter said.

"You're perfect for that, Walt; you know everyone." Sylvia was happy to see Walter taking charge again; he'd been moping around looking distraught for too long.

"I'll be in charge of food and beverages," Sylvia said. "I'll contact the vendors and make sure we're well stocked for that day. And I'll ensure that we have enough staff." There'd be some confusion, as she'd already broken contracts with their suppliers and let most of the staff go, but she'd explain the situation and make it work.

"What about merchandise?" Milly piped in. "I don't know a thing about putting on a tennis tournament or running a club, but I do know fashion and I know people love to shop. I imagine they'll pay good money to take home a souvenir from the biggest women's tennis match of the last two decades. What about cardigans or sweaters with The Island Club on the back, or sun hats? If it's a hot day, we could sell paper fans."

"I love the idea, Milly," Sylvia said. "But ordering personalized items takes weeks, months maybe, and we don't have that kind of time. And it requires money up front that we don't have at out fingertips." Walter nodded and Milly looked disappointed.

"What about items from our local boutiques? Could we set up a makeshift gift shop with items on loan from stores in town?" Milly asked. "We only pay for what we sell; they get a cut and we get a cut."

"I like it," Sylvia said. "Can you be in charge of that?"

Milly nodded, looking happy to participate.

The meeting went on with people chiming in making arrangements, assigning jobs. The camera crew talked about specific needs they had for filming—they discussed building a platform structure they could film from—and Walter brought up the need for additional seating around center court.

"What about national tennis brands?" Jonathan asked. "If we secure one of those brands, they could cover any structural additions."

"I had thought of that," Adele said. "Babolat strings, Wilson rackets, Dayton, Spalding—but I don't know if they're going to sponsor an event with two washed-up tennis players."

"Don't say that," Sylvia said. "Why don't you and I work on that together, Adele, and we can talk to them about sponsoring you and Margery too."

Sylvia had always loved to plan a party, to chair a committee, organize a charity gala—that's where she excelled—but this was intensely personal. As crazy and improbable as the whole thing had sounded at first, it was actually beginning to sound feasible, and, dare she admit it, quite exciting. She knew it was unlikely they could save the club, but she liked being part of a team in this way and loved working in partnership with Walter. Judith would see her parents working together to pull off this near-impossible feat, and they could at least walk away from it all with their heads held high.

When the meeting ended, Adele approached Sylvia and Milly.

"I need to train," she said. "I haven't played an actual match in twenty years, and I've only got a few weeks to catch up."

"Yes," Milly said. "But who will you train with?"

Adele laughed. "Robbie is not exactly my biggest fan, but I'll see what I can do to convince him or the other coaches to hit with me. But until they agree, I was hoping I'd practice with you," she said to Milly, then turned to Sylvia: "And you."

"I hardly think we're at your level," Milly said and laughed.

"No," Adele said, "absolutely not, but I have to take what I can get for now, and you two are it." She shrugged. "So will you play?"

"Well, sure," Milly said.

"All right," Sylvia said. "Between putting on the biggest event I've ever attempted and preparing to uproot my family and move to the desert, sure—why not take on some extra tennis too?" Sylvia said.

"Good," Adele said, not missing a beat. "Sylvia, you can be my eight o'clock. Milly, be ready at nine."

CHAPTER THIRTY-FOUR

Saturday, May 5—Match Day
ADELE

Margery tossed the ball high and whipped it into the far corner of the service box. It struck the ground, then shot past Adele like a long, low stream of jet fuel.

"*Merde*," Adele said under her breath. 15–love.

She had spent countless hours working alone on her serves, and she'd practiced relentlessly each day with anyone who would play. But no one, not even Robbie, who'd reluctantly agreed to hit balls with her, had been anywhere close enough to the level she needed to replicate the demands of this type of performance. *It's all right*, she told herself, *I just need to get used to the speed again*. She moved to the ad side and took a few steps back from the baseline. *Now*, she thought, *now I'm ready for her*.

This time, Margery served the ball to Adele's backhand, and Adele whipped it right back over and down the line. Margery lunged for it, but it was out of reach. 15–all. The crowd to Adele's right erupted with applause, and when she looked over, Milly and Sylvia were standing at their seats surrounded by all the women she'd been coaching—Betsy, Joan, Susie, Faye—all of them, all the women she had assumed would be through with her after her confession on live television.

Surprised and buoyed by their support, she crouched in the ready position. As soon as Margery threw the ball into the air to serve, Adele was on her toes. Racket back, *slam!* Hard and fast like an arrow into the service box. Margery rushed toward the net but couldn't get there in time. 15–30.

It suddenly sank in that after all this time, Adele was back on the court, playing an actual match against the very woman she'd destroyed her career over. If it hadn't been Margery, it would have been someone else who'd been at the receiving end of her wrath all those years ago. Adele's demise had been building for weeks, months, maybe even years before she broke. Now, standing here, she felt a surreal sensation, almost as if she were levitating a few inches off the ground from the energy and thrill of being back in the game. She was here, actually doing this, getting a second chance.

As Margery tossed the ball, Adele saw it go up at a crooked angle. Bad toss, she thought, but Margery hit it anyway, sending it right onto the net. She's nervous now, Adele mused, she'd hit a safe second serve.

But she didn't.

Margery shocked her by spinning the ball hard and fast crosscourt. Adele could barely get a racket on it. She managed to tap it back over the net, but it was a weak shot and Margery rushed the net, then hammered it down, sending the ball so high into the air that Adele didn't stand a chance. She backed up almost to the fence but couldn't reach. 30–all.

I'm going to take this point, Adele said to herself. She returned the serve straight down the middle and it hit the very back of the line. 30–40.

Margery served short, trying to catch Adele out, but she was already on her toes and leaping forward. That had always been her specialty. Had Margery forgotten that Adele could leap like a ballerina across the court? Adele volleyed to the left at a short and sharp angle. Margery was ready for her, reached her racket out, and shot it back. Adele sliced a backhand volley this time, a sharp angle to the other side, but Margery thought she was going left again and had already begun moving in the wrong direction. Adele won the first game.

God, I've missed this. A vibration buzzed through every inch of her.

The intensity, the fight, the desire to win was so strong, and in that moment, the last twenty-plus years of her life flashed through her eyes. Sad, lonely, regretful. She couldn't go back to that, not now that she'd tasted this.

At the changeover, the women on Adele's side stood and applauded furiously. Adele kept her head down and sipped her water. *Stay focused*, she reminded herself, yet a hint of a smile curled in the corner of her lips as she heard them call her name. What on earth? She had never smiled during a match, she had never let the crowd know she appreciated their support. Not until the win was securely in her pocket had she ever allowed herself to enjoy the game. It was her serve, her advantage. Adele took the next game. It was 2–0.

Margery grabbed a towel and wiped her face. She looked angry, and Adele allowed herself a glance. Margery was a few years younger than Adele—maybe forty-four, and still very fit. She clearly still played with some regularity, at least social matches, though Adele knew she hadn't competed with much success after the incident. She was strong and flexible and moved with confidence, but she wasn't as light on her feet as Adele; it took her a fraction of a second too long to change course when she needed to. Adele had prepared for the match by recalling Margery's strengths and weaknesses back when they were young: Did she rush the net? Did she prefer to stay back at the baseline? Her memory was imperfect. It had been so long, and everything was clouded with negativity and vicious rumors back then. They had overpowered her sense of the actual game by the time it began to fall apart.

When Margery turned and looked out at the hundreds of people who'd traveled from all over to see this match, Adele looked for the small white scar above her left eye. The papers said she'd had to have surgery twice after the incident but that her vision was almost 100 percent recovered after the second. Did it still affect her? Adele tried to stem the feelings of guilt that rushed back to her now, the regret for all the pain and heartache she had caused. She loved this game so much. She was sure Margery did too. Even if it had been an accident, Adele had taken tennis away from her, just as she'd taken it from herself.

She adjusted the green silk bandeau that she'd fixed around her hair that morning with her signature diamond pin. She'd been hesitant to wear the outfit that her sponsor, Lacoste, had sent—a white drop-waist dress with a green V-neck and green band at the waist, white socks, and the white lace-up tennis shoes, everything adorned with a small embroidered alligator logo. It was a chic outfit, but it wasn't her signature outfit, and she'd felt superstitious about wearing anything but her Jean Patou. But Lacoste was paying decent money for Adele to wear its clothes, and she'd earn a lot more if she won. Surprisingly, she felt good in it. The fabric was comfortable and more breathable than her old attire, and the style felt fresh and youthful.

The club had also been transformed. Walter had brought in stadium seating for the match, as he said he would. Adele thought he was crazy when he said it would seat a thousand people, but when she looked around, she didn't see a single empty seat. Sponsors had come pouring in, and multiple banners surrounded court 1, advertising local businesses too. A camera crew had set up on a platform mid-court. If she won the prize money, there was a good chance that she could help Sylvia and Walter keep this club, which would mean she could keep on coaching, maybe even playing. Not competitively, of course—this was a one-time opportunity—but she could potentially find players at her level. She could really start to live again.

Margery was up to serve once more.

Adele felt the heat in the very first serve as it aced past her. She stood way back for the next serve, but Margery switched it up and served short, too short for even Adele to reach. Then they began to rally, power shots back and forth, back and forth. The ball pounded so hard from one corner of the court to the next that white felt fuzz suspended in the air. Margery took that game and the next, tying it up 2–2. Then she won one more, taking the lead.

Adele began to worry. What if she didn't have what it would take to win? What if she lost when the world's eyes were on her? Had she made a big return to the court only to mess it up all over again and disappoint the very people who had brought her out of the shadows? For Sylvia and Walter, so much was riding on this. She'd gotten their hopes up; she couldn't let them down now. All of a sudden, it felt impossible and crushing. But, strangely, she had no desire to give up, feign injury, and default. No, she wanted to fight for this win. *I love this game*, she reminded herself; *I have always loved this game.*

Adele came back and they were head-to-head, going to a tiebreak at the end of the first set. Neither was able to cinch it. It was 5–5, then 6–6, then Margery was up 7–6. Adele brought it back 7–7. They could have gone on like this all day, but someone had to win by two. Adele served an ace. It whistled past Margery. Margery served and Adele returned and raced to the net, pulled her racket back as if she were going to swing big and hurl the ball crosscourt, but she remembered how to do this, how to fake out her opponent. At the last second, she lifted her racket at an angle in front of her like an ax and sliced down on the ball. Chop. It dropped just beyond the net and died, no bounce. Margery didn't stand a chance. Adele took the first set.

I remember this feeling, Adele thought as she looked up to her fans cheering her on, calling her name. *I remember the intense rush of pleasure when I'm ahead.* She also recognized the satisfaction in remembering the right shot in the right moment. This was as much a mental challenge as a physical one. She needed to stay sharp and use her head to think through the consequences of each movement.

The second set went on in much the same way. Painfully close, each woman inching her way up the scoreboard, tying it up, moving up, then tying again. Adele was exhausted. She was in shape and healthier than most women her age, but not nearly as fit as she should be for this kind of endurance competition.

"You can do it, Adele," Sylvia called out. "We believe in you."

"We believe in you, Adele," Milly repeated, and then all the women in that section began to chant, "Adele, Adele, Adele."

Adele felt something bloom inside her, an unfamiliar sensation—maybe love, gratitude, happiness? She wanted to win so badly. She wanted this for her friends. She wanted this for Sylvia so she could stay on Balboa Island and keep the club. She wanted this for Milly, whose confidence had surged since she started playing, and who, though she'd never told her this, showed a lot of potential, with good coaching, of course. She wanted it for herself, for her own pride and sense of accomplishment, to redeem herself, but strangely that mattered less now. She wanted the win for her friends and for the women who didn't abandon her when they learned her truth.

Early that morning, as she had sat on her living room floor stretching her calf muscles and hamstrings, she'd momentarily slipped into her old ways and begun reciting familiar phrases, the way she always had in the hours before a match, phrases that she'd believed helped to get her fired up, angry, and ready to demolish: *You are superior. Kill them. Slaughter them. Winning is everything.* All those years ago, her father's words had become her thoughts. Then she began to hear other words seeping in: *Tu es un idiot. You're slow. Tu joues comme un enfant. What are you thinking? You play like you've never picked up a racket.* But now it all tasted sour in her mouth. It didn't fire her up. It didn't fit her anymore. *Arrête*, she told herself, *arrête.*

Adele served, then rushed the net, volleyed the ball to Margery's feet, where she reached down to return it but could only pop it up over Adele's head and out. Adele was ahead in the second set, 5–4. At the next point, though, Margery changed her strategy. She lobbed the ball over Adele to the far-right corner. Adele managed to run far enough back to return it, but Margery hit a fast forehand with topspin to the baseline. She had Adele running from one side of the court to the next. Adele could outrun anyone in her day, but now she was winded—back and forth, back and forth—as Margery crept back up the scoreboard. Adele hit a high backhand but not hard enough. It fell into the net. Margery took the second set. Now it was anyone's game.

In her old life this was the point at which Adele would confer with her father, absorb his anger and insults, his way of igniting her rage and setting her game on fire. She had thought this made her stronger, meaner, tougher, but it didn't ring true anymore. She took a deep breath and tried to slow down her racing heart. *I love this game*, she repeated in her head. *There's nowhere I'd rather be; I may have lost that set, but I'll win the next.* Just saying those words made her feel calm and more in control. She wondered how much energy her negative thoughts had consumed in her younger days, how much her own self-debasement had sapped her strength.

She couldn't play tennis without thinking of her father and feeling all those swirling emotions in the pit of her stomach. Why had he done it? Why had her father pushed her so hard? She'd seen the way Milly treated her children, firm when she needed to be, but mostly loving, gentle, and encouraging. She'd witnessed Sylvia navigating the challenging teenage years, heightened and even more emotional due to their move, but she too handled her daughter with grace. She was sure there were times, behind closed doors, when both women lost their tempers or said things they didn't mean, but it was obvious that they loved their children whether they succeeded or failed. But maybe it had been the only way her father knew how to love. Maybe tough love was all he had known himself, and it was the only way he knew how to teach her. What if he'd been doing the best he could?

She took a long drink of water and wiped the sweat from her neck between sets. Milly and Sylvia rushed to her courtside.

"You look amazing out there. You're so graceful, so precise. It's like watching a fast and furious dance," Milly said. "Keep going."

"It's astounding," Sylvia said, leaning over toward her. "I've never seen anything like it in my life. It's an absolute honor to watch you."

"Thanks," Adele said. "I won't let you down."

The rest of the women cheered and clapped as Margery and Adele took their positions.

The third and final set started fiercely. Margery clearly wanted the win. Her serves were on fire, acing Adele twice in the first game, but in the third game she double-faulted twice in a row, putting Adele in the lead. Adele's next serves were equally fast and searing, but then, in a surprise move, Margery came to the net and crushed ball after ball. Adele had to adjust. She came up to meet her, but Margery managed to send the ball up and over her, landing it in. Margery was in the lead.

There's no place I'd rather be, Adele said to herself. *I love this game.* Slam. She shot it down the line, record speed. Margery missed. Then Margery took the next point and won that game. She was ahead 7–6.

"*Merde, merde, merde*," Adele said through gritted teeth, furious that Margery was ahead. But instead of making her shake, crumble, and search for anyone's approval to leave the court, give up, act out, it gave her razor focus.

Match point. They rallied back and forth, back and forth, speed and power erupting each time the racket made contact with the ball. Corner to corner, no one wanted to change it up, no one wanted to make the fault. Adele knew she had to end it, but the force of these shots was so great. Next one she'd change course, catch Margery off guard, and then she noticed the tiniest change in Margery's stance. Adele tried to move closer to the alley, but she was a second too late: Margery ripped the ball down the line, and it hit just inside the white line. Adele lunged for the ball, but the match was over.

Margery Horn had won.

Adele watched as her opponent dropped to her knees, put her hands together in prayer, and kissed the clear blue sky above her. Adele couldn't believe it, and yet she could. She hadn't trained enough to win, yet somehow, she had thought a win might still be possible.

She wouldn't get the prize money. The club would be repossessed.

She had let Sylvia down after all.

Sick with disappointment, she forced herself to look up to her cheering section, expecting her feelings to be reflected back in the women's faces, but instead they shot out of their seats and ran to her, more of them now—Milly, Sylvia, Joan, Maureen, Susie, Sadie, Faye, and Betsy—rushing from the bleachers onto the court, throwing themselves at Adele, hugging her. She could barely breathe and had to resist the urge to push them away. She'd lost—didn't they know this? But the women started jumping up and down, taking her with them, a pulsating, vibrating force.

"What are you doing?" she asked, almost laughing, as they began to loosen their grip. "Don't you know I lost the match? I lost!"

"Who cares, you were incredible!" Sylvia said.

"You're back," Milly said.

"Hardly." Adele tried to suppress her smile.

"You're back in the game, and you're a star," Milly said.

Adele couldn't quite believe it. She'd lost, and this was the reception she received. She peered over to Margery, where she too was being hugged and congratulated.

"*Excusez-moi*," Adele said to her friends. "Just a moment."

She walked to the net, and when Margery saw her, she approached. Adele held out her hand.

"Congratulations, Margery. That was a tough match."

"Congratulations to you also. You are still a force to be reckoned with," Margery said. "But I knew I could beat you if I had another chance."

It stung, but Adele nodded. "You won fair and square, and you have not lost your touch." She looked at the small scar, close-up now; it had a white sheen to it. Margery's fingers reflexively touched the spot. "I must apologize, Margery, for my terrible actions at Wimbledon. I am so sorry for the pain I caused you and for what happened to your career," Adele said, her eyes watering in spite of herself, as she heard the apology that she should have spoken years ago.

"Thank you," Margery said. "I appreciate that. I knew it was an accident, but I was too angry at the time to correct the reports. I should have spoken up."

Adele dropped her head. "And I want to say, I'm deeply sorry about the sleeping pill. I had completely lost my way. I would never—"

"Adele," Margery said, pausing until she looked up, "I didn't drink it."

"What? Yes, I saw you."

"I drank yours, the Perrier. You hadn't touched it."

Adele looked at her, confused. "But why?"

"You had an edge to you that day, a wild look in your eye. I don't know, I just had a strange feeling as I reached for the glass, and besides, I prefer sparkling water. I should have ordered that instead."

Adele put her hand to her mouth. Relief flooded her. "*Dieu merci*," she whispered.

"I'm so glad you asked me to play today," Margery said. "We should have done this a long time ago."

Adele nodded. "It reminded me how much I love this sport."

"Maybe we'll play again sometime. When you come to London next, perhaps?"

"Perhaps," Adele said.

Walking back to her friends, Adele was filled with humility and gratitude, but something nagged at her, a slightly unsettling feeling that told her she wasn't done with Margery just yet. She turned back.

"Margery, would you have lunch with me?"

Margery paused and looked at Adele for a moment.

"At my place tomorrow, before you leave?" Adele said.

Margery seemed to consider it. "All right. Why not?" she said. "For old times' sake."

"*Bien*," Adele said.

"Oh, but Adele," Margery said, "I'll bring the beverages."

CHAPTER THIRTY-FIVE

SYLVIA

Sylvia pulled a chair alongside Walter's desk in his dimly lit office and sat beside him. Flush with emotions following the match, they were sharing a burger and french fries left by the catering team. It had been incredible and inspiring to see Adele play like that. Even though Adele hadn't won, Sylvia was so proud and awed by her friend. She deserved every ounce of respect and congratulations that she'd received. And Sylvia was proud of herself and Walter for making it happen.

"Wasn't it marvelous, Walt, to see the club in all its glory? An event like that, packed to the brim with guests from near and far?"

He was watching her closely, a sad smile on his face. She wanted desperately for him to share in her own vision before it could evaporate.

"To see television crews filming on our property?" Sylvia continued.

It had been like a glimpse into the future of what might have been. But she could sense herself that the excitement of the day was wearing off, and an inevitable disappointment was setting in.

Walter glanced at the ledger sheets, teeming with scratchy notations, that lay on the desk before them. He gently took her hand. "I wish I had better news," he said. "Especially after all the work everyone put into this and how folks came together to make it happen. But the reality is, even with all those ticket sales and the advertising money, the food and beverage sales, they just barely covered the cost of everything we had to bring in for setup—the seating, the construction for filming, the extra bars, all the extra staff. We made some profit, but not enough to change the outcome."

Sylvia nodded. He'd been warning her all along not to get her hopes up. He'd been showing her the numbers, the money coming in and the money going out, just as he'd promised he would do, but she'd still held out hope for a miracle.

"I just wish we'd won," she said.

"I know. But the numbers are the numbers. This televised match would have given us a big boost if we'd been able to keep the club; it would have driven memberships, absolutely, but the bank will be in possession of this place by the time that happens."

Sylvia nodded. If only she could have done more.

"And, unfortunately, when they repossess a property as costly as this," he continued, "they try to recoup as much loan money as possible; that's why they'll eventually come after our little shack too."

"I was just starting to warm up to that little shack," Sylvia said, trying to lighten the mood, but neither one of them could manage much of a smile. "Well, we tried," she said. "We gave it our best shot, and that's what I wanted to do."

She had tried to prepare herself for this moment, for actually leaving the town she loved, the friends she thought she'd grow old with, but there was no real way to brace for this. In order to rebuild their lives, they'd need to live somewhere inexpensive, and the desert made the most sense. It was going to hurt; she was going to cry. Judith would be furious all over again, livid when she found out she'd have to change schools. But, Sylvia reminded herself, she had her family, they were safe now, and they would start over. They would come back from this.

Walter was watching her, his eyes filled with remorse, and he was about to speak, but she stopped him. "Don't, Walter, I don't want you to keep apologizing. You can't keep living with regrets. We are in this together. We're going to be all right."

He picked up her hand and kissed it. "We'll come in tomorrow to wrap things up and we'll hand over the keys on Monday."

She tried to smile. There was no way around it. The loss felt monumental now, and she was just going to have to find a way to live with it.

CHAPTER THIRTY-SIX

MILLY

On Sunday Milly and Lloyd sat on deck chairs and watched as Debbie and Jack built sandcastles down by the water's edge.

"They want me in New York in a week," Lloyd said. "It's not enough time to pack up and go, I know that, but maybe you could find out the name of Walter and Sylvia's real estate agent?"

"Sure," Milly said, staring out at the sailboats, the Pavilion across the bay, and the Ferris wheel at a standstill to its right. To think that Adele used to work there. What a waste of her talent. She wondered what Adele would do now that the club was closing.

"Milly? Are you listening to me?" Lloyd asked. "This is important."

She knew it was important, but she'd been trying to block it out and pretend that it wasn't happening. She'd put all of her energy into helping coordinate the big match. She'd made the club a decent amount of money by gathering for sale many special, local trinkets and gifts from the boutiques in town. The visitors had gone crazy for her selection, vendors selling out of everything by the end of the day, but that was all over now. The club was closing, her tennis lessons with Adele were over, Sylvia was leaving, and Lloyd was asking her impossible questions. Adele's loss, which had somehow felt like a triumph just one day earlier, now felt like Milly's loss too, and she was forced to look at the bleak future immediately ahead of her.

"What do you think?" Lloyd went on. "Should we let the kids finish school and the three of you join me in New York in the summer? Or should we all go together now and let them sell the house without us? Maybe it's better to show it if we're not here. It would be less cluttered without us."

She looked over at Lloyd, really stared at his profile for a long moment. She tried to imagine not seeing his handsome face, not seeing his soft hands, the thumb with the nail that grew in slightly bumpy after a childhood incident with his father's hammer, the small details that she had thought only she knew about. He was watching their children, and she saw his face change. She followed his concerned gaze out to the kids, where Jack's latest sandcastle attempt collapsed and knocked down the one he'd built next to it. Lloyd laughed tenderly as Jack continued to stomp all the sand down flat again and start over.

"He's resilient, that one," Lloyd said. "He must get that from you." He looked over at her and smiled, then turned serious when he saw Milly's face. "What is it, Milly?"

She took his hand in hers and swallowed. "I can't go to New York with you, Lloyd."

"Milly," he whispered.

"I'm going to stay here with the children."

"Milly, no, please."

"I can't do it, Lloyd. I just can't. I thought I was willing to stay and somehow put up with it here, on Balboa, where I have true friends, friends who feel like family and could hold me up, but I can't uproot all of us and move to the other side of the country. I can't start over again."

He looked down at his hand in hers and was about to speak, but he stopped.

"Who's to say it wouldn't happen again, Lloyd, with someone else?"

He shook his head but didn't deny it.

"I don't understand it, and I feel so ignorant for believing that you loved me for all those years. . . ."

"I do love you, Milly. I have always loved you."

"Not in the way a husband should love his wife." She paused. "I trusted you with my best years. I'm angry about that."

"You're right. I don't think I did it intentionally, but I'm sorry. I don't know how I can ever make that up to you."

"You can't," she said. "But you gave me two beautiful children, and for that I will be forever grateful." They both looked out to Debbie and Jack. Debbie was now burying Jack in sand, and they were both laughing. "I've been thinking about everything," Milly went on. "And I do recognize what a terrible situation you're in, that you've been in for many, many years. Maybe even your whole life. I understand now that you didn't choose this. You wouldn't choose this difficult path, and you shouldn't have to spend your whole life living a lie. You deserve to be happy." She blinked away her tears. "We both do."

She thought of Wes and wondered if the man Lloyd had fallen in love with had given him the sense of hope and possibility that Wes had given her. Lloyd deserved that as much as she did, but she wasn't going to stick around and be a part of it.

"There's something I need to tell you, Lloyd." She took a deep breath and waited for the courage to speak again. "I had an indiscretion too." She looked at him and expected to see shock and horror on his face, but he just looked out to the bay. "I'm not proud of it, but I knew you were done with me. I was sure you were having an affair with Beverly Douglas. . . ."

"Beverly Douglas!" he said, laughing now. "Good lord, she's a pill, a sweetheart, but an absolute pain in the behind!"

Milly somehow laughed too. All those imagined scenes she'd painted in her head, all those candlelit dinners she'd envisioned, their romping at some hotel on the studio's account. She shook her head.

"I don't blame you, Milly," Lloyd said eventually. "I haven't treated you the way you deserve to be treated, and I'm sorry for everything. But I love my children." He wiped a tear from under his sunglasses.

"I know you do," she said. "And they love you. We'll come out and visit as much as we possibly can. I've always wanted to go to New York." She tried to smile. "And you'll come back and visit us every chance you get. The cottage will always be yours, anytime you want. And when all this dies down, hopefully you can move back to Los Angeles, or somewhere around here, and we'll be parents to Jack and Debbie separately but together."

He nodded, wiping another tear, and she hated to see him this way, but she didn't see another path forward. He got up and walked down to the water's edge, picked up some rocks, and skimmed them out on the bay. After a while he returned to his deck chair and sat upright.

"They've given me a very generous signing-on bonus," he said. "It's yours. I'll write you a check this afternoon when we get back to the house. And I'll always do my part for you and the kids financially."

"That's kind," she said softly. "I'm going to take a job too—I don't know what yet, maybe something in town when the children are at school—so I'll contribute also."

"Thank you for understanding, Milly," he said, pulling her toward him and kissing her forehead.

"Thank you," she said. "For letting me go."

CHAPTER THIRTY-SEVEN

ADELE

Adele sat by the telephone and waited with trembling hands. Her local operator had transferred her to a traffic operator, who was now in line for a circuit to reach her mother in France. She'd been told to wait by the phone until a connection could be made, but it could be anytime that day. She made herself a cup of chamomile tea. She'd waited this long; she could wait a few more hours.

She jumped when the phone rang at 11 AM, even though she'd been staring at it, and when the operator connected them, there was static and then silence.

"*Maman*?" Adele said first.

"Adeline?" She sounded old and fragile.

Adele held back tears. "Hi, *Maman*," she said, speaking French. "I know it's been a long time, but"—she hesitated, then forced herself to get out the words that she'd been practicing since the early hours of that morning; she didn't know how long the line would stay connected—"I wanted to hear your voice."

"Oh, Adeline, you don't know how much I have longed to hear from you."

"I'm sorry it's taken me all this time." Tears streaked Adele's cheeks. She let them fall into her lap. "I didn't think you could forgive me."

"Forgive you? For what?"

"For Papa and his heart. It gave up after that day."

"No, my girl." Her mother let out a quivering sigh on the other end of the line, which shocked Adele, then she heard a younger woman's voice telling her she was too tired for this conversation, that she needed her rest.

"Please," Adele said. "Please let her speak."

"Adeline, it was not your fault. He was a damaged man. He was too forceful, too aggressive, too much for a child, and he realized too late. I would hope that was his greatest regret. It was certainly mine. I thought you blamed me and hated me for what we forced you into. You didn't tell us where you were. And I thought you didn't want to hear from me again."

"Oh, *Maman*," Adele said, grasping for the first time that all those years they'd both been alone and apart were needless. They could have been each other's comfort.

"I miss you," Adele said.

"I miss you too."

Adele heard the exhaustion and weariness in her mother's voice. "*Maman*, please, can I visit you?"

Her mother gasped and sobbed a little. "Yes. Please, come Adeline, come soon. Nothing would make me happier."

That afternoon Adele hastily rode her bike to the club and struggled to find a place to park it. Trucks had pulled up in front, and workers were in the process of dismantling the bleachers that had been set up for Saturday's match.

"I'm late, I'm sorry," she said as she rushed onto the court where Sylvia and Milly were sitting on the side bench in their tennis gear, looking miserable. They might have been excited at the match on Saturday, but here they were, two days later, and their disappointment was too thick to be concealed.

"You haven't missed much," Milly said. "We're not really in the mood to play."

"Why?" Adele asked.

Sylvia rolled her eyes and motioned to the courts and the pool. "Well, for one thing, we're losing the club. After today no more tennis, at least not here." She sipped her coffee and sighed. "I've got to say, I'm really, really going to miss playing with you girls."

"Yes," Adele said. "I wanted to talk to you about that."

"About tennis?" Sylvia asked.

"About the club. How much did you make from the event?" Adele asked. "There must have been at least seven or eight hundred tickets sold."

"We had over a thousand people attend, so with the tickets and the advertising and the food and beverage sales and the merchandise, we did well, about twenty thousand in profit." She shrugged. "Not bad for our first and only big tennis event. But not enough to make a difference. We were several months behind on payments. Walter's handing everything over to the bank this afternoon. We're probably not even supposed to be here, but I figured they could give us until the end of the day, at least, so we could stomp around this court one more time."

Adele nodded, but still no one stood up to play.

"I don't know what's going to happen after this," Sylvia said. "If they'll keep the club open, or if they'll try and sell it off right away." She shook her head. "It's such a shame, and I feel terrible for all the people, friends, who have active memberships." She looked to Milly. "Including you."

"How much did you need?" Adele asked.

"A lot. Today was the last day to settle the payments. We would have had to take out a new loan, but no bank is going to lend us money after this mess."

"Exactly how much did you need?" Adele pressed.

"What does it matter now?" Sylvia threw up her hands in exasperation, but Adele waited for her response. "Seventy thousand dollars," she said, finally.

Milly gasped. "That's a lot of money."

"It sure is," Sylvia said.

Milly stood and put on a forced enthusiastic smile. "So maybe we should just play? One last time?"

"Hold on," Adele said. "You said you made twenty thousand from the event?"

"That's right," Sylvia said. "It's not enough, Adele. I know you wanted this to work, but it's just not even close to enough."

"Well, the Lacoste people paid me to wear their attire, and Wilson paid me to use their racket. A little over ten thousand for sporting their gear on television, with a bonus of five more from each brand if more than ten million viewers tuned in. And I just found out from Rutherford that they did. I didn't get the winner's purse, but I got eight thousand in prize money just for playing."

"That's twenty-eight thousand! You're rich," Milly said.

"Hardly," Adele said. "But I live frugally."

Milly had begun to pace, bouncing the ball on her racket. Suddenly she stopped.

"Lloyd just wrote me a check for eighteen thousand dollars," she said. "It's his signing-on bonus for a job he's taking in New York. I need to save half to cover expenses and the mortgage, but if I had a job and a salary, I could invest the other half—"

"*Bien*," Adele burst out. "*Excellente!*"

"Oh gosh," Sylvia exclaimed. "I'm so grateful for what you two are suggesting here. But even if the three of us pooled our money together and had shares in the club, it still wouldn't be enough."

"You're right," Adele said. "We're still thirteen thousand short, and we'd need a cushion for the operating costs, but I think there's a way we could make it work."

"How?" Sylvia said, searching the sky, as if afraid to hear an inevitable disappointment.

Adele tried to suppress the slightest smile forming on her lips. "I've found an investor."

"Who?" Milly demanded.

Sylvia and Milly were holding their breath.

"Margery Horn," Adele said at last and let it sink in for a minute.

"Margery Horn wants to invest with us?" Sylvia said.

"That's right." Adele said. "We talked things over yesterday and we've made contact with Wilson. They want to sponsor an annual televised Grudges Match here at The Island Club, hosted by Margery and me, where former champions get to settle longtime rivalries and face off in a final match."

Milly clasped her hands together excitedly.

"Wait a second," Sylvia cautioned. "Let's think this through. Margery lives in London. Why would she want to invest in a club here?"

"She understands as I do that our competing days are behind us. This is a good opportunity to put some of our winnings to good use and hopefully give us decent returns. She's a smart woman. Just as she plays tennis, she's thinking three steps ahead, and she knows a good opportunity when she sees it," Adele said. "And the weather is a lot better here than it is in London, so she'll have a place in the sunshine to come and play."

Sylvia closed her eyes and shook her head as if trying to figure out if this was really happening.

"But there's one caveat," Adele said. "Walter would be part of the team, of course, director of operations, perhaps, but he would have to run all finances by the three of us." She shrugged. "No offense. But it's a lot of money, the only money I've got, and I can't risk losing it." She looked to Milly. "None of us can."

"Understood," Sylvia said. "He'd be relieved to not carry all the burden. That's what did him in last time."

"It sounds like we have a plan to be in business," Milly said, beaming.

"Oh my God." Sylvia put her hands to her mouth. "I can't believe this. And you're willing to put all that heartache and all those regrets from your past behind you?" Sylvia asked.

Adele picked up her racket and spun it in her hands, then she smiled. "I already have."

CHAPTER THIRTY-EIGHT

Two months later . . .
MILLY

Milly stood back and admired the display. She'd finally received the full shipment from Lacoste. It would sell out fast. Ever since Adele's picture from the match had been splashed across newspapers and magazines, people had been calling from around the country with requests for the dress, the bandeau, the shoes, even the socks! Shipments from other brands had begun arriving too, and she was expecting shoes, rackets, and bags in the next week or two, but the Lacoste collection was what all the women were talking about.

After seeing the local merchandise sell like hotcakes at Adele's big rematch, it had been Milly's idea to open a ladies' tennis shop at the club. She was hesitant to take charge of the endeavor at first—she knew fashion well but nothing about running a store—but Sylvia had held her to it and promised to teach her what she knew about working with accounts, paying invoices, and managing a small staff. She'd hired a young man to string rackets two mornings a week, and a girl to work the afternoons when Milly was with her children.

Milly had the next day off for the Fourth of July—the island's second largest event of the year after Bal Week. The American flag was already flying outside almost every home and storefront, the bridge onto the island was decorated with red-white-and-blue bunting, and the streets were filled with even more blue hydrangeas, red petunias, and white daisies than usual, adding to the charm and character that had attracted Milly to this island in the first place.

The beach would be swarming the next day, and, after a very busy month, Milly was looking forward to the chance to relax on the sand with her friends and their children. In the evening they'd all gather to watch the annual boat parade, which Wes planned to participate in. He'd laughed when he'd described to her how his old boat would chug along next to all those fancy yachts and sailboats, but he didn't care, he was just happy to be on the water.

"The rest of the holiday week is going to be busy," Sylvia had told Milly earlier in the day. "The courts are already booked, and restaurant reservations are full, so I'm sure there'll be gals coming in here wanting to shop."

"I'll be ready," Milly said.

She took one more look around the space, straightening the Wilson rackets that hung on the wall and running her hand along the collection of red, white, and blue swimsuits she'd arranged on the front table before locking up. She hurried off to catch the end of Jack and Debbie's tennis lesson.

The children were lined up facing the net. Adele moved down the line, gently tossing a ball in each child's direction and calling out when it was time to swing. Debbie got close, but most of them paused too long and swung after the ball was already behind them. A few of the younger ones, including Jack, dissolved into a heap of frustration.

"I'm tired," one boy called out.

"Me too," Jack joined in. "I want a Popsicle."

Milly stood quietly at the corner of the court, out of view, and hid a smile when she saw Adele close her eyes and take a deep, calming breath. This age was adorable and cute and funny, but it was also a test of patience. The children's class had only been in session for a few weeks, starting when Adele returned home from France, but it was already becoming clear they'd have to separate the children into different age groups and train more coaches as quickly as possible, because Adele was already in high demand with the adults.

"OK, let's try this a different way," Adele said. "Airplane tennis."

They held their arms out like airplane wings, rackets reaching toward the back fence. This time when they swung for the ball most of them at least made contact, and Debbie's soared over the net.

"Not bad," Adele said, looking back to see if the ball stayed within the lines of the court. "Not bad at all."

Milly had fifteen minutes before the lesson would end, so she sat down on one of the lounge chairs and put her feet up, allowing herself a rare moment to catch her breath. She'd never been so busy, nor had she ever felt this energized by how full and purposeful her life now felt. Over by the pool bar, she saw Sylvia, chic as ever in a pink belted dress and heels, giving a tour to a family of prospective members. They would join, they all did, once Sylvia walked them around the grounds, showed them the courts and the pool and introduced them to Adele, the star attraction. In the past two weeks Sylvia had also booked two weddings—one for that fall and one for the following spring—and membership was on a steady incline. Walter had already secured sponsors and was making plans for the following year's Grudges Match.

As Milly sat there, she considered her grand plan to move to the island earlier that year, a move that she'd thought many times might have a been a terrible mistake. It was clear now that nothing could be further from the truth. She was exactly where she needed to be. She had friends who supported her; a new job to discover; children who were happy and thriving; Leticia, who'd agreed to stay over and watch the kids one night a week to give her a break; and Wes, who'd insisted on cooking her dinner that evening. She had to admit, she had a lot of questions about how he might pull that off in his tiny onboard kitchen. But then she laid her head back and laughed. It was about damn time someone else made dinner.

AUTHOR'S NOTE

As a newcomer to the game of tennis at the age of forty, there was something incredibly addictive about the sport from the first moment I picked up a racket. In my high school days I was a cheerleader, so it was exciting to find a new sport that brought out my competitive spirit and challenged me to become a better player (still a work in progress!). But one of the most surprising benefits to taking up a new sport as an adult was the friendships that blossomed out of our time on the court. My family and I moved to California from New York City in 2020. It can be hard to build new friendships as an adult outside of your kids' lives, but tennis brought so many incredible women into my life, and it's these friendships that inspired much of this book.

Delving into the world of tennis for this novel, my research led me to French tennis champion Suzanne Lenglen, who was the number one ranked female tennis player in the world from 1921–1926. Known for her balletic style and brash personality, I was at first inclined to write about Suzanne, her real life and her death at just thirty-eight years old. However, I soon realized that I wanted to fictionalize her story, make her the inspiration but not the subject of the novel, and give her a scandalous past, and a different, happier ending. Since Adele Lambert is a fictional character, the dates of her Wimbledon championships and other tennis wins are all imagined.

I spent my teenage years in Southern California growing up just a fifteen-minute drive from Balboa Island, and anytime I visited, it always gave me a nostalgic feeling of walking into a little town that had been frozen in time. It was easy to imagine what life was like there in the 1950s, though there are certainly differences from how it is now. It's more populated, for one thing, and there used to be a beach in front of the Fun Zone, which is now all boat slips. And while there are certainly some fabulous golf, tennis, and yacht clubs near Balboa Island, The Island Club is completely fictional.

And finally, there's a reference to an article about Martin Luther King Jr. that was actually published a week after Easter in 1956. I chose to keep it in to provide context on the political climate of the time.

ACKNOWLEDGMENTS

While researching this novel I discovered the oral history program at the Balboa Island Museum of Newport Beach, which was an invaluable source of information, as was the abundance of resources at the Newport Beach Library—thank you for all that you do to preserve and promote the local history and culture. I was also incredibly fortunate to meet Theresa Elders, who generously shared her experiences—and even photographs—of her and her friends as a young women vacationing on Balboa Island during Bal Week.

I'm so grateful to my editor, Leslie Gelbman, who very patiently helped guide me (and occasionally reel me in) to make this the best book it could possibly be. Thank you to the entire team at St. Martin's Press for helping usher this book out into the world, especially Dori Weintraub, Erica Martirano, Brant Janeway, Austin Adams, Grace Gay, Vivian Rousseau, Lizz Blaise, Nicola Ferguson, Danielle Fiorella, Michael Clark, and Gail Friedman. It really does take a village!

I'm incredibly thankful to Stephanie Kip Rostan, the best literary agent an author could wish for, along with her team at Levine Greenberg Rostan, especially Courtney Paganelli, Meik Coccia, and Melissa Rowland.

I am indebted to my writing workshop friends Jennifer Belle, Donna Brodie, Barbara Miller, Meryl-Branch McTiernan, Steve Reynolds,

Steve Olsen, Matt Sack, and Suki Weston. You give the best and most brutally honest feedback.

My Thursday Author crew—Jamie Brenner, Fiona Davis, Lynda Loigman, Susie Orman Schnall, Amy Poeppel, and book maven Suzanne Leopold—I love our bookish friendship that took off over Zoom calls with wine during Covid. I have so much respect and admiration for you all.

Massive thanks to my parents Michael and Jayne Harrison and to my in-laws Mike and Ginny Ray for all of your support (and early reads of this book), and my forever early reader, Elisa Moriconi.

I am so grateful to my local bookstore PAGES for selling my books, for bringing our community together over literature, and for hosting the best launch parties. And a huge shoutout to all the bookstore owners and staffers, librarians, book influencers, bloggers, reviewers, and of course, the dedicated readers, without whom none of this would be possible.

And finally, to the loves of my life: my boys, Christopher and Greyson, and my husband, Greg Ray, thank you for always believing in me.

ABOUT THE AUTHOR

Yoshie Villarie

NICOLA HARRISON is the author of *Montauk*, *The Show Girl*, *Hotel Laguna*, and *The Island Club*. Born and raised in England, she moved with her family to Southern California when she was fourteen. She is a graduate of UCLA and received her MFA in creative writing from Stony Brook University. Prior to writing novels, she worked as a fashion journalist in New York City, where she lived for seventeen years. Now she resides in Manhattan Beach, California, with her husband, two sons, and a high-maintenance Chihuahua named Lily.